PROPHET ANNIE

PROPHET ANNIE

Being the Recently Discovered
Memoir of
Annie Pinkerton Boone Newcastle Dearborn,
Prophet and Seer

ELLEN RECKNOR

AVON BOOKS ◣ NEW YORK

This is a work of fiction. Names, characters, places and incidents either are the product of the author's imagination or are used fictitiously. Any resemblance to actual events, locales, organizations, or persons, living or dead, is entirely coincidental and beyond the intent of either the author or the publisher.

AVON BOOKS, INC.
1350 Avenue of the Americas
New York, New York 10019

Copyright © 1999 by Ellen Recknor
Front cover illustration by Raquel Jaramillo
Interior design by Kellan Peck
Published by arrangement with the author
ISBN: 0-380-79513-2
www.avonbooks.com

Library of Congress Cataloging in Publication Data:

Recknor, Ellen.
   Prophet Annie : being the recently discovered memoir of Annie Pinkerton Boone Newcastle Dearborn, prophet and seer / Ellen Recknor.
      p.   cm.
   ISBN 0-380-79513-2 (trade pbk.)
   I. Title.
PS3568.E284 P76   1999   98-54331
813'.54—dc21   CIP

First Avon Books Trade Paperback Printing: March 1999

AVON TRADEMARK REG. U.S. PAT. OFF. AND IN OTHER COUNTRIES, MARCA REGISTRADA, HECHO EN U.S.A.

Printed in the U.S.A.

OPM   10   9   8   7   6   5   4   3   2   1

PROPHET ANNIE

Tucson, Arizona
April 7, 1943

Ocain & Sons, Publishers
New York, New York

Dear Sirs:

   It's been near sixty years since I promised I wouldn't tell, but Johnny is gone to Jesus these last ten years, Sam Two Trees is dead for eight, and I can't see as how telling the truth now would hurt anybody except me. I'm just turned eighty-four, and I don't expect to be around long enough for it to damage me serious.

   Besides, I can't bear the thought of going through eternity with nobody knowing the genuine facts of what happened. As it stands, there is nothing permanent to mark the miracle of it but that book, which was ninety percent fabrication. Saying it was only nine-tenths lies is a kindness.

   By "that book," I mean Curiosities and Freaks of the American West, Volume III: The Amazing Powers of "Prophet Annie" Newcastle, *writ back in 1928 by one Mr. Ezra Bind Todd, God rot him. My Johnny would never call it by name, always called it "that book." I guess I got into the habit, too.*

Mr. Todd got all his "facts" fourth- and fifth-hand and did not even bother to interview Sam Two Trees, who was sure available, since he was back in the States then and cooking for the Waldorf-Astoria. Now, Sam had part of the true story. My Johnny, too.

And Jonas, of course, although since he was dead pretty much from the start, I don't know that you could count him.

But I am the only living person, then or now, to know the whole of it.

I have writ it all down, just like it happened and with nothing left out, and I hope that you will see your way fit to printing it up. I got it in there about Jonas and the castle, and Mr. P. T. Barnum and Lord Darrell Duppa and Aisha and the sisters, and Johnny and the El Galgo mines, of course, and how Sam Two Trees got to be a French chef. And, of course, that haunting business. It was a haunting and in no way possession: I'll stick to that forever, no matter what Mr. Todd's book claims.

I put in the part about the Devlin Gang, too, which Mr. Todd did not even mention in his book, since he didn't know beans about them. He just said as how I had a "mysterious disappearance," kind of like Aimee Semple McPherson, and left it at that. That's so low that I won't even comment on it. Anyway, he was more interested in when I was with Mr. Barnum and doing my prophesying and getting acclaimed—or reviled—against my will by the spiritualists and theosophists and such.

But like I said before, it's all in here. It took me near two years, and I wrote it mostly on paper sacks or whatever was handy. My neighbor lady works for a foot doctor, and after I got it done she typed it out for me, real neat. She fixed up my spelling, but other than that she didn't change a word.

She is a stony-faced gal (maybe you have to be that way when you're in the foot business), but when she brought my typed story over to me, she gave me a big hug, and then she went over and put her hand, real kindly like, right on Nebuchadnezzar, who she would never touch before.

Nebuchadnezzar is an African cheetah, stuffed, which I keep in my parlor by the Philco radio. He used to be up in the attic, but after Johnny passed I dusted him off and hauled him downstairs. He is good company, even if those glass eyes never blink. Although considering what I have been through in my life, I wouldn't be surprised if they did.

Now, I know that getting a real book published is not like in the movies, where some writer mails his story off to New York City and a couple days later they send him a box of books and a big fat check, and right away he's so famous that he marries Rita Hayworth or Bette Davis just before he takes to drink. I figure, what with the war on and there being a paper shortage and all, it might take a little longer before my book gets on the shelves. And naturally, I don't want to marry Bette Davis.

In case I am dead by then, you can send my money to my lawyer, Mr. Thaddeus Ward, who is instructed to give it over to the State of Arizona to help them fix up Newcastle's Castle, which is now a state park. I was up there a couple of years back. They take tours to see it, even if the roof is all caved in on itself and the stained glass has long been busted out and you can't even find the gardens anymore.

I'll bet Jonas Newcastle is rolling in his grave. Not that it doesn't serve him right, the old buzzard.

Sincerely,
Mrs. John Dearborn
(once known as Annie Newcastle, Prophet)

1

I want to say right off the bat that up until August of 1881, there was nothing special whatsoever about me.

I am not the seventh daughter of a seventh daughter, as has been said. I had never been pestered by premonitions or eerie feelings, and neither, so far as I know, had been anybody in my family. I had never been struck by lightning. I had no peculiar birthmarks, as has been claimed; neither was I born with a veil, or with a star in my palm.

And, up until that August, I had never heard any voices nor been hit by diving birds.

I was just turned twenty-two and had not exactly been living under a rock, so of course things had happened to me before. Just nothing of real excitement. I grew up normal—well, as normal as anyone could, living around Mama. I did my chores, looked after the boarders, went to church regular on Sundays and the ball games after.

I ran away and married a gandy dancer when I was seventeen; this was mostly to get away from Mama, although it didn't do much good. It turned out I was no more crazy about Mr. Tommy Boone than I was about Mama. When he got kicked in the head by a mule a few months later and died on the spot, I was more relieved than anything else.

Aside from a pocket watch and nine dollars cash, Mr.

Boone didn't leave me squat, so I had no choice but to move back to the boardinghouse, and to Mama. I took care of the lodgers, and of her. She was ailing then, and just lay in bed rereading all those letters from Mr. Jonas Newcastle. Mr. Newcastle was an old friend of the family. I sort of remembered his mother living with us—she was our first boarder—and she was older than God when she passed.

Mama would never let me see those letters, but sometimes she'd read a passage aloud. She read them like they had been brought down off the mountain on stone tablets, and Mr. Newcastle was Moses himself. Maybe even God.

Mama railed on and on about how I had ruined myself by running off with Mr. Boone, and made me promise not to mention it if and when I should ever run into Mr. Newcastle.

I thought this was queer. I also thought the possibility highly unlikely, since Jonas Newcastle was all the way down to Arizona Territory, and I had no intention of leaving Sycamore, Iowa. But when your mama is near twisting your ear off (and Mama was overfond of ear-twisting), I guess you'll promise anything, no matter how silly it seems.

Thereafter, if I'd forget and mention Mr. Tommy Boone in her presence, she'd holler, "No Tommy Boone in this house, Annie, no Tommy Boone, not now, not never!" Then she'd throw something, by way of punctuation.

Anyway, I did my work and put up with Mama and kept my own business. But I guess none of that means squat when the hand of Fate decides to grab hold of a body's strings and yank.

I got yanked good three times that August.

First off, there was Mama dying. I loved her, of course, but it was kind of a relief, what with her being sick for so long, and ornery as a sack of weasels even when she was in the best of health. I don't mean that disparaging. Mama was proud of her obstreperous nature. She worked at it like other women work at their needlepoint, always going for a more artistic pattern, a finer stitch.

I'd always figured that after she was gone, I'd go on running our family boardinghouse and have a nice quiet life as a widow woman. After all, Mama would be gone. What would she care if I mentioned Tommy Boone? I'd just go on cooking up breakfast, lunch, and dinner, and making beds, and collecting board money. Folks would say to strangers, "Take yourself to the Widow Boone's, for you'll get a square meal there, and a bed with no bugs."

But like always, Mama got in the last word.

We didn't own the boardinghouse at all, the lawyer told me while I hid behind my black veil. Mama had sold it a long time ago, right after Papa got killed on the CB&Q, to Mr. Jonas Newcastle. That was sure a big surprise. But the biggest one was yet to come: In return for sending us money all the years since Papa died (not to mention warm affection and family feeling), Mama had promised my hand in holy matrimony to the self-same Jonas Newcastle.

You may think it odd that my own mother would the same as sell me off to some geezer I'd met only once when I was just little and didn't remember, who was old enough to be my grandfather and lived fifteen hundred miles away to boot, and not even tell me about it until after she was dead. But that was what she did.

I couldn't refuse. Who could refuse a dying wish? Who could refuse Mama?

But I'm getting ahead of myself. Or behind, maybe. I wanted to tell you the second important thing that happened that August, which was my wedding day.

I did not come to it in a real optimistic mood—being opposed to it in the first place, but having no other recourse—and having spent ten days in travel.

Normally, I would have liked a good train ride. Sycamore, where I come from, was and is a railroad town. Carl Pinkerton was my daddy, God rest him, and he worked the night shift for the CB&Q. That's the Chicago, Burlington & Quincy, for those who don't know. He was a hard worker and made good money, but Mama was always after him because he wasn't rich like Jonas Newcastle, who had made something out of himself. Daddy would pretend he didn't hear. He'd just stare at his newspaper, or sometimes go sit on the porch swing by himself. If Mama followed him to the porch, he'd get up and take a long walk.

He died when I was twelve. It was a coupling accident. I always thought he'd probably had enough of Mama and the Newcastles, and when he saw that car rolling toward him he thought, "I can either jump clear and go on home and hear about Mr. Jonas Newcastle all through breakfast again, or I can just stay put."

He stayed put, and was crushed, dying instantly.

I grew up hanging around the train yards and breathing in their smoky, oily, burnt-metal smell; watching the engines come and go from the roundhouse; and making up stories about all the far-off places they had been and the folks, plain and exotic, they had towed. Once I got the bad news from Mama's lawyer that I didn't have a pot to piddle in nor a window to throw it out of—not to mention the betrothal—practically the only good thing I had to look forward to was that I'd finally get to take a long trip on a train.

Mr. Newcastle arranged for me to ride first class, so I had a berth. The dining-car food was pretty good and the scenery was real interesting, but I did not care for being on my own with so many strangers.

Plus, traveling was sure a lot more dirty than I'd been led to believe. The cars were so hot and stuffy that the only relief was to go stand outside on the little decks between cars or open a window, either one of which would have you caked with dust and smoke-grime in about four seconds flat.

And then there was the convenience. It was just this little place at the end of the car. You had to snap the curtains closed around you while you were fighting with your skirts, and with passing bodies all the time bumping you from the other side of the curtain. Why, people could see your feet while you were in there! I did not care for strangers staring at my shoes while I was tending to private business.

Anyway, while I was on the train I started reading Mr. Newcastle's letters to Mama. Not to snoop, mind you. I just thought they might help me understand who the Sam Hill I was marrying, since even after she died, all the arrangements had been made between Mama's lawyer and Mr. Newcastle, like I was some piece of property and they were deciding how to dispose of me.

Mama had saved every scrap that Jonas Newcastle had ever sent her, all in a hatbox, in packets tied real careful with black cord and sorted by year. I started with the first ones, written back in the 1860s, and they were pretty interesting. Jonas had volunteered for active duty when war broke out, but they slapped the rank of colonel on him and sent him north to Fort Defiance, up Minnesota way, to quell the Sioux uprising.

He was in his fifties by then—and I was barely walking—and I guessed he sure missed home because he wrote a lot and did a lot of reminiscing.

It seemed like my mama's relationship with Jonas Newcastle went back practically to before she was born. The Newcastles, Jonas included, were pioneers with my Grandma Frieda and Grampa Rudy. Jonas brought them—along with his own mama and sisters—out from Maryland back in the 1830s.

Well, I suppose Mama had told me something about that, too, but I didn't listen very good. Kids never do. But every once in a while the letter would make a reference back to those long-ago times.

Actually, Jonas talked about my grandma quite a bit. In one letter in particular, he recalled the pilgrimage and how they had just got as far as Illinois, then were stopped by the Black Hawk War. He went off and fought in that, leaving Grampa Rudy to look after the females in the party. But after he got back it took three years to convince the women it was safe to move on. Once they had pried the women loose, they crossed over the Mississippi and the Half-breed Tract; and then, one morning, Grandma Frieda—who was eight months pregnant with my Uncle Tad—just refused to climb back up in the wagon.

"No furder, Rudy," she said to Grandpa, although everybody heard her plain. "No furder am I goin'."

They stayed right there in the Michigan Territory, which later got turned into the great State of Iowa.

I had read up through about all the Fort Defiance letters by the time the train ended at Flagstaff, in the northern mountains of the Arizona Territory. I had to switch to the Butterfield stage line for the rest of the trip.

I spent four whole days being bounced practically bloody by that coach by day—up and down mountain trails that you held your breath on, they were so precarious—and waited out sleepless nights sweating and swatting bugs in the miserly shacks that passed for stage stops. About all they fed you in those places was salt pork and beans. Those kind of got your innards in an uproar, if you know what I mean, and did not help matters.

To top things off, my trunks had been sent on ahead— my hand luggage, Jonas's letters included, having gone along with them by mistake—and I had been wearing the same dress since Flagstaff.

So by the time we rolled into the town of Rock Bottom, I was ripe and grimy and mean. I could have bit the head off a live badger, had there been one handy to bite.

Before Mama died, she was always bragging on how her friend, Jonas Newcastle, was the second-richest man in Maricopa County. But from what I'd seen of Arizona in general— and now Rock Bottom in particular—that didn't sound so impressive. A possum with a little pocket change could probably have qualified for first richest.

There wasn't even a real stage stop. The coach just pulled up in the middle of the street, across from what might once have been a mercantile. The driver was in such a big toot to find civilization that he stopped barely long enough for me to get my foot off the step-down, and left me sitting on my backside in the middle of the road.

Not one soul came to my assistance. I found out later that nobody lived in town anymore, but right then I just thought they were all hiding away and awful rude.

Rock Bottom was hardly a town at all. I counted only a dozen buildings, none of them in anything close to good repair, and nothing all around but hard, gravelly desert and cactus and more desert.

There were no signs of life other than a spotted bitch, all matted and full of burrs, asleep on her back in an open

doorway—probably to keep clear of the tumbleweeds blowing lazy across the road. Somewhere a shutter banged in the
wind, and what glass windows there were had been mostly
busted out. The whole place smelled of dust and heat and
something else. Creosote, maybe.

I would have just sat there and cried if I hadn't been so
numb from everything else.

It's hard to explain the way I felt, on the inside. So much
had happened to me so fast, and all of it strange and foreign,
that about half the time I felt like I was having the worst
dream of my life and that none of it mattered, not being
real; that I'd be fine again if I could just stand it long enough
to get to the waking-up part.

The other half of the time I was just sad.

Anyway, I was up on my feet again, having grabbed hold
of a hitching rail, and was pounding the last of the road
dust out of my bustle and cussing Mama, when all of a
sudden something went *thump* right on the top of my head.

That just about did it. I turned around quick, thinking to
apprehend the culprit, but nobody was there. I called out,
"Who threw that? Come out, coward!"

But nobody did. The spotted bitch didn't even bother to
more than slant open an eye and close it again. There was
not a sound except the wind weeping through the holes in
the buildings and rattling loose boards, and the dry brushy
thumps of tumbleweeds bouncing across the road.

Just as I raised my hand to feel for a knot on my noggin,
I saw what had hit me. It was a little wren, fluttering its last
in the dust beside the rail post. It was dead before I could
reach down to it.

I don't know what the odds are for a bird falling right out
of the sky and smack onto a person's bonnet, but I suspect
I would have been wise to take it for a portent.

There was no time to dwell on it, though, for right then
the whole Newcastle clan showed up. I recognized Jonas
from an old picture Mama had—the white hair and spare
frame gave him away from a distance—and the ladies with
him could be none other than his two old-maid sisters, Miss
Jonquil and Miss Jessie.

With a lump in my throat, I watched them clatter toward me up the road in a spit-shined black buggy drawn by matched chestnuts. I cannot begin to tell you how strange that Sunday-go-to-meeting buggy looked dodging tumble-weeds and trailing dust all the way up the main street.

Of course, once they pulled up and climbed down, the Newcastles didn't exactly appear to have sprouted out of the landscape, either.

First off, while most everybody else I had met in the Terri-tory was brown as a nut, the Newcastles were all real pale, like they never went out in the sun. They were dressed real fancy, but the three of them appeared so dried-up and brittle that a good brisk wind would have snapped them apart. The sisters shared a big, lacy, ice-blue parasol and prattled nonstop, finishing each other's sentences.

"Aren't you—" said Miss Jonquil.

"—sweet?" said Miss Jessie.

"We're so—"

"—happy for—"

"—you and Brother."

"Oh, yes."

"Indeed. And you look so much like—"

"—your dear, dear—"

"Grandmother."

"Oh, yes."

"Blonde."

"Like new corn."

"Your grandmother to a *T*," said Miss Jonquil.

"It's almost eerie," said Miss Jessie.

Their words were real proper, but they were both jittery and nervous and maybe kind of embarrassed. They re-minded me of a couple of old porcelain teacups Mama used to have when I was a kid. They were cracked with age, and so thin you could see the light right through them. Real fragile and kind of pretty if you like that sort of thing, but useless and just for show, probably even when they were brand new.

Me, I favor things—and people—who'll stand up to their

purpose. Leastwise, that was what I told Mama when I accidentally broke those cups playing stickball in the house.

Anyway, both Miss Jonquil and Miss Jessie, smelling faintly of lilac water, had these little lace hankies they kept fluttering over their noses and daubing at their throats. They flicked their birdy old eyes at each other or down to their shoes or off into the distance, but hardly ever toward me, even though they chirped nonstop. I guess they didn't like the idea of their brother getting married after so many years, even to somebody they'd known years ago, when she was just a tyke.

Neither did I, but then, I didn't have much say in it, did I?

Jonas Newcastle, my intended, was not much help. He did no more than tip his hat, flush red over his long turkey neck, and say, "An honor," before he set to loading us all up in the buggy.

It was just as well, because my first sight of him had nigh on turned my insides upside down, and not in a good way.

He wore a black suit and tie—real formal and serious, like a German banker—and he appeared washed and just-shaved. His mustache was silver and waxed to a perfect curl, and he fairly reeked of bay rum, like he had doused himself a couple of extra times for the occasion. He leaned all the time on a fancy walking stick with a solid gold, ruby-eyed horse's head on the top.

But he was so much older than the gilt-framed picture Mama kept on the mantel, and he was none too young or handsome in that. In person, he was terrible thin, and so old and vulture-ugly that if there'd been another stage out of town I would have been on it, Mama's last wish or no.

But there wasn't another stage, and I *had* made that promise, so I gritted my teeth and tried to smile. I told myself that even though he looked like Ichabod Crane's great-granddaddy he was probably a nice enough man, once a person got used to him.

If they ever could.

So we all loaded up in the buggy, me up front with Mr. Newcastle and the sisters behind, and we set out. I watched the landscape as we drove, as much to keep from looking at Mr. Newcastle as anything. It wasn't nearly so pretty as the scenery up north had been.

Big hills jutted up in ridges—what I would have called mountains if I had not just ridden down on the stage through some real corkers—and the valleys in between them were rolling and lumpy and gravelly and sere. Every once in a while there was a raggedy sandstone outcrop that looked like about a hundred rattlesnakes were lying up there just waiting to fang me to death should I bolt and run, which, believe me, was on the tip of my mind.

The hills, through which passes had been blasted for the road, had some big stone ledges and upthrusts: dull black, patched with rusty-looking places. Mr. Newcastle, wafting bay rum when the breeze was right, remarked that it was volcanic rock, spewed up millions of years ago and molten hot from the center of the earth.

I believed him. It was the devil's own country.

Coming from Iowa, where everything is forty shades of green and grows so fast it's practically a nuisance, Arizona Territory—the part I was going to have to live in, anyway— seemed to me about the ugliest, most godforsaken place in the world. Not a blade of real grass, just brown, stickery, sun-beat bushes in clumps here and there, and every once in a while a mean-looking cactus. And everywhere in be- tween and around, gravel and rock and rock and gravel, and all of it black or rusty, like the land had bled on itself. I got to seeing it different after a while, of course, but on that day I felt like I had been banished to Satan's back sixty.

We wove through the desert hills for near an hour, though it seemed longer, what with the sisters chattering in the backseat about my mama and hadn't I grown up *tall* and wasn't I just like my grandmother, the spitting image.

Me, I nodded like a fool, every once in a while rubbing through my bonnet at the bump that bird had raised on my skull and thinking I had just made the biggest mistake of my whole life. I could have stayed home and worked in Miss Enid's Tasty Eats Café or the Widow Siddens's Ornament Emporium or Aunt Tot's Fine Foods. I could have been a wash maid, married another gandy dancer, scrubbed floors, slept in the street, anything but this.

Just as we emerged from another one of those passes blasted down through rusty-black rock, old Jonas reined the team to a halt, which got my attention again. He sat up as straight and proud as a man with time-bent bones is able.

Pointing ahead to the top of the next big hill, he announced, real grand, "I built it for you, Annie Pinkerton. Welcome to Newcastle's Castle."

I guess that after all the yammering my mama had done about his house over the last years—how the china came from Germany and the carpets from Persia and tapestries from England and France, and how it had taken seven years to build—I should have been prepared, but I was not. I don't think anybody could have been.

My jaw dropped practically down on my chest. What he was pointing at was a big, black, cut-stone, turreted mansion with stained glass eyes.

Three stories tall, it straddled the top of a black-rock hill with nothing but that ugly, heat-shimmered, scrub desert all around. A dozen or so buzzards, black as the castle itself, black as the hill it grew out of—and probably almost as black as my heart was toward Jonas Newcastle and Mama and life in general at that moment—circled overhead against a baked-white sky.

I had never seen anything so flat-out stupid in all my life.

I guessed Mama had spoken true, after all, about Mr. Newcastle being rich, although right at that moment I did not draw much comfort from it. Also, I could not think of a blessed thing to say. Nothing polite, anyhow.

Miss Jonquil said, "The vultures will go away. Sam Two Trees—"

"Butchered a hog," broke in Miss Jessie.

"For the festivities," added Miss Jonquil. She had her lips pressed tight together and her eyes narrowed to slits while she watched those birds.

Jonas Newcastle gave me a big, yellow, long-toothed smile, just a quick one, before he clucked to the team and we started toward the castle.

2

The wedding guests had beat us there and were clamoring for the show to get underway, which barely gave me time to wash my face and use the convenience, and for Miss Jonquil to throw about a whole bottle of *eau d'toilet* on me.

What happened next is pretty blurry in my memory, but eventually the ceremony got started, and I married the old geezer—him gushy-eyed half the time and leering the other half and wiping the sweat from his forehead nonstop—in the terraced cactus garden out back of that black-rock castle, with his two white-haired, humpy-backed sisters for my bridesmaids, and me still in my traveling clothes.

It was a big do, maybe fifty people, although since I had not seen another house and nobody lived in the town, I don't know where they all came from. There was a mariachi band and a long table heavy with cakes and pies and kettles of beans and stews and such. A little redheaded boy and a Mexican one walked up and down, swishing away the flies with tasseled sticks and stealing cake frosting on their fingers. Crepe paper streamers—red, white, and blue—were looped everywhere.

The crowd was real mixed. There were a lot of Mexicans, and an old, dignified Chinese man with a braid down his back, and an Englishman called Lord Duppa who got soused—more than the rest, I mean, for everybody was pretty drunk after a while—and went around spouting eloquent sayings. Sometimes it was in German, which I understood, and sometimes in what sounded like Italian, which I did not.

About half the people were real gussied up, the Mexican ladies especially, and the other half looked like they had not been near a needle and thread or a cake of soap since New Year's last. That bunch spent most of their time by the beer kegs and in the serving line. I saw one man alone go back seven times for more barbecue, the plate heaped each time.

Everybody, even the kids and the Chinaman, were about half-soaked in their own sweat, and one of the mariachis fainted from the heat. It was just as well. When a band has only five musicians and none of them are too careful about such things as notes, losing the third trumpet player can be a blessing.

Miss Jonquil and Miss Jessie took no part in the festivities. They mopped damp, wispy hair off their wrinkled, old-parchment brows while they picked at their roasted pig and jelly roll in the shade, and stared down their noses at the riffraff, you could tell they'd obviously had to invite, just to make a crowd.

Nobody said much to me after the congratulations part. Even when Mr. Newcastle had the first dance with me, he didn't utter one word. He held me clear out at arm's length—for which I was grateful—and waltzed me, real formal and solemn.

For a man with a gimpy leg, he danced pretty good. He only stumbled one time, but I sort of caught him so we could keep going. He gave me such a look when that happened! It only lasted maybe a half-second, but I felt sort of hooked to him, somehow, real close in my heart. But it only lasted a half-second, like I said, and then I was just dancing with a sweaty old man again.

I had one other dance, that one with the territorial governor. He had made a speech right after the ceremony about how proud he was to be there, and what a fine wife I'd make for Mr. Newcastle and how well-matched we were and all. I had to give him credit for saying it with a straight face.

After the dancing, I stood back under the crepe-papered ramada all alone, sweating big, dark stains into my dress and smelling my own stink. I kept wishing I was back home in Sycamore, with a cool morning breeze fluttering my curtains, and green outside my windows, and nothing more to worry about than getting breakfast for the boarders.

But I couldn't concentrate, what with the band making so much noise, so I just watched the sky clabber up while Mr. Newcastle circulated through the crowd, getting slapped on the back and more plastered by the minute. Sometimes I'd catch him staring at me, all moony, from across the throng.

The only one to be kind to me was the cook, who I took to be Sam Two Trees, the one the sisters had mentioned. He was youngish, my age or a little older, and he was dressed mostly like a white man. But you could tell he was at least part-Indian from his jet-black hair and high-cheekboned face, and the wide sash tied 'round his brow. He spent most of his time cranking the spit over a big roasting pit, and slicing off hog meat for the guests.

A couple times he just sort of turned up beside me, without my noticing how he got there, and handed me something to eat or drink. He didn't say anything. He'd just shove a plate of barbecue at me, then leave.

By the third time he showed up, I was pretty desperate for somebody to talk to, and it didn't much matter what about. As I took a glass of lemonade from him, I said, "A bird dived right out of the sky and hit me on the head."

He stared at me for a couple seconds, and I had just about decided that maybe he didn't speak English when he said, "What kind?" I guess I was expecting some kind of Indian talk, but he spoke just as plain as you and me.

"It was a wren," I said.

He pursed up his lips. "Not an owl?"

"No."

"You sure?"

It was nice to have somebody to gab with, but he was

beginning to irritate me. I said, "I think I know the difference."

He didn't seem to be listening. He stared out at the crowd for a couple of seconds, kind of absent, before he said, "I expect you do." And then he went back to his spitted pig without another word.

The afternoon faded. Clouds took over the sky, and the sun settled down into the hills. Lanterns were lit, and still the festivities showed no signs of petering out. It was nothing like back home in Sycamore, where folks talked soft and knew to go home by seven. Everybody except the territorial governor—who had left early so as to drive down to Hayden's Ferry before it got too dark—kept getting drunker and louder.

Just when I had decided the guests were never going to go home, and that I was just going to stand there, tired and sweaty and footsore and nervous for the rest of my life, the wind came up, hard and gritty.

Lanterns blew out, blew over. Revelers, their party clothes lit stark and hard in the lightning flashes, packed up their kids, pocketed what leftovers they could, and staggered on down to their horses and buggies. From the broad, black-pillared veranda, Mr. Newcastle shouted good-bye to their backs while Miss Jonquil and Miss Jessie flicked their hankies in the wind and murmured, "Thank you for attending, dear friends."

I just stood there, pressed against a rough stone column with my skirts blowing harder all the time, the twice-my-height castle doors open behind me like a big black mouth waiting to eat me up. I was unable to make my hand flutter a wave or my mouth form a fare-thee-well.

I wanted to call after the guests, "Take me with you! Don't leave me with these powdery-boned ladies and a tipsy old codger with mischief on his mind!"

But I didn't say a word, not even a whisper. I was fated by the plans of others to be sacrificed on the altar of matrimony, and I guess those invisible bonds Mama had tied round me gagged my mouth, too.

The wind rose up to nearly a cyclone and the thunder

was coming closer and louder, like Mama knew I was thinking about running off into the brush and never coming back.
Like she was hollering at me from heaven to finish what
she'd made me start, or else.

Then the skies opened up, and we rushed inside to track
water all over the fancy marble checkerboard floor. Mr.
Newcastle—who, outside of an "I do," had said no more
than maybe six sentences to me during the whole of our
acquaintanceship—whisked rainwater out of what was left
of his hair. He stretched himself into a great big dramatic
yawn and, between thunderclaps and over the noise of the
wind whining through the door cracks, announced, "Annie,
I believe it's time we retired."

Both his sisters blanched and stared at the floor as he
took my arm and led me, knees like jelly, past tapestries
from England and France and paintings from Italy, up the
wide, curving staircase.

And so there we were two hours later, Mr. Newcastle and
me, in the biggest bedroom of the biggest monster of a
house you ever saw, with a genuinely mean thunderstorm
still raging outside the tall stained-glass windows. And Mr.
Newcastle was doing his business with gusto.

Now, I was no stranger to the marriage bed. My late husband, Mr. Tommy Boone, had done me pretty much the
same way every Saturday night for the three months we
were married, though I admit he was not half so enthusiastic
as Jonas Newcastle.

Mr. Newcastle was all bony old elbows and knees and
his breath smelled like whiskey, and I was not enjoying the
process one bit. Sometimes the lightning would flare bright
and cast eerie colors through the stained glass and across
his face, making him purple and green and blue, like a
demon, a demon of the sere desert with a house built from
black rock a volcano had spewed up. And I was thinking
that I couldn't bear a lifetime like this, not hardly at all, when
all of a sudden Mr. Newcastle stopped doing his business.

He shouted out something that sounded like "Freedom!"

though it was hard to tell with the thunder and all. Then he slumped down on me in a heap, and made this rattly sound.

At first I just lay there and waited for him to start up again. What did I know? He'd done the same thing twice before, then hopped up in a minute, all spry and happy and sweaty. He'd poured himself another shot of bourbon, smoked a bit on his cigar, and then said, "I'm going to have another go at you, Annie girl." And then he would.

But this time he didn't hop up, even when I pushed at him, and pretty soon it came to me that he wasn't breathing.

It's only natural to be a little unnerved by a thing like that, isn't it? Your brand-new husband dropping dead in the middle of the wedding night and all, as sure as if he'd been poleaxed, and right when you were thinking you'd be just as happy if the old devil died.

Once I got past the initial surprise, I can't say I was exactly staggered. After all, he was seventy-six years old and a bachelor all his life, and therefore was a more than average enthusiast about the conjugal proceedings. I reckoned it was his pump that did him in.

Now, I don't mean to seem like I have got no feelings, talking about demons and old goats with bum tickers and all. I think anyone who knows me will tell you I've got a good heart. It was just that I didn't have much in the way of personal sentiments for Mr. Newcastle, except for that grudge I had against him and Mama for plotting my life. I suppose that if I'd known him longer I could have come up with some good things about him, some sweet sentiments. But a thing like that takes more than six or eight hours to cultivate.

Anyway, after I got him rolled off me, I stood over him for a minute and took a look-see.

I was the only one with Mama when she died, too, and she went with a cantankerous expression that even the mortician couldn't soften. Of course, that was Mama's way, and I remember several people at the viewing saying, "Don't Velda look natural!"

Mr. Newcastle, on the other hand, appeared downright overjoyed, with his eyes wide open and staring, and a great big grin plastered over his face.

Somehow, it didn't seem quite Christian.

It was a little scary, too, since he was lit entirely by lightning from the storm. The flashes were quick and watery with stained-glass color, and made me think of a book I'd read, where they used lightning to make a corpse come back to life, after which it learned to speak foreign languages and then went to Antarctica.

I lit a lamp and turned it up all the way. That helped some.

After I straightened his nightshirt and pulled on my shift and closed his eyes, I stuck my head out the door and hollered for assistance. It seemed like nobody would ever hear me over the storm. I finally decided I'd have to chance getting lost in that stupid castle of his and go find help.

I'd just gone back in to get my slippers when somebody rapped at the door. Mr. Newcastle's sister, Jonquil, stuck her head in. She had her eyes closed.

"Jonas?" she whispered, all flustered. "Brother? Is something wrong?"

I was too worn down to pussyfoot. I said, "You can look, Miss Jonquil. We are both decent, but I think your brother is dead."

She took a step in. "Jonas?" she said, real soft, then, "Jonas!"

White braid whipping the air behind her, she ran to the bed and threw herself on him practically full length. People started pouring through the door after that. Miss Jonquil was hollering and wailing and carrying on. Miss Jessie was so overcome with grief that she dropped a lit candle on the bedclothes, and it took two maids to beat it out. Sam Two Trees came in, too, and just stood by the door, holding his lamp.

They forgot about me, so I went and sat in a chair in the corner. I was feeling pretty cranky and a little unnerved, too, what with the circumstances of Mr. Newcastle's demise and the storm raging outside and having remembered that scary book. I was tired from the trip and sore from Mr. Newcastle's enthusiasm. Plus, it was so muggy from the storm and unnaturally hot that even with nothing on but a cotton shift, the sweat trickled down my back.

Finally, they remembered me. Miss Jonquil turned around,

her eyes all red and swollen in that powder-white face. She pointed a bony finger. "You!" she said. "You have killed Brother! What did you do to him?"

"I didn't do anything to anybody, Miss Jonquil," I replied in as even a tone as I could muster. "And he must have been glad to go. His last word was *freedom*. Besides which, it was him doing it to me. The third time was what got him."

Behind her, Miss Jessie flushed bright pink and covered her sunken cheeks with her hands. "Barn talk!" she said through bony fingers. "No barn talk in this house!"

"We might as well have barn talk, Miss Jessie," I replied, climbing to my feet, "since I was just the same as bartered to your brother like a brood mare."

And then I felt mean for having said it, for poor old Miss Jessie fainted dead away and had to be carried to her room by Sam Two Trees. Miss Jonquil gave me a dirty look before she turned her back, ignoring me entirely, and took up a vigil beside the body. When I spoke to her, she put her hands over her ears and wouldn't answer.

Finally I wandered out into the hall, then felt my way down the main stairs and forced open the big, carved front doors. Rain, blown hard, hit me straight on and plastered my shift to my body. I didn't care. It felt good, after doing what I was told for so long, to fight back against something. I battled my way out into it.

That wind was more creature than storm. It howled through the hills all around and tried its best to force me to my knees, but I kept pushing against it, struggling through the mire, until I was about a hundred yards down the drive.

Just then, lightning struck a big saguaro not twenty feet from me. I jumped at the flash and explosion, lost my balance, and landed, full out, in the rutted, flooding drive. With wet hair in my eyes and the stench of that scorched cactus in my nostrils, I hugged myself hard and started in to cry: big ragged sobs that weren't in mourning for Jonas Newcastle. I was just feeling terrible sad for what had happened to me and what Mama had made me do, and terrible angry that I'd gone through with it instead of standing up for myself.

I didn't know the last time I had cried. I sure had felt like it a lot, but I didn't. I didn't even cry when Mama died, not for the sorrow of her leaving, not even in the knowledge that I was fated to throw my life away at her behest. I was always raised up to do what I was told, and do it without comment or complaint, and to not show my feelings about anything, no matter how good or bad. Especially not the bad.

I don't know if that comes from the German side of my family or the Scots or from Mama hammering at me my whole life, or just from being an Iowan. But it was surely there. And somewhere along the way I had gone all dead inside.

So there I lay in the mud with the rain pelting all around and the numbness finally lifting off me, and feeling more horrible sad and sorry for myself than I could recollect, when the oddest thing happened.

The rain stopped, just like that. I could still hear the wind, still hear the rain pounding into the desert, but all around me was calm and still. Then, as if somebody had taken my head in their hands and gently turned it, I twisted 'round to look back up at the hill at Jonas's castle.

The rain had slicked its stone walls shiny as patent leather, and when another battery of lightning bolts flashed white in the sky behind it, it appeared, well, beautiful. Real forever-looking.

Right then, in that lightning-burst second, I knew it wasn't stupid or silly at all—it was exactly perfect. And I knew something else, too.

I blinked rainwater and tears out of my eyes. I felt my mouth stretch wide into a genuine smile. I had never in my life owned anything of value. I had never been the one to give orders, only the one taking them. I had never been allowed—or maybe never had the gumption—to be my own person. I wasn't even sure who or what that person was, but I was going to find out. And I was going to do it in a big, grand house in the middle of nowhere, with nobody to tell me what to do.

If I had known what was coming next, I doubt I would have been so full of myself. But I didn't know. And so, when it started in raining on me again, I stood up and danced in it.

3

Well, those are the first two things that Fate stuck me with that August. Mama's dying wish, and my wedding to Jonas. I sort of grouped the wedding and his passing together, since one thing happened so quick on the heels of the other. The third thing, the most important thing, was more complicated.

That first night in Newcastle's Castle, I slept downstairs in the front parlor, on a clawfoot, gilt-trimmed sofa. There were plenty of bedrooms upstairs, of course, but everybody was retired when I crawled back inside from the storm. It was easier to grope my way to the parlor than find a lamp and poke around upstairs for an empty room.

What woke me was the feeling of being watched. I lay there a minute, with my eyes still closed, wondering if Miss Jessie or Miss Jonquil was peering at me. Since it was a feeling of being stared at hard, I decided it was Miss Jonquil, probably pointing that bony finger at me again. I opened my eyes with a snap, figuring to startle her.

I felt pretty stupid when I realized I was all alone.

I crawled off the sofa and stood up feeling odd, like my head was stuffed and I was coming down with something. Well, not sick, exactly. Just real full. That's the best way to describe it: full.

Anyway, I was about halfway up the stairs when Miss Jessie called to me from below. "Do you want breakfast, dear?" she asked.

She had a funny expression on her face, like she wanted in her heart to be kind, but she was still wondering if maybe, now that I'd seen her brother off to his greater reward, I was planning on ferrying her and her sister across the Styx, too. She was sure dressed for the journey. She had got right down to the business of mourning, and was all decked out in black.

I said, "Thank you, Miss Jessie, but I'd like to get dressed first. Is Mr. Newcastle still . . ." I pointed upstairs, toward the scene of his demise.

I don't mean to seem callous, but about the first thing that had crossed my mind was that somebody had better haul him out and bury him quick. The rain had taken down the heat some—maybe it was only ninety degrees now—but it had got real sultry. It was eight in the morning and already the sweat was beading on my brow.

Miss Jessie, though, looked dry as talc, even in that high-necked black dress. She said, "Mr. Webb will be coming shortly."

I took Mr. Webb to be the undertaker, said, "All right," and started up the stairs again. I had taken about three steps up when I turned around and said, "That hat'll pop, you know."

Miss Jessie just looked at me, kind of startled. I was a little startled myself. We both just stared at each other for a time, nobody knowing what to say.

Finally, I said, "Thank you, Miss Jessie," and went up.

I was more confused than I thought, going 'round talking nonsense. I was also not much looking forward to sorting through my luggage with a dead husband at my back, but it was that or greet the undertaker in my nightie.

Miss Jonquil was still sitting with the body, although she must have taken some time away, as she, like her sister, was rigged in mourning black. I don't know where they had those dresses made, but I had never seen such scratchy-looking outfits in my life. I almost broke out in a rash just looking at her.

She said, "Good morning," real curt, then turned back toward the late Mr. Newcastle, which was just as well. Somebody had covered him all up with a sheet so I couldn't see him, but my nose knew he was there. And I was thinking, as I shimmied out of my damp nightshift and into dry under things, that the undertaker couldn't arrive soon enough.

I got my wish, because I had no more than done up my hair and pulled a dress from my trunk when I heard him coming up the stairs.

He walked straight into the room, Miss Jessie trotting at his heels. I held my dress up in front of me and hid in the corner. They didn't see me. That room was big enough to raise corn in.

He had his hat off, and held it over his chest. "A tragedy, Miss Jonquil," he said. I took the opportunity to slide the dress over my head.

"I am stunned," the undertaker continued.

"As are we all," Miss Jonquil replied.

"Such a vigorous man," said the undertaker.

I did up the dress's buttons and pulled on my stockings and shoes.

Miss Jessie sniffed, "Poor Brother," behind her hankie.

"So young," said Miss Jonquil.

"In his prime," said Miss Jessie before she blew her nose.

I stepped forward. "Excuse me?"

All three of them turned around.

I stuck out my hand to the undertaker. "I'm Annie. Mrs. Newcastle," I said. I didn't remember him from the wedding. I guess he'd been off burying somebody.

He introduced himself, since it didn't look like the sisters were going to do it.

"I am sorry we have to meet under such sorrowful circumstances," he said. I nodded and kept my face pitiful.

He mouthed a few soothing words, and then I said, "When's the service? It's awful hot. What I mean to say is, well, Mr. Newcastle's not getting any fresher."

Miss Jonquil appeared horrified, so I added quick, "I want to remember him like he was yesterday. Real . . . real vital."

"Vital, yes." Miss Jessie dabbed at her eyes. "That's just the word. Brother was such a vital man."

"A saint." Miss Jonquil had her hands all folded up, and slid me a sideways look. This morning, the sisters smelled like lemon verbena.

"Parson Brown will arrive momentarily, and services will commence in one hour," said Mr. Webb. "Or however quickly Sam Two Trees can dig the, uh . . . however fast Sam can dig."

Arizona has awful hard ground. The grave wasn't finished for four hours, and even then Sam Two Trees only had it about three-and-a-half feet deep, and that was with dumping water in the hole several times to soften it up.

"Are you sure it's deep enough?" I asked, just to be conversational. I had wandered out to the garden, which looked like the wreck of the Hesperus. There were Chinese lanterns all crushed and in the cactus. Storm-shredded crepe paper, the color leeched out of it, was tramped into the ground. Someone had cleaned up most of the buffet and taken the tables down, but the big pit for roasting the pig was still there, as well as some of the pig, and the flies were swarming. It stank.

I guess Sam Two Trees saw me looking at it, because he said, "Not right to bury a man where you just cooked a hog. I was tempted, though. Took us two days to dig that pit." He poured another bucket of water in Jonas's grave, then stood up and mopped his brow, the part the head sash didn't cover.

"Quiche," he said.

"Beg pardon?" I thought maybe it was an Indian word.

He said, "I had a quiche planned for breakfast, but not for this outfit. They always want a three-minute egg and dry toast. No imagination."

He hopped down into the hole again and swung his pick. He only did about an inch-and-a-half's worth of damage.

I said, "What's a quiche?" I admit I didn't much care, but

it was better than talking about what a boon to the whole of mankind Mr. Newcastle had been, like they were doing inside.

He stopped digging and looked up at me, studying my face. I guess he approved of what he saw—whatever that was—because he said, "Well, I'll admit it isn't exactly what you'd pick for breakfast. But I thought, with the wedding and all . . . It's kind of like a pie. An egg pie."

It sounded downright awful—who ever heard of an egg pie?—but he stared into the distance with an expression on his face like he was talking about his sainted mother.

". . . delicately seasoned," he went on, "in a golden crust. With cheeses. And artichoke hearts or smoked snake meat or bacon or mushrooms or chopped ground squirrel or—"

"Ouch!" Something had hit me on the head, and with force. I twisted around in a circle, holding my skull. A little blood trickled down. I turned all the way around to Sam Two Trees again. "Did you see that? Did you see who did that?"

He pointed to the ground. It took me a second to see the desert sparrow, lying in the party trash, dead as a hammer. The dust had not yet settled around it.

I could not believe it. I said, "Twice! Two times in as many days! Arizona birds are crazy!"

Sam Two Trees shrugged. "Buy a hat," he said. He switched to a shovel and went back to digging. Or trying to.

"Buy a hat? Is that all you can say?" I looked overhead. Nothing but blue-white sky, forever. "I want to know why every bird in the Territory wants to commit suicide on my head all of a gol-dang sudden!"

Just then, something brushed my shoulder. Someone whispered, *Annie?*

I turned. No one was there.

I whirled back around. "Tell Jessie don't eat that leftover pig."

Sam Two Trees propped both hands on the handle of the shovel. "What in the devil are you talking about?"

I didn't know why I'd said that, about pop-up hats before and leftover pig now. I didn't know where the words had come from, and it put a scare into me. So I said to him, kind of angry, "What are you doing to me? You're up to some funny business!"

He ran a thumb over his eyebrow, pushing the sweat away. "I'm just digging a grave and listening to a crazy woman. Never mind about the quiche. Nobody else cares, why should you?"

I slapped my hands over my head and ran to the house.

Somebody had thrown together an extra-long coffin. I don't know where they got the wood on such short notice. The sisters had dressed Mr. Newcastle real nice, in his opera clothes with a neck scarf and everything, although why anybody in Arizona would have opera clothes is beyond me. His opera glasses were in one hand and one of those collapsible stovepipe hats was in the other, in the folded-down position.

We put him in the coffin and said a few words of goodbye—Miss Jessie and Miss Jonquil more than me, for I had hardly known him, after all—and then Sam Two Trees nailed it shut. He and Mr. Webb and two Mexican men, who had shown up out of nowhere, carried it out to the garden, where the shallow grave was dug. Parson Brown was leading the show.

We trooped out after them, the sisters and me. I was searching the skies for birds, and wishing like mad that I had never heard of Jonas Newcastle or Rock Bottom, Arizona. I was also wearing a too-big, broad-brimmed black hat, which I had grabbed from the front hall out of Mr. Newcastle's things. I had my own hats, of course, but they were mostly packed away, and Mr. Newcastle's was closer.

I'll bet there were fifteen people in the garden, the same garden where Mr. Newcastle had danced with me and got drunk the afternoon before. They all looked as if they'd just dropped what they were doing and come to mourn. A couple of them looked pretty hungover, too.

They set the coffin down at the side of the grave. Everybody moved in close, all sniffily, and the preacher began to talk.

The coffin thumped, loud.

Everybody jumped. Well, at least I did, for it was like a gunshot. I admit I was plenty scared till I realized it was probably just his opera hat, snapping open. Sam Two Trees had the same idea, although he had to pry the lid up to assure Miss Jessie and Miss Jonquil that Jonas wasn't still alive and battering the lid to get out. While he was prying it, I remembered what I'd said to Miss Jessie that morning on the stair, and despite the heat, a little chill ran through me.

There was no time to comment, though. We all grouped 'round the grave again, and the preacher, the same preacher who had wed us, took up where he had left off. He hadn't gone a whole sentence when I felt a little *thwap* on my hat.

I jerked, but I didn't look up. I didn't have to. A house finch fell next to my shoe, its rosy breast shuddering one last time. Miss Jonquil glanced over and gave me a nasty look, like it was my fault.

I looked at the ground.

Parson Brown was talking about what a civic-minded citizen Jonas Newcastle had been—how he had twice saved the nation from the Indian Menace, and mined the valley, and given to the poor—when I was struck again. Another finch, this one's breast pale orange, dropped beside the first. Miss Jonquil took a step away from me—I didn't look up, but I could see those teensy pointy-toed shoes of hers—and the parson stuttered a bit.

"Jonas always took good care of his sisters," he went on, "and saw to it that Miss Jessie and Miss Jonquil never wanted for anything. No one knows better than they what a loss to us his death is, how much poorer are we all for his passing."

Two quick *thwaps*. I closed my eyes. I couldn't believe this was happening, and in front of fifteen strangers to boot. When I slitted my eyes to peek, two more finches lay in the dirt, already dead. By now, the crowd was giving me a wide berth and the preacher was stumbling over his words.

"Blessed be the name of . . . of . . ."

Just like that, it was raining birds. Finches, sparrows, swallows, and flickers pelted down, and every single one of them landed headfirst on my hat. I believe Miss Jessie gave out with a brittle scream, though I can't be sure it was her as I was running for the house by then.

I dashed inside and slammed the door closed behind me, and I was shaking so hard that my teeth were rattling. I told myself that it couldn't be me, it was these crazy Arizona birds! Maybe it was some Iowa scent on my skin that drove them mad, or maybe it was Jonas's hat.

I took it off and looked at it. It was dented up some, but other than a few stray feathers and a few flecks of bird blood, it was not damaged.

I had stopped shaking by then, and I walked back through the house, back through those big, dark rooms, till I found a window that overlooked the garden. Slowly, I pulled back the heavy velvet drapes. Sure enough, the funeral was back in progress with no diving birds to be seen. But all along the path of my retreat, there was a trail of tiny bodies.

I let go of the drapes, plunging the room into shadow again and letting loose a cloud of dust. I don't guess velvet can be easy to keep clean in the desert, but I sure went into one monster of a sneezing fit. I sneezed and stumbled my way out of that room, still sneezing, and it wasn't till I got back in the front hall that I heard somebody calling me.

I turned 'round and said, "What!" between sneezes, but by then my eyes were so teared up that I couldn't see for beans. *Hold your finger under your nose and press hard on your lip,* he said. I did it, and just like that, the sneezing stopped.

"Thanks," I said, looking up and sniffing.

Nobody was there.

"Hey!" I said.

Nothing.

"I know that voice. You called to me earlier, in the garden. Come out where I can see you!"

Still nothing.

Now, it was bad enough that I'd left home and married an old geezer. Worse that he'd died on our wedding night and left me his two old maid sisters to take care of. Worse yet that every bird in Arizona had taken a distinct dislike to me, to the point of killing themselves on my noggin. Wasn't

that enough trial? But now there was some joker trying to
get up a game of hide-and-seek with me.

Well, I wasn't going to play. I went into the parlor and
sat down in a heap on the big round ottoman—mauve velveteen, it was—and counted my woes. I wondered how
many birds there were in Arizona, and how long it would
take me to go through them all. I figured maybe I'd paint a
bull's-eye on my hat. Make it easier for them.

Having the house—and whatever money Jonas had left
me—was a boon, but I was thinking that it didn't offset a
bunch of birds with a grudge.

Annie?

I didn't look up this time. I didn't answer, either.

Annie Newcastle.

I kept my eyes to my lap.

Annie Pinkerton Newcastle! This time it was a shout that
nearly shook the black rock walls.

"What!" I yelled back. "Show yourself!" I added when I
couldn't see anybody, though it was hard to tell where it
was coming from. "Haven't I got enough trouble with suicide finches and dead people's hats? Sam Two Trees, is that
you? Are you throwing your voice in a cowardly manner?"

*Bully! You hear me! I'm sorry I called your grandmoth-
er's name.*

"What the dickens are you talking about?" For the life of
me, I couldn't locate the source of that voice. He had to be
somewhere in the room, it was that clear. I got up and
looked behind the drapes, but all I got was another noseful
of dust.

"What do you mean?" I said, once I got the sneezing
stopped. I peered under the sofa, then the divan. Maybe the
fireplace? It was surely big enough to stand in. "What about
my grandmother?"

When I said Frieda just before I . . . When I said Frieda.

I peered up the flue. "Nobody's ever mentioned Grandma's name to me except my mama, and she's with Jesus."
Then I thought about how mean Mama had been, and
added, "Well, she's with somebody."

You're not going to find me, my love.

Now, I thought that was pretty brassy, some total stranger calling me "my love" when he didn't even have the sand to stand out where a body could see him, and I told him so.

I can't. Not yet.

He was making me mad. "How do you mean? Show yourself this minute!"

I turned in a quick circle, hoping to catch a glimpse of him, but the person I saw was Miss Jessie. She had just come into the hall, and she was staring at me real funny. She said, "Dear? To whom are you speaking?"

"Is it you?" I demanded. "Are you throwing your voice?" Then, just as fast, "Don't eat that pork, Miss Jessie, don't eat it, it's gone bad, have the jelly roll instead. Chicago will win the pennant—fifty-six victories, twenty-eight defeats!"

I slapped both hands over my mouth. I didn't know what had taken hold of me. It was like somebody else was saying the words.

Miss Jessie put her narrow-veiny hands to her cheeks and called, "Sister! Sister, come quickly! Something's wrong with Brother's widow!"

There were a whole flock of people filing into the hall by then, the services being over, and Miss Jonquil came past her sister and into the parlor, running as fast as her brittle-stick legs could carry her.

"What's wrong? What's wrong?" she cried, her arms held wide, like she planned to embrace me. Or maybe smack me.

I backed up a couple of steps. "Nothing! Nothing's wrong except somebody is playing tricks on me, throwing his voice and—" There was that funny feeling again, like somebody else was using my mouth. "Mr. Alvarez, go home, your wife is in labor."

One of the Mexicans who had carried the coffin said, "*Si, Patron!*" real automatic, then shook his head, like he was trying to clear it. He raised an eyebrow, said, "*Señora*, excuse me," and scurried from the room.

Miss Jessie was still in the hallway, except now she looked like somebody had just shot her. She wobbled, and Sam Two Trees took hold of her arm and held her up.

Miss Jonquil was made of sterner stuff. To the crowd, she

said, "If everyone will repair to the dining room? There are refreshments." She waited while they shuffled away, all of them except Miss Jessie and Sam Two Trees.

"How dare you!" she snapped as she turned to me. Boy, she was sure changed from that frail little old lady who met me in town. I'll bet she could have brought down a bobcat with her bare knuckles. "How dare you make sport of dear dead Brother!"

She was mad all right, but you hadn't seen mad unless you'd seen Mama on a tear. Miss Jonquil might have thought to cow me, but it didn't work, not even a little.

I said, "It seems like somebody is making sport of me, Miss Jonquil. And I'll ask you not to use that tone. I did what I was told and came down here and married your brother and . . . and . . ."

That feeling was coming over me again. I was getting to recognize it. I said, "Mrs. Alvarez will have a girl, and they'll name her Ramona. Hey ho, we're off to the circus!"

Miss Jonquil looked startled, but then I guess she decided to pretend I hadn't said anything, because she started in on me again. I didn't catch what she said, though, because just about then, the voice said, *Annie? Can you hear me?*

"Who are you? Where are you?"

I was staring up at the ceiling then, it being the only place I hadn't searched.

Miss Jonquil grabbed my arm with bony fingers and tried to shake me, without much luck.

Annie, it's Jonas.

"No." I wagged my head. "No, you're dead. They just buried you." It was funny how I felt. It was like an insane person had just come into the room, and I was trying, real calm, to talk him out of stabbing the baby.

My hat popped up. Don't know why they buried me in that outfit. Smelled like mothballs. I hadn't worn it since '75. Say, this is getting easier. I believe I'm getting the hang of it!

Miss Jonquil had backed off, and Miss Jessie, having the frailer temperament, had fainted. Sam Two Trees hadn't noticed though. He was still holding her up by one arm like a rag doll, and he was staring straight at me.

I said, "You heard that, didn't you? Miss Jonquil?"

She made the sign of the cross, which I thought was real odd for a Baptist lady, and then she breathed, "She's mad. Grief has stricken her with madness." Her hands trembled as she covered her face. "Those birds have hurt her brain, oh, those horrid birds!"

Sam Two Trees looked square at me and said, "Ghost talker."

"What do you mean, 'ghost talker'? Didn't you hear him? I tell you, somebody's having a joke on me, and it's not funny, not one bit."

He's right. And the birds will go away. Well, most of them. I'm sorry about the other, but there's so much going on here! Voices talking, talking all the time, but I can't see the people. Can't always make out the words, but by God, the things I know! Poof, just like that! Sometimes it just leaks over into you.

"There! Didn't you hear him? It's plain as day!"

Sam Two Trees' face was stone. I couldn't read it anymore than when he was digging the grave or serving up barbecue. He said, "Heard what?"

One look at Miss Jonquil told me she hadn't heard either.

I whispered, "Mercy sakes alive." Then I sat down, hard. It was a good thing the ottoman was behind me, or I would have landed on the floor.

There, there. One bad thing about being dead, you can't touch anybody, not really. Oh, how I'd love to pinch your soft little nipples—

"Mr. Newcastle!"

No one else can hear, Frieda. Sorry. Annie. Annie dearest. Annie darling. My Annie.

Revelation overtook me, and I shot to my feet. "Frieda! You didn't shout freedom, it was Frieda!"

Miss Jonquil chose that moment to faint dead away, but I didn't have time to catch her.

"You said my sweet grandma's name while you were . . . were . . . while you were doing *that?*"

No answer.

"Mr. Newcastle? Mr. Newcastle!"

"Annie?" It was Sam Two Trees.

"What!"

"Put the vase down and help me with the ladies."

I hadn't realized I was armed. I guess it was Mama coming out in me. I thought I set the vase down careful, but it fell on the floor and broke anyway. I can't say I paid much attention. I walked toward Miss Jonquil, a black puddle on the floor, a black puddle with two thin white hands and a white face like paper floating in it, and she seemed to get farther and farther away with every step.

And in my head, I kept hearing Sam Two Trees say *ghost talker* like it was natural, like it happened every day of the week and twice on Sundays. But it didn't happen to me, it didn't happen in Sycamore, Iowa, not to nice people, not to any people! And then it finally hit me, for now I was no longer carried forward by the zealousness of the moment or the concentration or the anger.

I suddenly felt real light, like my feet weren't touching the floor or maybe I didn't even have feet. I had been talking to Jonas Newcastle's ghost, and nobody had heard him but me.

Ghost.

I guess it was right about then that I joined the crowd and fainted.

4

Now, I don't suppose it seems natural that a person could get used to a thing like being haunted, or that the folks around me could grow to accept it, even welcome it, but that is exactly what happened.

Oh, the sisters were upset, right at the first. They sent for the parson, but he said it wasn't his field. They sent for a priest, but the closest mission was nearly thirty miles away. By the time the priest got the message and realized it wasn't a joke and then came up to Newcastle's Castle, Mr. Newcastle had talked Miss Jessie and Miss Jonquil out of wanting him exorcised.

He talked the priest out of it, too. I don't know exactly what he said, since I was off someplace at the time. Mr. Newcastle most always booted me off to somewhere still and dark when he wanted to speak through my mouth. But Father Sebastian came in full of worrisome platitudes and cursing the works of Satan, and exited all smiles and praising the wondrous works of the Lord and kissing my—or, I guess, Jonas's—hand.

Me, I didn't have any say in it. Mr. Newcastle kept my mouth closed, my eyes blinded, and my ears stoppered for most of the while the priest was with us.

Well, three weeks later, Mr. Newscastle was still blabbering to beat the band—I could hear him plain as day when he was carrying on inside my skull—but we had made an agreement. He was to hold his peace during the nighttime, since all during the first week I had enjoyed no sleep at all, what with him all of a sudden shouting "Baseball!" or "Oil, it's going to be oil next!" All the commotion was all inside my skull, of course, so I was the only one to be disturbed; but still, a thing like that gets old the second or third time.

So he was to leave me alone while I was sleeping, and also during the days between noon and two, and again between six and eight in the evening. He was real good about it. Come noon, even if he was midsentence, I would say, "Mr. Newcastle, you are on the clock," and he would shut up quicker than a freshwater clam and not say another word until his time was up.

And I honored my side of the bargain. Oh, I was tempted, mind you. I guess they don't have clocks where he was, do they? But I had struck a bargain, and he was so good about stopping when I told him that I didn't have the heart not to tell him when to start up again. Mama always said that I thought with my heart and not my noggin. I guess she was right.

Anyway, it was coming September, and although the heat had not diminished appreciably, the crowds had swelled, and I do mean crowds.

At first it was Mexicans, maybe one or two, with their broad-brimmed sombreros in their hands, and then it got to be five or six people a day, and pretty soon all sorts of folks—Mexican, white, Chinese, colored, and tame Indians; poor and rich and in between—were making pilgrimages from all over Arizona Territory, just to talk to me.

Well, Mr. Newcastle.

They were all different kinds. Mothers, clad in black and weeping over lost children, wanting to make certain their little ones were safe in the arms of Jesus. Ladies who wanted their futures told, who wanted to hear of dashing young bucks or vaqueros just panting to carry them off.

Mostly, the men wanted to know where to dig for gold or silver, or if they'd make it big in the saloon or dry goods businesses, or where they could find the lost El Galgo mines. That last one got asked by about every fourth man.

We turned away most of those folks. Mr. Newcastle wasn't any good—at least, he said he wasn't—at telling people where to find a lost gold mine, or that they were going to find their true love on a Thursday. As far as babies in heaven went, he paid no attention to the dead nor the dying, unless it was somebody he knew personally. That, or maybe somebody famous.

He would have no truck with the blind that were led to that big black castle, or the crippled that came crawling. The deaf got turned away with their ears still plugged, and the lame limped off home the same way they'd come.

That's not my job, Annie, he'd say inside me while I was washing my face or braiding my hair. *That's not at all what I want to do. I don't know what's wrong with these fools!*

No, what Mr. Newcastle wanted to do was to orate. He took me over at first, and I'll be fried if I can remember a thing about those first few days. I'd just get all woozy in the head when he'd start in, and come to my senses at nine or ten in the evening, when the sisters pushed the last self-invited guest out the big front doors.

That's why I had to put a stop to it. Ghosts don't have to eat or drink or use the convenience, which I sure did.

See there? I just called him a ghost. The truth is, I still don't know to this day what was the right thing to call him. A ghost is something that lurks around, clanking chains and moaning and turning the halls chilly over in England or Scotland. Mr. Newcastle never once clanked or turned the hall cold. And trust me, I would have welcomed a cold hall that summer.

I asked him once if I could call him a spirit, and he got kind of huffy.

Why don't you just call me Mr. Newcastle? he said. And then his voice got real smooth and he added, *Or Jonas, if you like, Annie. After all, we've been—*

"Mr. Newcastle is fine," I said, and that was the end of the matter.

What he orated about mostly was the future. "The Coming

Majesty of the Age of Invention," Sam Two Trees said he
called it. Oh, he talked about horse races and baseball sometimes, and politics and war, too. And sometimes he talked
about folks he knew, like that time the day of his funeral
when he told Mr. Alvarez to get home quick, because his
wife was about to have a daughter.

But mostly, it was the future in the general sense, and
with a lot of his own personal life and times wrapped up
in it.

Anyway, that's what Sam said.

Sam was the one to keep me up to date on Mr. Newcastle's ramblings. Miss Jessie and Miss Jonquil were sure no
good at it. They had gone from scared spitless to puffed up
with pride inside of a week. By the time September rolled
around, they were charging a dime for admission to see me,
plus a nickel for lunch for those who didn't bring their own.

If, when Mr. Newcastle released me, I asked them what
he had talked about today, they'd only flutter and stammer,
and say things like, "Oh, he was wonderful! Wasn't he wonderful, Sister?"

"He sounds so bold, too!" the second one would add.

"Just like a young man again!"

"Oh, indeed!"

They were no help.

It was a Sunday, and Mr. Newcastle had called his lecture
quits at noon on account of the Sabbath. After lunch, Sam
Two Trees asked me if I'd like to have a ride on the desert.
Since I had got cabin fever real bad, being stuck in that fool
of a house with only short excursions into the gardens, I
said, "Sure," and fetched my hat.

We set off down the hill, me and Sam, riding the buggy
horses that had brought me there in the first place. We rode
and we rode, Sam up ahead, clad in his Indian togs and
head sash—orange that day—till that black old castle was
just a speck in the distance. And the whole of the time we
rode, the birds fell all around me.

Sam twisted in his saddle. "That hat works pretty good,"
he commented. A half-grown crow had just slid to the

ground, dead as a doornail. It was a biggish bird, and had made quite a thump.

"That it does," I said, and it was the truth. The evening after the funeral, Sam had rigged me a broad-brimmed hat, kind of Chinese-looking, out of scrap tin. "It works fine, but it makes a racket," I added. "Don't take me wrong, Sam. A little noise is sure better than a bloody scalp."

He nodded, then pursed his lips with thought. Two dead finches bounced from my hat to my shoulder to the ground while he mulled it over. Finally he looked up, all serious. "I'll glue some felt on it when we get back."

I said, "That would be fine."

I was glad, not only for the dulling of all those pings and thuds, but also because I thought the felt might make it cooler to wear. I swear, two minutes after we'd left the house that day, my head felt like a pork roast. Of course, I blamed it partly on my black dress—between Mama and Mr. Newcastle, I was in double mourning—but that tin hat didn't help one bit.

I didn't like to say anything, though, as Sam had made it special.

"Sam?" I said, more to fill in the time than anything else. "You know all about me, but I don't know a thing about you."

"I wouldn't exactly say I know your whole story," he replied. He was riding up ahead of me.

I stuck out my tongue at his back. "Well, you know some of it, anyway. All I know about you is that you're half-Indian and you work here and you cook a real good crusted beef roast—"

"Wellington," he said with a sigh. "Beef Wellington." He didn't turn around, but I knew he was rolling his eyes heavenward in exasperation.

"Right," I said. "Beef Wellington. But how come you're working here in the first place? Seems to me you could do a lot better. Seems to me there are a lot better places to cook than for a couple of papery old ladies in the middle of nowhere. Someplace where Miss Jonquil won't make a face and pick all the crust off your beef Wellington or scrape your holiday sauce off the vegetables, for instance."

He made a small shrugging motion with his shoulders and reined in his horse long enough for me to ride up even with him. "Hollandaise. And it's boring," he warned.

"I don't care. Tell me anyway. How'd you get here, and how'd you learn to speak such good English? Where'd you learn to cook so fancy?"

He smiled a little. "First off," he said, "it's easy to speak good English when your mother was white and you never knew your father. He raped her."

He said it so matter of fact that it took me a second to register it. And then, all I could think of to say was, "I'm sorry."

He shrugged. "So was he. After it was over, my mother snatched a carving knife off the table and stuck it eight inches deep into his side. Course, that didn't stop me. I'd already taken root inside her." His eyes flicked toward me, and he added, "Better close your mouth, Annie. One of those birds might miss your hat and head for your tonsils."

I closed my mouth with a click. "But you dress Indian sometimes," I said.

"My mother and her husband were missionaries on the reservation," he explained, reaching over to brush away the cactus wren that had just pinged off my hat and slid to my leg. "After Mr. Forrester died—that was her husband—she stayed on. A year or so later, she was making plans to go back east when my father raped her. Afterward—after she learned she was carrying me, I mean—she decided it might be wiser to stay on the reservation."

"And you took the name of that— You took your father's name?"

He shook his head. "I took my name. The name that the tribe gave me. I use it instead of a last name."

I screwed up my face. "Two Trees?"

"I had big legs when I was a kid. Happy now?"

Well, he'd solved part of the mystery, but not enough as far as I was concerned. I said, "But how'd you come to work for Mr. Newcastle? And how'd you learn to cook? I mean, I can see you learning regular things, like pancakes or fried chicken or roast venison, but how'd you learn to make—"

"—catfish galettes and quenelles," he broke in, "and choucroute garni—"

"That last one was the sauerkraut with pork chops and sausages?"

"Right," he said, and I could tell that he was pleased that I had remembered, even though we'd had it just two nights before. I guess he wasn't used to having his cooking appreciated.

He reined his horse around one side of a big patch of prickly pear and I reined mine around the other side, and when we came together again, I said, "Well, how'd that get started? They didn't teach that on the reservation."

Grinning, he shook his head. "You ask a lot of questions. But just to shut you up, I'll give you the short version. All right?"

I nodded.

"I met Jonas Newcastle," he began, "because he used to bring cattle to the reservation. In fact, I don't remember a time when I didn't know him. When mother died—I was eight—Jonas took me in. He didn't exactly raise me like a son or anything. After all, I was half Navajo."

He scowled. "An important man like Jonas can't have a half-breed following him around and calling him 'Daddy' or even 'Uncle Jonas'. But he fed me and clothed me and saw I was schooled, and when I got old enough, he sent me back east to further my education."

A sparrow hit me with quite a bang, but I paid it little mind. I said, "He sent you to cooking school?"

Sam laughed. "Not hardly! But while I was there learning about ancient Troy and gerunds and the anatomy of flowers, I happened to eat in a French restaurant. It was like . . . Well, it was a religious experience. I went back the next day and applied for a job as a chef's assistant. They hired me, and that was it. I quit school and started working full time. To make a long story short, Jonas found out and ordered me back home. So I quit my job and went."

I opened my mouth, but Sam beat me to the punch.

"Because I owed him, that's why," he said. "No more questions. We're almost there."

He reined his horse in halfway up a rocky hill and so did I, and we tied our mounts to a creosote bush in the shade of an outcrop. Then Sam slid his saddlebags down. "This way," he said, and started up, the bags slung over his shoulder.

I followed him almost to the crest, cactus wrens and thrashers sporadically diving to their fluttery dooms on my tin Chinese topper, and then sat beside him in a thin purply patch of shade made by the boulders in back of us.

Neither one of us talked. I guess that story had shut me up. I kept thinking how hard it must have been for Sam to come back here once he'd had a taste of the big city, and what it must have been like to be brought up in Jonas' house, part of the family but not part of it.

Sam opened his saddlebags, and brought out a big mason jar of lemonade from one side and two glasses from the other. He poured one out and handed it to me.

Pouring the second glass for himself, he said, "Are you alone?"

He meant Mr. Newcastle. I checked my watch pin. "For another twenty-seven minutes," I said. I had a long drink of my lemonade. It was warm, but it tasted past wonderful. Sam made it with lemons from the lower garden and mesquite honey, and he made it just right.

"Got a problem," Sam said, not looking at me, but straight out, back toward the house. It was just a black speck in the distance, riding that tall hill.

I was still thinking about French cooking. I said, "Why? Are you making holiday—I mean *hollandaise* sauce again?" The last time he'd made it, both the sisters had scraped it off their plates and made faces behind his back.

"No." He kept staring at the house. "Money problems."

I said, "Money problems? How could the Newcastles have money problems? Why, they've got the . . . well, they've got the biggest house in the territory, I'll bet, even if it's ugly.

All those tapestries and real china and the paintings from over in Europe!"

He still stared straight out ahead. He shrugged. "You were an expensive bride."

"What?" I gasped.

He finally turned to look at me. "Be quiet," he said. "You'll scare the hawks."

Frankly, I didn't much care whether the hawks were scared or not. I said, "What have hawks got to do with being broke? And what do you mean, I was expensive?" All of a sudden, I realized what a big bird a hawk is, and covered my head with my arms just in time for a suicidal Mexican dove to land on my hand, beak first.

Sam let me sit there like that—sucking my dove-stuck knuckles, and scared to death one of those hawks would see me and I'd be concussed by the next biggest thing to an eagle—for a good thirty seconds before he said, "Don't worry. They didn't show any interest when we crossed their territory."

I just stared at him. I couldn't believe he'd led me out here through a hotbed of hawks without telling me. And then I got to wondering why he'd said "they" when hawks are solitary. Maybe a couple of them had a nest nearby, but there being just the pair of them didn't make me feel any happier about it.

But rather than ask about killer birds, I said, "Back up. To where the Newcastles are broke."

He opened the jar and topped off my lemonade, saying, "You're a Newcastle now, too."

I didn't say anything. I pictured Mama, pointing her finger and laughing at me.

He capped the jar and made a level place in the dust to set it. "Miss Jessie and Miss Jonquil don't know," he said. "Old Jonas, he never told them. He never told them anything. He didn't think it was a woman's place to worry about money."

A wren banged off my hat and tumbled, in a soft little heap of feathers, next to the dove. I ignored it. "But you do."

He nodded. "Somebody's got to. All those dimes and five-

cent nickels they're charging would be a help, but Miss Jonquil's got 'em in a bag upstairs. Miss Jessie helps her count
'em every night. They think they're pretty."

He shook his head slow. "Jonas took care of everything.
They wanted a new silver service, and poof, there it was.
They needed frocks? The dressmaker showed up. When
Rock Bottom was a real town, they just picked out what
they wanted and walked off with it or had it delivered, and
Jonas paid. So you can see, it's up to you now."

"Why me?" I sputtered. "How come *I'm* the one? Why, I
could hop on a stagecoach right now and take myself back
home, up to Iowa, and—"

"Hush!" he whispered, lifting his hand and pointing.
"Watch!"

Like magic, five big bay-wing hawks had materialized
down on the flat. We don't see them in Iowa, getting mostly
the red-tailed variety or the little sharp-shinned hawks, but
I was salutatorian of my class and I knew right off what
they were. Perched on saguaro and prickly pear, four of
them watched the fifth. It was diving at something that
seemed to have run to the shelter of a brambly mesquite
thicket.

And then, two more left their perches. They went in opposite directions and circled back on the wind, coming at that
mesquite from opposite sides.

First, one dived at it, then the next, and then all five of
the hawks had taken wing, like they were hunting in a pack,
like they thought they were timber wolves. First one would
almost hit the mesquite, talons forward, and then it'd veer
away and another hawk would swoop down, fast and savage and beautiful. My heart was pounding, I can tell you.

"I've never seen the like!" I whispered to Sam, not taking
my eyes from those swooping, diving birds. Even though
they were a ways off, the air was filled with their rough
squeals.

"They're driving it," he said. "Watch. There, at the far
end."

Sure enough, they were going that way. And then, all of
a sudden, they stopped like somebody had blown a whistle

and the game was over. They flew back to their cactus perches. I held my breath.

And then a sixth hawk, one I hadn't seen before, rose up from the ground, a lifeless jackrabbit dangling from its talons. As he gained altitude, the other birds took the air and they left, following after him, heading to the west.

"Will they kill it?" I asked Sam Two Trees. "The other hawk, I mean. The one that got their rabbit." I was still breathless.

"No. The one with the rabbit is part of their pack. They'll share."

I made a face, because everybody knows what selfish birds hawk are. I said, "What?"

"In this place, with these hawks, they share. They band together in the desert. They have to, to kill prey and to fend off the owls that kill their chicks. This desert is the only place where the bay-wings pack up, where they hunt like wolves." He stood up, bringing the mason jar and his saddlebags with him. "I thought you should see."

I got up, too, shaking my head. "Well, I've never seen the like," I said.

"You said that already." He put the jar away, then held out his hand for my glass. "You got a letter."

Sam was sure full of surprises. First, that tale of his conception and birth and being taken under Jonas's wing, then that business about being broke—even though I still didn't see that it was any of my nevermind—and then those hawks. And now a letter.

"Who from?" I said, a little surly. I liked my surprises spaced out quite a bit wider than what Sam had them stacked up that morning. "I don't know anybody who'd write to me. Anyway, not so quick after leaving Sycamore."

He buckled up his saddlebags and started down the hill. "Wasn't from Sycamore."

Something thudded on my hat. I didn't look to see what kind of bird it was. I don't mean to seem like I was heartless, or that I didn't feel bad about so many little feathered souls going to Jesus on my account, but when a creature is committed to self-destruction and there's nothing you can do to

stop it, you get sort of blasé after a while. So I just skidded
down the hill after Sam. "Who's it from, then?"

"It came three days ago," he said. He was already over
by the horses and securing his saddlebags, and his back
was to me. "There were more, but this one was important,
I think."

"Three days?" A sparrow came diving straight for my face,
and I ducked so quick that I fell on my backside, just like
that. The sparrow ricocheted off my hat, and Sam didn't
even turn around.

I clambered to my feet, and while I was banging the dust
out of my skirts and wishing I'd never heard of Mr. Jonas
Newcastle, Sam said, "Miss Jonquil opened it and threw it
away. She throws away all your mail."

I was twisted 'round, beating the dirt out of my bustle
and coughing at the clouds of dust. "Opened what? Threw
what away?"

"Your letter. Here, let me get that for you."

He took my arm, gave my skirts about three good shakes,
then picked me up as easy as he'd pick up a thistle and
plopped me atop my horse. "Your letter," he repeated, looking up at me from that nut-brown face. "Your letter from
Mr. Barnum."

"From who?"

"Mr. P. T. Barnum," he said, mounting up. "He wants you
to be in his circus."

A couple of minutes later, it was time for Mr. Newcastle
to come in again, so Sam and I dropped the subject until I
had time to think about it. We rode on back to the house
in silence.

Well, Sam did, anyway. Me, I had to listen to Mr. Newcastle go on and on about his plans for the lower garden
and the upper, and how he wanted me to get another
lemon tree.

*Plant it by the wall, Annie, over in the corner. And make
certain Sam leaves a wide irrigation cup in the soil. Water
it every day—water it deeply, now—until it gets its roots
down deep.*

"All right," I said, trying not to think about Mr. P.T. Barnum and his circus. Of all the fool ideas! "A lemon tree. I'll water it."

When we got back and Sam was putting up the horses, Mr. Newcastle had me call the sisters to the front room. Having spent twenty-five minutes of his attention giving me orders on where to throw the daisy seeds next spring and who to order the lemon tree from and also the bougainvillea, I supposed he was inclined to talk to somebody else.

Once the sisters got settled and were leaned forward, all eager with their narrow, bony hands folded in their laps, he said, *"That'll be all, Annie."* The next thing I knew it was half past five and Miss Jonquil was getting to her feet. Miss Jessie looked a fright.

I yawned, and didn't bother to cover my mouth. This was one of those times when Mr. Newcastle just left, without being told, to go wherever it was he went off to. He'd left early, too, for which I was grateful.

I said, "Miss Jonquil? I trust you had a pleasant chat with your brother?"

Now, three hours is more than enough for a "chat" in anyone's book, and by the look on their faces I guessed it had been more like a serious discussion, but I couldn't just say that out, could I? Not to two old ladies a stiff breeze could have taken away.

Miss Jonquil put a hand down to her sister and eyed me, all birdy and staring. For a second she reminded me of one of those hawks, out on the desert.

"Just do as you please," she snapped. "Just be selfish. Go ahead! Think only of yourself."

Miss Jessie moaned. "But Brother said—"

"—to let her be," Miss Jonquil broke in, her frail old lady's voice a low, papery growl. She cast me a look that was more pit viper than human female. "And we shall. We certainly shall!"

She gave Miss Jessie another yank, but when all she pulled out of her was another moan, she just turned her back on the both of us and left the room, crossing that

echoey front hall like a stiff-backed soldier and marching up
the wide stairs.

If she was looking for dramatic effect, then she got her
wish. Both Miss Jessie and I watched the whole thing and
then listened till her door slammed before we looked at
each other.

"Miss Jessie?" I said. "Would you like something to drink?"
When dealing with old ladies, give them a glass of water
when you're in doubt, that's my motto.

But she shook her head no, and motioned me back down
on my chair. "You must forgive Sister," she said, digging
fitfully in her pocket. "She's—we've—just been given some
most distressing news."

At last her fingers found what she wanted and she pulled
out a tiny lace hanky, stiff with starch and ironed till I
thought the creases would never come out. She daubed at
her nose with it.

"News?" I said, more to fill in the conversational void
than anything else. I doubted Mr. Newcastle had told them
anything more than that he was having me plant a lemon
tree, but to those two, I guessed that could be cause for an
emotional upheaval.

"The news of our financial difficulty, of course," Miss Jessie said, and then she blew her nose into her hankie with
a real full-fledged goose honk.

I don't know which startled me more, that big noise coming from that tiny, frail woman or Mr. Newcastle spilling
the beans.

"You'll take complete charge, of course," she went on.
"And naturally, we shall follow Brother's wishes. You must
find it in your heart to forgive Sister. She'll apologize herself,
once she thinks about it a little." Miss Jessie shook her head
solemnly. "She always was headstrong. These last weeks,
with everyone coming to the house, have been . . ."

She paused, and I was waiting for her to say "horrid" or
"a strain on all of us," but what she said, finally, was "so
exciting! Why, we haven't had so much activity here since
the builders left. Of course," she added, leaning forward
confidentially, "they were the lower class sort. Craftsmen

and the like. And frankly, quite a few of your visitors have been, as well. But to hear laughter in the house again . . ."

She leaned back, fanning herself lackadaisically with that now-limp hankie and staring at the ceiling. "Brother told Sister to stop taking your mail. I told her she shouldn't, but then, she never did listen to me. I'm the weak one, you know. 'Poor Jessie, she always crumbles in a crisis.' "

She dropped her gaze from the ceiling to my face. "I'll have you know that when the very *president* of the Union Pacific Railroad came here for dinner and the aspic melted, *I* was the one who suggested serving fruit cup instead!" She gave a small but superior lift to her eyebrows. "Crumble? I should say I didn't!"

I said, "My goodness." This was about the lengthiest conversation I'd had with either sister since my arrival, but I found myself wishing that she'd get to the point.

Like she'd read my mind, she said, "At any rate, Sister won't open your mail anymore or throw it out. I told her she shouldn't, but she would have her way. And you're to follow Brother's instructions. We won't say a word."

She really had me confused. "What instructions, Miss Jessie? All he told me was where to locate the new plants in the garden."

She cocked her narrow head to one side. "Brother wants the garden changed?"

I waved my hands. "Forget I said that. What instructions?"

"Why, about our financial embarrassment, of course." She looked out into the hall, as if searching out eavesdropping spies. Lowering her voice to a whisper, she added, "You're to do whatever Brother deems fit, and Sister and I won't say a word. And . . . and we're to give all our lovely dimes and nickels to Sam Two Trees."

She paused, biting delicately at her lips. "I . . . I don't suppose we could keep just a few? I wanted to make a necklace of the shiniest ones."

I stood up and went to sit next to her on the davenport, taking her powdery hand in mine. It was cool and dry and soft. "I imagine that just a few wouldn't hurt a thing, Miss Jessie."

5

All during dinner and later on, after I went up to my room, I puzzled over how in tarnation Mr. Newcastle had known to tell the sisters about his money mess. In the end, it came down to one possibility. I hated to say it, but I suspected Mr. Newcastle had been listening in on Sam and me, when he was supposed to be off somewhere.

And then I started thinking: Where exactly did he go when I put him on the clock? Maybe he'd never gone anywhere at all. Maybe he just sat wherever it was he sat, and listened in on my private conversations!

"Mr. Newcastle!" I said, even though it was only a quarter till eight and I had fifteen minutes of "alone" time left. "Have you been eavesdropping?"

There was a sound like a yawn, and then, *What's that, Annie?*

"You heard me, old man." I crossed my arms and tapped my foot. It wasn't very Scotch or German, but it sure was Mama.

There was a long pause, and then, finally, he said, *Oh, all right. I can't help it, if that makes any difference to you. And I'm truly sorry about this money muddle. Really, dear Annie. I just didn't expect to pass on. Well, who would? But the house was so expensive and the furnishings . . . it was all for you, my angel, all for you.*

I sat down on the edge of my bed, my hairbrush in my lap. I was still hopping mad. Actually, I had been mad a lot of times just since coming to Arizona. As much as I didn't want to be like Mama, at least not in that way, secretly I admired the way it felt.

"You beat everything, you know that Mr. Newcastle? First you buy the boardinghouse out from under Mama. Then you kill her, for all I know—"

Certainly not! he broke in.

"Then you haul me all the way down here and marry me and then die on me—all the while shouting my sainted grandma's name—and then you start haunting me. And now, after I've been nice enough to let you speechify from beyond the grave for almost a month using *my* mouth and *my* body, Sam Two Trees has to tell me about your sorry finances because you're afraid to!"

All of a sudden, I realized my arm had gone numb and was creeping inside the top of my nightgown. I grabbed it with my other hand and said, "Mr. Newcastle! There'll be none of that!"

My arm was mine again, just like that, and Mr. Newcastle loosed a long sigh inside my head. *You're no fun, Annie. Wouldn't you let a poor old dead man—*

"No," I said, firm as a made bed. "What are you going to do about these money problems?" I began to brush my hair, as much as to keep my hands occupied as anything else.

I think the question is, more precisely, what are you going to do about them? he replied, kind of snooty. *After all, I'm dead. It's no skin off my nose. I don't even have a nose.*

I shrugged. I could be snooty, too. "Fine with me," I said. "Let your sisters starve. Let this spooky old castle fall to crumble and melt. I'm going back up to Iowa, where things are green and the hawks act normal and you can't fry an egg on the front porch. I'll get a job at Miss Enid's Tasty Eats Café, and I'll do just dandy, thank you very much."

Just like that, I heard a *whoosh* and all of a sudden I was pinned down on the bed, hands over my shoulders, and Mr. Newcastle was saying, *No you don't, Annie girl!*

His tone was not in the least kindly.

You're staying where I want you to stay, and that's not Iowa. You'll do what I want you to do. His tone softened some then—I guess he knew he'd scared me good—and he added, *You're special, Annie. I've made you even more special. Don't you like it? Isn't it fine to have them crowd at your feet and hang on your every word? Isn't it wonderful to know everything, to see it all?*

He still had me pinned. I couldn't feel my arms or my torso, and I was trembling in my soul. But I said, "I wouldn't know about any of that. You send me away, remember? It's your feet they're sitting at, your words they're hanging on. It's unseemly, that's what it is."

Oh, Annie, we could be such a team, you and I, he whispered, and I began to feel the numbness creep over the rest of my body.

"Mr. Newcastle?" I said, my voice coming out a little whimper when I meant it to be strong. "Mr. Newcastle? What are you doing?"

Oh, Frieda . . .

I watched my arms drift down and my hands cover my breasts, and I couldn't stop them, couldn't feel them, couldn't feel anything, like everything I was—mind, soul, hands, feet, everything—had suddenly shrunk so small they fit inside my skull, and I was pounding on the inside of it for somebody to let me out. Except nobody could hear me, I was so tiny and weak.

I tried to cry out, "Mr. Newcastle! Stop it!" but my lips wouldn't move.

Hush, he said, and it echoed all around me. I heard fabric rip, vaguely sensed it was my own hands doing the ripping, and shut my eyes tight against what I was afraid was coming.

And then I had no sense of time or sensation, just blackness, but when he released me, it was all at once. My body was somebody else's, and then it was mine again, just like that.

I remember I was tingling all over and felt like I was falling and falling and falling, but despite my ill feeling toward Mr. Newcastle, it was a strangely joyous thing. I was sweaty, too, and my belly was sort of thrumming, like all the muscles of my female parts were clenching and un-clenching all by themselves.

I didn't feel Mr. Newcastle anywhere close around. Maybe he'd got little, like I'd been, and was resting inside my head. I opened one eye, then the other, and sat up, slow. My nightgown had been ripped to tatters, and when I tried to fetch a new one to cover myself, my legs wobbled out from under me and I had to sit back down.

Soft, Mr. Newcastle's voice came to me as if from far away. *Tell me you've ever felt anything like that before, Annie sweet, Annie precious.*

"What . . . what is it?" I stuttered. I was panting, I realized.

It's love, my darling. Well, I don't suppose you felt it. Only the aftermath. But my stars! He sounded real strange, as if he'd done something wonderful for me when all he'd done was steal my body and make me feel like I'd run around that giant bedroom seventy-five times.

Or something.

Next time, he added, all full of himself, *I'll release you a moment sooner. Then you'll get, uh, more of the sense of it. Lord, if I'd known what women . . . that is, if I'd known what it felt like for them when they . . . when they, well, you know what I mean. Burst!*

He was talking crazy again. I tried to get up, and this time, I succeeded. I dug out an old robe and put it on, over the objections of Mr. Newcastle. He seemed to be of the hedonistic, not to mention smutty, opinion that I should just walk around naked as the day I was born.

"Dirty-minded old coot," I mumbled, and cinched the belt. I sure hoped this wasn't a sign of things to come, his pinning me down and all. He'd been my husband and I supposed he had a right to that sort of wedded gratification, but there came a time for certain things between a husband and wife to stop.

Like, for instance, when one of you is dead.

Well, let's get to the letters, little Annie, he said all of a sudden, sounding far too chipper.

I sat at the dressing table, where six fat candles dripped.

By their light, I brought the stack of envelopes to me—there turned out to be quite a few more than the one Sam had mentioned—and pulled out the contents of the first. Some of them had stains, but then, you'd expect that. Sam had rescued them from the garbage, after all.

There were letters from vendors and makers of everything from notions to tinned fruit to heavy farm equipment to remedies, all wanting my endorsement and willing to pay for it. Letters from individuals plagued with illnesses or doubts proclaimed a right to my healing or my reassurance. Letters from the clergy and table-rappers alike damned me for a fraud, or congratulated me on my great good fortune.

And then there were the letters from the exhibitors, the men who ran everything from carnivals and side shows to college lecture circuits, to the "The Greatest Show on Earth."

These were the letters in which Mr. Newcastle had the most interest, because they promised good wages for my service. One man offered a hundred dollars a week for sitting in a booth at the Luxemburg Hall in Denver and talking to people. Another promised "fifty dollars a week plus one-quarter of the gate" for a three-week speaking tour of the "Spiritualist Centers of the United States." Another, on the letterhead of the "Society of Theosophists," wanted to test my veracity, but offered no money.

Mr. P. T. Barnum offered me a year's contract at three thousand dollars for thirty-one weeks, plus one-tenth of the gate ("for your exhibition booth, proper"), for telling fortunes six days a week, plus a lecture on the seventh. Mr. Barnum's offer was by far the best, but his show season ended in October, and he was offering for next year.

"How do they know about me? I mean, you," I said, putting the last letter down and taking my feet again. I began to blow out the candles.

News travels fast, came the response, *particularly news like this. I think we should wait a bit, don't you, my dear?* he added. *Let's see what the rest of the offers are like.*

I snorted. "And how do you know there'll be more?"

He chuckled. *Annie. Really.*

I supposed he had a point.

The last candle extinguished, I made my way to the windows and opened them wider, in hopes that a breeze would come up during the night, and then I settled into bed.

"Good night, Mr. Newcastle," I said, closing my eyes.

Annie? Wouldn't you like to—

"No," I said.

Just once more? I'll let you—

"No."

He switched tactics, and went from soft to commanding. *You do realize I could make you do it again, don't you? I could make you do it all night and all day long, for weeks on end, if I wanted to!*

Then he seemed to catch himself, like he suddenly realized how that kind of pushy, I'm-Colonel-Newcastle-and-you'll-do-as-I-say-and-like-it nonsense got my back up. It frightened me, too.

His tone changed then, and he added, *I swear, girl, you're like a balm to my spirit. I feel like I'm twenty all over again! I've been good, Annie. I've waited three long weeks and a little more. Say yes, my little Annie-nipples, my wee buds, my sweet—*

I covered my ears, for what little good it did me since the voice was coming from inside. "Mr. Newcastle, it strikes me that the only reason you waited three weeks is that it took you that long to figure out how to do whatever it was you did, so don't be assigning any lofty motives to it. And stop calling me Annie-nipples. It puts a bad taste in my mouth."

And a sweet one in mine, my love, he replied.

I wanted to cry, I was so frustrated. There was no escaping him! I felt him, felt his appetites hovering all around me in the dark, felt him waiting for me to give him the word, any word, because I knew he'd have me with or without my say-so. He was just testing the waters, wanting to know where I stood on the matter so he'd know whether to chastise me or cajole me or sweet-talk me.

Finally, I said, "Mr. Newcastle, you're going to do what you want, anyway, so just do it and get it over with. But I'm going to sleep. Don't wake me up."

Ah, my darling! he crowed. *You'll come 'round, you'll*

see. It'll be glorious when you participate, but for now, I'm happy. Then, *Annie? Would you please remove your robe? I'd hate to rip it.*

Reluctantly, I sat up and shrugged out of it. At least it was good and dark. I said, "You'd just better get me covered again before one of the sisters comes bounding in here at six in the morning. Honest, Mr. Newcastle, I know I've got a wifely duty, but I never figured it would go beyond the grave. And I'll bet there are millions of married women who don't take their nightgowns off, ever. This is humiliating."

It's not supposed to be, sweetlet, he said, and I felt the sense of nothingness begin to creep over my body. *It's not supposed to be at all. It should be a triumph, a symphony! Now that's my good girl, that's my darling,* he soothed as I fell back on the pillows, unaware of my arms, my legs, my body, aware only that I was growing tinier and tinier and farther away.

The last thing I felt was a brush of warm air passing over my eyelids, then my lips, and the last thing I heard was, *Sleep while I make you mine again, beauteous creature, lovely Frieda. Annie, I mean . . .*

About ten days later—this was almost the middle of September—Mr. Newcastle got the offer he wanted.

" 'Boyd's Curiosities?' " I said, after we read the letter and he made his intentions known. "I've never heard of Mr. Boyd *or* his curiosities! Why not wait and go with Mr. Barnum? At least he's a brand name and not some upstart nobody's ever heard of!"

No, this is the one I've been waiting for, he said, and he would not be moved. *Besides, my dear,* he added, *we need the income.*

I was sorely disappointed, although I supposed he had a point. We'd starve long before spring if I didn't do something now. But I'd gotten myself worked around to being almost excited about the possibility of traveling with Mr. Barnum's sideshow. Every kid wanted to run away with the circus at some point or other, and I guess I'd managed to put myself in that frame of mind.

Back home in Iowa, you'd see posters from time to time, extolling the number of railroad cars used by different circuses, like you could tell their quality by the sheer footage they took up on the tracks.

Once a circus actually stopped in Sycamore, not because it was on their schedule, but because they needed repairs to a couple of cars and the locomotive. They only stayed a day, while the engine was in our roundhouse, and they weren't a very big outfit at all, but they set up over in Vern Maeder's cow pasture, east of town.

There weren't any tents or anything, seeing as how it was a real impromptu thing. But they had trick riders and jugglers and a lady who walked a tightrope and a sideshow and performing dogs and horses and a baby elephant that did tricks.

Mama wouldn't let me go to the sideshow. She said it would curse my womb, and that all my children would be born deformed. I didn't see as how it could affect them, since I was only about thirteen or fourteen at the time, but Mama had the last say-so.

Anyway, since Mr. Newcastle thought I should have a chaperone on the road (and I was secretly none too keen for any more traveling on my own), Sam Two Trees made ready to leave, too. He collected all those dimes and nickels from the sisters, and had two necklaces made from some of the coins plus some tiny little turquoise beads. The rest, he spent on stocking foodstuffs for the household.

He got hold of Mr. Alvarez, too, and convinced him and his wife and their kids to move into the castle, temporarily, to see after Miss Jessie and Miss Jonquil. Mr. Alvarez said it would be an honor.

The sisters, both wearing their sparkly new dime necklaces, were weepy the morning we left, but again, I had managed to whip myself up into a state of something close to excitement. At least, anticipation. I figured that as long as I was going to be stuck with Mr. Newcastle and his prophesying, I might just as well do it away from that ugly old house, around people. And even if it wasn't with a real circus, and even if I wasn't a kid anymore, it would be a change.

Except that as we pulled away—Mr. Alvarez drove us, so as to bring the buggy back—I turned one last time. There stood the sisters, on the big black-floored, black-pillared porch, the door yawning blacker behind them, and all around them that castle with its winking stained-glass eyes and turrets, that monstrosity Mr. Newcastle had built just for me.

Well, for Grandma Frieda, really. And it struck me that he really must have loved her like crazy to do something like that.

I was surprised when I felt a tear slide down my cheek.

"Second thoughts?" asked Sam Two Trees.

There, there, said Mr. Newcastle.

I wiped my eyes and turned my back on it. "I'll be fine," I said, and patted Sam's hand. "Just fine."

Annie? Mr Newcastle said to me all of a sudden. We were on the train to New Mexico, and he'd been quiet for a good bit, so it sort of startled me. But the next thing he said startled me more, because it was, *Why didn't you tell me you were married before? Why didn't you tell me about Tommy Boone?*

I was sitting in a window seat, with Sam next to me but strangers across, so I had to think at him instead of talk.

I just kept on looking out the train window, and thought, *I didn't figure it was that important,* and tried to seem like the act of marrying Tommy Boone had been as humdrum as frying up a batch of chicken. It wasn't far from the truth.

I'm very disappointed in you, Annie, he went on. *Very disappointed. And here your mother promised me a virgin! An untouched plum, an unsullied peach, a—*

"I get the picture, Mr. Newcastle," I said, right out loud. "You didn't get your saintly fruit." The ladies sitting across from me looked up, then looked at each other.

Beside me, Sam shook his head sadly and twirled his finger slow beside his temple. I jabbed my elbow in his ribs, but by then the ladies were out of their seats and moving up the aisle fast, chattering nervously in whispers behind gloved hands and feathery hats.

"See what you made me do?" I hissed to Mr. Newcastle.

Sam, who thought I was talking to him, shrugged and stood up. "Wanted the window seat anyhow," he said, then yawned. He settled down across from me in one of the ladies' recently vacated seats, stuck his legs, catercornered, up on the seat he'd just vacated, and gazed contentedly out over the landscape. "Better," he said, his eyelids drooping.

Annie, don't you lie to me again, Mr. Newcastle warned, although how he thought he could do me damage—more than he already had, anyway—was beyond me.

"I didn't lie," I whispered behind my cupped hand. "I just held back about Tommy Boone. That's not the same as lying. We were only married a couple of months before he got killed, anyhow."

But Mr. Newcastle would not see reason. *If you lie to me again, I can make things very embarrassing for you. If you . . . if . . .*

Strange, but right then I could feel that Mr. Newcastle was almost overcome with emotion. I got the feeling that had he been alive and in his own body, he would have been standing there, his gaunt face all bloodless and those bony old hands clenched into fists while he tried to hold himself back from pummeling me into next year. He was in the grip of a powerful sort of rage—from jealousy, I guess—that had leaked over from him into me. I don't mind saying it gave me a bone-deep scare.

. . . if you ever, ever *give me cause to . . .* He stopped himself then, and took hold of his emotional state. Or at least, I thought he had.

More calmly, he added, *If you ever lie to me again, or if you ever seriously fancy a man, I can make it very hard on you, Annie. Very hard indeed. Consider yourself warned. You're my wife now, and don't you forget it. Mine.*

And then he went away just like that, leaving me sitting on that sooty train, cactus rolling past the windows, and nobody to tell but Sam.

"Sam?" I said. I think my voice was shaking some, although it was less from Mr. Newcastle's threats than from that anger—no, it was more like indignation and outrage, I guess. That, and the sheer nerve of his thinking he owned

me, like a buggy or a plow or a dog. That might have been
true while he was living, but the law releases a woman once
her spouse has kicked the bucket, which Mr. Newcastle certainly had.

"Sam!" I said again, a little louder, but he stayed sound
asleep, his chin on his chest.

I got to thinking how strange it was that in a little bit
more than six weeks, I had lost Mama, gone all the way to
the Arizona Territory, got married and widowed in the space
of twenty-four hours, got myself infested by a ghost and
joined up with a sideshow on account of the ghost's immi-
nent financial embarrassment.

It struck me that the first few things should have been
more than enough to send me to the loony bin, or at least
give me a case of the vapors that lasted a year. And the part
about the deceased Mr. Newcastle taking up residence inside
my skull? Why, if I'd been living a century or two earlier, I
would have been burned at the stake if I hadn't killed myself
or gone crazy first. But there I was, in full possession of my
faculties and on my way to New Mexico to join up with
Boyd's Curiosities.

I tell you, the human mind is a treacherous and miracu-
lous thing.

Just when you want nothing more than to go crazy, just
for the relief of it, it puts on the brakes and says, "No, we're
not doing that today." And you adapt. You can adapt to all
of a sudden being motherless and in a strange country and
being the responsible party for a couple of old maids who
would not have given you the time of day under other
circumstances.

You can even adapt to a dirty-minded, cantankerous, and
deceased old curmudgeon of a goat forcibly taking up residence inside your brain and body, and even having his way
when it come nighttime.

And you can get to where it seems almost normal.

Now, if you ask me, my mind was under more strain than
God originally designed it for. But I guessed that since that
same God had let Mr. Newcastle come in and stay, he figured I could handle it.

6

I stopped stock-still. "Jumpin' Jehosaphat!"

Sam Two Trees put down our bags and took a long, straight-faced look around, and then nodded in agreement.

I said, "Have you ever seen anything like it?"

It was six-and-a-half days since we'd left Rock Bottom and the castle. We'd come all the way to Albuquerque, New Mexico, to meet up with the Boyd outfit, and let me tell you, it was something to meet up with.

The tent caught your eye first, crowded in front with customers coming and going. But then you noticed that to the sides (and in the back, I found out later) there were caravan wagons parked four- and five-deep and horse corrals and a cook tent and all kinds of exotic people going places with a purpose. I saw a man all covered in tattoos and a chubby woman with a beard, and a lady with a cheetah on a leash. Sam thought it was a skinny jaguar, but I was pretty sure it was a cheetah.

"Boyd's 101 Curiosities, Freaks, Incongruities, and Wonders of the Universe!" read the big black and red and white banner over the entrance to the tent. Under it was a smaller one, done in blue and white, that said, "Welcoming Prophet Annie Newcastle to Our Constellation of Stars!"

Bully! said Mr. Newcastle, as Sam paid our driver. All

around us, the air was buzzing with voices and laughter and excitement, and thick with the smells of popcorn and tamales and hot caramel buns.

Something thudded on my hat. "What's that 'Prophet' business about?" I asked, brushing away a dead wren. Its toenails had caught in my shoulder seam. "I'm not out of the Old Testament, I'm from Iowa!" I was craning my head all around, trying to figure out where that good caramel bun smell was coming from.

Sam just hoisted up the bags. "Come on," he said, leading me through the crowd and into the tent. "You can look at it later."

Right off, a fellow with sleeve garters yelled, "Stop, you two!" and jumped, one handed, over the little fence they had rigged to keep the wrong element out. He planted himself in front of us and said, "Can't you read? General admission, two bits." He held out his hand.

Sam started to dig in his pocket. I said, "Two bits? For the whole thing?" Split up between those one hundred and one acts, my share of a quarter wouldn't go real far toward keeping Miss Jonquil and Miss Jessie in groceries.

The sleeve-gartered man frowned. He was shortish and mustachioed and sandy-haired, and those sleeves he had hiked up were striped with blue. He said, "No, for two bits you get to see the museum part. You pay extra for the shows. Individual-like. Just the ones you want to see." Then he seemed to remember himself, and took a step back, throwing his arms wide.

"Hurry, hurry, hurry! The wonders of the ages! A pickled unborn calf with two heads!" he announced, so everybody could hear. "Another with five legs! Just two bits to see the museum, where you can touch a petrified piece of the One True Cross, nail hole included! The fabled Siberian snowman, stuffed and mounted and hermetically sealed in an all-around glass showcase! Only twenty-five cents to gaze upon the terrible man-eating tiger of Sumatra, shot by Mr. Boyd himself on safari in darkest Africa! The—"

"Sumatra's over by India, in Asia," I cut in. "That's a whole different continent."

Hush, Annie, Mr. Newcastle piped up. *I was enjoying myself.*

"Hush, yourself," I replied. "You can't just let people go around misplacing whole entire continents, even if you're entertained."

The sleeve-gartered fellow eyed me.

Sam said, "We're here to see Mr. Boyd. We have a letter. She's Annie Newcastle." He jabbed his thumb back toward the entrance and up at the banner.

The fellow started to say something, then stopped, like he was remembering, and then his face brightened. "*Sure!* You folks wait right here, and I'll get him. Mr. Boyd, I mean."

He hollered at the boy taking tickets in his stead, "Joey! Take over for a while!" and then turned back to us. "Sorry, ma'am. My name's Dilbert, Dilbert Croudy. Call me Bert. I'm Mr. Boyd's lead barker." He stuck out his hand, and both Sam and I shook it.

"Pleased," I said, then "What?" because Mr. Newcastle was saying something.

I said, tell him that I'm honored to meet him, too.

Bert looked from me to Sam. "Who's she talkin' to?" he whispered, fiddling at his sleeve garters nervously. "Is it . . .is it *him?* Is she witchin' him right now?"

That "witchin' " part sort of ticked me off, but I said, "Mr. Newcastle's glad to meet you, too."

To Sam Two Trees, he said, "Christopher Columbus! You mean to say she's not puttin' it on?" and pointed at me as if I was stuffed and mounted, like that Sumatran tiger he'd been hollering about.

Sam said, "Are you going to get Mr. Boyd? These bags are heavy."

Bert took the hint, and darted into the crowd.

I said, "Sam, you're a liar. I could hold those bags as long as you have. And I've seen you hoist a full-grown pronghorn buck over one shoulder and stand there talking to Mr. Alvarez for a half hour before you remembered you were hefting it."

As usual, he did his best to ignore my entire speech. Looking out over the crowd, he said, "I wonder who does the cooking for this mob . . ."

Mr. Newcastle had been jabbering in my head about something while I was talking to Sam. I had sort of learned to ignore it, seeing as how he was continually expounding on some kind of ray waves or the coming war with Cuba or Spain, or how I had hair like spun gold. He was always talking nonsense.

But seeing as how Sam wasn't listening to a word I said, I turned an inner ear to Mr. Newcastle.

. . . *and motorized carriages that don't need horses,* he was saying. *Those carriages'll put the horse right out of business in this country. Oh, folks will still keep horses, but only for pleasure riding. And shows! Why, people think we mistreat the horses now? Just wait for the future, when horses turn into rich men's baubles! Training with barbed wire! Exsanguination! Gingering and soring, whip welts worse than any New York City hack has ever known, and all for the sake of—*

"Mr. Newcastle?"

—fashion! All for a piece of ribbon and a trophy and a rich man's swollen pride! Why, when I was in the cavalry, we'd never . . . Did you say something, dear heart?

"Excuse me, Mr. Newcastle. I thought what you were saying was real interesting, but I think maybe you ought to save some of it up. You know. For later on, after folks pay their admission."

Annie, he said, kind of condescending, *I wasn't speaking aloud. I was speaking on the inside.* That's what he called it when he talked inside my head. I called it more like driving me lunatic.

"Well, just the same, Mr. Newcastle, put a cork in it."

Annie, I don't think I like your tone, he said. *You're changing from the sweet girl I married, that dear little girl from Iowa.*

"If you mean that girl who never got mad, or at least showed that she was, you're right," I said. "I've taken up Mama's cross, what with you pestering me all night, every night, and gabbing at me practically nonstop all day. I don't mean to say that I've got her gift for actual full-blown, red-faced tantrums, or that I can bring folks a block away out from their dinners with my poetic hollering and inspired curses, but you just give me twenty years. Then you'll see what I can do!"

There was no reply, and I said, "Mr. Newcastle?"

Well, I supposed I'd hurt his feelings and he'd gone off to sulk. That had happened before. But it was just as well, because right then Bert came back in the company of a fat-bellied, round-cheeked man with thick, white muttonchops. He had on blue pants and red suspenders and was in his shirtsleeves, and we must have caught him in the middle of his dinner, because he had a big white napkin tucked into his collar. He was smiling to beat the band, too, but his smile was all on the outside, if you know what I mean.

"Mrs. Newcastle?" said Bert, once they'd battled the crowd and had got up to me. "Allow me to introduce Mr. Boyd. Mr. Boyd, this is your Prophet Annie."

Mr. Boyd took my hand and pumped it up and down, and said, "Pleased! Pleased as punch! Delighted!"

"Glad to be here," I replied, after I got my hand free. I kind of stuck it behind my back and wiped it on my skirts. Something about him made my skin crawl, and besides, he was sweating something fierce.

"Got a crib all set up for you," he said, taking my arm.

"A crib?" The only kind I'd heard tell of were corncribs. For a half a second, I thought the folks at Boyd's were going to dry me out and throw me on the pile for winter fodder.

"A booth," Mr. Boyd said quickly, and started piloting me through the crowd. "Your salon. Your own little speaking hall! By the way, is the—" He stuck his lips next to my ear. In a hot fog of breath that smelled of onions and gravy, he said, "Is the entity with you at present?"

I pulled away from him, not enough to alienate him, but enough that his mouth wasn't practically on my ear. I said, "If you mean Mr. Newcastle, he was here a minute ago, but he just . . ." Well, I couldn't say he was mad and not talking, could I? So I said, "He stepped out for a few minutes."

"Ah," said Mr. Boyd, with a knowing look. I think that look irritated me more than anything else.

By that time we'd navigated the crowd all the way across the main tent to the other side. Now, the big tent—what I could see of it over the crowd's heads, that was—was circled all 'round and centered by what Mr. Boyd called the cribs. Each one had a big sign over a little stage, and barkers stood on some of them, encouraging folks to come on in and spend a nickel or a dime to see "The Wild Men of the Congo" or "Bartholomew the Bone Man" or whatever. I was trying to hear what the barker for High Priestess Aisha was saying when all of a sudden Mr. Boyd put on the brakes and pointed straight ahead.

He pulled himself up, all vainglorious, and said, "Here we are. And what do you think of your very own salon, Mrs. Newcastle?"

I scarce knew what to say.

First of all, the sign was bigger than most. It said "Angel or Devil?" on the right side, and "Saint or Sinner?" on the left. In between, in giant letters, it said, "Prophet Annie," and below that, still centered, it said, "The Clairvoyant Miracle of the Ages! She Stares Death in the Eyes to Wrestle the Secrets of the Future!"

If this was not bad enough, there was a painting, done real crude, of some fat girl with yellow ringlets and a yellow dress, holding her eyes up to heaven with her hands raised, palms up, and little stars dancing 'round her head.

It was all done up in garish colors, and in lettering so fancy with doodads and curlicues that you had to squint to make it out. It was the most god-awful thing I'd ever seen, and made that black castle of Mr. Newcastle's seem plain as a Lutheran church.

"Well?" said Mr. Boyd, expectantly, his fat cheeks shining with perspiration and something else. Greed, maybe.

"We had a sign painter all the way from Illinois," piped up Bert the barker.

Mr. Boyd remembered him then. He scowled and said, "Get back to work," then seemed to remember we were there, too, and added, "Run along, son."

Bert took off for the entrance without even saying good-bye, and I said, "It's real . . ."

I had to hunt for a word, on account of I was supposed to be nice to him. After all, there were the sisters to think of, not to mention me and Sam. We had about used up all our money settling up Miss Jessie and Miss Jonquil.

"It's real theatrical," I said at last.

"Just the sort of thing I expected," said Sam, all flat-faced. I stepped on his foot.

Mr. Boyd seemed to take our comments for the good, though. He clapped his hands together. "Oh, you love it, too! Wonderful! And I do believe he's caught a likeness."

"A likeness?"

"Of you, Mrs. Newcastle! May I call you Annie? Don't tell me you missed the portrait?"

I swallowed hard. "Mrs. Newcastle's fine. That fat girl's me?"

"Plump," Mr. Boyd said, just a hint of testiness creeping in behind his smile. "Pleasingly plump."

This time, Sam stepped on my foot.

"She's sure that," I said through gritted teeth, and trying not to hop. Sam might have been half Navajo, but he sure wasn't wearing moccasins. I added, "She's a blonde, all right," seeing as how that was the only thing we had in common. I didn't mention the two rouge-red spots on her cheeks that looked like a matched set of boils, nor did I draw attention to her double chins. Instead, I said, "It's a shame you didn't put a picture of Sam up there, too."

"Sam?" said Mr. Boyd, all of a sudden angry. "Who's Sam? Don't tell me this act's a double! I'm paying for a certified talent, not some table-rapper who needs a shill floating trumpets and working wires behind a curtain!"

This was early in my career, and I hadn't yet heard about the trumpet-floaters, let alone met any. "Mr. Boyd, this is Sam Two Trees. He's my chaperone, not my 'shill,' whatever that is, and I pay his salary myself."

He glanced over in Sam's direction, then back to me, his eyebrows working. "A tame Indian? No extra charge?"

"Half Navajo," I said, "though I don't see what that has to do with it. And no, no extra charge."

"No wires?"

"Nope."

"No duck calls, floating trumpets, or ghosts coming out of the fog? Not that I'd mind that, exactly, but I ain't paying more for it."

"None of that," I replied. He was really getting on my nerves, but I kept thinking about Miss Jessie and Miss Jonquil and that big old castle where they'd surely starve to death, and I tamped my newfound anger down.

I said, "Mr. Boyd, you get me and the spirit of Mr. Newcastle. Me, I just sit there. Mr. Newcastle does the talking. You can take up the duck calls with him, although so far as I know he's never quacked a note. And like I said, I pay for Sam. I'd hoped you'd supply him free room and board, though."

Mr. Boyd brightened considerably. "Certainly, certainly! No trouble. Just wanted to get things straight between us right off the bat, that was all. And now," he said, taking my arm again and turning me away from that mule-puke monstrosity of a sign, "if you'll come this way, I'll show you to your caravan."

A week later, I finished cleaning out the wagon. We were up in Colorado by then, outside some town I'd never heard of, and it was night. I rinsed my scrub brush in the bucket, and stood up. Hands pressed to the middle of my back, I stretched.

"Well," I said, "that's about the best I can do."

Sam, who was stretched out on one of the bunks, smoking a cheroot and reading, grunted at me. I suppose he thought he'd done his work for the day, having kept an eye to Mr. Newcastle while he was orating, and having made us braised prairie partridge stuffed with wild rice and onions for dinner.

It hadn't taken him but three days to talk the cook, Mrs. Bumbridge, into letting him into her outdoor kitchen, and by this time they were already trading recipes and cooking supper for about fifteen or twenty deformed, twisted, fat, skinny, hairy, or pontificating people.

He was in hog heaven.

I carried the bucket to the door and threw the dirty water out into the night. It was late, and lights still burned in a few tents and caravan wagons, but all in all, the place was pretty quiet. Even Esteban Murphy, the man with a stunted twin growing out of his shoulder, had stopped playing his mouth harp and gone to bed.

"What you reading?" I said, making a stab at conversation.

He didn't say anything, just wiggled the cover at me. It was a dime novel, *Panhandle Slim and the Lost Brigade*. There was a tall, thin cowboy on the cover, six-guns drawn and blazing. I swear, I don't know how he could read such tripe.

"Must be pretty good," I said, leaning heavily on the sarcastic.

"Fair," he said, without looking up.

I sat down on the other bunk, letting the bucket *thunk* to the floor and shaking my head. "Sam Two Trees, will you please put that book down and talk to me?"

He lowered it. He stared at me, that cheroot clamped between his teeth. "What do you want to talk about?"

He had me there. I thought for a second. I said, "Well, what did Mr. Newcastle talk about today?"

"Electricity and war. Mixed in with a lot of pioneering."

When no further information seemed to be forthcoming, I prodded, "War with who? About what?"

"The Hun." He took the cheroot from between his teeth. "Because somebody's going to shoot some archduke or something. Are you really interested?"

I wasn't. Although I had long since figured how to stick around while Mr. Newcastle did his prophesying—I couldn't get back in my own body, but at least I could see what he saw and hear what he heard—I usually went away. To be frank about it, he was boring. He mixed up all his personal hobgoblins and bugaboos and opinions in with the future, and a lecture about some war with the Hun or with the Spanish was likely to contain one part of the actual subject, and seven parts of Mr. Newcastle's experience in the Indian wars or hard-rock mining or animal husbandry, or why he was pretty sure Shakespeare didn't write his own plays.

I stared back at Sam just as stony-faced as he was looking at me, and said, "Interested? No, I guess I'm not."

He flicked his ash and picked up his book again.

He was the cussedest man! I said, "All I want is a little general conversation. If you're not going to talk to me, I might just as well take Mr. Newcastle off the clock."

He put his book down again. "Wagon looks nice," he said with a sigh. The threat of Mr. Newcastle always got him. I could get away during those lectures, but poor Sam had to sit through every one, lest Mr. Newcastle get on a subject he shouldn't. Like for instance, the personal life of Annie Newcastle.

I said, "Thank you, Sam. I wish I could get my hands on some paint. Maybe some fabric for new curtains, too."

I'd managed to get our caravan clean, but it still looked shabby. The outside was all right, I suppose, but inside, the yellow-checked curtains were rotted and stained so you could barely see the pattern, and the paint was chipped on the cupboards and alongside the built-in beds. It was peeling on the walls, too.

There'd been bed bugs when we first moved in, and I'd had to throw out all the bedding, which meant we'd had to sleep on boards for the two days it took us to get new mattresses rigged.

I shuddered to think what kind of shape the other caravans were in, for that old skinflint, Mr. Boyd, had said this one was his finest traveling accommodation.

Sam was staring at the wall, at one of the peeling places. He said, "I can get paint. I'll get it tomorrow, if Jonas'll shut up on time. Maybe some cloth, too." Then he hiked an eyebrow, which pushed against his head sash. He said, "Why? You thinking of having company over?"

I folded my arms. "I don't know what you mean."

He put the book down, fanned open and spine up, and hiked himself on one elbow. "Sure you do. That saddle tramp. The one you were trying so hard not to make cow eyes at."

I think I turned red. Anyway, I sure felt the heat race into my cheeks. I said, "I don't have the slightest idea—"

"The one with the dimples," Sam said, cutting me off. He swung his legs over the side of the bunk and sat up. "And the dark, wavy hair." He made his voice all girlish, and rolled his eyes for that part, teasing me. Then he lowered his voice again and gave me that flat look. "You remember."

Sure, I'd seen that fellow—who could help but see him? He'd been leaned up against a tent pole while my barker was heaping lies upon the crowd. He'd cracked peanut shells while he stared at me with those sly green eyes, those white teeth smiling in a way that made my knees all wobblety and my spine go to mush.

"All right," I said, avoiding his gaze and looking instead at the chipped paint next to his knee. The top layer was green, and there was some pink and white under it. "I saw him. So what?"

Sam grinned. "You see him pay money for two of your shows, too?"

My jaw dropped, but I snapped it shut. "He's interested in the future, that's all."

"Nobody," said Sam, hauling up his feet again and lying back, "is *that* interested in the future. Especially the way Jonas tells it." He stubbed out his smoke in the pickle jar lid he used for an ashtray, and picked up *Panhandle Slim*. From behind it, he said, "You get a look at the fellow he was with?"

"What fellow?"

Chuckle from behind the book. "See?"

I felt myself turning red. At least Sam had the decency to keep his dime book between us.

"Big, tall drink of water," said Sam. "About six-five, six-six?"

I couldn't for the life of me remember him. All I recalled was that cowhand.

"Well, for your information, your friend was—"

"He's not my friend," I said, a little cross—and a little guilty, too. "I never even spoke to him."

"Well," drawled Sam, "friend or not, that tall hombre he was with was Pat Garrett."

"Who?"

Sam put his book down. "Do you mean to tell me . . . ?" He sat up partway, his elbows propped behind him. "Don't you know Pat Garrett? Billy the Kid's pal? Don't you read the newspapers?"

I stuck my nose up in the air, I guess. "And when would I have the time, what with Mr. Newcastle and all?"

Sam flicked his eyes heavenward. "William Bonney is Billy the Kid—or was Billy the Kid. He got shot last July by his good friend, Pat Garrett. That barker—Bert, the one at the front gate?—he spotted him and told me."

The name Billy the Kid did ring a bell somewhere, but I couldn't figure what for, except I thought it was for something bad. "What'd he do?"

"Billy or Pat?" Sam said, rolling toward me and pulling out his fixings. He began to roll another smoke.

"Billy."

He stared at me. "You're fooling! Billy the Kid?" His dark eyes crinkled with excitement, and he struck a match and lit his smoke. "Why, he was deadly! Killed at least fifteen men—some say forty! Haven't you ever heard of the Lincoln County wars? Or the Regulators?" The match burnt his fingers then, and he shook it out, swearing under his breath.

"You don't need to cuss at me," I said. "It's not my fault if I don't hone in on the crime section of the newspaper. Criminy, you act like he was some famous stage actor or the president or something instead of a curse on the populace!"

"Well," Sam said, "he was famous. Still is! Maybe not like an actor, but famous." He blew smoke out through his nose. "And Marshall Pat Garrett is the man who shot him down. Funny about that. They say they were best friends. Makes a person wonder if Garrett wasn't just putting Billy out of his misery. Still, you'd better keep it in mind if your saddle-tramp friend comes back, though. If he's running with Garrett, it could mean he ran with the Kid, too. Bound to be trouble."

He said it just like I didn't have trouble enough already, what with Jonas Newcastle using up half my life and me spending the other half worrying about the sisters back in Arizona. Not to mention, was I going to have to spend the rest of my days traveling with a freak show.

"He won't be back," I said with finality, though I was half-wishing it was a lie.

"Yes he will." He took a drag on his cigarette. "And while we're at it, do you think you could hold off Jonas tonight? I'd like to sleep in my own bed."

"Hold off Jonas?" Sam was sure one for switching horses in midstream. "What do you mean?"

This time, it was his turn to color up. "It's just . . . Well, I don't like being waked in the middle of the night, that's all."

"Waking you up? Who wakes you up?"

He rolled to his back again and stared at the ceiling. "You do. With all your moaning and gyrating and . . . Oh, hell. Forget I said anything."

"Oh Lord!," I gasped, then clapped a hand to my mouth. I had thought Mr. Newcastle was on his honor, what with me and Sam sharing a wagon, but now it appeared he was having his way with me every time he got the urge. I didn't know whether I was more embarrassed for myself or angry at Mr. Newcastle. Either way, it wasn't Sam's fault. I went with the embarrassed part first.

"Sam," I said, not looking at him, "I could just die, honest. I swear, it's not me, it's Mr. Newcastle."

"I know that," he muttered, and I could hear the fluster in his voice. "Just forget it, all right? It's not so bad, sleeping outside, on the ground."

"No, I won't forget it. Mr. Newcastle was supposed to be on his good behavior, and now I learn that he's been keeping up his goatish ways, and without asking me first! If it happens again tonight, Sam Two Trees, don't you get up and go outside to sleep. You just shake me. Shake me hard and call my name till I answer you. I'll fix Mr. Newcastle's wagon."

*   *   *

That night, I woke to Sam shaking me like a rag doll and saying, "Damn it, Jonas, let her go!"

"Stop!" I shouted. "You're going to break my neck!"

Sam let go of me right away, and I fell back on the pillow. I was soaked with sweat and felt real odd, like there wasn't enough air in the caravan. My whole body was all tingly and buzzing—not bad, just strange—and I felt kind of swollen all over.

"W-what happened?" I asked, even though I pretty much knew the answer. "Is he gone? Mr. Newcastle, are you there?"

Sam said, "He's gone," and Mr. Newcastle said, *Damn it, Annie!* at the same time.

I ignored Sam, and said, "Jonas Newcastle, you listen to me. I have had it with you just coming in whenever you want and swiping my body for your perverse pleasures, and there'll be no more, do you hear? No more!"

For a second, Mr. Newcastle was silent, and I had a brief moment of relief, thinking I had startled him all the way out and he was gone for good. Either that, or he was just holding back, building up pressure for the big blow. But then he said *I'm sorry* just like a kid digging his toe in the dirt. *Forgive me?*

I sighed. Maybe I'm soft, but I couldn't stay too awful mad at him. He was just a randy old buck, that was all. "All right, Mr. Newcastle," I said. "But you have got to stop this. Poor Sam is going to catch his death out there, and I don't take to it too kindly, either. You know what I mean."

Saturdays and Wednesdays? he said. *I'm a man, after all. I have my needs. And you're my wife.* That last sentence had a bit of a threat in it, so I said, "All right. Saturdays and Wednesdays. But that's all. I remind you that you're dead. Why, by law you don't have any rights at all!"

Inside my head, he barked out a cruel laugh. *The law? That's a good one, Annie. You have a sense of humor!*

I hadn't heard him that mean since he bawled me out about Tommy Boone on the train, and I have to admit it frightened me. I clamped a lid on it, though, and said sternly, "Mr. Newcastle, you are going to have to learn what is mine and what is yours, and what I'm just lending you out of the goodness of my heart."

Sam, who naturally couldn't hear Mr. Newcastle's part of the conversation, warned, "Don't make him mad, Annie."

"He's already mad, Sam," I said. And then, to Mr. Newcastle, I added, "I'm sitting here in practically a foreign land, taking part in nothing better than a freak show so that I can keep your addlepated sisters in meat and bread and jam, and keep that silly roof over their heads. I didn't have to do this, you know, but we made what I thought was a gentleman's agreement. I—" I felt Mr. Newcastle leaving, kind of leaking out of me, and said, "Hold on there, mister. Don't you leave when I'm talking to you!"

I was full-blown Mama right about then, and to tell the truth I was enjoying myself. "I could have just gone back home to Sycamore after you croaked," I went on, once I felt him pulling back into me. "I could have gone anywhere, to California or Paris, France, or Timbuktu, but no, I stayed on because I felt sorry for those old ladies. You coddled them so terrible for so long that they don't know which end is up."

But Annie—

"Don't you 'but Annie' me, Mr. Newcastle!" I was heading downhill and gathering speed, like Papa used to say, and I admired the feeling. "You scared me about Tommy Boone, I'll admit it. But I hadn't thought through my possibilities yet. Well, I've thought through them now, and if anybody has the upper hand in this, it's me. You say you can make it bad for me, but I can make it worse for you. How'd you like to be locked up in the loony bin, Mr. Newcastle, tied down with restraining belts and ropes? How could you take your pleasure then?"

Annie, you don't mean it! Annie, my sweet, you wouldn't put yourself through—

"I've got to tell you, Mr. Newcastle, it wouldn't trouble me any. If I'd be free of your pestering and your endless speeches, I wouldn't mind all the ropes in the world."

"Annie!" Sam hissed. He'd crawled over to the corner, and

was hunkered down underneath the rack where we hung our clothes, looking at the ceiling like any minute a bolt of lightning was going to come down out of it. "Don't push him!"

"Oh, hush up, Sam," I snapped, racing with anger, steaming down that hill at one hundred miles per hour. "Mr. Newcastle, you answer me!"

All right, he said.

"All right?" I said, twisting my head around. "All right what?"

All right, Wednesdays and Saturdays, he said. *And I won't scare you anymore.*

"And?"

There was a long pause, but finally he said, *And I'm sorry, Annie.*

"All right, then," I said, sort of disappointed the argument was over. It made me feel, well, sort of powerful. I fixed my covers—all that time, I'd been uncovered in a scandalous fashion—and felt my cheeks heat up belatedly.

"Sam?" I said, hoping he'd been too flustered by Mr. Newcastle to notice that I was half-naked, "You can go back to bed now. Mr. Newcastle has agreed to hold it to Wednesday and Saturday nights. Maybe you can bunk with Bert or one of the others when he comes."

Sam slunk toward his narrow bed. I supposed he was feeling ashamed for hiding under the clothes during my tantrum, but I was too tired to say anything. Now I knew why Mama always took a nap after one of her yelling spells.

He climbed in, saying, "Is he gone?"

I studied on the inside of my head for a second. "Just me in here," I said, and rolled over. "Good night, Sam."

"Good grief," he muttered.

7

Well, Mr. Newcastle was on his good behavior for the next few days. My "saddle tramp," as Sam had dubbed him, didn't show up all the next day or the next or the next. I figured he'd moved on and it was just as well, but I was secretly sorry to see it. I swear, I had never in my entire life had such a physical reaction to another human being!

It wasn't just that he was rogue-handsome, or powerful-muscled or broad shouldered, or even that he had—as Sam had so perspicaciously pointed out—dark, wavy hair and dimples. They weren't just dimples, mind. They were cut deep in his cheeks, long slashing furrows above a strong, square, clean-shaven jaw and a thick mustache. Above were those jade-green eyes, as green as I imagined the sea to be in deep, sheltered, secret places.

If he never came back again, I was certain I'd remember him all my life, down to the last button on his sky-blue shirt, the thatch of hair that slipped down onto his forehead when he took off his hat to a passing lady, and the little lines that winged out at the corners of his eyes when he caught me looking.

I wondered if he had that effect on all the ladies, or if it was just me. If it was everybody, he must spend half his time reviving fainting spinsters and schoolgirls, not to mention widows and matrons.

Tough as it was, I had managed not to think about him too much, and that was because of Mr. Newcastle. I'd bawled the old rapscallion out, all right, but I figured it didn't pay to tempt fate. The cowhand wasn't coming back, and there was no sense in stirring up the old goat in my noggin, so I just put a lid on it and tamped it down.

But by then, another interesting thing had happened to help me push aside the green-eyed saddle tramp.

Among the acts at Boyd's there was a lady, an elegant and exotic sort, who billed herself as High Priestess Aisha. She was about forty-five or fifty, and she used cards to tell fortunes—five cents for three questions. She wore uncommon theatrical dresses. I forget now what she called them, but they were done up in bright fabrics, and each was one long yardage of cloth that she wrapped around herself in a clever way and belted, so that when she was done you couldn't tell it from a sewn dress.

She had medium-dark skin and jet-black eyes and a long regal nose, and wore big, gold hoop earrings and bracelets, and a gold pendant with a gold symbol on it. A tall turban of the same fabric as her dress wrapped her head, and she spoke with a strange accent.

Sam told me he thought she was Egyptian, but then, nobody was real sure, since she told everybody a different story.

High Princess Aisha had a cat. Not a friendly little tabby you could pet on your lap, but a big cat. It wasn't a skinny jaguar, like Sam had thought before, but an African cheetah. They are the fastest land animals there are—leastwise, over a short distance—and the only kind of big cat that you can trust to be a pet. The ancient Egyptians, before the time of Moses, used to train them to run down game. Maybe that's where Sam got the idea Aisha was from Egypt.

Anyway, the cats name was Nebuchadnezzar, and Aisha said he had come from darkest Africa when he was just a kitten. Most everybody was afraid of him, Mr. Boyd in particular, so she kept him on a leash like a dog even though he wouldn't have hurt a fly. He lounged in the back of her little fortune-telling cubicle by day, being so quiet that the folks having their fortunes told didn't even realize he was there. By night, he slept in her caravan.

I had only seen him from a distance the first few days we were with Boyd's Curiosities, but I had admired him. Cheetahs are tall cats, built kind of like greyhounds with that little waspy waist and long legs and a small head. They have spots—not rosettes like a leopard, but just plain spots—and dark tear lines at the corners of their eyes. I wanted to see him up close, but I didn't get a chance until we'd been with Boyd's for about ten days.

I was walking out toward the makeshift corral the men had pitched at the edge of camp, thinking to stretch my legs and take a gander at the distant mountains. Ching Toy, the Chinese contortionist, was following along, picking up the birds that fell from my hat and putting them in a bucket to sort later for the stewpot. There is no telling what some folks will eat, I guess, especially folks from as far away as the other side of the world. I tried not to think about him eating them but I suppose it was kind of a relief, thinking that those flickers and wrens and such hadn't died for nothing.

Anyway, I was almost to the horse pen when I caught sight of Aisha's cat, stretched out in the cool Colorado grass beside her wagon, watching the horses. The tip of his long tail was thumping the ground while he watched a couple of ponies kicking up a ruckus.

I stopped stock-still. *Regal* was the only word I could think of to describe the way he looked in the last slanting rays of the sun. I had heard that Mr. Boyd was always threatening to kill and stuff him, but I couldn't imagine those alert gold eyes traded for glass, or sawdust in place of those tensed muscles. Never in my life had I seen anything so beautiful as that cat.

"He doesn't bite," said a voice behind me. It was Aisha. "He is a clever puss, aren't you, Nebuchadnezzar?"

I was just thinking the same thing, because while I was standing there, not ten feet from him, no birds had hit my hat. Of course, it might have been a coincidence, but I said,

"I swear, he's the most handsome creature I've ever seen, ma'am! He's a cheetah, isn't he?"

She nodded, pleased that I'd known.

"Mind if I stick around for a bit?" I was wanting to test him, to see if he really *was* scaring the birds off me. The possibility of being mauled didn't even cross my mind, to tell the truth. I was just plain fascinated.

Ching Toy cast a suspicious eye toward the cat and went stomping off with his bucket of birds, and Aisha swept an arm out, bracelets jangling. "Please," she said. "Come and sit."

Don't do it, Annie, piped up Mr. Newcastle from inside me, kind of panicked. I guess maybe he was afraid of cats.

But I thought right back at him, *Go away, Mr. Newcastle. I remind you that you're on the clock!*

He grumbled some, but he went off, and Aisha and I sat down: me on a wooden stool and her on the caravan steps.

"You are Prophet Annie, are you not?" she said, folding her arms. "You are the girl the birds dive at."

"Yes'm," I said. I was sort of relieved she didn't mention Mr. Newcastle's ghost yakking through my mouth.

She turned out to be a real nice lady. She told me that as a young girl, she'd come all the way from Morocco with her new husband. They got a place in New York City and he had a good job doing fancy leather tooling and they were doing fine, but he was killed in the Irish riot of 1871.

She shrugged her narrow shoulders. "Funny. He was neither a Catholic nor a Protestant, just a poor Muslim bystander. I have detested the Irish ever since." She looked at me, her eyes suddenly narrowing. "You are not Irish, are you?"

"No, ma'am," I said quickly. "Scots and German. Though I admit I have no prejudice against the Irish myself."

Right about then, Nebuchadnezzar sauntered over and pushed his head against my hand and I starting scratching it. I know it sounds odd but it felt real natural, chucking that big old cat behind the ears and under his chin. He started purring and I guess I grinned.

"You have not lost a husband to them," said Aisha, still on the subject of the Irish.

"No," I said, looking at Nebuchadnezzar. "I lost my husbands to a mule kick and a bum ticker, respectively." I didn't see any harm in mentioning Tommy Boone's demise, even if Mr. Newcastle was listening.

"Ah," said Aisha, as if she got some big revelation from this, and then she said, "Let me see your palm."

I held out the one I wasn't using to pet the cat, and she squinted at it in the fading light. "Yes," she said. "Two gone, and one who waits."

"I don't think I'm waiting for anything in particular," I said, although it struck me that I sure was waiting for Mr. Newcastle to move on and leave me be. I didn't say that, though.

But Aisha shook her head, the turban wobbling, her earrings clanking. "No. You will marry again. And this time," she added, lifting her almond-shaped eyes to meet mine, "it will be a love match."

I think I blushed. The first thing I thought of was that green-eyed cowpoke, but I shoved him right out of my mind since I didn't know where Mr. Newcastle was. I pulled away my hand and mumbled, "If he's out there, I sure don't know about him."

Aisha just smiled. And then she said the darnedest thing. It was, "I will die very soon, you know." My mouth fell open, and she said, "Don't look shocked, little one. I am not sad, I am ready. It is a lonely life with no husband, no people. I have seen it in the cards. It is a time like this when one is happy to know the future, so that one may prepare for it. I want you to take Nezzy."

By this time he had crawled halfway into my lap, his chest across my knees and his head pushing against my bosom, and the rumble of his purr vibrated my whole body. Even though he was squishing me I had to admit that he was past fine, but I said, "No, Aisha! Why, you hardly know me! Plus, I can't believe you're going to die. You can't be more than forty, and you look hale and hearty to me."

She shook her head. "Thank you, but I am fifty-six," she

said with a faint smile. "I feel as if I have lived twice that many years, though. It will happen within the week. Two weeks at the most. And then you must take my Nezzy for your own. He likes you. Besides, haven't you noticed? While he is at your side the birds stay far away."

That was sure true. I hadn't felt one *ping* or *thump*. Besides, Mr. Newcastle didn't seem to care for cats, which was also a big plus in Nebuchadnezzar's favor. Still, I didn't like the idea of Aisha up and dying, not when I'd just found out what a nice lady she was.

I said, "If it'll put your mind at ease, I'd be proud to take him when the time comes, and I promise he'll always have a good home with me. But you keep him for me for now. I surely do admire him, but I hope you'll understand that I don't want to have to collect him for a good long time."

She smiled. "Excellent," she said, rising with a fluid motion. "Come, and I will show you how to take care of him. Did you know that the cheetah has feet like a dog? Their toenails do not retract, you see . . ."

Boyd's Curiosities traveled through the countryside at a fairly fast clip for something that seemed so ungainly. Every other day or so, the roustabouts would be out there in the evening, taking down the big tent and packing it up, the exact same way every time.

There were more folks paid to help move the show than there were performers in it, for that "Boyd's 101 Curiosities, Freaks, Incongruities, and Wonders of the Universe" turned out to be more like thirty-five actual acts, the remaining sixty-six being things in jars or stuffed monsters cobbled together out of five or six animals, and the like. Two times in Colorado, somebody lost the petrified piece of the One True Cross, nail hole included, and they just brought out a new rock and drilled a hole in it and carried on, business as usual.

Anyway, once the roustabouts had us packed, we'd hitch up our horses and line up in a long, long row, and then we'd be off for the next county or the next territory. By the time Aisha's first week was up, we'd moved across most of

Colorado and were inching steady toward Utah. Eventually, the scuttlebutt had it, we'd turn south so as to miss winter in the high country. We'd wind our way down through Arizona, and end up in Tombstone for Christmas week.

Sam was happy about this, for we'd pass close to Newcastle's Castle and he thought we'd better look in on Miss Jessie and Miss Jonquil. Not that he didn't trust Mr. Alvarez to tend to them—he held Mr. Alvarez in the highest esteem. I just think he was worried that the sisters would get their hands on some of the money we'd been sending and paper the walls with it.

Aisha still showed no signs of turning sickly, despite her warnings of death and doom, and I was delighted. Not that she'd mis-predicted, of course, but that . . . well, I guess it was that she'd mis-predicted, after all. I enjoyed her company, for she had lots of stories about how it was to live in Morocco when she was younger, and her first days in New York, when she and her husband couldn't even speak English and were trying to get along.

For my part, I told her about Grandma Frieda and Grampa Rudy, and how their parents came over from Europe not speaking English either. The difference was that their parents never did learn it. Grampa Rudy grew up speaking both English and German, and Grandma Frieda grew up speaking nothing but German, even though she'd been born in the U-S-of-A.

Grandma Frieda was Bavarian and Grandpa Rudy's people were all Swiss and Austrian, but back then they all got lumped together as Pennsylvania Dutch, even though some of them lived in Maryland. Anyway, they were newlyweds when they moved next door to the Widow Newcastle. That was back in the late 1820s. Grandma Frieda and the Widow got to be bosom friends, even though Grandma could only speak German and was barely sixteen. She was even younger than the Widow's kids, who were all grown up but still lived at home.

I guess the Widow Newcastle got to be like a mother to Grandma Frieda, who had lost her own ma early. I have been told that the Widow taught her to speak and read

English, and tried all her life—without success—to convert Grandma from Martin Luther's teachings to the Baptist church.

"This Widow Newcastle," said Aisha, looking up from the coverlet she was knitting. It was a crisp, clear evening, we were somewhere in Colorado, and she was sitting on the steps of her caravan, needles whirring. I was sitting in the grass with Nebuchadnezzar flopped across my lap. In the distance, we could hear the roustabouts hard at work, packing up the tent. "I don't understand. Your name is Newcastle, too, and you say this Widow was like a mother to your grandmother. Was your Mr. Newcastle her great-grandson?"

I was glad it was night so she couldn't see the flush I felt burning my cheeks. In the weeks Sam and I had been with Boyd's, I guessed Aisha had never had time to take in my show, and she didn't know how old he was. I guess nobody knew that. I mean, she was accustomed to me mumbling to him all the time, but that was all she knew about him.

Right then, I knew I couldn't just blurt it out. It was the sort of thing you had to back into.

You might as well say it, said Mr. Newcastle, in a jovial mood, although he hadn't said a peep for at least an hour and I thought maybe he'd gone off for the evening on account of the cat. He didn't like to be around Nezzy. *I'd enjoy hearing it as well!* he added. *Go on, Annie, say it.*

"It's kind of a long story," I said to both Aisha and Mr. Newcastle, and moved my leg. Nebuchadnezzar had gone to sleep on it, and now it was going to sleep, too. When I moved it, it felt just like soda water. Maybe Mr. Newcastle was so brave all of a sudden because Nebuchadnezzar had nodded off.

Aisha started the needles moving again. "I have time, and the night is young. Besides," she said, tipping her head back toward where the roustabouts were working, "who could sleep with all that racket? Tell me the story of your life, Annie."

Well, I told her all about the folks coming west and stopping in Illinois on account of the Blackhawk War and all, and how when they finally got moving again Grandma

Frieda made them stop in Iowa. Grandma and Grampa took the land they stood on, and the Newcastles had their farm over the next hill.

"It was good land?" Aisha asked, intent on her needles.

"The best," I replied. "Like the books say, it had good black topsoil and a salubrious climate. Still does."

Aisha smiled. "A regular ten-cent word, salubrious. Go on."

"My mama grew up on our farm," I continued. "When she was seventeen, she married my daddy—he was Bill Pinkerton—and he came on the farm, too. During her married life Mama was pregnant eight times, not counting miscarriages. I was number seven, and the only one to live past the ten-day mark."

Aisha shook her head slowly. "Sad to see so many children die," she said.

"I suppose," I said. "I only saw the one that was born after me, when I was about three, maybe three and a half. I remember it was winter and the ground was frozen. It died right off and they put her outside the window, in the cold box, till somebody could dig a grave. I snuck her out and played with her. She was like a little baby doll, you know?"

I stopped, remembering that little blond angel of a baby. I guess she was my earliest memory, lying dead and perfect in my arms. Perfect, except for being so cold, of course.

"Daddy found me and took her away," I went on. Aisha was waiting. "He didn't get mad or anything, just took her away and sent me up to bed. But anyway, Mama went on. She always did, I guess." I smiled. "Mama had aspirations to the upper classes, and everything she did was just so, you know? She wouldn't give an inch, and she was stubborn and she talked all the time, mostly about what people had done wrong with their lives or their clothes or their table manners or if they looked at her funny on the street."

"Ah," cut in Aisha, her needles moving again. "I know that type. Like Mrs. Akbash, back home. She was so meddlesome and vile that—" She looked up. "Do not take exception, child, for I do not mean that about your mother. But they beheaded Mrs. Akbash's husband on account of something she had said, and it did not curb her tongue one bit."

I said, "I guess Mama and Daddy were lucky they didn't live in Morocco."

Then I told about Daddy. He wasn't a large man, only two inches taller than Mama, and weighing maybe half as much. Whenever there was heavy lifting to do, Mama did it. He was a Scotsman, second generation to the United States, and used to get ribbed all the time because of our last name. "Solved any crimes lately, Pinkerton?" people would say like they were the first one ever to be so clever. He got pretty tired of it, I guess, but he was always good-natured and would give them a smile.

Daddy had blue eyes, too, but darker than Mama's, and sandy hair and a big mustache that tickled. I remember him laughing a lot when I was little, a boom of a laugh almost bigger than he was. After I got to be eight or nine, I don't remember him laughing much at all. I guess life, or maybe Mama, had got to him by then.

I never did understand why they had wed each other in the first place, they were so different. Once, when I was about ten, I asked Daddy why Mama was so mean to us all the time. I loved her, of course—a person should always love their mama—but it seemed like about the only joy she took in life was yelling to make me or Daddy feel bad. Daddy just patted my hand, real soft, and said, "She lost a lot of babies, honey." And then he turned away.

"That didn't make any sense to me, Aisha," I said. "If a woman had lost so many of her babies, don't you think she'd be especially tender with the one the Lord let her keep?"

"Life seldom makes sense, little one," she said with a soft smile. "Only Allah is constant, and we cannot understand his ways. But you've told me about your parents, and I wanted to hear about *your* life, yours and Mr. Newcastle's."

"Sorry," I said with a shrug. "I guess the problem is that I'm all tangled up in my family. I can't say about me without saying about them, too."

"Very well," she said, taking out a new ball of yarn. It

was too dark to see what color it was. Off in the distance the roustabouts dropped something heavy, and we heard the thud and then the cursing. Aisha ignored them. "Do your best," she said.

"Well, I wasn't raised on the farm," I began. "In 1863—that was during the Civil War—Grandpa Rudy lost his leg to a neighbor's new steam-powered threshing machine, so he and Grandma and my mama sold off the farm and moved to town into the big house on Cedar Street. Daddy and Uncle Tad were away at war, then. That is, Daddy was at war and Uncle Tad was at Andersonville. Anyway, when they came home, I guess Daddy was pretty happy about the move to town. He had never liked farming. He had a kind of mechanical mind."

"Annie," Aisha said, to get me back on the track.

"Sorry," I said, and moved Nezzy again. Well, I moved his head. You can't move a cat that weighs that much without a block and tackle.

"Jonas Newcastle was in his fifties then," I said, looking at Aisha to see if it was all right to talk about *him*. She made no sign, so I just went on.

"Jonas was already a big man," I said. "I mean, politically. He volunteered for duty, too, but they didn't send him south. On account of the Sioux uprising, he got assigned to Fort Defiance, up in Minnesota. He was a colonel. According to Mama, he limped home late in 1865, visited with his mother and his old-maid sisters for three months, then sold off his farm and went west."

Aisha opened her mouth, but before she could say anything about getting to the point, I added, "That was how we got into the boardinghouse business, by letting rooms to Jonas Newcastle's mother and sisters."

"Oh," she said. "I didn't realize you had a boarding-house."

"*Pinkerton's Rooming House*," I quoted. "*Reasonable Room and Board to Christian Railroad Men of Good Character.* We had a sign."

"Ah," she said.

"Anyhow," I continued, "Mr. Newcastle gave his mama

and sisters most of his farm money, but they weren't of a mind to buy their own house. Besides, the Widow Newcastle wanted to be near my grandma. The trouble was that Jonas had done real well by himself raising hogs out there on the farm. He had three live-in farmhands and a maid and a cook for the house. I guess, after they moved in with us, my mama got stuck with being the maid for his mother and sisters."

I leaned my head back against the wagon wheel and stared up at the stars. "She never minded that, I don't think. She always looked on the Newcastles like royalty, like they deserved waiting-on just because they were breathing."

"You sound bitter, Annie," said Aisha, and clucked her tongue.

Surprised, I turned to look at her. "I don't think I mean to be. Duty runs deep in my family. She just figured it was her place to take care of them, that was all."

Aisha raised a brow, but she didn't say anything.

"Anyway," I said, "by the time I was five, both my grandparents and the Widow Newcastle had passed on. The Newcastle sisters—Miss Jonquil and Miss Jessie—were still alive but long gone, Jonas having struck it rich and sent for them. I don't remember them much. Mama had got used to the extra income, though, and just kept letting out their rooms."

"Stop." Aisha reached to turn up the lantern's wick. "So far you have told me all about your mother and your father and your grandparents and your friends, the Newcastles. When, dear child, do you tell about yourself?"

I filled my cheeks with air and blew it out through pursed lips. Frankly, I was kind of irritated. I'd never tried to say out the story of my family before, and even though I was barely hitting the high points, I was sort of enjoying it. Besides, I'd already said as how I was all tied up in kinfolk, but I guess she didn't see the point. "All right," I said. "Now."

"Really?"

Really? echoed Mr. Newcastle, who'd been quiet, so far, through the whole thing.

"Really," I said to both of them. "I'll try my best. I'll tell about the trains, all right?"

Mr. Newcastle gave an enthusiastic, *Oh, yes!* and Aisha didn't say no, so I started out, "The Chicago, Burlington & Quincy had a red-brick roundhouse about a half-mile from our house. It seemed like it went on forever, both up and around. It could handle sixty engines and tenders at a time, and was the biggest facility of its kind west of Chicago." I said it proud, for it was what had put Sycamore on the map.

"Us kids—my cousins and I—used to go there to play, though we weren't supposed to. It was always roaring with commotion, like a cave full of dragons and thunder, and in the winter you couldn't see the roundhouse roof for all the steam and smoke pouring through the vent pipes. Sometimes men who knew Daddy would let us come inside to watch them push an engine around before they drove it onto one of the side tracks.

"I have loved trains all my life," I confided. It was the first time I had said it out loud, and it got me feeling all warm with the memory. "I like the noise and the burnt-metal smell of them, the steam jetting when you stand beside them, and the rattle and roll when you're inside and going somewhere new."

I told Aisha about the roundhouse, too, how it was kind of like a big doughnut with a bite out of it, the bite being the wide doorway engines came and went by, and the hole in the middle being the roofless circle where the turntable was. On the turntable was a stretch of track long enough for a locomotive and its tender, which is pretty gol-darned long. Sixty side tracks fanned out from it, like wheel spokes. Those were all under the roof, and that was where men like my daddy worked on the engines.

But the turntable was the thing that held my interest. Two men could hand-push one of those giant engines around to any track they wanted to lock it into, for the turntable was on bearings and would go 'round as slick and smooth as if it were buttered, but it still seemed magical to me every time I watched.

Mama would get awful mad if she found us by the train yard, and she'd haul me home by my ear, carrying on the whole way. "You go into that roundhouse one more time, you'll go deaf like Old Mr. Wells! You want to have to use an ear trumpet all your life?" Or, "You stay off those tracks! What would Mr. Newcastle say if you caught your foot in a switch and lost a limb?"

Back then, I never could figure why it mattered what Mr. Newcastle thought or said, or why Mama cared, what with the whole Newcastle family being either dead or gone off to the western territories and of no importance to me. Mama never lost touch with Jonas, and I'm not sure how old I was when she started sending him pictures of me. I must have been pretty small, though, as I don't recall a time when I didn't have to face the photographer's flash once a year as "a remembrance for our dear friend."

About the only time Mama was in a genuinely cheery mood was when she had just received a letter from Mr. Newcastle. She made a real ceremony out of reading Mr. Newcastle's letters. She'd go sit in the parlor all by herself, in the red plush chair we had mail-ordered from the Sears catalog, and which I was never allowed to touch. She'd stare at the envelope for a while, holding it real careful, before she'd slit it with a brass Chinese dagger she kept for the purpose. And then she'd read it over and over, pausing between readings to smooth the pages over her broad lap and stare out the window, her fingertips touching just the edge of the paper.

"Now it's back to Jonas Newcastle and your mother again," said Aisha. Her needles were in her lap and she was looking at me down her aristocratic nose. "What about Annie? Were you even a part of this family?"

"Yes," I said, a little cranky. "I'm getting to that part, all right?"

One of Aisha's brows cocked up. "By all means, then."

"Mama never read Mr. Newcastle's letters out loud," I said, feeling a little ashamed of myself for having snapped at Aisha, "but sometimes she'd tell us parts of his news. 'Mr. Newcastle's mines are bringing up a goodly amount of silver and tin,' she'd say, or 'Miss Jonquil Newcastle has got herself a canary bird. Imagine that, a canary bird in the wilds of

Arizona!' Later on, when Jonas starting building his big house, the letters got thicker and she told us more.

"She'd tell me about this room or that—there was only me to tell by then, because Daddy died in a coupling accident when I was twelve—and all about how thick the walls were, and which rooms had marble floors or stained-glass windows. The china and silverplate had been ordered all the way from—"

I stopped because Aisha was looking at me real odd. She said, "I'm sorry you lost your father, child." She had kind of a strange look on her face, like she didn't know whether to be amazed or sorry or just smack me.

"Thanks," I said, trusting it was one of the first two, and just like that, I felt the wetness pushing at the back of my eyes. Most of the time, I tried not to think about Daddy— about how much fun he'd been and what a comfort, about how he'd smelled of pipe smoke and trains and bay rum, and how his laugh had filled a room—because it always led me to thinking about how he'd killed himself down there in the train yard to get away from Mama.

"He was a good man. He used to take me to baseball games in the town park on Saturdays. He . . ." I wiped my eyes and said, after a couple seconds when I couldn't speak at all, "I don't want to talk about him, if it's all the same to you."

Aisha sighed and shook her head, although in a kindly way. "Well. I suppose we could have more about your mama, then."

So I told her how about how Mama would yell so loud that the neighbors would come out on their front lawns to see who was getting killed, and how she once chased a boarder three blocks with a broom for being a divorced man and having hid it, and how I married Tommy Boone to get away from the hollering and the ear-pulling. I told her how that didn't work out very well what with Tommy getting killed and all, and how even during those last two years after Mama took sick and I was running the boardinghouse single-handed, she was keen on Mr. Newcastle's letters.

Mama would tell me more things about the house, and if

my attention wandered—which it often did, as I had no interest in some fool and his folly of a house fifteen hundred miles away—she'd throw something at me, or yank my ear if she was close enough.

"You pay heed, Annie Pinkerton," she'd say. "This is important for you to know."

After she died, I guess I found out why it was important for me to know, and why it had been Jonas Newcastle this and Jonas Newcastle that for all those years. I also found every single letter he had ever sent her—the ones I was reading on the train, back when I first came to Arizona. They filled a whole hatbox, and were bound up with black cord, in packets sorted by year.

She never saved one letter my daddy wrote her from the war.

Aisha stopped me about there. It had got awfully dark, and the roustabouts had stopped working for the night, I didn't know when. Nebuchadnezzar had wandered off my lap and was under Aisha's caravan, sprawled out and fast asleep.

"Just a minute, Annie," she said, and I noticed she had put her needlework away. "This Jonas Newcastle—the old one, the one who came west with your grandparents, the one who was older than your grandmother and who built the castle—is this your roundabout way of telling me that he is the very same Jonas Newcastle you married?"

She was right. It sounded almost perverse on the face of it, and even more so when you took into account Jonas calling out Grandma's name the night he died, and the fact that I had just that second figured out that Mama was secretly in love with him, too, for the whole of her life. But I didn't say this. I was too embarrassed. I just said, "Mama promised my hand to him. It was her dying wish."

That's right, said Mr. Newcastle. Actually, he kind of gave me a jolt popping up just then, when I was feeling sort of squished inside. I'd forgotten he was listening. *And I'm ignoring that "some old fool and his folly of a house" business,* he added, *only because you told the story well. Although you could have got more in there about my cavalry days. I was quite the—*

"Not now, Mr. Newcastle," I said.

Well, hurry up. Today's Wednesday. Don't you want to go to bed?

"Hold your horses," I hissed, and he went away.

All during that and for a time thereafter, Aisha sat very still, her hands clasped around her knees. Finally, she looked up at me. "You married a man in his seventies because you promised your mother, a mother who did nothing but make your life miserable and chase people with brooms and probably—I am sorry to say this—as good as killed your father?"

I was shocked. Here I was just beginning to get a grip on the situation after twenty-some years of living it, and in the space of an hour of listening, Aisha had put her finger smack-dab on the money.

"Well," I said, embarrassed at how slow even a salutatorian can be about some things, "I didn't promise her, exactly. It was her dying wish. The lawyer read it to me. It was in her will."

That Velda, muttered Mr. Newcastle in admiration. *I had no idea!* Then he made a yawning sound, although I don't know how he did it for he'd already told me he didn't get sleepy over on the other side. Tired, yes, but not sleepy. *Aren't you weary, Annie? Don't you want to go to bed?*

I said, "Five minutes, Mr. Newcastle. All right?"

Aisha was shaking her head. "Look where this nonsense has taken you. From your nice town of Sycamore to this wild country where you travel with oddities and freaks, and to sitting in the grass and talking to an old fortune-teller and the dead ghost in your head."

The "dead ghost" was kind of overdoing it, but you didn't argue with Aisha.

She stood up in a cloud of the sweet mimosa she always wore, her bracelets rattling softly, and crossed her arms. "Some promises, my little prophet, are best not kept."

8

That night, after Mr. Newcastle had taken his pleasures and released me and I had come back into myself, I got to thinking about what Aisha had said, and even more about what she didn't say. She'd said I talked about my family and not me, and she was right. Of course, I was so woven into them that I guess I thought, right up until that night, that everybody else was the same way with their kin.

But they weren't. Not Aisha, not Sam. Not even my papa, who never talked about his family at all. Of course, what with Mama being around I don't suppose he had much chance.

But I thought, as I lay there in the dark all by myself, that I had got lost somewhere in the bosom of that family. I was my mama's daughter and servant and pawn and can to kick down the road. I'd been my papa's little girl. I'd been Tommy Boone's wife, then widow, and now I was Jonas Newcastle's widow. Still his *wife,* to hear him tell it.

I'd talked about my family like nothing I ever did was important except maybe looking at those trains, like Mama was the center of everything else, and I guess that was right. Mama had been the center because she claimed it, and she had such a rank temper that we all fell right into line.

But where did I come in? Where did I start, and where

did Mama or Daddy or anybody else stop? It was like there were hundreds of pieces of me scattered all over, like a bunch of jigsaw puzzles that had got mixed up and put in the wrong boxes. I didn't know which pieces went with my puzzle and which were hooked into Mama's or Daddy's or Grandma's or somebody else's.

I reckon everybody has some pieces of their puzzle that ease over and connect with other folks, but mine? Mine was all lost in my family's.

I thought about the girls I'd gone to school with, how they mostly did what they were told and didn't speak unless they were spoken to. Did any of them have their own puzzle put together? Had they found the pieces? Probably not. They'd probably spend their lives cleaning up other people's messes and waiting hand and foot on their families until they died in childbirth or just plain wore out, and would never, ever think to ask themselves the question that Aisha had asked me.

I thought about the boys I went to school with, how most of them had gone on the farm or into business and had married those girls. I guess I'd never really thought about it before, but I swear: Those boys' lives were so different! Why, they could go off to work of a day, whether it be in the field or in a store or down at the train yard. When they came home, they didn't have to do a lick—they each had a wife to cook and sew and wait on them; a wife who didn't stop toiling when the whistle blew at six, but just kept on.

They had all the fun in bed, and got to smoke the cigars instead of scream in pain when the babies came. And if they should happen to take a shine to the idea of California or New Mexico, well, the whole gol-dang family went right along with it, even if it was the woods of New Hampshire or the plains of Kansas they were pining for.

America was a democracy, but a family sure wasn't.

Well, I had charge of a family, too. Not the one I was originally saddled with, but I was the sole support of the sisters. God gives you what He gives you, I guess. I was out on my own—there was Sam, but it wasn't like he bossed me around or anything—and I was making money and sending it back home.

I sat straight up in bed and said "Crimeny!" right out loud.

I suppose you'll think I was a fool and a half, but it honest to gosh hadn't sunk in till just that second. I was important to somebody—not just as their pet or their servant, but as their sole support. They counted on me!

Of course, once I thought on it a little more, I realized that the sisters weren't exactly sitting around lighting candles to my picture or praising my name. They just expected to be taken care of, like they always had, and they didn't much mind where their support came from.

But all the same, I had the role of breadwinner. I had a job, even if traveling with an exhibition of freaks was sort of an odd one, and my life mattered for something.

I suppose you'll think that's strange, my saying that my life mattered. But to tell the truth, I'd never thought about it in just those terms before. I'd always sort of sleepwalked through life, I guess. I'd never shown much emotion on account of Mama. I've said that before. But I never once balanced Annie Pinkerton Boone Newcastle against the whole of humanity, against the possibility that there were choices for me, that maybe—just maybe—I didn't have to do what was expected.

Granted, of late folks had expected me to do some pretty unusual things, but I'd adapted myself and done them. And look where it had got me!

Well, I was there and that was that. No use crying over spilt milk when the pail's already over the cliff, like Papa used to say.

So I resolved right then and there to try and figure out Annie Pinkerton Boone Newcastle, who she was when she stood all by herself, without any other person's influence—including that of the late Mr. Jonas Newcastle.

All of a sudden I got a chill. "Mr. Newcastle?" I said to the darkness. "Are you here?"

But he didn't answer me. He was off somewhere, flitting in the vapors.

*   *   *

The next day we were off to the next town, all in a long line of caravans and wagons. The weather was nippy and I had on a fleece jacket, but no hat. Aisha had taken to letting Nebuchadnezzar ride with me and Sam when we were moving, and his presence put the kibosh on diving sparrows and their kin.

Me and Sam and Mr. Newcastle were singing "Lorena," which is an old song from the Civil War. Mr. Newcastle liked to sing and he had a pleasant voice, but let me tell you, it's hard to keep your place, melodically, when there's another voice in your head singing the baritone part.

After that, we launched into "Ten Times the Bloody Fight," then "Hoist Your Voice Up to the Lord," and then "Beetles on the Hedgerow." Mr. Newcastle was about to swing into "Send My Heart Home in a Box of Salt and Bury It Next to My Ma," but I was used up. I said, "Mr. Newcastle? Could we take an hour or so off? I swear, my singing parts are about worn out."

Certainly, Annie! he said, real jovial-like. He was always in an especially good mood on Thursdays and Sundays, after taking his pleasure the night before. *You two carry on, then,* he added, and just like that he was gone.

"I was hoping we'd sing that song where the dog dies, Jonas," said Sam, who'd been enjoying himself.

"He's taken off," I said. "And you mean 'Old Blue Has Gone Up Yonder Where the Streets Are Paved in Knuckle Bones.' "

Sam nodded. "Yes. That one. And I'm surprised Jonas stayed around as long as he did, what with him." He tipped his head back toward Nezzy, who was lying crosswise in the narrow space behind us, watching the land go by.

"Don't put on, Sam," I said, smiling. "You like Nezzy and you know it. It's Mr. Newcastle who can't stand him, though I admit he was pretty nice about it today."

He adjusted the reins in his hands. "I suppose so. How's Aisha doing on that prediction?"

He meant how much longer did she have before she proved herself wrong. I said, "Well, she said she was going to die in two weeks at the outside, and this is the eleventh day."

"Looks like she's going to make it."

I didn't say as much, but I had an idea that some of the men, Sam included, had been betting money on Aisha. I just hoped his money was on her living. I said, "Speaking of money—"

"Were we?"

I made a face at him. "I need some cash. I want to buy some pencils and notebooks in the next town." I had got it into my head that the only way I figure out what was me and what was somebody else was to write it down in a list.

"Can't afford it. Say, that's a big one!" he said, reining the team around a pothole that looked deep enough to hide a whole family of badgers.

I waited till we'd cleared the pothole, then I said, "Sam Two Trees! You mean to tell me that we're already out of cash? How can that be? I'm making good wages!"

He shrugged. "I sent it all off. You can wait for your pencils and paper till next payday, can't you?"

This made me kind of mad. Here I was the one earning the money, and I didn't get to see but the fraction that Sam doled out to me. I said, "Well, maybe I'm the one who ought to handle the money from now on."

Sam set his mouth. "Fine by me."

"Maybe I should decide who gets what."

"Fine."

"Maybe that way I'd have an extra nickel or dime when I want it."

Through clenched teeth, Sam said, "Fine," again.

He didn't turn to look at me. He just kept staring straight ahead, straight between the horses pulling us, and I couldn't read his face. I stared ahead, too, feeling every rock those wood wheels rolled over. I hadn't expected it to be so easy. I'd expected a fight out of Sam, or at least a little argument. Here I'd counted on feeling smug, and all I felt was a kind of queasiness, like I'd just spat on the wooden Baby Jesus up at the First Lutheran.

After a minute or two, Sam said, "I suppose I'll just go on home then. Seeing as how you don't need any help."

I turned toward him. "Huh?"

"There'll probably be a stage in the next town," he said, still staring at the horses. "Will you be able to handle the team all right? If you can't, I'll ask—"

"Just a consarned minute!" I cried. "You can't just up and go back to that black castle! Why, what would I do without you? Mrs. Bumbridge can't make that Pâté de Cham— de Crem—"

"Pâté de Campagne," he said, and I saw a flicker of a smile cross his face. Not a big one, but a flicker. "That was good, wasn't it? No one realized I substituted prairie chicken and ground squirrels."

"It sure was good," I said with enthusiasm. "And nobody makes that apple Charlene like you do."

"Apple *Charlotte,*" he said, correcting me, but the smile stayed on his face this time. "It was luck I found those apricot preserves in the back of the kitchen wagon. Of course, the rum was easy . . ."

"I never tasted such a thing," I went on, and added, "it fairly sent my mouth to heaven."

It was the truth, too. In fact, three days beforehand that skinflint Mr. Boyd had nearly fired Mrs. Bumbridge, saying that she didn't do any cooking anymore. Of course, she did, what with fixing breakfast and midday meal and keeping the coffee on all the time, but Sam had said he was just her assistant and that she cooked the dinners. She didn't—she didn't know an Apple Charlotte from a road apple—but that was Sam, lying for her so she could keep her job.

Well, I told myself that relegating responsibility was part of having it, and if it was a choice between Sam handling the money or having no Sam at all, I guessed I could do without pencils for a while.

I put my hand on his arm. "Sam, don't go. Please? We'd all miss your cooking something terrible, and you can keep on handling the money."

He studied on this for a few seconds, his lips pursed together and his brows all frowny, and then he took a deep breath and let it out. "All right, Annie," he said. "I'll stay on."

"Thank you," I said, just as we hit a pothole. I nearly fell out of the seat, and he shot out an arm to grab me at the last minute.

"Big one," he said, after I'd got myself straightened out and Nezzy calmed down. That in itself was a job, let me tell you. That cat didn't like to have his perch jostled more than necessary and he'd tried to jump out of the wagon three times before he paid any attention to me.

"I think we're all going to live," I said, turning around to face front again. I checked my blouse for rips and hands for scratches. I was unscathed.

"Speaking of your friend, Nezzy," said Sam, "I asked Ching Toy what he did with all those dead birds he used to toss in his bucket."

"What?"

Sam made a face. "Well, first he pulls out the big feathers."

"Just the big ones?"

"Wing and tail. And then he builds a fire in his little cooker and gets the oil bubbling. He takes those birds, guts and beaks and feet and all, and dredges them in—"

"Stop!" I shouted. "Don't tell me. Please."

By this time, all the towns looked about the same and I had stopped wondering where we were. I just went to work each day in the tent, let Mr. Newcastle do his speechifying when the time came, and moved on to the next town. The crowds were getting bigger though, I did notice that. Two days after that little tiff with Sam, there were so many people that they took up all the seats and stood two-deep in the back. We had to turn away sixteen others.

"You're sure getting popular," I muttered to Mr. Newcastle as I took the stage.

Of course, he said, kind of cocky. *I am, after all, brilliant.*

"Plus which, you are dead," I remarked. "Don't forget that part."

You don't need to remind me, he said, a little huffy. *As if*

I didn't know. Don't you think I feel half a fool, sitting up here all the time in your skirts? What I wouldn't give to put on a pair of britches again! What I wouldn't give to take a good long piss standing up!

"Mr. Newcastle!" I hissed. The crowd was still noisy, but I always thought they were going to hear us talking. His part, I mean, because his voice rang out so clear in my head.

He laughed, and then he said, *You're a goddamned pantywaist, Annie, but I wouldn't have you any other way. I thought I'd speak about the Indian Territory today. They're going to open it up, you know. Going to kick the Indians off and let the settlers have it.* And then, before I could say a word of surprise, he started singing, *Just north of Texas, the reservation's grand, Just south of Kansas, on that Indian Nation land . . .*

I clamped my hands over my ears—for what little good that did—and said, "I don't care what you talk about!"

He stopped singing right about the time I realized the room had got real quiet and everybody was staring at me. *Going to be a big hit in the twenties,* he said.

I guess I blushed. I cleared my throat and then, like usual, I began to recite my little speech, which began, "Good afternoon, folks. My name is Annie Newcastle, as some have called prophet . . ."

After I finished the introduction, I sat down in the wooden chair on the little platform and said, "You may enter, Mr. Newcastle."

Naturally he'd already entered, but I was saying it more like he was going to enter the room. I felt myself going numb as he took over my body from the toes up, and then I heard him talking, as if from far away.

Good day, good ladies and gentlemen. Today I will speak of the coming glory for our nation, a time in the not-too-distant future when that parcel of land called the Indian Territory will be—

I stopped listening. I went away.

Now, I never knew where I went when I went away. I'd just dribble away to nothing, and then *bang!* I'd be back in myself and it'd be several hours later. I sort of had the idea

I'd been sitting in a rocking chair someplace nice—kind of warm and homey-like and real safe—but I never, in all the time Mr. Newcastle was with me, could recall a thing about it.

I can say that I got no rest while I was away. I'd get my body back just the way Mr. Newcastle had left it: with my throat all scratchy and talked-out after a long lecture, or covered in sweat and tingly after a night visit.

I sure had a sore throat when I came back that day. The crowd was making its exit, and Mr. Newcastle said happily, *Bully show, Annie, just bully! They seemed interested. Some people even took notes! It's about time I was taken seriously.*

He said that last bit every time and, also like every other time, I said, "They've always taken you seriously, Mr. Newcastle."

Well, I believe I'll be off, my dear, he said, also like always.

But this time I stopped him. "Where do you go off to? Is it the same place I go when you're speechifying?"

Heavens, no! he said, and he sounded shocked. *I go to the white room. Lots of books, lots of people to listen to—I can't exactly see them, though—and lots of things to learn. You don't go there. You go to the holding porch.*

"The holding porch?" I had thought it would have a more glamorous name than that! "What's the holding porch?"

But he was gone, off to his "white room."

Sam, tucking a newspaper into his back pocket, came up to the stage. He held out his hand and I took it. "Good show today," he said, helping me down. He was dressed like a white man today, in Levi's and a blue shirt and jacket. With Sam, you never knew from one day to the next whether you were going to get a Navajo brave or a cowboy or a French cook. I liked him any old way.

"My throat's sore," I said. "Feels like Mr. Newcastle was stubbing out matches on it."

"Not surprised. Put on your hat." I did, and Sam lifted the flap. We went out the back way, down toward our caravan. "Jonas talked for more than three hours. It's past five o'clock."

He was right. The sun was low on the horizon, and there

was a distinct nip in the air. Ching Toy was on my trail, following at a distance with his bucket. He'd already picked up two meadowlarks.

I said, "Hadn't you better go to Mrs. Bumbridge's cook tent? You won't have much time for making supper." I felt bad for having let Mr. Newcastle go on so long. Not that I could have stopped him. Sam's suppers were usually fair complicated and took a long while to whip up.

But he shrugged. "Already snuck out twice. It's easy tonight. Potatoes au gratin with ham cubes, green beans amandine. I made the four big trifles yesterday, for dessert. Everything's done."

This last part he said sort of absently, because he had pulled the newspaper out of his pocket and was reading it. Another bird *pinged* off my hat, but I paid it no mind because I was staring at the page Sam was studying. "What are all those numbers?" I asked.

"Stocks," he said.

"No, really," I said, having seen no cattle listed. "What are they?"

"Stocks," he repeated. "What they're selling in New York. Things like grain futures or railroads or ladies' clothing."

I twisted my face. "What?"

We got to the caravan and Sam opened the door. "Annie, you really are naive," he said as I went up the steps. I turned to scowl at him, but before I could open my mouth, he explained, "See, when a business gets big—this is the simple explanation—sometimes it goes public and they sell shares in it."

I must have looked like I wasn't getting it—which I wasn't—so he said, "Pretend that Jonas's mines hadn't all played out. Pretend that the Silver Princess was still coughing up ore to beat the band. But say that all of a sudden, it stopped. Now, you know that there's more silver, but it's going to take more money than you have to blast your way to it."

"Must be in the next county, then," I said. "Dynamite's cheap."

Sam rolled his eyes. "Just pretend, all right? So what you do is you decide how many shares you want to sell, and—"

"How do you do that?"

"I don't know," said Sam, gritting his teeth. He was always more emotional when he wore his white man's clothes. "You just figure it out, all right? And then you keep more than half—say, fifty-one percent—so that you have the controlling interest, and you sell the rest. You get the money to blast to the silver, and when you dig it out and sell it, then you split the proceeds."

I was lost. I said, "With who?"

"With the people who bought the shares!" Sam shouted.

I shrank back a bit in surprise. I'd never seen Sam yell before. I said, "Don't holler at me!"

"Sorry," he replied, and sat down on his bunk. He waved me to my bed, opposite it, and then said, "It's like this. Pretend that you made up a hundred shares and you kept fifty-one. Usually there are a lot more, like a hundred thousand or something, but let's just say one hundred for the sake of argument."

I nodded.

"And say that after you hit the silver, you had enough left over after covering your costs—labor and materials and so on—that you could declare a dividend. That's the profit. So, let's say there's a ten-thousand-dollar profit."

"I did pretty well, didn't I?" I piped up.

Sam ignored me. He said, "Ten thousand dollars divvied up between a hundred shares means a profit of a hundred dollars a share. So you get to keep five thousand one hundred for your fifty-one shares, and send everybody who bought a share one hundred dollars."

I sank my chin on my fists. "Doesn't seem fair. I did all the work."

"But you couldn't have done it at all without those forty-nine people each buying a share and financing you."

I thought this over. "This is a one-time deal, isn't it?"

He shook his head. "Nope. For always. Of course, you can always buy up the shares, if you have a mind. And people can sell them to anybody they like. And before you ask, no, you can't buy them back at the same price. It's like wagering. If a person buys stock in something, he's betting that the stock will go up, be worth more. And then when and if the price of the shares rise, he sells them and makes a profit. See?"

I sighed. "It sounds crooked to me. Everybody else is making money because I couldn't afford a little dynamite. All those people who've never even seen the inside of a mine are betting with my money!"

Sam threw up his hands. "But if they hadn't invested in your mine in the first place, you'd be flat broke! You'd be starving to death on the streets, or working them. You'd be—"

Somebody knocked at the door, and we both jumped a little. I answered it.

It was Aisha, with Nebuchadnezzar. I saw Ching Toy behind her, mumbling Chinese-talk under his breath and walking away with his bucket. "Come and have supper," said Aisha happily, "and then we'll play!" She riffled a pack of the tarot cards she used to tell fortunes, while her earrings caught the last rays of the sun and sparkled them over her cheeks.

"Still sounds crooked to me," I whispered to Sam over my shoulder, and then, "Sure thing!" to Aisha.

"So it's not illegal?" I said to Aisha. We had just finished up our supper of Sam's potatoes au gratin and green beans and trifle—I went back for seconds on that—and were walking back toward her wagon, to the sounds of the roustabouts dismantling the show. Nebuchadnezzar led the way, his shoulders pumping up and down.

"It's not illegal at all, Annie," she said again, sighing. I guess I'd been harping on it all through dinner. "I promise you, it's all on the up and up. I can see why you say it's twisted, but—"

"Crooked," I said, correcting her. "It just seems like those men who are betting . . . oh, never mind. I never knew gambling was so organized, that's all. All those fellows sitting around in New York City, deciding just how much everything in the whole U-S-of-A is worth. Doesn't seem Christian, somehow."

Aisha tilted her brows. "It seems distinctly Christian to me."

I remembered then that she professed the Muslim persuasion, and my cheeks went warm. "Sorry," I said. "But you know what I mean. I swear, nothing's what it used to be! Well, what I *thought* it used to be."

Aisha laughed. "For Annie Newcastle, things are much changed," she said as we reached her caravan. Bracelets clanking softly, she motioned me toward a blanket on the grass, and after she lit the lamp she sat upon the caravan steps. "Life is a little like this traveling sideshow, my darling. What is offered is not always what one receives, and both are far from the truth."

"For instance?"

She smiled and smoothed her skirts. There was a bit of gold thread woven into her garment, and it sparkled softly in the lantern light. "Well, your friend Ching Toy is not Ching Toy, and he is not Chinese. Did you know that? His true name is unpronounceable, and he was an acrobat in the royal court of Siam. A little trouble with one of the king's two hundred consorts, and, well . . . He is here now, and still has most of his body parts."

I stared at her.

"And then we have the Nairobi Twins," she said.

"What about them?" I asked. I knew them by sight. They were billed as the Two-in-One African Slave Girls, and they were joined by a knot of flesh below their waists.

"They are not from Nairobi, and their names are not Jasmine and Spice. They are Doris and Marjorie Johnson, bred of three generations of freed men, and they were born in New Hampshire." She shrugged. "Well, they *are* joined at the hip. But take Baffling Bob, there. The Gill Boy." She nodded toward Bob, who was sitting on his steps and smoking a pipe, three caravans over. "He is no boy, to start with. He is thirty-five if he is a day, and those are not gills in his neck, they are scars made by an inept barber."

I guess I looked at her funny, because she explained,

"They were both drunk at the time. But when Baffling Bob is in his tank of water, he breathes through a glass tube, not through the gills he doesn't have. Take Swami Rashimani. He isn't a swami. He isn't even from India. He's—"

"Aisha?" I interrupted. That was rude, I guess, and I have to admit it was pretty interesting to get the inside story on folks you worked with, but I had just remembered something. "What's the white room?" I figured if anybody at Boyd's would know, it would be her.

"The white room?" she asked, tipping her head. Her turban wobbled.

"Something Mr. Newcastle said," I explained. "I asked him where he went, and he told me he went to the white room. Well, come to think of it, I asked him once before and he said he didn't know. But now, leastwise, he says he's going to this white room. He says they have books there, and people to talk to."

Aisha stroked her chin thoughtfully. Nezzy, who was lying in the grass behind me, gave me a shove with his head and I reached around to scratch him.

Finally, Aisha said, "I cannot help you, little one. I have never come across this 'white room.' Do you go there, too? I mean, in the times when you surrender control of your body to him?"

I shook my head. "I never remember. It's just like lost time to me. He says I go to something called the holding porch, though."

Aisha laughed. "You say that with such a scowl, Annie! Is it so awful?"

"It's not that," I said. "It's not that at all. I mean, I can't remember being there or anything. But it's that *name!* The holding porch. Honest, Aisha, it's like I'm being held out there with the eggs and the butter and the milk during wintertime. Like I'm not even good enough to go inside to the parlor or the waiting room and sit by the fire!"

Aisha started to laugh again, but this time she had the decency to cover her mouth. "Oh, Annie," she said, sitting forward over her knees. "Don't be so put upon. I cannot know for certain, of course—not yet—but I think this holding porch is just the place for you. After all, it is likely that only the dead can enter the house. Well, whatever that house stands for. The holding porch is the in-between, neither a place of death nor a place of life, I think. It is not time for you to go inside to the waiting room just yet. Allah or Jesus or God, whatever name we call Him by, will judge us soon enough."

She's right, Annie, said Mr. Newcastle suddenly. *The porch is fine for you.*

"He's back," I said to Aisha. "Mr. Newcastle. Just this minute."

"Ask him," she said, chin in the palms of her hands. "Ask him about this holding porch, and then tell me."

I nodded. "Well, Mr. Newcastle?"

He made a sighing sound, then said, *Aisha's mostly right. I admit I'm surprised. She's very perspicacious for a female. Can we go now?*

"He says you're mostly right," I said to Aisha. "He says you're smart." I left out that "for a female" part. Mr. Newcastle could be awful rude—sometimes without knowing it, but sometimes on purpose.

"Ask about the white room," she urged.

No, said Mr. Newcastle, before I could open my mouth. *That's not for civilians, Annie. I've probably told you too much already. Come along, now. Let's go to bed. Aren't you tired?*

"Just hold your horses, Mr. Newcastle," I said, then to Aisha, "He says he's not supposed to talk about it. He says he told me too much already. Sorry."

Aisha sat up straight and smiled. "Ah, well. I shall find out soon enough, I think. He is urging you to leave? Is it Saturday?"

See? crowed Mr. Newcastle. *Even the card reader knows about Saturdays!*

Reluctantly, I gave Nezzy one last pat and stood up. "Yes," I said with a sigh. "I suppose Sam's already over at Bert's wagon."

"He's helping with the tent." She pointed toward a knot of roustabouts lugging a rolled piece of canvas to its wagon, and I spied Sam's head for a second when they passed near a fire. "Are you certain you cannot stay a bit longer? We have yet to read the tarot."

Annie, entreated Mr. Newcastle, *it's late. It's almost nine!* I could almost see him stamping his foot and staring at his watch.

"Tomorrow," I said to her, and lifted a hand in good-bye.

I have always wished I'd stayed a little longer, always wished I'd let her read my cards, always wished we'd just set a spell and talked, because the next day—the fourteenth day, right on schedule—while we were en route to Heber Creek, Utah, Aisha's caravan and two others slipped off a narrow canyon road. The edge of it just crumbled away. Aisha was killed, along with Samson Hernandez (the strong man) and his family, Bartholomew the Bone Man, and six horses.

Nebuchadnezzar, who had been riding a couple of caravans back with me and Sam, leapt off our wagon, breaking his tie-line, and scrambled down the hill. It took the rest of us considerably longer to get down there since it was pretty much a sheer drop. We had to go ahead to where the climbing was easier and then backtrack.

Sam and I split up in order to better search for her. Caravans had been shattered like so many matchsticks on the rocky canyon bottom. Possessions were strewn in the creek and the banks, up and down it for a good quarter mile. A fire burned where somebody's broken lantern had got mixed up with somebody else's lit cigarette—Bartholomew's I supposed—and I could hear a horse groaning somewhere.

Aisha had been thrown clear, but that had not saved her. I found her on the creek bank in a nest of boulders, Nebuchadnezzar lying beside her body, nuzzling her hand and chirping at her to get up.

I knew she was dead right off. Nobody could have been twisted and bent like she was and still be alive. I sat down beside her, beside Nezzy, the tears dripping off my cheeks and nose, and buried my face in Nezzy's neck.

All around me, I could hear the carnies moaning and weeping, hear the thuds and scrapes as timber was moved to uncover another victim and another, heard the wails of the women when they pulled Samson Hernandez's broken and bloodied children from the wreckage, and I sobbed all the harder. I jumped at the shot when they put that horse out of its misery, but I never raised my face from Nebuchadnezzar's neck.

I just kept thinking that Aisha was probably the only true friend I had ever had, outside of Sam, and that a couple of weeks wasn't long enough to have known her, not nearly.

There, there, soothed Mr. Newcastle. *There, there.*

"Go away!" I wept into Nezzy's fur. "Leave me alone, you dirty old ghost! You could have stopped this!"

I assure you, Annie, there was nothing I could have—

"Go away!" I shouted, lifting my head. "Go away, Jonas! Go off to your white room and leave me with my friend!"

He was gone, just like that. But as I focused my swollen and burning eyes, I saw Mr. Boyd staring at me from down the creek. I couldn't look at him and I buried my face in Nebuchadnezzar again.

A few second later, Nezzy's low, mournful chirps changed to a growl that I felt more than heard. I opened my eyes to see a pair of boots, and above them Mr. Boyd's big trousers. I didn't look above the knees. I didn't have to.

"Is she dead?" he asked. I heard the sound of a match striking, then smelled tobacco.

"Yes," was all I could get out.

A spent match dropped, not a foot from my face.

"A tragedy," he said. "A terrible thing."

I didn't answer.

"Samson and his whole family, Bartholomew, and now Aisha," he went on. "Not to mention three caravans and six horses."

"I suppose those caravans and horses were worth a good piece of money," I said, feeling my face grow hard. I had never much liked Mr. Boyd, but right at the moment I felt that dislike swelling to a new level.

"Indeed they were!" Some ash dropped next to the spent match. "You're the only one who's commented on *my* loss,

Annie. Why, replacing three acts is hard enough, but those caravans were—"

I launched myself at his knees, driving my shoulder into his shinbones and dropping him to the rocky ground. I had never done anything remotely like that in my whole life, not even when I was a kid, but something took me over. Not like Jonas Newcastle taking me over, not at all: It was more like some kind of primal emotion, some need to just haul off and slug somebody. I might have been saving it up all my life for the way I flew at Mr. Boyd then, for the way I beat at his stomach and face and shoulders, crying and shouting nonsense all at the same time.

Then somebody grabbed my arm and hauled me up, and I took a swing at him, too, and didn't realize it was Sam until I'd already punched him in the shoulder. But the fight went right out of me. I just flung my arms around him, and wailed, "Sam, oh Sam!"

He held me tight, murmuring, "Cry, Annie. Cry until you can't cry anymore," before he said, "Leave us, Mr. Boyd."

"Not until I get my cheetah," came the answer.

I turned my head to find Mr. Boyd up on his feet and dusting off his trousers. I thought I'd punched him good, but I guess it is hard to do serious hurt to a fat man, what with the padding and all. Nebuchadnezzar was sitting a couple of feet from Sam and me, his hackles raised, and this time I didn't have to feel his growl. I could hear it.

"No," said Sam.

Mr. Boyd hooked his thumbs through his red suspenders and stood up straight. "I've sustained a lot of damage today, Indian. I want that cat. He's a menace. Just listen to him growling! I want him stuffed and mounted and in my museum where he can't hurt anybody."

"You mean, where he'll draw a crowd," I sniffed. "Nebuchadnezzar is mine, Mr. Boyd. Aisha promised him to me and you can't have him."

"Nonsense!" Boyd snapped. "Why, Aisha owed me money! I'll take that cat and call it even." He made a grab for Nezzy's collar, but Nezzy hissed and spat and he drew his hand back before it was halfway there.

"No," said Sam.

"That's right, Mr. Boyd," said a new voice. It was Baffling Bob, the Gill Boy, who was standing behind us, along with a growing crowd of teary-eyed show folk. "Aisha told me herself she wanted Annie to have Nezzy if anything happened to her."

"Aisha, she say Nebuchadnezzar go to Annie," piped up Swami Rashimani, his beard in curlers, his eyes red.

"That's right, Mr. Boyd," echoed Bert, the head barker. "I heard her say it myself."

Mr. Boyd flushed bright pink. He said, "I ought to fire you, Annie Newcastle! Stealing from your employer! Taking goods that don't belong to you!"

"I'm not stealing," I said, now that I had some control over myself and had half the show there, backing me up. "Nebuchadnezzar's mine, and you can't have him to kill and stuff. And go ahead. Fire me! See if I care!"

Sam squeezed me extra tight to shut me up, but he said, "Yes, fire her. Fire your main attraction. Fire the girl that brings in record crowds."

"Record crowds?" I wheezed into his shoulder.

He ignored me—although he eased up his grip some, which was a good thing because I was about out of air—and behind him, Bert and Swami Rashimani and Mona the fat lady and everybody else nodded their heads and murmured, "The best we've had," and "He can't fire her!" and "He'd be slicin' his own gullet."

I guess Mr. Boyd forgot himself, forgot where he was standing, forgot all those dead bodies around him, because he shouted, "Then Bert's fired! And you, Bob! And—"

"They go, and I go," I broke in.

"No more write-ups in the papers," Sam said. "No more front-page news, no more folks coming in from fifty miles away, no more—"

"Oh, all right," Boyd said through clenched teeth. His face was crimson by then, and his hands were stiff at his sides and balled into fists. "You!" He swung out an arm, and the fist changed into a finger, pointing right at Bert the barker. "Dilbert! Sort through this mess and salvage what you can."

He stalked off toward where we'd left the wagons, and his back wasn't turned five seconds before people were coming up to me, touching my shoulder or my hair, and saying how sorry they were and crying along with me.

We gently lifted the bodies and bore them up to the wagons, Nezzy walking solemnly alongside Sam as he carried Aisha's broken body. He put her in the back of our caravan, on my bed, and I covered her with a blanket.

We buried our dead in the next town. Clutched in Aisha's hand, all crumpled into her cold, slender fist, was the tarot card she'd been holding when she died. It was number twenty-one, Judgment. That's the one where all the people are rising out of their coffins and floating up to heaven. They looked happy, those people, real expectant. If it had been the Death card, I might have taken it away, but I didn't take this one. We buried it with her.

We didn't make it to Tombstone for Christmas after all. For the first two-and-a-half weeks of December we were snowed in near the town of Flagstaff, Arizona Territory. In Flagstaff, Mr. Boyd had wired all the towns down the line with the news that we were delayed, but that didn't help any of us feel better. The show was stopped, and so was our pay.

Sam grumbled about how stupid it was for anybody— "anybody" meaning Mr. Boyd—to think they could just move forty-two wagons through the mountains in the middle of winter as pretty as you please, but I guess I didn't mind it too much. I was still grieving over Aisha and not much in the mood for crowds.

For all of Sam's carping, Mr. Boyd had sure changed his tune. He'd got almost pleasant right about the time we buried our dead—and I mean right then, while we were standing at the graves—and this was because he bought a paper. One minute he was all sour and cranky, and the next he was holding my arm and helping me to my wagon and asking if I needed anything.

It was the Heber Creek *Sentinel* that he had under his arm. Now, the *Sentinel* didn't have anything in it about our catastrophe, because that had just happened and newspa-

117

pers take a while to get out. But the headline read, in big bold print, "GIRL PROPHET TO VISIT OUR CITY."

Now, you'd think that a place like Utah—and especially a place called Heber Creek—would not have been very welcoming of "Prophet Annie" Newcastle, let alone have put up with a story about a female prognosticator being smack on the front page of their paper. Utah is as thick with Mormons as a turkey egg is with freckles, and a town with a name like Heber Creek? Well, let's just say that I'd been planning on spending my prophesying time having a good nap. The Latter Day Saints don't much take to prophets who aren't in the Book of Mormon.

But Heber Creek turned out to have a fair population of Methodists and Baptists and a few Catholics, and they welcomed me with open arms. I was still awful shaken up about Aisha, but that next day when Mr. Newcastle took me over for the lecture, there were one hundred and seven people in the audience to see me. It was a record crowd, and they had to hold it in the main tent, with folks sitting or standing betwixt the exhibits of petrified frogs and the stuffed Sumatran tiger and glass cases full of preserved whatnots and impossibilities.

Mr. Newcastle spoke for almost three hours by my reckoning, and that evening he did it again for a crowd of ninety-seven, and the next afternoon for an audience of one hundred and twenty-eight, not counting babies on their mothers' knees. I figured we had just about the whole town in there at one time or another. Sam said it was more like they all came twice. The non-Mormons, I mean. And some of them, too.

Anyway, what had got them so eager was this story in the paper. It called me "an auger for our times" and "a modern Ezekiel," although I didn't see what Ezekiel had to do with it, because the Lord sure hadn't spoken to me out of any wheel of fire in the sky. The only things coming out of my sky were suicide birds, and the only one talking to me or through me was Jonas Newcastle. If these old-time prophets had known about his carnal desires or some of the peckerwood things he said to me—people walking around on the moon, my foot!—I guess any one of them would have just turned him into a pillar of salt or smote him with a tongue of fire.

On that first day, my eye caught the headline, but that was all. I didn't read any further. I think you'll understand when I say that my mind was in other places. But Sam had got a copy and saved it for me until I was up to paying attention, which was sometime the next week, when we were heading south toward the Utah/Arizona border.

"What's it mean by 'and there are fortunes to be made by paying rapt attention to Mrs. Newcastle's oration'?" I dropped the paper to my lap and stared at Sam.

"Just what it says, I reckon." He flicked his eyes over to me, then back at the road ahead. We were on our way to Pullet Bend, Arizona, for the next day's performance, and we still had nearly thirty miles to go.

"But what fortunes?" I asked. "Jonas doesn't talk about money, and he won't say where a fellow should dig for gold. He just babbles about the cavalry or pig farming and such."

It's hardly babbling, said Mr. Newcastle, who'd been rapt as I read the paper. *Why do they say it's you doing the prophesying and not me?*

Sam clucked to the horses. "Don't forget, Annie. He talks about the future, if you can sort it out of all the ranching and mining and Indian fighting."

"Don't tell me you believe him, too! I admit, Jonas is right on a few things, little things, but—"

Sam stopped me. "When did you start calling him Jonas?"

I had to think. I guessed I had started it out there, by the canyon creek where the wagons crashed and Aisha and the others died. I'd been blaming him for it, for not seeing that in the future, and I guess I'd started calling him Jonas right about then. To my mind, calling him Mr. Newcastle implied that I had some respect for him.

I said, "It doesn't matter. Do you mean to tell me that you're taking for truth everything that comes out of my—I mean his—mouth?"

It most certainly does matter, said Jonas, all huffy. *I*

thought you were calling me by my first name because you liked me!

"No reason not to believe him," said Sam.

I ignored Jonas and said, "But all that malarkey! Maybe he's saying something important during those lectures—I admit I plain don't listen—but he's always jabbering to me about little bitty clocks you strap right to your wrist that'll tell you what time it is in Sweden. That, or men walking around up on the moon or some President who's gonna get himself shot in Dallas or some songwriter named Cold Porter."

Cole Porter, said Jonas. *Cole, Cole, Cole!* He was sounding real annoyed right then, but I, like a fool, just kept on ignoring him.

"He harps on flying machines and driving machines and space rockets, says people are going to shoot themselves up in the air and fly around the world! He says a colored lady's going to be President someday, and we're going to bring home rocks with bugs in 'em from the planet Mars, and some crazy man in Germany's going to kill twelve million people!" I cried, and the sound of it woke Nezzy.

"Can you imagine?" I said. "Why, I'll bet that's more people than there are in the whole world! I think he's gone plum crazy, that's what I think, and if he's—"

All of a sudden I couldn't move, I couldn't talk. I was seized by a paralysis so overwhelming that the first thing I thought was lockjaw, then lock*body,* then *Jonas!* He had shut me down so quick and overwhelming that for a half-second I thought I was shut out for good, that he'd closed the door on everything but my eyes and my brain.

"Annie?" said Sam.

I couldn't answer him, and Jonas Newcastle, that vile creature, said inside me, *Mock not thy husband, Annie Newcastle! It was bad enough when you kept me to Saturdays and Wednesdays, bad enough when I found out you'd been married before, bad enough when you took in that damned cat, but this mocking I will not stand. Remember the train? Remember when I said I could make you sorry? Well, now's the time, wife!*

My body stood up and I went with it, terrified I'd fall under the horses and be crushed by the wagon. But Jonas had other plans for me. While Sam said, "Annie? Annie?" over and over, my fingers went to the buttons of my dress and my mouth moved and I began to sing.

"I've got you under my skin," came the lyrics and strange tune, straight from Jonas Newcastle, straight out of my mouth.

Horrified, I realized I'd undone—Jonas had undone—most of the buttons on my bodice. My underwear was showing to the whole world, and as I looked down, my fingers went to the little bow at the top of my camisole.

The wagon stopped and I couldn't hear Sam anymore, couldn't hear anything. I could see that people had jumped off the caravans ahead of us and were running back, their mouths moving but no sound coming out. Inside my head, I pleaded, *Please, please, Jonas! Mr. Newcastle! Stop it, please!*

But he didn't stop. He just kept singing—now it was some caterwaul about a girl called Roxanne, and how she didn't have to turn on the red light—and then the bow was undone and my top was coming down. Mortified and wanting to die, I saw something out of the corner of my eye—a quick movement—and then . . . nothing.

I woke up in darkness, and it took me a second to realize I was in our caravan, in my bed, and not dead. I reached down to the floor and my hand found Nebuchadnezzar, asleep and breathing deeply, his ribs rising and falling.

I searched the inside of my head for Jonas, but the low bastard had gone off someplace, probably to that white room of his. I wished I could tell somebody in that white room what devilment he was causing me down here (for some reason, I always thought of that white room as "up there" somewhere) because I was pretty sure if they knew what he was doing—whoever "they" were—they'd slam his fingers in the cookie jar pretty gol-dang fast.

All of this happened in about five seconds, and in the sixth, I became aware of a terrible pain in my jaw. The hand that had been on Nezzy flew up to touch it. "Ouch!" I said out loud, for it was hot and swollen, and it felt like at least one of my teeth was loose.

"Sorry about your jaw," came Sam's voice in the darkness. He struck a match, and for a second I saw his face on the other bunk, all bright gold while he lit his cigarette. Then he shook it out and all I could see was the red, floating glow on the end of his smoke.

"What happened?" I asked. My mouth felt like I'd borrowed it from somebody else and it wasn't a good fit.

"How much do you remember?"

"I remember the whole horrible thing," I said, "up until I was pulling down my top and singing, 'Walk the streets for money,' and something about not caring if it's wrong or right." I felt my face get red-hot, and added, "What the heck kind of a song is that, anyway?"

Sam grunted. I couldn't see if he was tickled or disgusted, but he said, "I punched you. Couldn't figure what else to do. You didn't give an inch when I tugged your arm or tried to pull you down. Jonas sure uses that body a lot stronger than you do."

I rubbed my jaw again and said, "I don't remember that part. But I thank you anyway. Did I . . . Was I . . . ?"

"You were still decent when I knocked you out," he said. "But just barely. What got into Jonas?" he tried to say it real calm, but I could tell he was worried. More than worried.

"My fault," I said. "He was punishing me. He told me on the train that he would."

"The train?"

So I told Sam about how Jonas had given me that lecture on the Atchison, Topeka, and Santa Fe, and about how I was married before, and how Jonas didn't like to be mocked.

"I swear," I said at the end, "he sounded like something out of the Bible. 'Mock not thy husband, Annie Newcastle!' he said." A shiver took me, and I clutched at my shoulders.

"That's Jonas, all right," came Sam's voice. He took a draw on the cigarette and the end glowed bright for a second. "Always came across like the Lord God Himself when he was riled about something. I remember when he brought me back from school. Not school, really, because I was cooking at that restaurant, remember?"

I nodded, even though Sam couldn't see me.

"He picks me up in town in that undertaker buggy of his and says, 'Suffer thee not an ungrateful child, sayeth the Lord.' I didn't remember that particular phrase being biblical, but he was so mad I didn't mention it. After all, he'd taken me off the reservation, hadn't he? 'My will shall be thy will,' he says, 'and thou shalt serve in my house for seven years.' And then he just picked up the reins and drove out to the house—that was before the castle was finished, and we were living at the old ranch—and he didn't say another word."

I rolled to my side so that I could pet Nezzy a little easier. "What'd you do?"

"Well," Sam said, "I owed him." He took another draw on his smoke. "My seven years is up a year from this coming January."

"Sam!"

"Like I said, Annie, I owed him. Besides, somebody had to be there to look out for the sisters and clean up their messes. Old Jonas, too. He would have gone broke halfway through putting up that monstrosity of a castle if I hadn't been there. Those workmen'll steal you blind if you give 'em half a chance."

It hit me then, *bang,* like a gunnysack full of bricks. I wasn't the only one who'd done what I was told and didn't speak until I was spoken to. Men had to do that, too, at least Sam had, and he was still doing it. I had a whole new feeling for him, although I didn't know if it was respect or pity. Maybe some of both. Maybe kinship, too. He had the same as lived my life, even though he'd lived it fifteen hundred miles away from Sycamore, Iowa.

I didn't say anything, though. I couldn't say anything.

Soft, he said, "Listen to me, Annie. You've got to guard your thoughts. Don't make fun of Jonas or complain about what he's telling you. Don't think about that Tommy Boone of yours. Just go along with whatever Jonas wants, all right?"

Just like that, Mama's mad took hold of me. "Why should I?" I practically shouted, anger pumping hotly through my veins. "How long's this going to go on? When do I get my life back? What about *me*?"

There was silence for a minute, such a long minute that I was just about to apologize, then Sam said, "I don't know, Annie. Maybe it'll go on forever. Maybe till the day you die."

All my insides sort of went splat. The implications of Jonas Newcastle haunting me for the rest of my days seemed a load too heavy for a mortal woman to bear. To tell the truth, I hadn't given much thought to it, about how long he planned to stay around, I mean. I'd sort of had it in my mind that someday I'd be shed of him, that I'd make enough money to buy a little house with a garden somewhere, that I'd be happy.

I guess I hadn't really thought about it at all, not till that minute.

Over the next few weeks, while we were snowed in at Flagstaff, I thought about it a lot. There's not much else to do besides ponder when you're stuck in a town that's already seen everything your show has to offer three times or more. Of course, one or two of the leading citizens—and the not-so-leading—would slog their way a half mile through the snow every couple of days to have a private audience with me. That's what Mr. Boyd called them, anyhow, a private audience, like I was the Queen of England or something.

Me, I just felt sad all over. Empty, too. Aisha was gone, and Mr. Newcastle was still getting over his snit-fit, but only made his presence known when there were paying customers. He didn't even come on Wednesdays and Saturdays anymore. Sam was kept busy cooking for the whole mob, on account of Mrs. Bumbridge had slipped in the snow the second day in Flagstaff, and broken her right arm.

Baffling Bob (the Gill Boy) tried to cheer me up, and so did Mona and the others, but they finally left me alone to sulk in my caravan in the company of Nebuchadnezzar. I guess I was a sorry case, all right, but at least I got to know Nezzy real good. He was quite a cat. He'd chase a ball through the snow and bring it back—so many times that I thought my arm was going to fall off—and he seemed to know what I was saying to him.

Before, I'd thought he was real handsome and certainly a help with the birds, but I'd just thought he was kind of like an overgrown barn cat, only more intimidating when you first met him.

Except he wasn't like that at all. He was kind of like a dog—well, kind of like a real big dog in a cheetah suit. He slept a lot, and even when he was awake he could be deaf as a post if he didn't want to hear you, but he was one heck of a watchcat.

One night some fool came creeping through the drifts to the campsite and tried to get into our caravan, and let me tell you, it was Katie bar the door! I was up and Sam was up and that cheetah charged out and chased our burglar right up a tree. He would have gone after him if we hadn't grabbed his tail and pulled him down.

That fellow was scared white when we got him out of the tree, and had already been through five caravans, including Mona the Fat Lady's. His pockets were full of geegaws and money, which we relieved him of before we gave him over to the Flagstaff sheriff. In turn, the sheriff made Nebuchadnezzar an honorary deputy, with a tin badge and everything. We clipped it on his collar.

Of course, personally, I figured it had more to do with that burglar having swiped a plate full of chicken legs out of Mona's wagon along with everything else. Nezzy was a fool for chicken. I didn't say anything though. I was real proud of him.

Anyway, Nezzy and me were best buddies by the time the pass was clear and we pulled up stakes, but I was still no better off, Jonas-wise. Oh, he'd begun to talk to me some by then; I suppose he couldn't do without his Wednesdays and Saturdays. He never mentioned that little scene he'd caused and neither did I, but the fact that he could maintain a residence in my head until doomsday kind of put a damper on things.

Since our schedule was off and we were passing close to home anyway, Mr. Boyd allowed that we could put into

Rock Bottom over Christmas and spend the holidays at the castle.

Still wearing mourning black, Miss Jessie and Miss Jonquil were delighted when we all rolled up in front that morning, the wagons trailing a quarter-mile down the road to the house. They gave both Sam and me a brittle hug, and had their hankies out to blot their tears. Of course, they weren't so overjoyed when Mildred the Bearded Lady and Esteban Murphy, the man with the stunted twin in his shoulder, came up on the porch to join us. But I have to say that they—meaning the sisters—took it pretty good, all in all.

They even made up to Nezzy—well, sort of—after a bit. It helped that Nezzy purred and licked Miss Jessie's hand just a little and then curled up at Miss Jonquil's feet. They were still leery, but you could say they were smitten.

Miss Jessie had been holding my mail in a couple of rain barrels, but she'd saved the important-looking ones separate. There were three letters from Mr. P.T. Barnum. I read them in order. The first one said as how he was looking forward to having me join his circus come spring, and to report to headquarters in March. The second one asked why I hadn't replied, and included a contract. The third one was kind of worried, in between the lines, and said as how he'd reconsidered, and wouldn't I like to do a tour of the East Coast, and furthermore, he was still waiting for my reply.

So I signed his contract, which promised much better terms than originally offered, and wrote and said as how I was bringing Nebuchadnezzar and Sam and if he didn't like it he could call the whole deal off. I didn't think he would, though. A hoodoo woman who travels with an Indian man and an African cheetah is bound to be more conducive to good press than one who doesn't. Anyhow, I sealed the envelope and gave it to Mr. Alvarez, with instructions that he mail it after the holiday.

I didn't mention it to Mr. Boyd. He'd been offering me more money and bigger signs and a better caravan (although I didn't see how he could do that last part, since he'd said at the start that the one he gave us was his best), if only I'd give Barnum the heave-ho and stay on with him.

That evening, after Sam and Mrs. Alvarez and Mrs. Bumbridge had managed to roast a whole steer and everybody had oohed and aahed over the castle and the caravans and wagons were all parked in neat rows on either side of the drive, we had a party.

After a real good supper of beef—and corn and little potatoes that Sam had put up in seasons before—and caramel custard, Mr. Boyd was in such a good mood that he took the sisters down to see the petrified piece of the One True Cross. Of course, everything was all packed up, but he lifted the canvas tarp back so they could take a peek at the Sumatran tiger and some of the other doodads.

"It was stunning!" said Miss Jessie, all agog and breathless after they'd come back up the hill.

"Simply amazing!" said Miss Jonquil. She dabbed at her forehead with a starched hankie.

"We've never seen anything like it—"

"—in all our lives!" finished Miss Jonquil. "They have the Twenty-third Psalm—"

"—written on the head of a pin!" said Miss Jessie.

"And a sea monster and a stuffed penguin," added Miss Jonquil.

Miss Jessie clutched her hankie in her hand and held it to her heart. "Oh, the sea monster! Did you ever see anything so terrible, Sister?"

"And the preserved hand of a giant ape and an elephant's tusk and an unborn calf with two heads!" Miss Jonquil went on.

"And the desk of President Lincoln!" said Miss Jessie.

"And George Washington's wooden teeth!" said Miss Jonquil.

I didn't believe I'd ever seen them anywhere near so electrified with enthusiasm. It was a good thing the Siberian snowman and the Tasmanian Terror were packed up at the front of the wagon so Mr. Boyd couldn't show them to the sisters, too. With all those glued-on fangs and claws and grisly appendages, Miss Jessie and Miss Jonquil probably would have fainted dead away.

Later, we built a big fire in the parlor hearth—it wasn't

snowing where the castle was, of course, but it got fair nippy at night—and some of the acts performed for us.

Testo the Great juggled seven plates, then five vases and the fireplace poker. Bruno Krump, the strongman, lifted that big mauve velveteen ottoman with Mona the Fat Lady sitting on it.

Ching Toy, our contortionist, had gotten over being mad about there being no more birds for his dinners, and fair turned his body into a human pretzel. Nezzy did his one trick, which was jumping through a hoop for some beef scraps, before he curled up by the fire and went to sleep.

In between, Bert announced all the acts—not like at the show where he was trying to get folks to spend their quarter, but quicker and more to the point. Somehow friendlier, too. And all through it, Jonas cheered (well, inside my head, anyway) for every performance. He could be nice when things were going his way and he was entertained.

After all the acts had performed that were going to and the show folk started drifting out toward their caravans for the night, I got to wondering why he hadn't asked to speak to Miss Jessie and Miss Jonquil. They were his sisters, after all, and he hadn't seen them for a spell.

I asked him about it, but he just said, *It's late, Annie. We're all tired. Aren't you tired?*

As always, it was his subtle way of convincing me to go to bed. Now, both the sisters were looking a little droopy— as much from all the company and excitement as from their brother's lack of interest. I said my good nights, then took Miss Jessie aside. I felt a little closer to her, what with her having confided in me that story about the railroad president and how she thought to serve fruit cup after the aspic melted.

Besides, Miss Jonquil had already gone upstairs to bed. I think she'd been crying, although it was hard to tell. Whether they were mad or happy or sad, the sisters always looked like they could burst into tears at the drop of a hat.

"Miss Jessie?" I said to her on the wide marble staircase. "It's been a real long day. How about we all tuck up for the night? Tomorrow morning, Jonas'll have a nice long con-fab with you and Miss Jonquil, I promise."

She brightened considerable, and even patted my hand when she said her good nights.

I went up to my room, sinking into that soft mattress that seemed miles wide after the caravan bunk, and didn't even wake when Mr. Newcastle finished doing his business. In fact, I didn't wake until early the next morning.

The smell of coffee, good coffee, came to me first, and I opened my eyes to find Sam standing over me, a big smile on his face. He'd been dressing white the past few weeks, but today he had on his Navajo duds. Well, except for the apron. It was green and white checks with pink piping. He wafted a big steaming mug of coffee under my nose. I loved my coffee, and he knew it.

"Morning," he said, handing it to me. "Sleep okay?"

Careful not to wake Nebuchadnezzar (who was snoring beside me with his head on the pillow), I sat up and sipped the coffee. It was just right. "Fine," I said, and took a greedy gulp. "Better than fine. I'd almost forgot what a real bed is like. Thanks for the coffee, by the way." I set the cup down for a second to slide open my bedside drawer, pulling a lumpy, wrapped package from it. Handing it to Sam, I said, "Merry Christmas. I made it myself, so don't complain or I'll get my feelings hurt."

Sam laughed. "Same to you," he said, and produced a gift for me from behind his back.

"Thanks!" I said, smiling at the wrapping paper. He'd drawn little Nezzys all over it.

"Open it later," he said with a wink. "Crepes and canned berries for the holiday breakfast. Strawberry, raspberry, and blackberry."

I frowned. "Those kinds grow in Arizona?"

"No," he said with a proud sort of smirk. "But they grow for me in the shade garden out back. The secret's extra water and only morning sun, and netting to keep the birds out. Lots of compost, too. We had a big crop last year and I canned about sixty jars, which is about fifty-five more than Miss Jessie and Miss Jonquil will eat in the next ten years.

Gonna get the use out of 'em. Now rouse yourself up off that goose down and come to breakfast."

Yes, let's, said Jonas, as I swung my legs over the side. To tell the truth, I could have stayed in that soft bed about two hours longer. *Strawberries again!* he added. *Haven't had strawberries since I vacated the earthly plane.*

"Since you died, you mean," I muttered. "And you're not going to have them today, not until you talk to your sisters."

Sam was halfway out the door, but he overheard me and paused. "Jonas back?"

"He comes and goes." I put on my wrapper. "Lately he's been sticking around a little more."

I want my strawberries! Jonas shouted, just like a little kid on the edge of a tantrum. The sheer volume of it made the inside of my skull ring.

That scared me a little bit, but I figured, what could he do when I was here in my room? He couldn't cause me physical harm, for he'd feel the aftermath every time he took my body over.

I stood firm. "Your sisters first, Jonas, then the berries. They've been pining to talk to you since yesterday afternoon. Why, I saw Miss Jonquil sniffling into her hankie on the way upstairs," I added, laying on the guilt.

Sam was shaking his head. "I would've thought the two-headed calf would have held her a day. Oh, well." He went through the door, saying over his shoulder, "I'll save you some breakfast. And wake that lazy Nezzy-cat up."

All right, Annie, said Jonas, in a more normal tone. In fact, it was so normal that it unnerved me more than that shout had.

I didn't let on, though. I sat down before the mirror and began to brush out my hair. "What are you up to, Jonas?"

Me? he said. *Nothing, little peach. Nothing at all.*

I could tell he had something up his sleeve, but I didn't press him. I already had a plan, which I figured was guaranteed to knock the wind right out of his sails.

*   *   *

But what are we doing all the way out here? Jonas argued.
*It's Christmas Day! We should be at the castle, singing carols
and drinking cider and burning a Yule log!*

After the sisters and breakfast, I had gone straight to the
barn and saddled up one of the buggy horses and ridden
directly out on the desert, so far that I couldn't even see the
castle anymore. Nezzy wasn't with me. He'd eaten nearly a
whole haunch of beef the night before, and after he'd gone
outside to do his business, he'd stretched out under the
nearest caravan and gone back to sleep.

I had my tin Chinese hat, though, and the birds were
making up for lost time. I'd forgotten just how annoying all
those pings and thuds could be, and then I wondered if
maybe I should stop and pick them up for Ching Toy.

Let him find his own birds, said Jonas, kind of nasty. *And
turn this confounded horse around. I want to go back home!*

"Nope," I said, trying to act sure of myself, which I wasn't
at all. "I rode all the way out here with a purpose in mind,
Jonas. I'm going to talk and you're going to listen."

Goddamn it Annie! he thundered. *Rein this bangtail
around this second, do you hear me?*

I believe my eyes got a bit wide, but I said, "No. Jonas
Newcastle, you and me are going to have us an agreement,
one we can both stick to. And it doesn't include you shouting at me or cussing or raising your voice in any way, shape,
or form. You understand?"

Well, it seems you *can shout,* he said, real snotty, just like
an eleven-year-old girl whose dress is prettier than yours.

I stopped the horse and closed my eyes for a second,
which only brought more birds. I bet you that five of them
hit me and slithered to the ground just while I was sitting
there.

Finally, as calmly as I could, what with being so mad at
Jonas and the dead birds falling and all, "I'm sorry if I
shouted. I didn't mean to. And you've got to stop shouting,
too. This is my body, you know. My hands, my feet to walk
with and mouth to talk with."

I started the horse moving again. "You're just borrowing
it. You used up your body and now it's gone and buried,

and you're a guest in mine. An uninvited guest, I might add. If I were you, I'd be ashamed to be such cranky company. If I were you, I'd be a lot nicer."

But I am *nice, Annie, my pet, my flower!* he said right away, all creamy. *I'd be nice to you more often if you'd let me. Wednesdays and Saturdays aren't enough to—*

"Jonas, no!" I said, and smacked my own hand when it started to get too familiar. That part didn't hurt, but after Jonas gave up control, which he did right off, the sting that followed sure did.

"That's not what I mean by being nice," I said, trying to rub my hand and guide the horse and brush a dead finch from my shoulder all at once. "What I mean is—Say! Is that one of our men, clear out here?"

A lone fellow had just stepped from behind a big grove of prickly pear. He slowly limped toward me—us—and waved.

That's funny, said Jonas. *No horse.*

"Maybe it got hurt," I said. "He's dragging his leg."

First the left and now the right, said Jonas, his voice laced with suspicion. *Turn the horse around, Annie.*

"We can't leave a man out here," I said, and waved back at him. He was dressed like a saddle tramp, in rough clothes and a broad-brimmed hat and chaps. He had a gun on his hip, too, but then, that's normal when a body is out in the wilderness. Even I had a rifle in the boot, although I scarce knew how to use it. Sam had made me bring it.

I gave my horse a little kick, goosing him toward the man, who fell down right about then and lay there in the gravelly dust, not moving.

Annie! Turn around this instant or I'll—

"Or you'll what, Jonas? Take me over?" I reined in the horse and stepped down. "I've got a surprise for you." I crossed my fingers and hoped it would work.

For a few seconds, it was war inside me. First Jonas would take a leg, then I'd take it back. Then he'd try for an arm or even a finger or a leg again, but if I concentrated, I could always push him out. Of course, I couldn't push him out of my head, but I didn't let him know that.

Annie, he said, and he sounded about as used up as I felt. *Please! Leave that man lay! Go back and get Sam.*

"And that's another thing," I said, ground-tying the horse, taking down my canteen, and walking toward the fallen cowpoke. "That was real mean of you, Jonas, practically keeping Sam an indentured servant for seven years just because you were mad at him for cooking in some restaurant."

I knelt beside the man and uncapped the canteen. He was medium-size but muscled up, so far as I could tell, and wore a faded plaid shirt, the sleeves rolled up past the elbows. Gently, I pushed his shoulder back until I could see his face, and then I held the canteen to his lips.

"Mister?" I said softly, bending to him. He was dark and kind of ugly-featured.

"Mister?" I asked again, and suddenly he grabbed my arm.

I tried to pull back, but he held me firm, far too firm for a man who has just awakened from a swoon, and said, "Are you Annie Newcastle who tells the future? The one folks call a prophet?"

Well, I figured it was some fellow who had seen my show. Imagine that! I thought how surprised he must be to be waked up from his faint by a famous person. Well, sort of famous. He had probably grabbed my arm to make sure I was real and that he wasn't hallucinating.

"That's right," I repeated kindly. There was just a smidgen of pride mixed in, though I did my best to hold it back. "I'm Prophet Annie Newcastle. Now, do you think you can stand? We'll just get you up to the castle and—"

He sat up, *bang,* just like that. Still hanging on to me for dear life, he shouted, "I got her, Ike, just like you said! I got her and she's the right one!"

10

"What do you mean, you got me?" I said, giving my arm a tug. It didn't do much good.

"Just what I said," he replied, with all the warmth of a toad in winter. He smelled a lot riper, though. Taking me with him, he stood up and started to dust off my skirts with his hat.

I smacked at it, shouting, "Let go of me, you fool! Who are you and what do you want?"

"Howdy, Miss Annie," said a new voice. I turned—well, as much as I could with that pockmarked man still clinging to my arm—and saw another fellow coming out from behind the prickly pear and leading two horses, a gray and a buckskin.

This second man was a little taller and so bone-clanky thin that he could have almost given the late Bartholomew the Bone Man a run for his money. About thirty or so and almost good-looking, he was mustachioed, with one of those funny little goatees that are just a dot of fuzz right under the bottom lip. Every time I see one of those, I want to scrub it off. And when he swept off his hat I could see that he had sandy hair, cut all crookedy.

He pressed his stained hat to his shirt, gave a funny sort of bow—clumsy, I mean—and said, "Ma'am, I'm Ike. Ike Tackett? You may have heard'a me?"

Now, he'd said that last part like maybe I should've heard his name or read it in the papers, like maybe he was the mayor of some big city or a leading citizen or something. That's how he said it, all proud. But he didn't look like any kind of leading citizen I'd met—and I'd met quite a few in the past couple of months—and I'd never heard the name Ike Tackett mentioned. I said as much.

He looked so disappointed that I sort of wished I'd lied. He recovered right away, though, and said, "Well, I reckon you travels a good bit with your prophesyin' business. Anyhow, that feller what's hangin' on your arm is my half-brother Gobel. Gobel Tackett. Don't s'pose you heard'a him, neither?"

I shook my head. "He's about to cut off my circulation, though."

"Sorry, ma'am," said Ike, hat still clutched tight to his chest. "Ease up a mite, there, Gobel."

Gobel loosened his grip, but not so much that I could pull away.

Ike went on, "See, me and Gobel got different mamas. Same papa, though. That's why we's both Tacketts. Now, Jubal, he's got the same ma as Gobel, and Mike, he's got the same ma as me, but we's all Tacketts just the same. Yes, ma'am, the same blood."

I gave him a little nod. I couldn't think of anything to say. Truthfully, I plain couldn't figure out what those two yahoos were up to. They were too polite to be robbers or killers. Not that I'd ever met any robbers or killers, mind, but I figured that sort to be plenty tough. I didn't believe they'd be the kind to call a lady "ma'am" or take off their hats or dust her skirts or talk about their mamas.

Now, I'd already shouted inside my head for Jonas, but the coward had fled and was nowhere to be found. He was probably hiding in that white room of his, shivering and quaking or whatever ghosts do. Some war hero. What did he do back in Minnesota when the Indians attacked, I wondered?

I said, "What is it you gentlemen are wanting?" I figured it best to call them gentlemen, even though that ugly Gobel was still hanging on to my arm in a most ungentlemanly way.

Ike Tackett said, "Miss Annie, that is, Mrs. Newcastle, ma'am we . . ." Brow furrowed, he looked down and scuffed one boot in the dirt, back and forth. I looked at Gobel, but he was picking a dead sparrow off his sleeve and staring at it, his face all screwed up.

"What?" I asked again.

Ike looked up. "Reckon Badger could tell you better'n me. It were his idea, ma'am."

"Badger?"

"Yes'm, Badger," Ike replied, at last settling his hat back where it belonged. "He's a'waitin' down the road a piece."

Just then another bird hit my hat. All three of us gazed at the body as it fell to the desert. "That sort'a thing gonna happen a lot?" Ike asked, still staring down. He didn't seem put off by it, just curious.

"Yes," I said.

"Dang," he replied. And then, without missing a beat, he said, "Gobel, help Miss Annie—I mean, Mrs. Newcastle—up on her horse, there."

"Thank you," I said, as the pocked-faced Gobel led me to my horse. I figured as soon as I was mounted I'd give it a kick in the ribs and get back home pronto, except Gobel snatched the reins away.

"Hey!" I said, and the Mama in me popped out. I cried, "Give those back!"

Ike blanched and backed off a step, but Gobel said, "Nope," just as wood-faced as a cigar store Indian. It was the first thing out of his mouth since he'd shouted to Ike that he had me and I was the right one. He climbed up on the buckskin, still holding my reins. "Gonna go see Badger."

"Well, I don't want to go see Badger!" I crossed my arms. "I want to go back to Newcastle's Castle this minute! If this Badger person wants to see me, he can come to call there." I made a snatch for my reins, but Gobel held them away.

"Ma'am?" said Ike, still acting a little nervous, like he thought I could snap my fingers and send them up in smoke.

"I'm real sorry, but you're gonna have to come with us. See, we needs you."

"What on earth do you need me for?" I snapped as he stepped up on his gray. I took a deep breath and pushed the mad back. This wasn't easy, since it was like a hot poker goading me. But I did—sort of—and added, "I'm not worth any ransom, and I don't have any cash money on me."

Ike, slouched in the saddle, evened up his reins. "Badger'll tell you, ma'am."

We started to move forward, away from the castle. Gobel led my horse and Ike rode on the other side, just close enough that I couldn't jump off. Well, I suppose I could have slid over her rump, but they would have had me in two leaps if the horse didn't kick me first.

All the mad left inside me was directed, right at that minute, straight at Jonas Newcastle. I sent him a lengthy silent curse. I called him names so terrible that I'd never said them out loud in my life, much less thought them. I figured that'd rile him enough that he'd come forward, but all I got for my trouble was more silence.

I guess the mad went right out of me about then, and all that was left was fear. Seems funny to say it, how a person can trade one emotion for another just as you'd changed your hat, but it happened. I tried not to show it, though. I kept my chin up and my back straight, even though there was nothing more I wanted to do than to just disappear off that horse in a puff of smoke, like Rhubarb, the magician's rabbit.

I tried not to think about them raping and torturing and murdering me and such on account of they were so polite, but I had little luck. Jonas had told me that Stenholm Krieger, the mad murderer of Denmark, was real polite to his victims, too. Or would be.

I really wished he hadn't told me that.

Trying to hold my voice steady, I said to Ike, "Am . . . am I being kidnapped? For ransom? Like I said, nobody's got any money to pay for me." And then I thought that I shouldn't have said that, because they'd probably just slit

my throat right there in the desert and leave me lay in a
pool of my own blood.

But it was too late to take it back. Turned out it didn't
matter anyway, because Ike said, "Yes and no, ma'am. See,
we're . . . Well, cain't you wait for Badger to tell you? I
'spect he can do it a whole lot better'n me." All of a sudden
he smiled, and added, "If you don't mind me sayin' it,
ma'am, that's a right purty dress you got on."

Well, it was plain and it was blue, but it was clean and I
suppose that made it pretty to him. I said, "Th-thank you,"
still wondering if I was going to be killed. Maybe they'd
stop up ahead and pull their guns. Maybe Ike'd carry around
a bit of my skirt fabric as a memento.

"Got a sister, too, me and Gobel," Ike said as we rode
on. He was riding a little ahead of me, his horse's rump
even with my horse's neck, and he didn't look back at me.
"Name's Mimi. Her ma's different. I mean from mine and
Ike's, and from Gobel and Jubal's. Her ma's a Frenchie
woman. Now, she was from down 'round Tucumcari,
weren't she Gobel?"

Gobel just kept riding, but Ike said, "Yep, that were it,
Tucumcari, and she were Daddy's fourth wife . . ."

As he prattled on, we steadily left the hills and Sam and
the sisters and Nebuchadnezzar behind, moving farther out
across the plain. How I wished I'd brought Nezzy with me!
If he could chase a burglar up a tree with such fervor,
he'd've sure as shooting made short work of these raggedy
Tackett brothers. But Nezzy was back at the castle, still full
as a tick and probably dreaming of the yellow African veldt.
I ached to be there with him.

Little by little, I started to relax—I mean, they hadn't killed
me yet and Ike's voice was sort of soothing. He was up to
his daddy's seventh wife by then and never asked me a
question, nor turned to see if I was listening or not. He kind
of put me in mind of Mrs. Schuyler back home, always gabbing and rambling, and never an ear for anybody else's
news.

They hadn't even bothered to tie me up. We were just
riding along like we were going over to Aunt Hester's house

for some after-church pie, while Ike brought us up to date
on his family.

". . . when we come up to Phoenix and bought that bull
for daddy, remember, Gobel?" Ike rambled. "Yep, that were
it. I reckon that must'a been eighteen and seventy-nine in
March. That's when he were married to Lois Jane. She were
number eight. Now, when we got the bull home, Daddy'd
been in the homebrew again, and he took a hankerin' to
steppin' up on him. The bull, I mean. Course, he was
soused. Daddy was al'ays soused, wasn't he, Gobel? So we
roped that old bull and threw a saddle on him and . . ."

I guess I didn't listen. While Ike's monologue washed over
me, I began to study them. Gobel Tackett hadn't said a word
since we'd mounted up. He looked as dark and swarthy
from the back as he did from the front, and sat his horse like
a two-hundred-pound bag of grain, all heavy and poured in
the saddle. His backside never shifted, but his shoulders
and neck bobbed with his buckskin's gait, and he never
looked 'round.

On the other hand, the sandy-haired scarecrow that was
Ike Tackett was staring out at the desert ahead, gabbing
away with kind of a pleased and lofty, half-amazed expression on his lean face, like he'd just communed with the Holy
Spirit or something.

He rode just as slouched as his half-brother, but a lot
looser, like his joints weren't all connected. They were as
unlikely a pair to be brothers—even half-brothers—as I had
ever seen. Other than a last name, the only thing they had
in common, so far as I could tell, was a couple of real
bad haircuts.

Suddenly, it struck me that they weren't paying the slightest bit of attention to me. And it came to me at the very same
moment that we were about to skirt a good-sized manzanita
thicket. By good-sized, I mean maybe fifty or sixty feet
across and about as long.

I eased myself back up on the saddle's cantle.

Nobody looked, and Ike just kept talking. He was on wife
number nine, now, and I was half-inclined to stick around
just to see how many wives Daddy Tackett had got up to.

But I pushed myself back until I dropped off the saddle entirely, onto the horse's rump. Still, they took no notice. Ike was telling some story about a wolf, now. I supposed the wolf got number nine. Daddy Tackett's wives always ended bad.

I closed my eyes and said a little prayer to God that this mare wasn't overly spooky and that she wouldn't jerk forward or worse, kick back. And then I just slid backward, off her croup and past her tail.

I landed in a silent crouch and stayed there, holding my breath. That mare hadn't missed a beat. She was still walking along, letting Gobel lead her.

"And then that dang ol' lobo skittered left," Ike was saying, "straight into the deepest, darkest, skinniest, most low-ceilingedest cave you ever did see . . ." Neither brother took the slightest notice of my exit.

I made myself stand up. My knees were shaking something fierce, but I managed to scramble over to the thicket, and then got down on my belly and started worming my way into it.

Oh, it was terrible! First, you cannot imagine the critters—bugs and such—that take shelter in those thickets during the daytime. Things I can't and won't describe slithered over my hands and crunched under my knees. There was thorny things growing in with the manzanita, and they scratched my hands, snagged my sleeves and bodice, caught my skirt and ripped it. Dust rose in little puffs, sent up by the smallest movement of my hands, and within seconds my nose was plugged and I was having to breathe through my mouth.

Still, there was no sound of the brothers galloping back, no shouts of, "Hey! Where is she!"

I thought I'd just crawl a few more feet in and then wait. Maybe wait until dark, until the Tacketts had given up looking for me—that is, if Ike ever shut up long enough for them to notice I was gone. Then I'd start to walk back, and Sam would ride out to meet me and Nezzy would be with him, and we'd have a big old hug fest and I'd never wander off on my own again as long as I lived.

I kept on inching, getting used to the bugs going *crunch*

and the twigs slapping at me and the thorns digging at my skin and tearing my clothes. But then I heard something, something that sounded like a hissing kettle at first, a kettle just before it whistles.

I froze. Even back in Sycamore, Iowa, timber rattlers have surprised many a plowman, and you are taught when young what a rattlesnake sounds like. I figured it to be coming from off my right side, maybe four feet away. The sound faded, then grew louder, back and forth, like this snake couldn't decide if I was friend, food, or foe. I was afraid to turn my head and look, lest the motion of it tempt that devil to strike.

I do not know how long I crouched there, listening to that ungodly hiss, but it was long enough that my shoulders and knees ached, and the sweat was dripping off my nose despite the balmy weather. I was even beginning to wish the Tackett brothers would come back, and that they'd shoot it—although Ike would probably talk it to death first.

I remembered Sam telling me that the snakes went away in winter, that they hibernated or something, and I thought that he ought to be here instead of me, stuck crouching on his belly in the manzanita and the stickers, listening to that "hibernating" rattler sound his warning.

I called and called inside my head to Jonas. I figured he might know some trick for escaping vipers, but he didn't answer me, not even with a peep.

And through it all, that warning sound just kept rising and falling, rising and falling. *Go away!* I thought, my joints trembling with fatigue. *Go away and bite somebody else!*

And just then, my shoulders gave out. I dropped the three inches to the ground, so scared that I barely registered the pain above my elbow, and only vaguely realized the rattling sound had stopped.

I just lay there for a second, my cheek in the dirt, listening. There was a slither, the sound of a sinuous body shifting tiny pebbles as it slipped away, and then nothing but the scratch and hum of insects.

My arm was pounding. It came to me just like that, and I whipped over on my side, not caring if that rattler was all the way gone or not, not minding the sticks that poked me or the dust that fell in my eyes.

It had bitten right through my sleeve. Two fang marks and a few drops of blood marked the site, and there I was, miles from the house, miles from help, and with no horse.

A real thin, high sound was coming out of me, although I wasn't trying to make it. I tried to back out of that manzanita too fast, and all my flailing did no good. I just got more twisted up in sticks and leaves and those sticker plants, and that horrible, airless shriek just kept getting louder and louder. To my ears, anyhow. I doubt you could have heard me ten feet away. That's how it is with hysterics, I guess. I'm ashamed to say it now, but I have to tell the truth. I panicked.

Not for long, though. Jonas popped into my head and my body and stopped my struggle. I didn't even try to push him out this time.

Hush, Annie, he said, real firm, and then used my fingers to tear away my sleeve in sure, long motions. *Hush and be still.*

I minded him, and let him take me the rest of the way over. I went away to my holding porch.

I woke up in a bed. Not my feather bed, nothing any-where near so grand, and not in my room, either. This place was dark and dusty-smelling, and the walls were, so far as I could tell, hammered planks. Not too good a fit, either, since light came through the cracks in thin, mote-filled slivers.

I started to sit up, but my head pounded like somebody was building a railroad in it. My arm was giving me fits, too, and I lay back down. I didn't remember the snake until just then. You know what it's like when you're waking up? At first, everything's just fine, and then *bang!* The weight of the world hits you.

It was that way for me. I remembered the snake and the Tackett brothers and the carnival and Mr. Barnum and Jonas all in one fell swoop. Well, Jonas, because just then he said, *Lie still, dearest.*

"Where am I?" I whispered, clutching at the thin quilt that covered me. "What the dickens is this place? What's going on?"

You might better ask when *it is,* he said. *You've been unconscious for nearly two days. If I hadn't stepped in and screamed for help, you'd still be lying in the manzanita. You'd be dead as a post, too.*

"You mean those Tacketts have got me?" I asked, surprised. Annoyed, too. "You mean you gave me up to those two fools?"

When you're snakebit, he replied, *two fools are better than nobody at all.*

I reached across and felt my arm. It was swollen, but felt cool to the touch. I took that for a hopeful sign.

Yes, said Jonas in agreement, *it's quite a bit better. You were out of your head until last night, though.*

"Out of my head?"

Oh, ranting and raving and talking foolish, he said. *Not much of it made sense. I only peeked in every now and then. You're going to love Badger Jukes, by the way.*

He said that last part kind of snide, like I wasn't going to like Badger Jukes at all and I'd soon figure out the reason. I was just about to ask him what he meant when he said, *Bully! Here he comes.*

Well, there'd been a door in that dark wall, and when it opened, the light near to blinded me. I couldn't see a blessed thing against the glare except for a short and wiry silhouette, like a stick man's shadow. He came toward me.

I shrank back, as much from the stink of him as anything else. I reckoned that sometime in the last week or so he had done an unfriendly thing to an ill-tempered skunk.

He bent over me.

"Well!" he said, and his voice shocked me. It was high, the next thing to a girl's. "It's awake!" he said. "How's you feelin', sugar pie?"

I had almost laughed at that girlie voice, but something besides politeness kept it from coming out. Just his presence and well, something I couldn't put my finger on, had broken my arms out in goose bumps.

"Well?" he said. "I asked you a question."

"I-I'm fine, thank you." I wished I could see his face, something more than that black shape against the light. Then again, maybe I didn't want to see it.

"Good. Glad to hear it," he went on. "How's that arm a'yourn healin' up?"

His fingers plucked at my quilt, but I brushed them away. "It's fine, too," I said. "What is this place?"

He laughed, a thin cackle that set my teeth right on edge, it was that scary and out of place. Macabre, Miss Jenson would have said. She was my teacher back in Sycamore, for the third and fourth grades.

I think I cringed.

He finished laughing, just like a spigot turned off, and said, "That's for us to know and for you to figger out, sugar pie. 'Cept you ain't figgerin' it out. Just know that we brung you out so far that there ain't nobody a'goin' to find you. You's ours to do with."

By this time, I was about half-frozen with fright. I mean, there I was: snakebit in some falling-down shack out in the smack-dab middle of nowhere, with naught for company but three crazy fools who might do anything. Mr. P.T. Barnum was going to have to call off my tour, Sam was going to have to French-cook for somebody new, and on top of everything else, Jonas had disappeared again.

No, I haven't, Annie, Jonas said right then, and his voice had never been so welcome. *They don't mean to hurt you. Actually, they're scared silly, and it's me they want to talk to.*

"To you?" I said, right out loud.

The man who'd come in said, "What are you talkin' about?" real cranky, and then he stood up and backed off a step. "You talkin' to him now?" he whispered, and he sounded spooked. "That haunt?"

The step back and the change in his voice set my mind at ease, at least for the time being. I might be scared of these boys—and the little high-voiced one would bear watching—but they were more frightened of me. I said, "Would you be Badger Jukes?"

He yanked his hat right off his head. "How'd you know that?" he whispered. "Did . . . did you witch it?"

See what I mean? said Jonas, and I could tell by his tone that he was full of himself.

"Yes," I said to Jonas, "I see. Is it safe for me to get up?"

Nobody answered, not Jonas or the little man, so I sat up slow, my arm thudding, then put my feet over the side of the bed. You couldn't exactly call it a mattress.

"Do you have something I could make a sling out of?" I asked. When Badger just stood there, clutching his hat, I added, "For my arm."

"W-who's talkin'?" was all he said, and it took me a second to figure out what he meant.

"Me," I said. "Annie Newcastle, I mean. The sling?" It came to me that I was still in the same dress I'd been in two days ago. Not that I supposed Badger minded much, or could even tell. My eyes had started to tear up from the sheer sour skunk stench of him. I could taste it, too.

And my stomach was hurting. I didn't suppose anybody'd had the presence of mind to feed me a little broth while I was sick. Frankly, I doubted these boys knew what broth was.

All of a sudden another figure appeared, and hunkered down to fit through the door. All I could see was his shape, but I knew that long, lanky frame.

"By cracky!" he exclaimed. "I believe Gobel has saved her, Badger!" He stuck his head out the door and shouted, "Hey, Gobel! You done healed her!"

Somebody outside grunted.

"Hello, Ike," I said.

He pulled his head back inside and took off his hat. "How do, ma'am," he said.

"I was just asking your friend for some cloth to make a sling for my arm. I'd like to wash up, and I'm hungry."

"I'll take care'a that right now, ma'am," Ike said. "Yes, indeed, right this minute. We got a real nice spring out here for washin' in, and I believe that tortoise Gobel's roastin' is nigh on near ready."

I felt my whole face pucker, but Jonas said, *Don't say it,*

Annie. Play along with them, and I'll have you free of these miscreants before nightfall.

"Tortoise," I said and smiled, although the thought of it made me sick. "Oh boy."

Well, Ike brought me water for washing and drinking. While they left me alone to clean myself up and tend to other urgent matters, which don't need mentioning here, I had a long heart-to-heart with old Jonas.

It seemed that the two days he'd mentioned were kind of shaky, and when pressed he thought it might have been three, or as much as four. When I was unconscious, he couldn't get in. But a few times when I'd been having fever dreams, he slipped in for a look-see and a listen.

Gobel had taken care of my arm out on the desert, and here in the shack. Ike had fetched and carried for him, and Badger had just stood around, scratching himself.

"What's he look like, anyway?" I said. "Badger Jukes, I mean. Is he one of the Tacketts' brothers?"

You wouldn't want to take him to the church social, Jonas said. *And he mentioned kin in Arkansas, although I take it we wouldn't wish to meet them. His name's Jukes, after all, not Tackett.*

"Well, I didn't know," I said, ringing out my cloth over the water. At least, I hoped I was over the water. It was too dark to see what I was hitting. "Jukes could be his middle name or something. Lord knows, Ike and Gobel have got enough brothers and sisters."

Thirteen, by my count, he said, *although I'm confused about the twins their father had by Maybelle. Did they live when the javelina got in the house?*

"Hey!" I said, kind of cross. "You weren't gone after all, back there when he was telling that story and I was scared spitless! That was pretty mean of you, Jonas."

I was thinking, that was all, he said.

I didn't press it.

Jonas also told me we were in the mountains. That explained why the water Ike brought was so fresh and cold, and why I started shivering the second I took off my quilt covers. But beyond the mountains and the relative elevation, which I gathered he could tell from what was growing there or the soil or something, Jonas wasn't too sure of just exactly *where* we were. He said there were maybe three different mountain ranges we could be in. I did not find this satisfactory.

We were out cold for most of the ride up, he finally snarled, after I'd asked him for about the fourth time to be more specific. *It is* my *fault you let yourself get bitten by a snake?*

"Oh, just like I planned it!" I said, rinsing my armpit with a wet rag. It was as cold as all get out, actually, especially when a person was stripped down and wet.

I went on, "Just like I said to myself, 'Gosh, nothing much is happening today. I believe I'll ride out and get myself stuck full of stickers and fanged by a poisonous snake. And while I'm at it, I believe I'll get myself kidnapped, too, just to break up the tedium of living.'"

Very funny, he said, grouchily. *You remind me less of your sweet grandmother with each day.*

I dabbed at my snakebit arm with the cloth. Even if it was on the mend, it still hurt like nobody's business. I said, "I swear, Jonas, you don't remember Grandma Frieda very well at all! Why, when she'd let fly at Grampa Rudy, everybody for three blocks would dive under their bed or lock themselves in the chifforobe. Why do you think everybody in Sycamore called her Fiery Frieda? Where do you think my mama got her mean streak?"

Of course, I didn't say that Grandma Frieda's obstreperous attacks—what she called "old Scratch gettin' de uber hand"—were far apart and short-lived, or that she was always especially nice to everybody afterward and made us apple strudel.

I don't believe it! Jonas thundered. *Not sweet Frieda! Not that fair Dutch flower! She didn't have a mean bone in her dear little body!*

The inside of my head rang with his ranting, but I said, "Fine," and pulled my sleeve back down. Jonas had ripped the other one clean off out there on the desert. "Don't believe a word of it, then. Doesn't make me any—never mind. The truth's the truth whether you want it or not."

Oh, he whispered, *little Frieda,* and the way he said it—all let down and sorrowful—made me feel bad for having told a little lie, or at least not the whole truth.

Not bad enough to take it back, though.

While Jonas thought that over, I found the long cloth—more like a rag, I suppose—that Ike had brought me, and started fixing it into a sling. It was darker than sin in that shack, and I was clumsy tying it, just like I'd been clumsy with the buttons on my dress. When your fingers on one hand are swollen to the size of sausages and don't work any too well and it's dark to boot, a buttonhole can be a real tricky thing.

"I wish we had more hands, Jonas," I muttered. Then, "Jonas?"

He'd fled the scene again! Doggone it if he wasn't getting downright flighty all of a sudden. Well, he'd been flighty—not to mention pigheaded—all along, but now was hardly the time to flutter off to his white room.

I shouted, "Jonas Newcastle!" one more time, but he was all the way gone.

The door banged open, blinding me with light, and I heard Ike's voice. "Ma'am? Ever'thing all right?"

I sighed. "Fine. Have you seen my tin hat?"

"Should be right in back'a you, on the stove."

That was how dark it was in there with the door closed. I'd been standing two feet away, and I hadn't noticed my hat, let alone the big old potbellied stove it was on. I settled the hat on my head and said, "Don't you gentlemen believe in windows?"

Ike wrapped the quilt around my shoulders, took my good arm, and led me outside. While I squinted and rubbed my eyes, he said, "Ain't our'n. We just come across it. Reckon the feller who built it boarded up the winders to hold off Apache. Been dead a good while, but we still buried him."

I stopped rubbing my eyes. "What?"

Ike, his face now clear and well-lit by what I took to be

the tree-filtered light of midday said, "I wouldn't worry none if I was you, ma'am. I don't reckon none of them'll bother us."

I swallowed hard. "Worry? I never do." I had tried to make it come out bold and nonchalant, but I don't believe I had much success.

"Yes ma'am," he said, and led me toward the fire.

The cookfire was down the hill about ten yards from the cabin, and about twenty feet up a rise from a little creek. All around, aspens and little pines and sycamores shivered in the light breeze that sang through their limbs. Underneath, ferns were thick and green and studded with tiny purple wildflowers. Imagine that! Just a few days past Christmas, and flowers! Under any other circumstances, I would have been happy to be there.

Well, except for the birds. The boughs were thick with them, and they had already sighted me. Six or seven had already killed themselves on my hat.

"Why'd you build a fire out here instead of up in that big old stove?" I asked, mostly to take my mind off the questionable chunks of meat roasting over it.

Ike looked away, probably to shield his eyes from flying beaks and small talons as much as anything else, and shifted his toe in the dirt.

Gobel, who was tending the fire, looked up. "I reckon," he said, his ruined face all stony, "it's 'cause that's where we found what was left of the feller we buried."

I said, "Oh," but it sure didn't cover what I was feeling. On top of everything else, a good-size tortoise shell lay to one side, all messy with bloody entrails. The flies were having themselves a real picnic, let me tell you.

I looked away. I have always been real fond of turtles and tortoises. Back home, I had a pet box turtle named Violet for six years, until Mama got riled up one day and threw her clear across the street. I took her out to the country and turned her loose the first chance I got.

I figured I had to live with Mama, but that poor turtle sure didn't.

"Smells fine, Gobel," said Ike happily. He sat me down

on a log and brushed away the lark that had just fallen into my lap. He hollered for the absent Badger to join us, and then he said, "They's beans, too, ma'am. Can I scoop you up a batch to go with your tortoise?"

"Lovely," I replied, remembering to stay as pleasant and polite as I could. "Except I'll just have the beans. My stomach's still a little queasy." That was no lie. Just thinking about that poor tortoise was enough to do it.

Ike picked up a dented tin plate, brushed away a dead finch, and began ladling beans onto it. They were runny, and didn't have the scent of any seasoning whatsoever. Sam's cooking had spoiled me, that was for sure, but even when I was cooking for the boarders back home, I knew to doctor things up with a bit of ham or onion. At least salt.

He handed me the plate and a fork with two tines, and said, "Whatever you say, ma'am. An' after you fills your belly, maybe you could . . . mayhap you'd tell a mite about your . . . your powers?"

I didn't answer. I just ate those tasteless beans with the birds banging off my hat, and tried not to think about the gutted tortoise. Or the poor nameless man those Indians had folded into his own stove.

11

Badger Jukes didn't join us until about ten minutes later, and when he did he took away the rest of my appetite. I had never seen anyone quite like him, not even Charlie Snodgrass back home, who lived in the alley behind Kent's Furniture Store and Carpentry, and who was feeble and kind of strange-looking on account of he was got by his uncle raping his mama.

First off, Badger Jukes had orange hair. When I say orange, I mean it was fiery, the color of scraped carrots. He had watery, light blue eyes, one of which stared in at the bridge of his nose no matter where the other was looking. As for his other features, they were small and fine, with one ear a little bigger than the other.

But when you looked farther down, he had one arm that ended in a sort of club. At first I thought it had been mangled in farm machinery, or something like it. But upon closer inspection, I saw he had only three fingers—well, two fingery things with no joints whatsoever, and a little nub of a thumb out to the side. The "fingers" were cleft deeply, back to the wrist. It was like somebody had taken an ax to his hand and split it down the middle, then sewn the two fingers on either side together so they looked like pincers, except there were no signs of scarring whatsoever. I guess he had been born that way.

He sat down a couple of feet from Gobel, across the fire from me, and took up a plate. "What are you starin' at?" he said in that high, girlish voice.

"Nothing," I replied, and kept my attention on my plate. By this time, I wasn't doing more than shifting those tasteless beans around and trying to hold my plate so no birds would land on it. Besides, Badger was upwind from me, and the stench wasn't conducive to eating.

"Reckon you was lookin' at my arm," he went on. "Reckon you think I should'a been in that there freak show you was with."

Something in his tone told me it wouldn't be the best idea to venture an opinion, so I looked up and said, "Did you see me at Boyd's?"

"Yeah," he said around a big mouthful of beans. "Seen you there with a couple'a pards'a mine. Back in October, maybe November. That's when I got me the idea to swipe you."

"Ol' Badger," piped up Ike. "He's a crafty one, he is."

"Shut up," Badger said, and Ike went back to his plate. He turned to me again. "See, I got plans for you. What with you prophesyin' the future and all, I reckon you's a gold mine just waitin' for the right prospector to come along."

He laughed then, and let me tell you, it had an effect on me like fingernails on a chalkboard. Both my arms—even the one that was swollen—burst out in goose bumps.

"If there's something you wanted to know," I said, holding back the urge to rub them down, "you should have just asked Mr. Newcastle. The spirit, I mean. For seven dollars to Mr. Boyd, Jonas gives private audiences. You didn't need to go to all this trouble."

Ike moved away from me a little, like he'd just remembered I was haunted. Gobel concentrated on chewing his tortoise.

"Sure, we did!" said Badger, testily. "We did, too, need to swipe you, if we wants to know—"

He stopped mid-sentence, because Gobel had suddenly popped to his feet. "Rider," he said, without expression, and picked up a rifle I hadn't seen.

While Gobel headed down into the trees and Badger scurried uphill, Ike shut me up in the shack. "Prob'ly better, ma'am. Kept you outta the birds," he whispered quickly, and then he shut the door, leaving me in darkness.

Well, what could I do? I felt my way over to the bed and sat down, praying the whole time that whoever Gobel had heard wasn't an Apache. I sure didn't want to end up stuffed in the stove.

And then, suddenly, I realized it could be a rescue party. If it was Sam, I sure hoped he wasn't alone. That Badger Jukes fellow had blood in his eye.

I don't know how much time passed. Maybe five minutes, maybe fifteen. It's hard to tell when you're in the dark, trying to hold your breath still and your heartbeat down to a quiet roar. But then I began to hear sounds. Arguing, and somebody—or somebodies—tramping through the brush with a horse. It came closer to the shack, and pretty quick I could make out the words.

"You did what?" came a new voice. "I swear, you knuckleheads beat everything!"

"Well, why's it dumb, Johnny?" said Ike's voice. He sounded like he was whining. "We take her, and then she can tell us all the gold shipments! Badger says—"

"Don't tell me what Badger says," growled the one called Johnny. "Badger can hardly speak English, let alone think in it. And you should know better. Listening to a Jukes! Listening to a man who's dumb enough to poke a skunk with a stick!"

"Still smells a mite skunky," admitted Ike.

"Well, I'm goin' to cut Badger's plans short," said Johnny. I heard boot scuffs just outside, and then his voice loud, right on the other side of the door. "I'm going to have a word with her." He paused, then asked, "You boys didn't rough her up any, did you?"

The door started to open, letting in a wedge of light, but then it slammed shut again. At the same time, Badger's voice said, "Hold on, there, Devlin! If'n you're thinkin' how you'll set her free, I's here to tell you that you's wrong."

Somebody sighed—Johnny, I thought—and then he said,

"Badger, why don't you go back to Arkansas? Why don't you go back there and marry your sister and have lots of red-headed, wobble-eyed, pincer-armed babies?"

I gasped, then clamped a hand over my mouth. Those were fighting words for sure, and any second I expected to hear a gun sing out, or at least the sound of fisticuffs.

But Badger said, "You know I cain't marry my sister, Johnny," and there was a tinge of sadness in his voice. "Buttercups's already took by my brother, Weasel. Ain't no more Jukeses left to marry up with, less'n them outcast Jukeses up to Missouri got one to spare. And don't say as how I should take myself up there an' look," he added, a little self-righteously. "Them Missouri Jukeses was outcast for a reason. We has vowed to plug 'em on sight. And besides, I won't be the one to besmirch the good Arkansas Jukes name with their rogueified, thinnish blood!"

By this time, I was gripping the edge of the bed. I had never heard such a conversation in my life, and never hoped to again.

"Can we get back on the subject?" said Gobel. I hadn't heard him come up, but he must have.

"I was just saying that I'm about to turn this little flower free," came Johnny's voice. "Here, Gobel. Take my horse down to the picket line, would you?"

"Why come?" shouted Badger. I heard the sound of a horse being led away. "We took her, and she's our'n! We ain't even had us a chance to ask her no questions yet!"

"You can't just run around kidnapping folks, Badger," Johnny said patiently. "It's not civilized." And then paused, like maybe he was thinking that Badger Jukes and civilization didn't have too much in common, anyway. He added, "It's not smart."

"Didn't see you askin' if it were a smart thing when we robbed that stage last month," said Ike softly.

Johnny just replied, "That was different."

Now, I'd been all set to like Mr. Johnny Devlin right up till that second, but stage robbery is a low profession indeed, if you can even call it such.

"Shut up, Ike," he said, and opened the door.

At first, I couldn't see him just the same way as I couldn't see Badger when he first came in, what with the light blaring in behind him. He was just a big black shape. He came over to the bed and went to help me up, but I let out a yelp and pulled back.

"She's snakebit," shouted Gobel, from off a ways. I guess he could hear alright, though.

"Take the other arm," Ike said.

"Sorry, Miss," whispered the black shape called Johnny. In spite of myself, I admired his voice. It was deep and rich, and he sounded like he genuinely meant his words. "Can you move?"

"Diamondback bit her three days ago," Ike offered. He was leaning in the door, by then. "Swole up somethin' fierce an' turned purple an' black an' got blood blisters all around. Gobel fixed her up good, though."

"Still," Johnny said, taking my other arm, "it's got to hurt like the devil. Easy, Miss. Let's get you out in the light."

"Aw, we already done had her out in the light once already," said Badger as we emerged. "Birds all over the damn place!"

I was blinking again, but I saw him scratch his thin little belly with that three-fingered claw. I found myself thinking he should have taken up gainful employment with Mr. Boyd and billed himself as Badger the Lobster Boy.

"They fed me," I said, mainly to get my mind off Badger's claw. A thrasher bumped me hard just above the ear. I put my hand to it, and then I looked up at Johnny.

I near about to died. He was that cowpoke—*the* cowpoke—from Boyd's, the green-eyed man who'd come to see my show with Pat Garrett all those months ago. I'd tried to forget about him, and I'd been almost successful right up until that second.

"It's you!" I cried without thinking. I forgot all about getting my hat, forgot all about the birds. My knees gave out.

"Easy there, sis!" he said. He caught me with one arm and sat me down on a little boulder, just outside the shack's door. I swear, it felt like his arm left a scorch mark. It was a good thing Jonas had run off to his white room or wherever, because I was feeling so wonderful and strange and goose-pimply and breathless that it had to be bad.

"Just look at her," he said, and then ducked to avoid a sparrow. "What the hell?"

Ike produced my hat and put it on my head with a "Here, Johnny," but I can't say I paid much attention to that, or to the blood trickling from where the thrasher had hit me. Because all of a sudden Johnny's name seemed prettier to me than any other I'd ever heard. Johnny Devlin. Johnny Devlin. Annie Devlin.

Stop it! I told myself, and pinched my bad arm to reinforce it.

I cried out from the pain, and Johnny put a big hand on my shoulder and said, "Look what you fools have done! There're probably search parties out all over the Territory by now." He batted the air with his other hand, and said, "Christ! Have the birds gone crazy?"

He could have just stood there forever swinging at the birds with one hand and the other on my shoulder and I wouldn't have minded a bit. That hand *belonged* on my shoulder.

"We've got to get her back, and the sooner the quicker," Johnny went on.

No, you don't, I thought dreamily, as something *pinged* off my hat.

"Crikey," spat Badger. "She ain't even witched nothin' for us yet. At least let her witch the gold shipment!"

Yes, Johnny, I thought, feeling that hand burn itself to me. *Let me "witch" something for you.*

"Christ, Badger!" he said, and snorted. He took another swipe at the air. "You spent too much time listening to that damn Kid."

Badger lowered his voice, hissing, "Billy *knew* things, Devlin." His claw twitched.

But Johnny said, "Billy didn't know—" He batted away a sparrow. "Billy didn't know his ass from a tree stump. This girl can't 'witch' anything, except maybe birds. Don't you know a carnie trick when you see it?"

I sat up straight and pushed his hand right off my shoulder. A goldfinch just missed my face. "What do you mean, a 'carnie trick'?"

"Oh, come on," he said, stepping back. It was as much to get away from the birds as anything, I guess. A smirk teased at the corner of his mouth, and I knew he was holding it back just to be polite. That got me madder than anything else. "You don't have to pretend for us," he went on. "We're all men of the world." He glanced at Ike and Badger and added, "Well, some of us are. I saw your show twice, remember?"

"No, I don't," I lied. Sam had told me later, but I hadn't remembered myself, so I guess it wasn't a total fib. "And I'm no fake. I am inhabited by the spirit of Mr. Jonas Newcastle, the celebrated entrepreneur of the Arizona Territory. He was an officer in the Sioux uprising and a big rancher and he owned mines. He was my husband until foul fate took him from this earthly plane on our wedding night. The birds came with him."

I was all het up, sorry to say, but that Johnny calling me a fake had got to me more than I'd thought possible. Now, Badger could have called me a fake and I'd have said, "Thank you very much, and good-bye," but Johnny Devlin? That was a different story.

He just stared at me.

"See?" said Badger, smiling all superior. Well, as superior as he could look with that funny eye turned in all the time.

"Yeah! See?" said Ike, as three swallows plowed into my hat, *bang, bang, bang*.

Johnny rolled his eyes heavenward. "Jesus, save me from morons," he said, so soft the others didn't hear him, but I did. Then he stopped, lowering his face to mine, and said, "All right, then. Produce him."

Jonas? I called in my head. *Jonas?* But he didn't answer. He was still prowling around in the white room and either wouldn't answer or couldn't hear me.

"I can't right now," I said, a little snotty, my nose up in the air. "He is incommunicado."

"I see," said Johnny. He reached out to push the third

swallow from my shoulder. Badger and Ike exchanged confused looks.

"He goes off sometimes to read and to talk with the other
ghosts," I continued, fully aware of how lunatic I sounded—
and looked—but unable to stop talking. "He goes to this
white room, and I can't contact him while he's in there."

"Ah," said Johnny. And then he stood erect again.

I was about to lambast him with several of Jonas's predictions, when, behind him, I saw Gobel. He was coming up
the hill through the trees, and he was carrying several big
parcels tied with string. He hefted one over his head, and
cried, "No more'a that dang scrubby tortoise! Johnny
brung bacon."

A waterfall of saliva attacked my mouth. I hadn't realized
how really hungry I was, I guess.

Ike started trotting toward him, with Badger close behind.
Johnny helped me up and said, "I suppose we can sort this
out later. Can you cook?"

"Of course!"

"Can you do it with all those birds doing . . . whatever it
is they're doing?"

I ground my teeth and squared my shoulders, and the
latter motion sent a deceased warbler the rest of the way to
the dirt. "I reckon I can," I replied, deadly serious, "if you
don't mind a few feathers in your dinner."

He studied me for a second. "I was going to say, as long
as there's some salt and pepper in there with 'em," he said,
just as stony-faced as I imagined myself to be, "but come to
think of it, I'm not overfond of beaks with my bacon."

He swept an arm toward the cabin door, motioning me
inside, although he did not close it. Then he left me to join
the others near the fire, where Gobel was already un-
wrapping the victuals.

I was feeling pretty low. Not only about all those dead
birds and Sam and the others out there searching to no
avail—and about Jonas having skipped out on me again—
but about that cowhand. That stage-robber, I mean.

Every time I so much as looked at Johnny Devlin, I

couldn't help but feel all queasy in my innards and warm in my sitting parts. That's how much he affected me. I tried not to look at him, tried not to hear him, but that cabin door only faced one way and I couldn't help but take him in.

I suppose that I could have turned 'round and just stared into the dark of that shack, but that would have left me too much alone with myself. I was not much in the mood for solitude of any sort.

So I sat inside the door, far enough back that the birds didn't much beset me, with my fists propping my cheeks and staring at the dirt floor. I heard the men talking back and forth, scuffing the dust and dry weeds with their boots, heard the clang and thud of spoon hitting skillet. And I thought about Jonas Newcastle: about how agitated he might get if he found out the fellow at this camp was the same fellow I'd been all moony over. Was still moony over, to tell the truth, even if he didn't believe in my powers.

Although, in truth, I could hardly blame Johnny for not believing. I was the one that was haunted, and I had got used to it. It seemed normal, now. But, when I was back home in Sycamore, if somebody had told me of a lady whose dead husband spoke out loud right through her mouth and told the future, I would have laughed myself to a sideache. I hesitate to think what Mama would have done.

So I couldn't really hold it against him. That he didn't just accept the whole thing, lock, stock, and barrel. I suppose I would have wondered about him if he did.

Still, there was a haunt to contend with, and a jealous haunt at that. It struck me about then that Jonas had listened in on that whole conversation—well, speech—that Ike had said out about his family, and I hadn't known he was there. If I was getting better at controlling him—I'd established that I could push him right out of my body when I put my mind to it—he was getting better at hiding from me.

All of a sudden, I realized he might very well be with me that second.

Took you long enough to figure it out, he said from some-where inside me. He sounded real satisfied with himself. *Two can play at this game, you know.*

"That's not very fair," I whispered to the dirt. "Now I'll never have any privacy!"

Was it fair when you kicked me out of your legs? He laughed. *Say, that was funny! Kicked me out of your legs!*

I didn't smile. I just sunk my fists deeper into my cheekbones and said, "You're mad, aren't you?"

Over what? he asked, archly. *Now what could I possibly have to be upset about? That you pushed me out of your body when I was only trying to keep you from getting into this mess in the first place? Or that you're all gaga over some thieving saddle tramp? These are only the high points, you realize. I could go on for days.*

"Jonas," I began, but he wouldn't shut up.

When I think of all the marvels I've told you about! We're not supposed to do that, you know. No, not supposed to do it at all! At least, I don't think so. But out of the goodness of my heart and my overwhelming love for you, my dear Fr—I mean Annie—

"I'm not Frieda!" I shouted, just as a shadow fell over the patch of dirt I was staring at. I looked up.

"Nobody called you Frieda." It was Johnny Devlin himself, and there was a curious look on his face, like he couldn't decide whether to hug me or send for the loony wagon.

I said, "You're beautiful," and then slapped both hands over my mouth. To this day I don't know what possessed me to blurt out those words. Oh, they were true, that's for certain sure. I just don't know why I said them right out loud.

But even as I felt my face burn red hot, he looked at me, steady as you please, and said, "You're beautiful, too, Annie."

And then he seemed to forget why he was standing there. He turned around and walked down toward the fire, and he was halfway there before I realized he was carrying a plate, probably my plate, in his hand.

He seemed to realize it then, too, and came back up the hill. "Here," he said, holding it toward me. He didn't look at me. He appeared to be sort of dazed. "Brought you some . . . uh . . ."

I managed to force out a "thanks" and took the dented plate from his hands. He turned and took two steps, and then he stopped. He stood for a second, his back to me, before he twisted his head over his shoulder. He opened his mouth, then closed it again like he wanted to say something but couldn't figure out what. Then he turned away, and I heard him mutter, "Oh, hell," before he went back down to the others.

You are going to think I am crazy, but I knew right that second that I loved him. That scared me more than anything else, even Jonas.

All the rest of that afternoon and into the evening, I sat or paced inside that shack. I tell you, I was an unholy mess, or so Mama would have said. All I could think about was Johnny Devlin, picturing us in a little white house with a picket fence and a rose garden, just so, or maybe in a big hacienda down in South America, where he'd be free from the law dogs on his trail.

That's how far I got. I was even thinking of the whole darn legal system as law dogs.

I had us rich as Croesus and living in Europe, I had us poor as church mice and living on love in a Chicago slum. I had us making out just fine on the farm, with him plowing the fields and me carrying his lunch out to him, and him wiping his brow with the back of his sleeve and giving me a big kiss. I had us with two kids, then six, then seven. I had him running for mayor in a suit and straw hat, and pretty soon I had him running for senator, orating from the back of a train, with all the women fainting dead away because he was so handsome. And me, all kindly but smug, on account of I knew his heart was mine alone.

When you're bitten by love so hard and deep it makes a snakebite look like a love peck, I guess that's the way your mind works, especially if you're a lady in your twenties and love has never touched you before. It's a miracle my feet even reached the ground, I was so caught up in foolishness.

I kept thinking about those green, green eyes, magic eyes the color of Chinese jade and new spring grass. I'd never seen eyes like that before. Not just their color, but their frame. They were all sooty-lashed—thick, long, curled-up lashes like mothers prayed for their girl babies to have, and so dark! When he smiled, little wings came out at the corners and his eyes fair danced; when he frowned, they darkened like a storm at sea.

His nose was long and straight but not too long, his lips full but not too full, and the cleft in his chin gave him an air of . . . Well, I don't know what it gave him an air of, exactly, but I kept wanting to press the tip of my baby finger into it.

And his dimples. Oh, his dimples! The furrows bracketing that lush mustache went so deep and straight and matched up so regular, you wondered God didn't give them to every-body just to make the whole race more attractive.

His cheekbones were high and distinguished, his hair was thick and the color of dark walnut and cut short, his ears matched each other, and his neck went all the way, both up and down. All this was set on a pair of shoulders that looked like they could heft a horse for a good five minutes. Below that was a lean waist and slim hips and long, straight legs.

Well, all right, they were a little bowed. But then, you'd expect that from a man who spent as much time on horse-back as he likely did. And it was hardly noticeable.

And he was clean, his clothes were washed, and he was shaved. This may not seem a big thing, but compared to Gobel and Badger and Ike, he almost smelled of roses.

I guess you can see why I was smitten. Anybody would have been. There I was, in the middle of nowhere, with the most drop-dead handsome fellow I had ever had the distinct pleasure to lay eyes on, let alone meet, and he had said I was beautiful.

Beautiful.

Of course, I'd said it first, but I wasn't thinking about that part just then.

The fact that he didn't come back up to the shack again, sending Ike with my supper at about sundown, didn't faze me a bit, nor did it stop me daydreaming. Neither did the threat of Jonas Newcastle, who had yet to make another appearance.

I forgot about all things unpleasant. My head was in the clouds and my innards were in an uproar, and all I could think about was Johnny Devlin, Johnny Devlin, Johnny Devlin.

Just after sunset, the object of all this adoration came walking up the rise, carrying a lantern. You know how people say their hearts come up into their throats when they're having a real emotional experience? Well, that's just how I felt when I realized it was him. I was certain all those sweet fantasies I'd been having about him and me showed on my face.

I didn't have much time to be flustered, though. He stopped outside the threshold and raised the lantern so that it lit our faces. I don't know about mine, but his looked like a million dollars.

He looked right at me and asked, "Everything all right?"

I nodded and tried to smile knowingly, but I think it came out more like a silly grin.

"Well," he said, and hesitated, looking past me into the shack. His eyes flicked back to me again. "I'll be taking you down to the flats in the morning."

"Why?" I said, before I thought. I seemed to be doing a lot of that lately.

"So you can go home, of course," he said, his brow creasing.

I wrested my mind away from what a handsome forehead he had, and said, "Don't you want to ask Jonas about a payroll or some such?"

He shook his head. He said, "I hope these boys haven't inconvenienced you, Miss Annie," and that "Miss Annie" cut me like a knife. Here I'd daydreamed us through about four countries and the U.S. Senate and umpteen kids and grandkids, and he was calling me Miss Annie?

I couldn't think of a thing to say. I just turned around and walked to the bunk—it was only about five feet from the door—and sat down in a heap.

I stared at my lap, but I saw the light come closer, and

then his hand setting the lamp on the dirt floor. His fingers touched my brow, and I swear, the shivers just came coursing through me.

"Still feverish," he said, soft, and then, "You're shaking."

I nodded. How could I tell him it was just because he'd touched me? He could have done anything to me right then, and I would have let him, and gone along with it. He could have asked me to rob a stagecoach or kill somebody or dance around the fire bare-naked, and I would have said yes and done it gladly.

Doesn't it beat everything? Just when you think you've about got the world handled and nothing can get to you, it's staggering to all of a sudden find you have no self-control—not to mention no morals whatsoever—when it comes to a certain person. Later on, I was kind of shocked at myself, but right then I was just a quivering heap.

"Lie down," he said, and I guess I did, and then he pulled the covers up over me. "You got up too soon," he went on, tucking me in just like I wasn't going crazy, just like everything was normal. "Snakebite's nothing to fool with. I ought to horsewhip that Ike."

He said that last part—about horsewhipping Ike, I mean—under his breath. It came out all low and rumbly and burrowed its way into my spine like he'd said a love poem.

You can see how bad I had it. I doubt anybody's ever had it worse.

It was a good thing, though. I was so choked up with emotion and overwhelming adoration that I couldn't blurt out that he didn't have to take me back or that I loved him or that I'd follow him right to the gallows, if it came to such. All I could do was try to swallow that lump in my throat.

He looked at me a little quizzically, then stood up, taking the lantern with him. "You stay put now, you hear?" his voice rumbled. He was smiling kindly. Not a big smile, just a little one around the edges, like he was worried but trying to cover it up. "Everything's going to be all right. I'll get you back home before you can say . . . well, whatever you carnival folks say."

And then he went outside and closed the door behind him, leaving me in pitch darkness.

Open or closed my eyes still saw black, so I closed them. I was more tired than I thought, because right away I started sinking down into sleep. Just before I got there, though, a voice came into my head. Jonas Newcastle's voice.

He said two words to me.

Ungrateful slut!

12

The next day, the last of the fever had fled. My arm was still swollen up like a watermelon and I carried it in a sling, but I was thinking straight—really straight—for maybe the first time since before Mama died.

Ike had shaken me awake and put me on my horse while I was still half-asleep. Nobody else had been around—no sign of men nor horses, which I thought was queer—but he'd just hushed me and handed me up my quilt, then mounted up himself. While I tucked it around me and craned my head, looking for even a peek at Johnny Devlin, Ike led me down the hill. We went by way of a crooked little trail that went back up almost as much as it did down, then over another hill, then another.

I could see then that we were in the foothills and not the mountains, like they'd told me, because every once in a while I caught a glimpse of real mountains peeking through the trees, and rising up against the white morning sky all blue and gray and hazy. I guess we must have ridden for a good two hours, and Ike babbled the whole time.

He talked about his pa, he talked about his brothers and sisters, he talked about all those stepmamas he'd had. He talked about everything under the sun, but mostly I just let it flow over me without his prose hardly getting me damp.

I had other things on my mind, things even more important than Johnny Devlin's whereabouts.

Mainly, that I couldn't find Jonas.

Now, you're probably thinking this was a good thing, and that he was gone for good after being so mad at me the night before, and that I should have thrown a party and danced on a table. But I wasn't jubilant, not one bit. I was scared.

Jonas had pulled this disappearing trick before, and I suppose it had worked out all right, but he hadn't been half so mad then: before, he'd been like a spoiled little kid, all snotty that he hadn't got his way, and full of "I'll show you!"

Last night, though, the anger had been more. His cranky old man's voice had been all bitter and mean, and his tone full of venom. But still, it had been more than that. Something I couldn't put my finger on.

I felt so empty! Before, I'd thought I could tell when he was gone, but now I realized my senses had been dulled over the last few months by his constant presence. Even when he was gone, he always kept one toe in the water, so to speak, even if I hadn't recognized it as such at the time. That stuffy feeling I'd had, the first morning after he died, had never gone all the way away. But now? There was a feeling of almost unbearable lightness, like I'd float out of the saddle if I didn't hang on to the horn, float right up out of my skin.

That, and I'd never felt so alone.

Was this the way it had been before, I wondered? Does everybody feel so disconnected, so untethered, so hollow and alone every day of their lives? I suppose they wouldn't, having had nothing to compare it to. I suppose they just go along, just get on with it, never knowing any different.

But I had gone all cold inside my narrow innards, inside my clanking bones. There was nothing to hold me steady, no other presence to shore me up or keep me from turning into vapor.

And then there were the birds. The absence of the birds, I mean. Since we'd started out, not one sparrow had crashed

into me, not one wren had dived and died. In fact, I hadn't
seen a bird, let alone heard one, the whole blessed day.

And Ike, he just kept on talking, never expecting an answer, never realizing anything was wrong, never missing the
flutter in the trees or the constant birdsong. He just looked
back every few minutes to make sure I hadn't taken another
dive off my horse or got chomped by another rattlesnake.

He needn't have worried. The possibility that Jonas was
really gone this time was plenty to keep me glued to the
saddle, so far as I could be glued. I didn't know for how
long he'd be gone. Maybe he was gone forever. You'll say
I'm crazy, but the thought of that froze my marrow. Here
I'd hated having him around and wanted him to depart as
badly as anybody's ever wanted anything.

But now that he'd vamoosed, what would I do about the
sisters? What would I do about the castle? What would I do
about Mr. Boyd and Mr. P.T. Barnum and all the folks who
were depending on me?

Both as a living man and a dead one, Jonas had put me
in an almighty fix, and now he'd climbed out to let me sink
or swim before he'd even so much as taught me to tread
water. If he ever came back, I had half a mind to pull one
of Mama's tricks and take after him with a broom, if I could
just figure out how to do it.

On top of everything else, I didn't understand why Johnny
Devlin had sent Ike to take me back, or where those other
boys had gone to. I asked Ike about it first thing, but all
he'd do was shrug, twiddle his sandy mustache, and talk
about his brothers and sisters some more.

Now, I knew that I'd gone a tad overboard the night before, dreaming up all those versions of my life with Johnny
Devlin when I'd probably never see him again. I could
blame part of it on the fever, I supposed; but to be honest,
I knew that I would have imagined it anyhow, with or without a temperature. Just maybe not so colorful, with all those
details and such. I supposed he was naturally one of those
fellows that women went wild over, and I had followed in
their silly, swooning footsteps.

In any case, I was mad at myself for daydreaming so

intense, and for making Jonas so all-fired angry at what he had to consider my outrageously adulterous behavior—thoughts, anyway. But at the same time, I couldn't help being disappointed to the bone that Johnny hadn't come along, that he'd just taken off like that. I had this terrible ache to see him again, and it pained me that he hadn't cared enough to stay. I'd thought—hoped—that he was feeling something for me like I was feeling for him.

About noon, we came out of the trees at the sloping edge of an old beaver meadow. Ike helped me down, saying we had to rest the horses, which was all the same to me. Between Johnny and Jonas both running out on me (not to mention the birds), I was too depressed to care. He pulled off their saddles and staked them out to graze on the long, pale winter grass, my sorrel and his grey. While I gnawed on the jerky he gave me, he talked some more.

I was fully prepared not to listen—I had never known anybody to jabber on about nothing like Ike Tackett—but something he said perked my ears up.

"That Johnny!" he said gleefully, right in the middle of some story about his brother Mike, and slapped his knee. "Them boys is gonna be fit to be tied."

"What's that?" I asked casually, trying not to appear too interested. With a thumbnail, I picked a globby string of dried fat off my jerky. "What'll they be fit to be tied about?"

"Cause they been sent on a fool's errand, that's why. Ain't you been listenin' to a dad-blamed thing I said?" He looked a tad irritated and that little smudge of a chin mustache gave a twitch to one side. But then he remembered himself—or rather, remembered who he was talking to—and said, "Ma'am, sorry, ma'am. Cause they's been sent down to Tucson to roust out ol' Evil Eye Harrison."

"Who's he?" I asked, figuring to ease the conversation around to Johnny Devlin a bit later.

"He's a she, ma'am." Ike put his hat back on his head and offered me the canteen. I accepted. "Johnny told Gobel an' Badger they dasn't mess with a witch-woman like you," he went on. "Not unless they had a protectin' spell cast over 'em first. They went to have ol' Evil Eye make 'em a mojo."

Before I could ask, he lifted a little hide bag, like an Indian's medicine pouch, out of his shirt. It was strung 'round his neck with a thong, and was all stained with old sweat and dirt. He said, "I got me this'un maybe three years back. Bought 'er off'n a *curandera* down Sonora way, right after Johnny saved my hide from those goat herders."

I was truly tempted to ask more about the goat herders and how Johnny'd saved him—more, I admit, to find out about Johnny than anything else—but I decided to sort of work my way toward it, indirect. I handed the canteen back and wiped my good hand on my skirt, having finished the jerky. The other one was still in its sling. "Curandera?"

"Mexican witch," he said real serious. "More like a *bruja,* I reckon. They's real strong and can heal you up when there ain't no doc around. Does magic with herbs and such. The one I seen made me a charm against bullets." He flicked the little bag with his fingers.

"Gracious sakes," I said, trying to keep a straight face. "Does it work?"

"Ain't been shot since I had it," he announced, then leaned toward me conspiratorially. "Now, Evil Eye Harrison's from Loo-siana. She makes hers the Frenchie way, with that voodoo magic." He sat up again and shrugged, tucking his charm back inside his shirt. "All the same thing, I reckon. You know any'a them voodoo spells?"

I shook my head, at a loss for words.

He leaned toward me again, stopping to glance over his shoulder like the trees were going to hear, and tell on him. "That feller what you have talk through your mouth? That Mr. Newcastle? You reckon he'd come out for a spell? Johnny said not to pester you with it, but I just gotta know somethin'."

"I don't think I can call him up," I said nervously, trying not to be rude and scooch away. Even though he was a good sight fresher than Badger Jukes, Ike didn't smell a bit good up close. "Um, Mr. Newcastle is . . . that is, he—"

"Doesn't exist," boomed Johnny Devlin's voice. I would have known it anywhere, even in the biggest crowd in Chicago.

As much as his voice had set my spine to tingling, those words sort of got my dander up. I stood and looked up into the trees, and sure enough, there he came between the sycamores, covered in sun dapples and leading his bay horse. He looked just like a picture, and for all that I wanted to be mad at him, the sight of him made my insides all clutch together and my head feel light.

Ike had stood up, too, although I didn't notice until he stepped in front of me. He waved a hand and said, "Law, you must be half-Injun, Johnny! Where'd you leave them two?"

Johnny didn't answer him. He walked on out into the clearing's edge proceeded to unsaddle his horse. It was a fine one, clean limbed and real breedy looking about the head. Back in Sycamore, a horse like that would've brought a pretty penny, and I supposed it was no different here.

He eased the saddle to the ground, slipped off the bridle, and cracked a hand over the bay's rump, saying, "Go on, old son."

While it trotted on down to the other horses, he sat himself on a log. "Since I don't see a fire, I suppose coffee would be too much to hope for," he said to Ike. He hadn't looked at me once, which was probably a good thing, since I am inclined to believe I was standing there with my mouth gaping like a sunfish pulled into the raft.

Oblivious to me, Ike replied, "I can sure make some, Johnny, yessiree," and bent to his saddlebags.

But Johnny waved a hand. "Never mind. I'll live without it. Hey!" he said, looking up. "What happened to the birds?" He turned his head, sweeping a glance over me. That glance was like a beacon of fire and I believe I blushed bright red, because my face got hotter than a smithy's forge.

He looked away real quick, like he was embarrassed, too, and said to Ike, "You got any of those sugar biscuits left?"

He must have just said the first thing that popped into his head, because Ike looked kind of surprised. He screwed up his face and said, "Ain't had none since we was down to Tombstone last August. You all right, Johnny?"

"Fine," he grumbled, his face still turned away from me.

And then he said, "Sit down." Well, Ike sat down right there in the dirt, like he was a dog and Johnny had just given him a command, and it was all I could do to hold back a snort. But Johnny rolled his eyes and said, "Aw, Jesus. Get up, Ike. I mean the girl."

By this time, I had got back a little more control of myself, and I said, "I don't want to sit down. And I have a name, you know. It's Annie Pinkerton Newcastle, if you have forgotten, and you can use any part of it you please. Ike didn't say where he was taking me on this trip. Are we moving to another hideout?"

At last, Johnny twisted to face me, and in spite of myself I felt the hot flush race up my cheeks again. He was so handsome it made your heart hurt!

He didn't talk so handsome, though. Not this time. He scowled at me, saying, "I told you last night. We're taking you back to where we got you. Where *they* got you." He tipped his head over toward Ike.

I sat down in a heap. I remembered, all right, and to say I was disappointed was a vast understatement. And something else. I was mad, too.

I guess it showed on my face, because Ike hissed, "Don't tick her off, Johnny. She might witch you!" like he thought I couldn't hear him, but Johnny Devlin just gave a small, exasperated snort.

"Christ," he said under his breath, and then he turned to me. "Miss Annie, I'd like to apologize on behalf of this whole sorry batch of lamebrained, waffle-headed morons. I told 'em not to—"

"Not to what?" I said, and the anger in my voice surprised even me. "Not to snatch me clear off to who knows where? Not to let me get bit by deadly snakes? Not to close me up in some dingy old shack with a dead man in the stove, or not to let me wake up to find I'm being held prisoner by two loony Tacketts and a crazy, skunk-stinking man with a lobster arm? Or are you going to apologize for insulting me right and left and saying I'm a charlatan and I'm faking Mr. Newcastle? I think that if you're going to apologize, you should at least give me some idea of where you're starting."

By the end of it, I was shouting, and Ike looked like he'd been poleaxed. Johnny didn't, though. He looked just as mad as I was. Hands balled into fists at his sides, he rose up, slow, and glared down at me.

"I told them not to grab you," he said, the words precise between clenched teeth. "What came after that, I've got no control over."

Ike flicked his eyes from Johnny to me and back again, and whispered, "Johnny?"

"And nobody insulted you," he went on, paying no attention to Ike, just staring straight at me with those narrowed green eyes. "You're a carnie playing carnie tricks. I know, because I saw your act twice in Colorado and once in Utah, and I just said the truth."

"Utah?" I whispered, more to myself.

Ike's eyes had gone wide. "Johnny!" he hissed.

I wasn't paying much attention to Ike, though, and despite the fact that I was still a little stunned at that Utah business, I stood right up. "The truth? How can you even begin to know the truth? You don't know diddly about me! All you know is what you think you figured out from watching me on stage, and that wasn't me at all. Why, I'm not even there when Mr. Newcastle gives his shows!"

"You've been reading your own signs too much," Johnny hollered, "and it's turned you crazier than a bedbug!"

Ike whined, "Johnny, please don't—"

"Shut up!"

We had both turned and shouted at Ike at the same instant, and he was almost as surprised as we were.

"Start saddling the horses," Johnny said after a second, real clipped. And when Ike just stood there, his mouth hanging open, Johnny added, "Now!"

He had such a commanding voice that Ike just turned and grabbed up Johnny's saddle, and scurried down the hill without so much as a by-your-leave, and the whole business startled me so much that I nearly went with him. Probably would have done, too, if I hadn't been so mad.

I said, "You don't have to go yelling at Ike because you're mad at me. Which, by the way, you've got no right to be in the first place! I was just minding my own business, riding on my own property, when—"

"I'm not mad at you," he cut in, though his words were belied by a forehead deep in furrows. Those green eyes were about to boil, too.

I flung my arms—well, my good arm, anyway—up in the air and shouted, "Then who the devil are you mad at?"

"Me!" he hollered. Then, "Gobel and Ike! That goddamn Badger!" All of a sudden he swept the hat off his head and banged it against his thigh with a cry of "Christ on a crutch! *Everybody,* all right?"

I stuck my nose up in the air. "There's no need to raise your voice."

"I wasn't!" he shouted.

"Yes, you were!" I hollered back. To tell the truth, I was enjoying myself. Fighting with him took my mind off his dimples, at least, although he was powerful handsome when you got him riled up.

But he stopped yelling all of a sudden and stared at the ground and twisted that hat back and forth in his long fingers, and finally, he slapped it back on his head.

"Fight's over," he announced in a normal tone of voice. He looked away from me, toward Ike, down the hill. "I'm taking you back, and that's all there is to it. I'm sorry about them kidnapping you, but I'm doing my best to fix it, and it'd be a sight more pleasant for everybody if you'd just calm down and—"

"Look out!" I shrieked, and launched myself straight for him.

He put his hands out—to catch me or ward me off, I don't know—but I shoved my good shoulder into his midsection, catching him off balance. I didn't push him all the way to the ground—not that I didn't try, mind you—but I did shove him out of the path of Nebuchadnezzar, who had leapt from the cover of the forest and just missed us by an inch. I felt him brush against my back as he passed.

Things happened awful fast. I cried, "Nezzy!" and dropped to my knees. He had just turned and started toward me, all full of cheetah chirps and growls, which are the friendliest of greetings, when I realized Johnny had pulled his gun.

I raised up just in time to knock his hand away. The shot went wild, singing into the trees. Then I saw Ike running up the hill with his rifle in his hand and Johnny aiming again and Nezzy skittering off to the side and hissing at Johnny, and I screamed, "Don't shoot, you fools!"

I ran to Nebuchadnezzar and flung my arms about his neck, even though the snakebit one still pained me, and soothed him as best I could. Between his hisses, I said, "Put your guns away. He's just happy to see me, that's all! There, there, Nezzy. Good old kitty to find me. Good old lovely puss-cat."

And then I realized that if Nezzy was all the way out here—wherever "here" was—Sam couldn't be far behind. Maybe Sam and a whole rescue party.

Ike had huffed his way up the hill, and stood five feet from Johnny with his mouth agape and his rifle swinging, all but forgotten. "Oh, Jesus," he muttered breathlessly. "Oh, Jesus, Johnny, she's witched it. I told you, you shouldn't be a'hammerin' at her like that. She's witched a lion-cat right out of the air!"

Johnny just said, "Shut up, Ike."

Nezzy was still skitterish, but he had calmed down enough that I let my bad arm drop. It hurt like sin from just raising it up like that. "I didn't 'witch' Nebuchadnezzar," I said, "and he's not a lion. Sam's probably brought him to scout for me. He's probably coming up the hill right this minute, and he's most likely not alone."

Ike said, "Let's go, Johnny," and then slapped himself in the head. "Aw, cripes. Your horse run off when that . . . that leopard sprung outta the woods!"

Nezzy hissed at the sudden movement, but he sat still beneath my arm. "You'd better go find him, then," I said to Johnny, who seemed to be paying no attention to Ike. "And he's not a leopard. He's an African cheetah."

"Who the hell is Sam?" asked Johnny, his forehead creased. He'd holstered his pistol, but his hand was still on its butt and he was watching Nebuchadnezzar like one of Sam's bay-wing hawks eyeing a jackrabbit.

"He's my friend, if it's any of your nevermind."

One of his dark eyebrows cocked up. "He that Indian that travels with you? Your boyfriend?"

I lifted my chin. "My traveling companion and chaperone," I said. "You'd better leave, you know. There are plenty of women just pining to be kidnapped and stagecoaches waiting to be robbed."

The minute the words left my mouth I wanted to reel them back in. Johnny Devlin looked, for just a fraction of a second, like I'd slapped him.

He recovered fast, though, and frowned at me. "I might just do that," he said, all cold.

I wanted to cry. Isn't that silly? Here I hardly knew the man, and I already wanted to tell him I was sorry and ask him to forgive me and throw my arms around him and kiss him right square on the lips. I stammered, "I didn't mean, that is, I'm sorry I—"

He turned around just as I stopped midsentence, for we both heard somebody crashing up the hill through saplings and brush, and then Sam's voice shouting, "Annie! Annie, are you up here? I heard a shot! Here, Nezzy! Kitty-kitty-kitty?"

For somebody who was supposed to be half-Indian and therefore stealthy, that Sam sure made a lot of noise. I guessed he had worn his white clothes.

Johnny turned back to face me, and his expression had altered. It was softer, almost yearning, if a man can be said to look that way, and I had a chill. A good kind of chill.

He said, "If you're ever . . . I mean, maybe if you . . . Aw, hell."

With that, he turned and went skidding down the slope after Ike, who was just weaving his way into the woods on the far side of the meadow.

"Johnny?" I called after him. "Johnny Devlin!" But it didn't do any good. Either he couldn't or wouldn't hear me. He just kept going until he disappeared into the trees.

I sat back, pulling Nezzy into my lap. Well, his front parts, anyway. Scratching his chin, I said, "You sure know how to make an entrance, kitty cat. But couldn't you have held this one off for five minutes?" I closed my eyes and dropped my forehead against his ear, and whispered, "Utah! I'll be danged!"

Nezzy chirped at me and started to purr.

Sam broke through the trees then. He was riding the other buggy horse, which whinnied down the hill to its friend, who was still tied in the meadow. Sam had a great big wrap-around smile on his face.

"Annie!" he cried, fairly leaping from the saddle. I heard more riders coming through the trees, but I didn't have much time to think about it, because Sam was on me like a bluebottle fly on a bucket of hog guts, hugging me and talking a mile a minute and patting Nezzy all at once.

I managed to disentangle myself from both Sam and Nezzy about the time Testo the Great rode up to join the others. Sam was fair mauling me, he was so happy to see that I was alive and well, so I didn't get a look at them until then. Testo was there, like I said, and Bert the Barker and Mr. Alvarez, and they all were grinning to beat the band.

"Thank God," Sam said for about the fiftieth time. "Thank God you're all right." And then his expression darkened a little, like maybe his relief was wearing off and he was getting ready to yell, and he said, "Why'd you run off like that? Don't you know we were worried sick? Boyd's taken to his bed, he's so frazzled!"

I guessed he would have, seeing as how I was his cash cow. I also guessed they hadn't seen that trail of three sets of tracks back there in the dirt where Ike and Gobel had snatched me. Or if they had, they didn't realize it had anything to do with me. I said, "Sam, you are all white when it comes to tracking somebody."

He twisted up his face. "Huh?"

I opened my mouth to tell him about Gobel and Ike, but instead, what came out was, "Easy with that hugging. Can't you see I'm hurt?"

Well, there was a big fuss made over my arm. Sam had me ease it out of the sling and turn it all around so he could see, and even though it was practically all healed up, Testo had his pocketknife out and begged to slash it. I had never known jugglers were so bloodthirsty.

Bert made me a better sling out of a couple of bandannas, and Sam gave me his coat, although I gave him some argument in return. After determining I was all right, Mr. Alvarez went down to get my horse and left the others to stew over me.

In all the hubbub, I just said a few words about being bit by a rattler, and how these fellows had found me and tended me. I was pretty vague about it. I didn't say as how I'd been kidnapped, because that would have implicated Johnny, and for some reason I didn't want to get him into trouble.

Not that he wasn't in enough trouble already, what with having held up that stage and all and being in cahoots with Badger the Lobster Boy, which is how I was thinking of him right then, and the Tackett brothers. I just couldn't bring myself to add any more kindling to the bonfire.

At last, the men decided I was fit to travel—something I could have told them right off the bat if they'd only given me a chance—and we mounted up, me in Sam's coat and him clutching my frayed old quilt around him like a shawl.

"We can make the castle a little after nightfall if we don't tarry," he said.

"Then let's not burn any daylight," I answered, and whistling to Nezzy, started back through the trees the way they'd come. And all the time we were going down that hill, I kept thinking, *Utah, he came to Utah to see me, too.*

Despite the absence of Jonas, I found I was smiling, for his absence had been in some way filled, just a little, by something strange and new.

Contrary to what Sam had promised, it was almost ten o'clock when we got back to the castle. If we hadn't had such a bright, full moon to travel by, I suppose we would have had to stop and camp overnight. Anyway, I was about frozen to death by the time we got there, and Sam had to be even colder. After Miss Jonquil and Miss Jessie came fluttering out on the porch to join the throng—and we had picked up quite a number of Boyd's people on the way up—we all went into the castle and built the fires high.

Mrs. Alvarez made hot chocolate with cinnamon for everybody and served it in her bathrobe, her long black braid swinging back and forth over the plaid flannel. Sam stuck his feet in a bucket of hot water. Mr. Boyd woke up at all the racket and came down the stairs—his nerves were so frayed that he had moved inside the castle—and he danced a little a jig in his nightshirt. Then he remembered himself and made his excuses, but not before he reminded me that time was money, and he hoped I had been taking good care of Mr. Newcastle, and then he winked.

I just smiled at him, or tried to.

Nobody really pressed me for details about my absence. I guess saying I had been snakebit—and having the swollen arm to back it up, complete with fang marks and the brand of Gobel's knife—let me off the hook. I guess that when you're bit by a snake, folks are just happy to have you alive, and understand about the delirious part.

The gunshot took a little explaining, but I just told Sam that one of my "Good Samaritans" had fired it into the air to lead the search party to me, and then had taken off. I said he was real shy. Sam kind of wiggled his eyebrows, but he just let it drop.

The next day my arm was a little smaller, but Jonas was not back. By the time the troupe got ready to pull up stakes so they could start the tour again in Phoenix, my arm was normal-looking and didn't hurt, but still there was no Jonas and no birds.

Sam was the only one I had told about Jonas having run out on me. I couldn't help but tell him, since he noticed almost right away that no birds came around, even when Nezzy was far off, nosing jackrabbit holes. He had kept my secret, but now it was time to fess up to Mr. Boyd.

It was the night before they were to leave, and everybody had gone to bed except for Mr. Boyd, who was in Jonas's study. He had all but taken over since Christmas, and lately was even bossing Mr. and Mrs. Alvarez around. I crept down the hall and stood outside the door for a minute, staring at the fan of light that emerged from underneath it, and then took a deep breath and knocked.

"Come in," he said.

I turned the crystal knob.

"Ah, Annie!" he said, real jovial. Mr. Boyd was always jovial until you crossed him, which was just what I was about to do.

"Mr. Boyd, there's something I have to get off my chest," I began, and then I told him about Jonas disappearing and how I'd tried to call him back—was still trying, but with no luck. "And that's why I can't go with you," I finished up.

He looked like he was going to explode, his face got so red, and I stood behind a tall chair, holding its backrest like a shield.

"Why didn't you tell me this before?" he demanded. I was glad we were alone in the study with only one lamp lit. I don't think I could have stood to see his face in the full light. "Why'd you wait until just this precise moment?"

"Well, I—"

"Why'd you just stand silent when I wired Y.T. Smith and Lord Duppa? They're expecting you! They're expecting *all* of you, if you take my meaning."

I scuffed my toe on the rug and stared at it. "Sorry," I said. "I thought he'd come back by now."

"Sorry doesn't cut the mustard, Missy!" he boomed. "Do you know who Lord Darryl Duppa is? He's British! He's an earl or a count or some fool thing! He's an important person, and he's waiting to meet you! Why, he even christened, whatyacall, Phoenix! If it hadn't been for him, they would have called it Pumpkin Flats! Lord Duppa is—"

"He was the drunk at your wedding," interrupted a new voice. Sam opened the door the rest of the way and stepped inside.

"The drunk?" I asked. "Everybody was pretty well sozzled, as I recall."

"He was the one who kept reciting poetry in Italian and French, and pissing off the terrace when he thought nobody was looking."

I said, "He pissed over the garden rail?"

Sam shrugged. "Guess nobody else was looking after all."

"Hang the pissing!" shouted Mr. Boyd. "Why can't you come with us anyway? Fake it like everybody else!"

I guess Mr. Boyd didn't have much faith in his acts. I said, "Why, Mr. Boyd, most of your people aren't fakes at all! The juggler really juggles and the contortionist really contorts, and the—"

"You don't mean to tell me you actually believe you can call up Jonas Newcastle's spirit!" he said. "I thought that was all part of your act, just pretendin', you know? You mean right from the first, you thought he was real as eggs?"

I had never heard that egg thing before, but I decided to let it go past and said, "It was real, Mr. Boyd. Except I didn't call him up so much as he just walked in and took over."

He held his hands out to the side and looked up at the ceiling. "You're a lunatic, pure and simple. If I'd known for one second you thought you was the real thing, I—"

"Mr. Boyd?" Sam broke in, shaking his head. "You would have taken her on just the same. I didn't see you questioning her gift that day we met the show in New Mexico. You were real glad to have her."

"Nobody asked you, Indian," Boyd growled.

"And nobody asked you to go around insulting people," I said, stepping forward and leaning on the desk. "Nobody asked you to take over this house like you owned it, ordering special tarts and pastries in the middle of the night like it was a fancy hotel. Nobody asked you to set up your business office in Jonas's own study."

He leaned back in his chair—Jonas's chair—to get away from me, but I wasn't finished. "I've had about enough of you saying *Indian* in that tone you always use, like it was a dirty word or something. I've had about enough of you eyeing Nebuchadnezzar for a rug. I've had about enough of your cheapskate ways and your pinching every last penny till it screams. If it wasn't for Bert the Barker and Bob the Gill Boy and Mona and Mrs. Bumbridge and all the others— and especially Aisha, who you never grieved over, not once—I would have taken my trade elsewhere a long time ago."

Boyd puffed out his cheeks and slapped his hands flat on the desk. "Now see here!"

"No, *you* see here," I said, and I was so mad I was all shaky inside. "I'm not going with you because I can't. Jonas has gone off someplace, maybe to that white room, or maybe he's gone for good. The only contract I have with you is a handshake and my word, and I freely admit I am defaulting. The Prophet Annie you hired doesn't exist anymore. She went away when the haunt went away, and I don't know when—or even if—she's coming back. I wouldn't know how to fake it, the way you say. I'm no liar, at least not on big things. I wouldn't know where to start!"

Boyd sputtered something, I couldn't make out what, and Sam took my arm. He led me out into the hall and closed the door behind us just as Mr. Boyd shouted, "I'll seek legal recourse! You ain't heard the last of this, girl!"

"He won't do a thing," Sam whispered. We walked toward my room. "He hasn't got a legal leg to stand on. Of course, Barnum is another matter. You signed something, didn't you?"

I stopped, and Sam stopped with me. "Lord," I said, putting my hands to my cheeks. "What am I going to do?"

"When are we supposed to meet him?"

"March," I said, "March in Baltimore."

"Well, this is the third of January," Sam said thoughtfully. "That gives you all of this month and February to try and scare Jonas up. Are you trying?"

I nodded. "Trying so hard my brain is sore." It was the truth, too.

Sam smiled—not with his teeth, just his lips. "That's quite a temper you're sprouting, Miss Annie."

I said, "Mama just takes me over sometimes."

The smile widened to a grin, and he shook his head. "No, I don't think that's your mama. I think that's pure, unadulterated Annie Newcastle. No, don't make a face. It's nice to see you growing a backbone."

I didn't know what to say. I just stood there like a fool, but Sam laughed and bussed me on the forehead. "Thanks for the sweater, by the way."

"Oh! You're welcome. Did it fit?"

"Like the proverbial glove," he said. "That rickracky business on the front's real handsome." He meant what I'd intended to be a Navajo design. "How'd you like what I gave you?"

I slapped a hand to my cheek. "I never even opened it! I guess that morning was so busy, what with the sisters and all, and then I got, um, snakebit, and . . ."

"Well," he said, "you go ahead and open it up, then come down to the kitchen, little ghost talker. I'm going to ply you with fresh-made ice cream and hot jam, and shortbread right out of the oven, and when I get you good and sticky and full, I want you to tell me what *really* happened while you were gone."

13

Well, Sam got me sticky, all right. I wore his Christmas present to me, which turned out to be a necklace, with a cunning solid gold charm of Nebuchadnezzar that had little chips of topaz for the eyes. We ate nearly a whole freezer-crock full of his good vanilla-bean ice cream with hot raspberry jam drizzled on it, and I 'fessed up and told him the whole sorry story. It was embarrassing, having to tell about what a fool I made of myself over Johnny Devlin, but I left out no details.

At the end of it, I figured he'd plop his hands on either side of his waist and glare at me down that long, regal nose and say something like, "When you louse things up, Annie, you surely don't fool around."

But he didn't. He just took off his apron and moved around the big oak table to sit beside me, and slid his arm over my shoulders without saying a word.

And what did I do? I bawled like a baby. All those pent-up emotions about Jonas Newcastle and Johnny Devlin and the whole dang situation just came surging up like a flash flood. By the time I finished crying on Sam's shoulder, we were both pretty spattered with my tears.

"There, there, Annie," Sam said at last, and handed me a fresh handkerchief. I had about used up the first one he gave me.

I blew my nose with an unladylike honk. "Thanks," I said. "I thought for sure you'd ride me about how I'd messed up things for you and the sisters."

He lifted a brow, and I added, "Well, not for you so much. But for Miss Jonquil and Miss Jessie and the castle and everything. With Jonas gone, I don't know what we'll do."

I started to sniffle again, but Sam dried my eyes. "That's enough," he said. "Whether Jonas comes back or not, we'll be all right. I can get odd jobs around town."

But of course, there wasn't any town, Rock Bottom being dead as a hammer and long deserted. I was about to point this out when Nezzy came strolling in, looking for a handout.

"Well, hello, hero," said Sam, and proceeded to slice him off a chunk of the beef roast left over from dinner. In the time Boyd's people had been camped out front, I suspected Sam had gone through a whole herd of cows, not to mention three or four flocks of chickens and a pronghorn or three.

Nezzy swallowed the beef in one gulp, then settled down in the corner to have a bath. Sam said, "Sorry there's no chicken," to the cat, then turned to me. "Annie, things have a way of working out. Quit your worrying over the sisters. I mean it. We have more important things to talk about."

I cocked my head. What could be more important than those poor old spinsters starving to death? I said, "What, for instance?"

Sam clucked his tongue. "Your Johnny Devlin, for instance. Annie, you're in love!"

I turned my head to the side even as my face grew hot. To the wall, I said, "This seems hardly the time to talk about it. If it wasn't for him, I mean, if it wasn't for me thinking about him, Jonas wouldn't have left and we wouldn't be in this mess."

"Ah, but you did." He touched my face with his fingers, and turned my head toward him. "You did, Annie," he said kindly. "And if it's of any interest to you, I believe I can tell you a little about your Johnny Devlin."

Surprised, I said, "How could you know anything about him?"

Sam rolled his eyes. "Because I read the papers, Annie. If you'd ever read any part of the newspaper except what they write about you, it'd expand your world a goodly bit."

Well, I guess he had a point, although he didn't have to be so consarned condescending about it. But I bit my tongue and said, "What?"

He leaned back in his chair and smiled. "Your Johnny Devlin's a famous man, Annie."

"Famous?" I had never personally met anyone more famous than the acts in the carnival.

"Why, Johnny Devlin's wanted all over this territory and New Mexico!" Sam said, proud as a peacock to be doing the telling. "I'm not surprised that was him with Pat Garrett. Why, he probably knows the Earps and Doc Holliday on a first-name basis! Probably that little girl they going to execute over in Hanged Dog, too!"

Well, he had me skunked. I said, "Who are these people?"

He shook his head and looked at me through slanted eyes. "The Earps? The Earps run Tombstone, down south," he said. "There's been a big hoorah in the papers about them lately, on account of that shootout. And that Kincaid girl said she knew 'em. Of course, that was before. They tried her in Hanged Dog—that's about forty-five miles to the east as the crow flies—for murder and barn burning, except they fooled around waiting for a Kansas City hangman, and he brought some newfangled contraption with him that blew up the town."

It was my turn to shake my head. "You lost me."

"They lost her, too," he said. "It's in all the papers, Annie. Or was, till this Earp thing took over the headlines." I must have looked real blank, because he added, "It's a bunch of brothers named Earp. One's the sheriff and the rest were deputized, along with Doc Holliday, who used to be a dentist but who's now a gambler and a dangerous gunfighter."

"A dentist?" I asked, making a face. "Doesn't sound too dangerous to me."

"Anyway," said Sam, through clenched teeth, "these cattle rustlers called 'em out and they had a big gunfight. All right?"

"What's this have to do with Johnny?" I asked. Just saying his name made me all shivery.

Sam shook his head and heaved a sigh. "I only meant that they were famous, and that your Johnny's famous, and that he probably knows them since he runs with Pat Garrett. Most famous people know each other, don't they? And you're a hard person to talk to, Annie."

I disregarded that last comment, and asked, "Well, what's he famous *for?*"

"Stage jobs," Sam said with satisfaction. He was likely glad to be back on the subject again. "He sticks up stages. And not just any stages. The Devlin Gang has something against Fortesque Potter, because they only rob the stages his processed gold is on. Well, wagons, too. They started shipping it with an armed guard last week. It was in the *Bugle.*" He pulled a paper from his back pocket, unfolded it, and pointed to an article headed, "POTTER PICKS TIMES BY BIBLE."

I screwed up my face. "What's the Bible got to do with it?"

"Because—Oh, all right, Nezzy." Nebuchadnezzar had come up and was nuzzling his hand while eyeing the roast. Sam sawed off another chunk. He tossed it in the air amid little droplets of blood—it was very rare—and Nezzy snatched it in midair, just like that.

"Because he uses the Bible to pick which route his wagon's going to take, and what time," he continued, wiping his hands on a tea towel. From the corner came the sound of Nezzy munching down that beef, and Sam turned to look at him. "You're going to get fat, you know. A fat cheetah is a sorry thing."

I picked off another piece of shortbread. All that crying had sort of worn off my full feeling. "He uses the Bible?"

"Bibliomancy, I think he calls it," Sam said, still looking at Nezzy. "He just opens it at random and picks a page and a verse, and that's the date and the time. Don't know for certain how he picks the route." He turned to face me again, and took a piece of shortbread for himself. "That's probably why those fellows grabbed you in the first place. To get you to ask Jonas when the next shipment was."

I had already figured that out, but to be polite I nodded and said, "Oh. Except Johnny didn't believe in me. He made them bring me back."

"Good thing for you he did," Sam said. "That one you called Badger? Well, the papers call him the Arkansas Claw, and he's a piece of business, let me tell you. He was born that way, I guess, with that funny arm. They say there are a few other things wrong with him, too, if you peel him out of his clothes."

All the hair on my arms stood up. I said, "Don't tell me what they are."

Sam nodded. "Even the Apaches won't touch him. They think he's an evil spirit. Anyway, the Arkansas Claw beat a pregnant Englishwoman near to death down at the Paiute stage stop last spring. Would have done her all the way to dead, too, if the stationmaster hadn't fired off a shotgun. They managed to save her and the baby, but it was touch-and-go there for a while."

I swallowed my shortbread, and it went down dry and sideways. "Why'd he do it?" I finally croaked.

Sam just shrugged. "Bored, I guess. Maybe she said the wrong thing. You never can tell with that type. Here, you need something to wash that down with."

He fetched glasses of water for the two of us, then tossed Nezzy a piece of shortbread before he took another himself.

"Those Tackett brothers you were talking about?" he said, chewing. "I heard that one of 'em murdered three whores over on the Colorado river at a place called Stinky Molly's." Then he looked up at me and his neck turned red. "Sorry. Didn't mean to say 'whore' right out like that. A soiled dove, that's what I should have said."

I shook my head. "The word doesn't bother me any. Which Tackett was it?" I had a hard time picturing Ike doing a murder. Maybe it was Gobel.

But Sam said, "I don't know. There are about twenty of 'em. Tacketts, I mean. Can't keep 'em straight. But one way or another, they're all on the wrong side of the law. They say you can't go wrong if you just shoot a Tackett on sight."

"And what do they say about Johnny Devlin?" I asked, trying to move Sam away from the malformed and the much-married and back to the subject.

"Depends on who you ask," he said cryptically, and threw Nezzy another piece of shortbread.

I said, "Sam, I'm asking you."

He shrugged. "That's a very good question. I can't say, personally, but you ask ten people and you'll get ten different answers. Even the papers disagree. Oh, they all agree that he's an outlaw, don't get me wrong. They just sorta disagree on his motivations."

I was leaning forward. "Why?"

"Well," said Sam, taking an idle wipe at the tabletop with his dishcloth, "some folks'll tell you that he's just mean. I don't believe he's ever killed anybody, but there are those that'll pin every killing west of Dodge City on him. Course, they're the militant ones. Same ones as would crucify you for a witch."

I nodded. I knew the type.

"At the other end of the spectrum," Sam went on, "there's those that say he never so much as swatted a fly or took a penny that wasn't his own."

"Even I'd have a hard time with that," I said. Nezzy had got up again, and was shoving his head up under my hand. I began to scratch his ears.

Sam broke off another piece of shortbread and popped it in his mouth. "It's all in how you look at things," he said around the shortbread. "See, he only holds up those gold shipments. Fortesque Potter's gold shipments, to put a fine point on it. And there are folks that swear that old Fortesque Potter stole that gold from Johnny Devlin's father. At least, stole the land it was on. Some say it was a crooked spin of the roulette wheel, and that Potter's men killed him as soon as the papers changed hands."

A little shiver went through me. Here I'd thought I was hopelessly in love with an outlaw, and that I'd spend the rest of my days pining outside a prison or rigged in black, visiting a graveyard. But this new information sparked a joyous sort of excitement in me. All of a sudden, Johnny Devlin wasn't just a devilishly handsome but common criminal, hiding out in the woods with blood-spilling riffraff: He was the wronged party, with a murdered father and thieved land and gold, and he was just trying his best to right it.

"I don't think I like that expression," said Sam, jerking me out of my reverie.

I did my best to make my face blank, and tilted my chin up. "I'm sure I don't know what you're talking about, Sam Two Trees."

"Right," he said, like he didn't mean "right" at all. His face got stern, and he added, "Don't start thinking he's some kind of Robin Hood. There are a lot of stories running around. I just told you the two at the opposite ends. I know you're soft on him right now, but he's not the sort of fellow it's a good idea to be soft on, if you get my meaning. He keeps bad company, for starters."

"I wouldn't say I was soft on him," I said, staring down at Nezzy's head. I was still scratching behind his ears.

"Well, whatever you call being crazy in love with somebody you hardly know," he said, a bit more kindly. "If you want to call it infatuated, or that you've got a case on him, or that you're just making calf eyes at each other, it's all the same to me. Words aren't important, it's the feelings. And all I'm doing is telling you that nothing's going to come from whatever this thing is between you and Johnny Devlin. Nothing. Keep that in mind, and you won't get hurt. Not more than necessary, anyway."

I wanted to ask him why he thought nothing would come of it, why he thought that Johnny Devlin wouldn't ride right up to the castle and propose to me on bended knee. But just thinking about it—thinking about saying that right out loud to Sam in the middle of the castle kitchen—made me feel silly and small.

So I kept my mouth closed, and Sam and I sat there for a while longer in silence, tossing pieces of Scotch shortbread to an African cheetah in a fairy-tale castle in the dead dark center of an Arizona night.

* * *

Boyd's people left that next day, tearily waving good-bye as their caravans kicked up lazy dust on the road south. I had real mixed feelings. I was awful sad to see the carnies go, especially Mona the Fat Lady and Bert the Barker and some of the others who had been good friends to me. But I was sure glad to see the back end of Mr. Boyd.

Just before his wagon disappeared from sight, that avaricious old devil stood up and shook his fat fist at me. I just did a little jig on the porch and bowed to him as he went over the crest of the hill and out of sight. I expect he was too far away by then to see me sticking out my tongue.

"Well!" said Miss Jonquil, who had seen my dance.

Miss Jessie, who hadn't, said, "Now at least we'll have—"

"Brother all to ourselves," finished Miss Jonquil as she turned her gaze back to the road, and I felt my heart sink.

"And you, too, of course, Annie dear," added Miss Jessie, patting my wrist with a frail hand.

I guess Sam saw my fallen expression, because he said, "Ladies? I wonder if we could step inside? I have some painful news to convey."

Sam was always just grand with those old ladies.

Anyhow, I took the coward's way out and let him break the news about Jonas. Afterward, I didn't see the sisters for days, as they had both taken to their beds from the shocking news that Jonas was really gone.

I spent the following days catching up with the papers—discovering them, Sam said. All right, I suppose I had not been one for the news, although I never would have broken down and admitted it to Sam, but all of a sudden I had a real yen to find out as much as I could about Johnny Devlin.

I didn't, though. It seemed he hadn't committed a recent crime, so the news was fair sparse. There was still more talk about that mess down in Tombstone than anything else. At least I learned something about the Earp brothers and Doc Holliday, so Sam didn't think I was such a dunce anymore.

I also helped in the garden. Now, you might not think there could be much to garden in January, when the civilized world is decently blanketed in snow, but in Arizona it's pretty surprising what will grow. Sam put in some roses he had ordered the summer before, and I tended the peas and string beans and tomatoes and potatoes and lettuce that Mr. Alvarez had started in our little hothouse.

Usually Sam would have strung up nets to keep the birds from the vegetables, but what with Nezzy prowling about they seemed to have stopped coming around the castle proper. They just chirped at us angrily from the paloverdes and cactus on the perimeter.

The sisters eventually got over their second mourning for Jonas and tried to help me in the garden. But Miss Jonquil picked all the little yellow flowers off my tomato plants because they looked "untidy," and Miss Jessie tried to level out my potato hills, so I had to throw the ladies out.

I wasn't mean about it, though. I set them to taking an inventory of the flatware, which I figured would take them a good week, seeing as how they had to discuss every fork and spoon. It ended up taking them halfway through February, as the debates over the pie server and the grape scissors took longer than expected.

I fretted over that contract I'd signed with Mr. Barnum. Word had got out locally that I was no longer Jonas's vessel, so the crowds we'd experienced at the beginning didn't appear. But it seemed nobody had told Mr. Barnum and I didn't hear from him, though every time Sam went down into Rock Bottom to pick up the mail, I held my breath.

And I couldn't get Jonas back.

I tried everything. I prayed. I stared into space for hours. I rode out to the place Sam had taken me and watched the bay-wing hawks. I tried talking aloud to Jonas, pleading with him, then demanding that he come back, citing the death by starvation of his poor sisters if he didn't.

But nothing worked. One night, late in February, I even took a spin at the Ouija board. We'd had a drop-in visitor that day, a man who had danced with me at my wedding and who Mr. Boyd had railed at me for "disappointing" when I declined to go on with the carnival. His name was Darryl Duppa, although he went by Lord Duppa, and a bigger package of walking, talking, humbugging malarkey I had never met, not even when I was with Boyd's carnival.

He said he spoke about six languages, although nobody could be sure since we didn't speak them either, and told all about how he'd come to America to seek his fortune and find excitement. He was a nice enough looking fellow, I supposed, and was dressed in an out-of-date but fancy suit of clothes. Nobody could put away the whiskey with more rapidity, and the drunker he got, the more fabulous the stories he told became.

We settled in that vault of a parlor after dinner, and the sisters hung on every word that came out of his mouth. They were naive to a fault—and after all, he had been a good friend of Jonas's. Sam and I just sort of listened politely, watching the decanters go down while his level of animation and the pitch of his orations rose.

By about nine o'clock, just when I was thinking of making my excuses and going to bed, Lord Duppa stood up all of a sudden, right in the middle of some story about fighting off Apaches single-handed. Nebuchadnezzar growled at him, but he didn't notice.

"By God!" he said, just as clear as a bell, although his account of the Apache attack had been slurred by a good quart of Scotch whiskey. "My dear Miss Jonquil and Miss Jessie, didn't Jonas have a Ouija board somewhere in this mausoleum?" And then he looked straight at me and said, "That's just the ticket, Mrs. Newcastle!"

He always called me Mrs. Newcastle, even though I'd said, "Call me Annie," about six times.

Miss Jessie's face lit up. "Why yes, Lord Duppa," she said. "Now that you mention it, I do believe Brother had one."

"In the attic," said Miss Jonquil, rising delicately to her feet. "I know just where!"

"Do you think we could speak to Brother again?" asked Miss Jessie, her thin-lidded eyes full of hope.

"Better the board than a flawed receiver," said Miss Jonquil with a sideways glance at me. And then she and Miss Jessie trooped up the stairs in a swish of fabric and a flurry of dusty whispers.

"What's a Ouija board?" I asked Sam.

He didn't have time to answer, though. Lord Duppa stuck his thumbs in his vest and said, "A yes-yes board, my dear. *Oui* is French for yes, and *ja* is the affirmative in German. Put them together, and you had a Ouija board. Of course, the English and Americans have bastardized the German pronunciation of the latter syllable into 'gee,' but I suppose that sort of thing is to be expected." He shook his head and muttered, *"À tort et à travers,"* under his breath.

I was about to open my mouth and ask what it meant— the Ouija, I mean—but Sam stepped on my foot right after I got out the "What—" When Lord Duppa cocked a brow, I finished up, "What do you suppose is, um, keeping the sisters?"

"Ah!" he said, brightening. I guess he cared more for an audience that was consistently dazzled by his presence, because I turned my head to follow his gaze, and there came the sisters down the grand staircase, a flat wooden box held between them. They were smiling so wide I thought their faces would crack, like too-thin porcelain.

Lord Duppa went to meet them, and I whispered, "Holy smokes, Sam, you didn't need to bust my foot!"

"Never ask him to explain anything," he groaned, "unless you want weeklong company. It looks like it's an over-nighter already."

I said, "But what's a Ouija board? And furthermore, where's the attic?"

"It's a bunch of hooey," Sam whispered. "And where do you *think* an attic would be?"

Lord Duppa and the sisters joined us before I could answer, and Lord Duppa carried the box over to the round table under the windows, where Miss Jessie liked to spread out her jigsaw puzzles. There wasn't a puzzle on it then, though, and he opened the box and lifted out a folding board and a little wooden thing shaped like a trivet and about as big as your hand.

"Come, my friends!" he said real grand as he set the box down on the floor and opened up the board. "Gather 'round! Pull up a chair!"

Well, we all did, with less or more enthusiasm, the sisters being the most eager and Sam the least. He had a real pained expression on his face. Me? I was just curious.

On the board were printed all the letters of the alphabet and the numbers zero through nine, plus the words *yes, no,* and *maybe.* Lord Duppa set the trivet on the board—it had a little glass window in the middle, so you could see the letters through it—and then he said, real serious, "Shall we all clear our minds?"

Miss Jessie giggled a little, but Miss Jonquil put the kibosh on that straightway. Lord Duppa closed his eyes and then so did the sisters, and I followed suit. Then Lord Duppa said, "Attend me, my friends!"

Well, we all put a finger on the little trivet—real light, Lord Duppa said, so as to not overly influence it—and then he said, "Spirits! Hark unto me! Spirits, are you there?"

Well, I didn't know what to expect. There we were, all hunkered around an alphabet board with our fingers on this stupid trivet. I had it in my mind that any second Mrs. Alvarez was going to bring in a steaming pan of enchiladas and ask us would we kindly move our hands away so that she could put it down.

Then all of a sudden the wind kicked up. It just went from still to howling in a finger snap. The sisters cringed, but Lord Duppa grinned. I suppose he was pretty well lubricated by then, but even I jumped a little.

"The spirits are here," Lord Duppa said, real ominous.

Sam rolled his eyes.

"Speak to us, O Departed Ones!" Lord Duppa went on. "Identify yourselves!"

Well, I'll be jiggered if that little trivet didn't start to move! I was overcome with awe right at first, but as it circled, I began to wonder who was moving it.

It stopped on the *J* first, then the *O*, then the *N*, and pretty soon it had spelled out JONAS. I knew right then it was a fake, because I didn't feel him in the room, not one single bit. I kept my mouth shut, though—mainly because of Sam, who squashed my foot again about the time I started to open my mouth.

While the wind blew outside, shaking the bushes and sending little bits of gravel pinging off the window panes, Lord Duppa carried on quite a conversation with "Jonas." Jonas's rheumatism was bothering him a bit, it seemed, and heaven was just like the sisters had supposed it to be, all pearly fence-work and solid gold streets.

I couldn't figure out why, if heaven was so perfect, Jonas would still be beset by the rheumatism, but I kept my mouth shut.

Everything was fine, he said, although he evaded the sisters' question about where he'd put the Pennywhistle Ink Stain Remover. And then he was gone. More like Lord Duppa's finger got tired, I guess. I noticed that the wind had died down, too.

"Beautiful," said Miss Jonquil, a serene look of satisfaction on her face.

"Indeed," said Miss Jessie, and wiped away a tear.

"An enigmatic and wholly astonishing event," said Lord Duppa. He mopped his brow and intoned, *"Magna est veritas!"* And then, suddenly brightening, he said, "Ladies, I believe that this calls for a bit of liquid refreshment."

"Calls for something, all right," Sam whispered to me in disgust as we stood up. "He's pretty goddamned grand for somebody who lived in a saguaro-rib, no-roof ramada in the middle of nowhere for years, sucking down mescal like there was no tomorrow."

I hissed, "Shhh!" but I needn't have bothered. Lord Duppa was already across the room, pouring out the last of the decanter of Scotch, and the sisters were fluttering after him. Just for a second, they looked like an old painting of women going to greet their son or nephew when he's been away at war. The firelight washing up gold on their dark skirts made their skin seem warmer, more alive.

It didn't last more than a half-second though, and then they were back to being two dizzy old maids, swoony, silly, and trotting after a man half their age just for the attention.

Sam stepped away, shaking his head, and I had just turned back to the table to push my chair in when a bit of movement caught my eye. I blinked, thinking I'd stared toward the fire for so long and it had fuddled my eyes. But it moved again—the little trivet on the Ouija board, I mean. Nobody was touching it this time. At least, nobody living.

I watched, spellbound, as it slowly spelled out WAIT. I stood there, waiting, and after a pause, it moved again, this time spelling out, AFTER THEY GO. And then it stopped.

"Sam?" I said, still staring at the Ouija board. The word came out kind of funny, not sounding like me at all. "Sam?"

"Yes? What?" He came up behind me.

I couldn't seem to take my eyes away from the trivety thing, even though it had stopped moving and was now just sitting there like a dead rock. "Sam, something—"

"Sam?" echoed Miss Jonquil's voice from across that big old room, and Sam turned away from me. "We seem to be out of whatever Lord Duppa is drinking," she said. "Could you please see to it?"

For a couple of sweet old ladies, the sisters could sure put their uppity shoes on. Sam nodded and left the room, just like that.

Well, I didn't know what to do. Was I supposed to wait in the room, or by the table, or just in the house? I decided to play it safe. I pulled out my chair again and plunked myself right beside that hoodoo board, all the time wondering why Jonas would chose to use that when he could have just popped into my head, like always.

Also, I still thought it strange that I didn't feel him at all. I don't mean with my fingers, like you'd feel a tweed jacket, but that kind of feeling I always had inside me when he was around. I don't know how to describe it. A sense of fullness, I guess, or maybe like you weren't alone.

You know that feeling you get when you're all by yourself in the house, but you could swear somebody's looking at you? I guess everybody has that sometimes. Well, that's kind of what it felt like to have old Jonas rattling around in my head, even when he wasn't talking, even when he was off in his white room.

I know it's going to sound funny, but my head always felt bigger, too, besides feeling stuffy. When he went away, it felt as if somebody had sort of let half the air out of it. Out of all of me.

But I didn't feel any of those things, the things that would have told me he was back. I was purely mystified. Kind of scared, too.

Sam came back blowing the dust off a fresh bottle of Scotch, and the ladies and Lord Duppa talked on a while. I kept one eye on that Ouija board, but the trivet didn't move again.

"Come join us, Mrs. Newcastle," Lord Duppa said at one point. "You're so far away over there. And you look like you're afraid that board will bite you!"

The sisters thought that was real funny and laughed and laughed. Of course, they thought everything Lord Duppa did was so gol-danged refined and witty, him with those shiny elbows and that hair in sad need of a barber.

He put me in mind of Lester St. Ives, back home in Syca-more. Lester had an accent, too—a lot fancier one than Lord Duppa—and claimed to be royalty although he always ad-mitted in a whisper that he was bound by secrecy not to divulge just what his title might be. He hardly ever washed, and he lived in the cheapest room at our boardinghouse for the year that I was thirteen. It's true that he got little checks from England fairly regular, but for my money, I don't think there was any title or lands or big houses or anything. I think his kin were probably just paying him to stay as far away from them as possible.

At any rate, the party wore on for about another hour, Sam slumping in a chair and looking bored sometimes and peevish at others, while the sisters perched on the edge of the blue horsehair loveseat in fluttery awe of our guest.

By about ten-thirty, Lord Duppa was so blasted that he couldn't even balance his elbow on the mantelpiece any-more. He slithered down the marble to the hearth and landed on his backside, right in the middle of a sentence. He didn't seem to notice, though—leastwise, he didn't skip a beat in his oration. Sam helped him up—still pontificat-ing—and Miss Jessie said, "Dear, dear, we've kept the Lord up too late!"

"And that," Lord Duppa said to no one in particular, "is how I came to own an illustrious medicine hat stallion, once the prized possession of the mighty Cochise himself!" He slumped again, but this time Sam was there to catch him.

"Shame on us," Miss Jonquil said behind her hand. "The poor man's asleep on his feet!"

"Mein Gott, mein Gott," he groaned, pointing toward the ceiling with one finger. *"Es wurden mir übel."* Finally he was talking something I understood, that being German. Half the time I didn't understand the English he babbled, but I got this—he said he felt sick.

Frankly, I couldn't figure out why he wasn't keeled over. He was already pretty much fried when he showed up that afternoon, and had put away a quart and a half of the good stuff since then. By rights, Sam should have been nailing him in his coffin instead of helping him up the stairs.

"Good night, dear friends!" he slurred from the top landing. "Until the morrow!"

"A fascinating man," said Miss Jonquil, staring after him.

"So gallant," said Miss Jessie.

"And brave," said Miss Jonquil.

"Standing off all those—"

"—Indians! And taking tea with—"

"—Her Majesty Queen Victoria—"

"—herself!"

"I do admire his company," said Miss Jessie with a dreamy sigh.

"Of course," warned Miss Jonquil, "we must remember that he does tipple a bit, Sister."

I couldn't stand it any longer. "A bit?" I said, and both sisters turned to look at me. I guess they had forgot I was in the room. "If you ask me, it's a miracle Arizona has got any liquor left, what with him guzzling it so fast. He could keep a distillery busy all by himself!"

Miss Jessie looked shocked that I'd say anything untoward about our guest, but Miss Jonquil snapped, "At least Lord Duppa didn't lose Brother!"

"Sister!" gasped Miss Jessie.

"I didn't 'lose' him," I replied. I was a little hurt, but I tried not to let it show. "He left me. He left you, too. That coward left us all in the lurch."

Miss Jessie started to cry, but Miss Jonquil's eyes got real big. "Take that back," she said.

I was pretty stirred up by then. I got to my feet and said, "I will not. It's the truth. And your Lord Duppa didn't call up Jonas on that board. The words he spelled out didn't even *sound* like Jonas! When's the last time you heard your brother say words like 'an enchanting vista, fit for the eyes of fairest Helen'? That's your Lord Duppa talking, not Jonas. I believe he was moving that trivet thing, because Jonas wouldn't—"

"Planchette," piped up Miss Jessie from behind her hankie.

I let out a little huff of air. "Well, I believe he was moving that planchette thing all by himself."

"And how do you explain the howling of the wind and the tapping of the window glass?" said Miss Jonquil, her chin up, her brows arched.

"A dust devil," I said. "A wind flurry. Why, you see dust devils every day from the house! Sometimes they go spinning out across the desert six or eight at a time. And those taps on the glass? Nothing but pebbles tossed up by the wind."

Miss Jonquil's chin was still in the air, but it was trembling a little, and all of a sudden I wished I'd kept my big mouth shut. She said, "You have your explanation then, but we have ours. Come, dear Sister."

Without another word to me, she escorted Miss Jessie from the room, across the marble-tiled, echoing entrance hall, and up the staircase, into the dark.

I sat back down with a thump. If I'd been closer to the fireplace, I would've just grabbed the poker and beat myself over the head with it, I felt so bad. I was so busy lecturing myself for having yelled at those two poor brittle old ladies that when I heard the scratching, I jumped.

The Ouija board was moving. Well, not the Ouija board, proper. The little trivety thing. The planchette.

All by itself, it went to the *H* and paused, then the *E,* and so on, until it had spelled HELLO ANNIE.

I was hanging on to the edge of the table with both hands. "Hello, yourself," I said in a whisper that came out quavery. "Is that you, Jonas?"

The planchette moved again. This time it spelled out DONT BE SILLY.

I cocked my head. From upstairs, I heard Lord Duppa singing. Italian opera, I think it was. He didn't have a very good voice, although it was loud enough.

I was too self-satisfied to pay much attention, though, or even to remember to be scared of the hoodoo in the board. Sort of proud, I said, "I didn't think so. I would've felt him."

The planchette started moving again, and this time it spelled out YOURE LETTING NEZZY GET FAT.

I sat up straight, a burst of joy coursing through my veins and a grin stretching my face. "Aisha!"

14

HEAVENS CHILD BE CALM the planchette spelled out, and then, TOO HARD.

I was about to ask what she meant by "too hard," when I noticed a sort of fuzzy golden light in the chair across the table from me, a fuzzy light full of sparkles that grew until I could make out a blurred, shimmering form. And gradually, the form began to look like Aisha.

"Allah is merciful," she said, her image still wavering, like a mirage on the desert. Maybe I heard her words with my head, maybe with my ears, but I'll swear till the day I die that I saw her lips move. "Your Lord Duppa is such a pig! I could not get that planchette away from him to spell a thing!"

"Golly," I replied, squinting at her, trying to make her outline come all the way into focus. She was wearing that red and gold wrap dress I had always thought was so pretty, and a big tall turban to match, and there were blurry glints of gold at her ears and her neck and her wrists. Surprised, I said, "They let you wear ear-bobs in heaven?"

She laughed, and the sound of it—so genuinely joyous and just like old times—made my heart sing. "You see what you wish to see," she said, still smiling. "I am pleased to find you in such good spirits. We have been worried about you."

Now, I could still make out the back of the chair (as well as the still-life painting on the wall) right through her, but she was real as real. I said, "We who? Is that old crank Jonas there with you?"

She laughed again, though it was more like a snort. "I should say he isn't! But your grandmother is here, and your father. And others. Your father watches over you, you know."

My eyes got kind of hot, and I whispered, "I always felt like . . . like he was close to me, you know? No offense to you Aisha, but why didn't he come?"

She reached out and put her hand on mine. I felt no warmth of flesh, no pressure, just a tingling sensation. "It is very difficult to cross back," she said, very serious. "It is almost impossible when you are as far along the path as he is."

I tilted my head. "What's the path?"

"Well," she said, smiling a little, "he calls it the tracks. It is just our way of saying how far you are from death, and how near to the new life. He has moved far down those tracks, but I have lingered. I came to tell you not to worry."

I was pretty gol-danged confused, but I asked, "Worry about which thing?"

"All of them," she said. "And none of them. Jonas is pouting in the record room, that's all. He will return to you. He has nowhere else to go."

I said, "The record room? He always told me he went to the white room."

"The same," said Aisha, patting my hand. It felt a little like if you were riding on a train, but the only part of you that could feel the buzzing, vibrating motion of it was the back of your hand.

"Jonas Newcastle is confused, that's all." She shook her head. "There he is with all of time's great thinkers, living and dead and yet to be born. Plato, Mary Wollstonecraft, and Socrates; Carl Jung and Descartes, Nostradamus and Dorothy Parker; Diogenes, Cleopatra, Confucius, Aristotle, Jack Benny: why, there are thousands! But does he speak to them? No. Is he marginally aware of their existence? No. Your Jonas isn't even supposed to be in there!" she said.

She stood up then, and Nezzy followed her as she walked toward the fireplace. No, not walked. Floated, more like, still translucent and shimmering.

I said, "What do you mean, Aisha?"

"I mean," she said, turning toward me, "that it's a mistake. Someone made a clerical error, that's all, and now Jonas is in the library, with the records of everything that ever has been and ever will be, from the conception of time until its end. Which, of course, are one in the same. But this is no time to talk of abstract philosophy."

Her form flared a little, glowing brighter and more solid for a moment. "The fool," she added under her breath,

"Who made the mistake?" I asked, although I knew even then that Aisha's visit was going to bear a lot of thinking about, and for a goodly bit of time. She'd thrown so many new things at me that I was dizzy. "Did God make the mistake?"

Aisha's aura calmed down a bit, and she smiled. "Dear Annie, God doesn't make mistakes. He—or she or whatever you wish to call it—simply gets . . . distracted. The universe is a very large place, you know. So many things to attend to! No, someone made a bookkeeping error, that's all. And now Jonas is in the Akashic library crouched under a reading table, grumbling to himself and totally unaware that he is not alone. The error will be corrected, but all in Allah's good time. Or the accounting department's."

Nezzy had walked over and, purring loudly, curled himself at Aisha's feet. Well, where her feet would have been if they were on the floor. As near as I could tell, she was hovering about four inches above it.

"We will convince him to come back to you," she went on, which was a good thing since I was speechless, "so stop your worrying about Mr. Barnum and the sisters Newcastle. And Annie?"

I swallowed hard. "Y-yes?"

"About your Johnny Devlin. All good things are set in stone, you know." She paused, as if listening to something

I couldn't hear, and then she added, "Well, some stones are bigger than others. But only the bad things are written in mud. Be of good cheer."

And then she started to fade.

"Aisha!" I cried. "Aisha, come back! Will you come again?"

By then she had gone down to a golden glimmer, right in the place her belly used to be. The wind kicked up again, blowing like crazy, and Nezzy got to his feet and cocked his head.

"Good-bye, little one, good-bye!" I heard her say, just before a hand reappeared from the golden mist to sweep over Nezzy's head, ruffling his fur with static electricity that crackled louder than the fire. Then the hand and that gold glow winked out, just as though it had never been there, like Aisha herself had never been there at all.

The wind stopped blowing all at once. The only things that remained were the dying fire and a cheetah rolling on the hearth, lost in a spasm of unearthly joy.

The next day I stayed in my room, for Lord Duppa was still with us and Sam was busy trotting after him and the sisters. I'd said I wasn't feeling well, which was just about the truth of it. Aisha's ghostly appearance had thrown me for a real loop, so much that I was half sick.

By about ten-thirty, lying in bed and staring at the big vaulted ceiling hadn't gotten me anywhere—and hadn't brought Jonas back, either—so I got myself up and dressed, and started in to pace.

By eleven-thirty, my stomach got the best of me and I headed downstairs to put some food in it. I met Miss Jonquil on the stairs. We both stopped, me up two risers from her, and there was an awkward silence.

"I'm sorry, Miss Jonquil," I said at last. She really should have been the first one to apologize after her accusing me of losing her brother and all, but I spoke first since I didn't want to stand there until next Christmas. Also since I felt bad about rising to the bait and yelling at her. "I'm sorry about last night, I mean. I shouldn't have said anything about Lord Duppa."

She twisted that thin line of a mouth, and then she said, "You're correct, you shouldn't have. However, I shall accept your apology." She walked up the stairs, passing me, and when she was up a ways, she called back down, "Sister will be another matter." Then she turned her back and went the rest of the way up, then down the long hall. She never looked back.

I stared after her with my mouth hanging open. I had been gracious enough to apologize when she had been in the wrong, and she hadn't even had the decency to be a little nice about it. By the time I got to the kitchen I had closed my mouth, but I was talking to myself.

"She'll accept my apology, will she?" I said as I opened the cupboards, one by one, looking for who knows what. "Couple of vile old women, that's what they are," I grumbled as I slammed the cupboard doors and started on the lower cabinets. "After all I've been through, after all I've done for them!"

I slammed the last cabinet and slumped in a chair just as Sam and Mrs. Alvarez came through the back door. Mrs. Alvarez had her apron full of fresh-picked snap beans, and Sam carried a basket filled with oranges straight from the tree.

Sam saw me and grinned. "Finally decided to come down and mingle with the common folk, eh?" He settled the basket on the big worktable, while Mrs. Alvarez emptied her apron on the tabletop. Snap beans were everywhere.

"How do you feel about fresh quail au l'orange for dinner?" Sam said, still smiling. "We don't have any ducks, but I believe I can shoot enough quail by suppertime. Especially if you lock Nezzy up."

"Who owns this house, Sam?" I asked, ignoring his question entirely.

He kind of looked at me funny, but he said, "You do. Why?"

"Am I the boss of everybody here?" I asked.

"Technically speaking, yes. I suppose you would be."

"Then, would you please ask Miss Jonquil not to be so consarned cranky to me all the time?" I twisted my skirts in one hand. "I didn't lose her brother, Sam, and I'm tired of being accused of being an inadequate vessel. He's the one that vacated!"

Sam came around the table and took my arm. "If you'll excuse us, Mrs. Alvarez?"

She hiked a brow and muttered, *"Si,"* and he led me outside to the garden he'd just come in from and sat me on the bench beside my tomato plants.

"Strange you should ask me to talk to Miss Jonquil about Jonas," he said, "because this morning she told me to speak to you about the very same thing. You had a little argument over Lord Duppa's veracity?"

I nodded, expecting that next he'd tell me that Miss Jonquil was really sorry, but just too proud to apologize. He didn't, though.

"Well," said Sam, leaning against the overhang post, "you've got to understand about Lord Duppa, and about the sisters. Questioning his authority in any way, shape, or form is like . . . Well, you might as well tell 'em the Bible was writ last Thursday by a bunch of fifteenth level Masons. Same thing. Blasphemy, as far as they're concerned."

I twisted my face. "But he lied! He outright lied to everybody in that room, saying Jonas was shoving that thing around, talking to us! Why, Aisha said Jonas has been under a table in the white room with Socrates and Diogenes this whole time—well, they're not under the table with him, just in the room. And he hasn't been pushing anybody's trivet around for a parlor game."

Now it was Sam's turn to make a face. "What in the blue-eyed world are you talking about?"

I had sort of remembered the reason I was upset in the first place and forgot enough about the sisters to be reasonable. I patted the seat next to me and said, "Sit down. This is going to take a while."

It sure felt good to get the story out, and Sam didn't ask a question or try to stop me until I got all the way to the end. And then, all he said was, "I'll be diddly damned."

"Well," I said, patting my hair, for the wind had kicked up a bit, "all I can say is the sisters are sure going to be surprised when Jonas shows up again and tells them Lord Duppa is an old fake. Well, a middle-aged fake, anyway. Can we go in?"

I started to stand up, but Sam pulled me back down again. "Have you told anybody else about this yet?" he asked me.

"No," I replied. "Just you. Why?"

He scratched under his head sash. He was dressed Indian that day. He said, "Well, don't. Don't say a word. Let's just keep this between you and me for the present, all right?"

He patted my hand, and I found myself staring at it. "Why, Sam Two Trees!" I said, jumping right to my feet. "You don't believe me! You think I dreamed it all up!"

He grabbed my wrists. "Calm down, Annie."

I tried to pull away, but he held me fast.

"Settle down! It's not that I don't believe you, exactly. It's just . . . well, how'd you feel if some woman walked in here and announced she'd had a visit from a dead fortune-teller, who informed her that her late husband was hiding under Nostradamus's chair in some mythological library in the sky but that he'd be back momentarily?"

I yanked on my arms again, and this time he slung me to the side, so that I sat down pretty forcefully on the bench beside him. I said, "Ouch! I'm not 'some woman.' And let me go, you fair-weather friend!"

But he didn't let go. He said, "All right, let's try this. What if I were to come up to you and say that I'd just seen Moses in the back forty, and we talked for a spell, and he told me not to worry, that I'd get to France and to cooking school just as soon as I got off the train ride from the planet Venus."

I gave him a dirty look, but I slumped back and stopped fighting him. "I didn't know you wanted to go to France, Sam."

He rolled his eyes. "You never asked, but that's beside the—"

"Well, that's a pretty far stretch to think of, that somebody maybe wants to go to France!" I cut in, sticking my nose in the air. "I won't even comment on that Venus part. Why, I could have just as well asked you if you wanted to go to

Siam, or be the heavyweight champion of the world, or sing opera in Rome, Italy!"

"Christ!" he said, and took his hands off my wrists like I had the plague. "Never mind," he said, all disgusted. "Go. Do what you want."

Nobody in the world could look more disgusted than Sam Two Trees when he put his mind to it. I just sat there and so did he, both of us staring straight out at nothing in particular, and both too stubborn to talk first.

Finally, I said, "Going to France is different."

"I should say so," he replied, not looking at me. "It's a far piece from a dead woman telling you about a dead man who's the victim of some angel's clerical error and is therefore hunkered under a mystical table in some white room. No, you're right. France is a lot more exotic."

He had me, all right. I took a deep breath and let it out slow, then said, "Sorry, Sam. I guess when strange things happen to you a lot, you begin to think they're ordinary."

He nodded. "I reckon."

"I won't tell anybody," I said. "Feel better?"

He sighed and turned toward me, stretching one arm along the back of the bench. "It's not a question of how I feel, Annie. Even if Aisha's right, even if she really did appear to you, you don't know that Jonas'll get here in time for you to meet Mr. Barnum. I have a feeling that those folk on the other side have a strange conception of time. I mean, their clocks must run different or something. In the time it takes Aisha to have a cup of coffee, why, you and I could both grow old and die."

I snorted. "I don't think Aisha has need for coffee where she is."

One corner of Sam's mouth quirked up. "You know what I mean. They're bound to be on a different timetable. And I wouldn't take what she said about Devlin too seriously, either, if I were you."

"All I said—"

"I heard what she said, and I heard the way you told it to me," he cut in. "Don't go getting your hopes up. She didn't exactly say that the two of you'd live happily ever after. In fact, when you get right down to it, she didn't say much of anything. Anything you could bank on, I mean."

I crossed my arms. "You're awful calm for somebody who's about to get thrown out on his backside. This is important! One year with Mr. Barnum—even a couple of good months—would keep Miss Jessie and Miss Jonquil in tortillas and fish forks for the rest of their lives! And furthermore, Aisha *did* mean that I'd see Johnny again, I know she did. Jonas is going to see the error of his ways and come back till they get that paperwork straightened out, and everything's going to be just fine!"

I didn't know it till I said it, but that's what I believed. Oh, I'd done a load of wobbling and mental fence-riding since Aisha's visit, but when push came to shove, I had said out the truth of what I expected, and common sense be hanged.

Sam pursed his lips. "That's the way it is, is it?"

I nodded. "Yes, it is. I feel it in my bones. But Sam," I added, "if you don't want me to say anything, I won't."

He tipped his head once, said, "Good," and stood up.

I put my hand on his arm. "Sam? I've got to know one thing."

"Yes, Annie," he said soft, covering my hand with his for a second. "I know. And I believe you." He added a sort of sarcastic, "God help me," under his breath, and I stomped down on his foot just at the moment we heard Lord Duppa coming 'round the side of the castle.

"Judas Priest!" hissed Sam, hopping on one boot. "What'd you do that for?"

"La donna é mobile qual piúma al vento," came Lord Duppa's voice, in that off-key baritone. *"Muta d'accento e di pensiero . . ."*

"What is that?" I whispered, although there was no need. Lord Duppa's singing—if you could call it that—was loud enough to drown out a church pipe organ going full tilt hallelujah.

"It's *Rigoletto,*" said Sam, and then he gave me a push. "Inside, quick!" he urged. "Before he gets to the high note!"

*   *   *

That night, Sam and I suffering through another diatribe by Lord Duppa—this time he orated upon the spawning cycle of the Pacific salmon, buffalo hunting on the open plain, and the state of the classical dance in Russia. Mostly. There were a few other topics mixed in there, but they sort of washed over me, and the liquor just kept flowing over Lord Duppa. Through him, I mean. Sam whispered to me that if Duppa invited himself to stay one more night, he'd drink us out of Scotch whiskey altogether.

The sisters were civil enough to me. I guess Miss Jonquil only had it in her to be rude in private. At any rate, she and Miss Jessie sat rapt, soaking up every word that issued from Lord Darryl Duppa's mouth as eagerly as he tilted the decanter.

For myself, I was mostly in my own world and thinking about Jonas. I needed him to come to me again, of course, if for nothing but purely for financial reasons. The sisters were his and the castle was his, even if he'd built it for me, and so it was up to him to provide for them and it. But he'd been gone for so long—nearly seven weeks, by that time—that I had got used to being alone in my own body again.

I admit I was half-dreading his return.

I decided that things were going to be different, though, if and when he came back. Real different. The new rules might put him in a mind to run off again, but I couldn't tolerate him the way he was before.

And I decided that the next time I met Johnny Devlin, I was just going to say right out that I loved him, and damn the consequences. I suppose people would have thought that real odd, that I'd plan to do a bold thing like that when I'd only known the man less than a day, and I suppose they'd be right. But some things just *are*. If Aisha was right and all the world's blessings were set in stone, then he'd say, "Why, I love you, too, Annie darlin'. Why don't we get hitched?"

I guess you could say I had the whole world figured out that night. Yes, I had it all figured. I was feeling pretty smug, in fact, sitting there, listening to Lord Duppa drone on. I was ready to pack my bags and get on that train and meet

Mr. Barnum in Baltimore—that's where the tour was to begin, Baltimore—with or without Jonas.

I just knew he'd show up in time. Probably right at the very last minute, if I knew that old buzzard. But he'd come. Aisha would see to it.

And so, when it was around a quarter to ten and Miss Jonquil put in a request for the Ouija board (and threw me a sidelong glance), I smiled and said to say hello to Jonas for me, but I was going upstairs.

"So early?" said Miss Jessie, who, by the looks of her, had forgiven me. She always was the more tenderhearted of the sisters.

"Sleep well," said Miss Jonquil, and turned her back. She walked away from me, toward the lure of the Ouija board, and it took all the strength of will I had not to blurt out that she was a silly old fool and that her precious Lord Duppa was a trivet-shover and a charlatan.

"Oh dear," muttered Miss Jessie, who was still near me, and watching after Miss Jonquil. She muttered, "Sister, Sister," under her breath.

I decided to push Miss Jonquil's rudeness out of my mind—I was too all-fired happy to let it plague me—and smiled at Miss Jessie. "It's all right," I said kindly. "I guess I ate too much of Sam's quails with orange sauce. They've about put me to sleep."

Miss Jessie touched my arm with a bony finger. "All right, dear Annie," she said, giving me a dry little smile. I thought we were thinking the same thing, which was that we weren't going to talk about Miss Jonquil and the quail with oranges was just a cover-up for deeper conversation.

But then she leaned over and whispered, "Myself, I don't care for mixing foods. Fruits and meats, that is. But one must put up with one's servants' little peccadilloes, if one wishes to keep them. We are so far away from the good agencies!"

I watched her join the others, shaking my head the whole time. Just when I thought I had those two figured out, one of them would toss a great big buttonhook into the gears.

I said my good nights to Lord Duppa and Sam, and went

up to my room, muttering to myself the whole way. Those old women! After Sam had practically given them his services free and taken care of them, not to mention put food in their mouths, Miss Jessie still considered him a servant! Probably Miss Jonquil, too. Why, if it hadn't been for Sam taking care of all of us these past few months, I don't know what we would have done!

Just because he didn't call attention to what he was doing, it didn't mean he wasn't doing it.

By the time I got to my bedroom I had worked myself into an uproar, and consequently did a little slamming and banging while I was getting ready for bed. Of course, it had been sort of a slam-and-bang day. Earlier in the evening, while Lord Duppa was pontificating on the spawning habits of salmon, Sam had confided to me that I'd knocked two of the cupboard doors off level.

As I ran the brush through my hair for the last stroke, I reminded myself to apologize to him, come tomorrow. After all, he'd likely be the one fixing them. As usual. It struck me that all I did was make messes and expect Sam to clean them up. I was as guilty as the sisters, in my own way.

I vowed to do better.

I said my prayers—God might be preoccupied in the far left corner of the universe, but I reckoned he still had time to listen. I crawled into bed, snuggled into the covers, blew out the lamp, and closed my eyes.

I don't know what time it was when I woke up, only that it was dark. My body was in such an uproar that I didn't have the presence of mind to look at the clock. My legs were twitching and kicking wildly, my arms and hands gyrated to two separate and warring tunes. My body was writhing so bad I thought my spine would snap, and my head felt so full that it was about to explode!

I tried to open my mouth to call for help, but my jaws were clamped shut like I'd come down with the tetanus, and all I could do was thrash.

Blast your hide, came a voice I knew too well. *Stop it! Hold still! Quit fighting me, you little catamount!*

And you quit trying to murder me, Jonas Newcastle! I

called back, in my mind, for that was what he was surely trying to do.

And then my limbs stopped their convulsing, just like that.

Oh! said Jonas, kind of surprised. *I'm in already.*

I wiggled my toes, just to see if they'd obey me, and when they did, I snapped, "Well, what did you think, you old goat?"

I was kind of surprised to hear my own voice, out loud in the middle of nothing but black.

How should I know whether I'm in or out? he grumbled. *After the way you shoved your way clear on the desert—*

"I what?"

After you threw me out of your legs like that! he said. And then he added, a little arch, *Before the snake got you, in case you don't remember.*

I remembered. "Sorry. But at least you know I can do it."

He didn't answer, but I knew he was still there. It felt like we took up the whole room, we were so big. I struck a match and lit the lamp, as much to make sure that I hadn't really grown from wall to wall as to "shed a little light on the subject," like my papa always said.

When I turned up the wick, everything looked just like always.

Why'd you do that, Annie? said Jonas, and suddenly his tone was all creamy.

I tightened my mouth. He was still randy after all that time in the white room. A person would have thought a lengthy spell with great philosophers—even if he couldn't see them—would have put him in a loftier frame of mind. I crossed my arms and said, real firm, "Don't you try that on me anymore, Jonas Newcastle!"

Try what? he said, all innocent.

"You know what I mean," I replied. "There're going to be some new rules if you plan to stay around. And the first one is no more Saturdays and Wednesdays."

Tuesdays and Fridays, then? he said real matter-of-fact, like he was penciling it into some celestial appointment book.

I sighed. "No, Jonas. Never. No more."

What do you mean, never? he thundered.

There was a time when that ominous tone would have scared me silly, and wondering if I'd look up and find it was raining frogs. But no longer.

"Never," I said with finality. "I've got a line on you, Jonas Newcastle. You're stuck. It's either here with me or huddling under some table up in that white room, and I'll wager you're sick of huddling."

What?

"Hush. Now, I figure you don't have much time left, seeing as how you're a mistake in the first place, so you'd best make hay whilst the sun shines, if you get my drift."

What do you mean, I'm a mistake! he roared.

"You don't know?"

Know what? You've certainly got a lot of bark on you to call me a mistake!

While he complained at length, I smoothed the covers over my chest and turned the lamp down a mite. "Jonas?" I said at last. "Jonas, stop hollering. You're giving me a headache."

I'm certainly not a mistake, he huffed. Funny, but the way he said it put me in mind of Miss Jonquil. *Of all the unmitigated gall, of all the nerve, of all the—*

"Maybe I put it wrong," I interrupted. "What I meant to say was that Aisha visited me and we had quite a—"

Ha! he said, all full of himself. *Aisha's dead! She couldn't have visited . . . Oh.*

"Oh, indeed," I said, when he lapsed into an embarrassed silence. "She told me you're in something called the Akashic library. It's where all the great thinkers of the world are, dead, living, and yet to be born."

Ah, said Jonas, in a self-satisfied tone. *I always knew it! At last I've been given the recognition that I sorely lacked in my corporeal form. But I haven't seen anybody. I've heard whispers, just murmurs on the wind, as it were. But there's no one in that drafty place but me. Aisha was mistaken. Or perhaps,* he said thoughtfully, *I'm in a class by myself!*

"Jonas?" I said, and I tried to be as kind as I could. "That's what I'm trying to tell you. See, up there in heaven they've got clerks, same as down here. And one of them made a little mistake."

Mistake?

I nodded, though there was no one there to see it. "You can't see anybody because you're not supposed to be there at all. It's just . . . what did Aisha call it? A clerical error. They're trying to fix it, but until they do you're either stuck there in that white room all by your lonesome, or here with me."

A what? A clerical error? he cried, so loudly that my whole head rang with it. *I'm Jonas Newcastle,* he shouted inside me. *Colonel Newcastle, a hero of the Blackhawk War! The Sioux War! A pioneer of the territories, by God! I'm some-*body! *I'm no 'clerical error'!*

I gave a little shrug. "Sorry to squash your daisies, Jonas." I sat up and pulled the lamp toward me. "But that's just the way it is. I can't do anything about it, and neither can you."

He didn't answer me, and I knew he'd gone off to pout and grumble in private. But I was smiling. He was still inside me. I could feel his metaphorical toe in the lake of my mind, leastwise. And once he calmed down—and I figured that'd take until long about breakfast—he'd see reason and every-thing would be just peachy again. Well, most everything.

I blew out the lamp and settled into the best sleep I'd had in months.

15

When I came downstairs the next morning, the sisters had already taken their breakfast. They sat outside on the flagstone patio, the one where they'd perched in the shade on the day of my wedding. I could see them from the breakfast room window, chattering away. The sisters were animated and buzzing like elderly bees around Lord Duppa, who, although I could scarce believe it, was looking a tad bored.

"What's he drinking?" I asked Sam when he brought in my eggs and bacon. There was buttered toast and a fresh orange, too, sliced real fancy, and little bits of lemon peel set here and there, all curly and just for show. Sam was quite the one for what he called "presentation."

Sam followed my pointing finger to Lord Duppa's glass. It didn't look like his usual Scotch, and had some green stuff in it.

"Mint julep," said Sam, helping himself to a slice of bacon off my plate. He sat down, sighing. "He finished off the last of the Scotch at breakfast. Jonas's private stock of twenty-year-old Scotch malt whiskey, aged in smoked oak barrels in the dungeon of a baronet's castle on the misty moors of Scotland." He bit off a chunk of the bacon. "I should be in mourning," he said, chewing.

"He's going to go, isn't he?" I asked.

Sam nodded dejectedly. "I give him until noon, at the latest. Might take him that long before he can sit a horse. He always leaves as soon as the Scotch is gone, and now, what with Jonas having departed the mortal coil, we're not likely to order more shipped in."

I broke the yolk in my first egg, and dipped my toast. "Well," I said around a mouthful, "I sure hope he doesn't leave until Jonas pops up."

Sam looked at me like I'd just put a cocked shotgun to his head. "What kind of an idiot thing is that to wish for? Hell, I can barely stand two days of the pie-eyed old buzzard. I didn't sign up for a couple of years!"

I smiled and turned the lazy Susan until I got to the cactus jelly. "Might not take so long as a couple of years," I said, scooping out pink, see-through jelly with my spoon. "Might not even take a couple of hours. As a matter of fact, he might already be back."

Sam reached out and stopped my jelly hand halfway to my toast. Lit up like the Fourth of July, he whispered, "Is he . . . is he back?"

Well, if I'd known Sam was going to react with such enthusiasm, I wouldn't have teased him. He looked like he was about to stop breathing.

"He is," I said, and just like that, Sam dropped my wrist and jumped up and commenced to do an Indian war dance around the breakfast table!

"We're saved!" he hollered after he'd circled it twice. He threw his arms in the air and shouted, "Hallelujah and pass the biscuits!" and then he went back to his dance, singing louder and lifting his knees up even higher than before.

I was laughing like crazy, and Sam pulled me up and into the dance, him singing Navajo, me singing nonsense, and both of us giddy as two loons. That was, until I looked up and saw Miss Jonquil at the door. I stopped midstep, and so did Sam, and I guess we both did look pretty foolish. She was staring at us like we'd both lost our minds, and Sam stood up straight, took the orange slices off his head and the lemon peel off his ears, and said, "May I help you, Miss Jonquil?"

She stood there for a second, like she was trying to remember just how the etiquette books said a lady should react in such a situation. And then she said, "Lord Duppa is leaving," like she was the Queen of England. She turned and walked away, as stately as all get out.

We watched her go down the hall and turn into the main dining room, and only then did Sam close the door. The minute it latched, I collapsed into giggles. Sam laughed and started picking toast crumbs off my shoulders, and saying, "Land sakes, Annie, we've sure made a mess."

He was right. In our enthusiasm, we'd spread most of my breakfast over each other for war paint, and we—along with the walls and floor—were splotched with egg yolk and cactus jelly and orange slices and toast bits.

"At least you helped make this one," I said, still grinning. I grabbed a napkin off the table and began to wipe at the walls. "Usually it's the sisters or me you're cleaning up after. Sam," I said, sobering, "I'd like to say right now that I'm sorry."

"Oh, that's all right," he said, his attention on the floor. "The yolk's still wet, so it won't stick. When did he come back, Annie?"

"No, not the egg yolk," I said. "The messes, I mean. All of them."

Sam was on his hands and knees, under the table. "Annie, stop changing the subject!" he called. "Tell me about Jonas!"

Well, you can see how it was. I gave up trying to apologize—for the time being, anyway—and told him about Jonas's visitation. "And he's still with me," I finished up. "He's off someplace pouting, but he's still there. I can feel him." And then I remembered why Miss Jonquil had come back to the breakfast room in the first place. "Hadn't we better go say good-bye to Lord Duppa?"

Sam got up off the floor and dusted his pant legs. "I suppose," he groused. "We can only hope we've missed him. On the other hand," he added, brightening substantially, "maybe Jonas'll put in an appearance!"

We had no such luck, though. After Sam got Lord Duppa up on his horse and Duppa swept his hat a couple of times, recited some Shakespeare, and then said a quote in what I guessed to be Italian. He rode off, weaving down the road toward Rock Bottom and points south.

"A wonderful man," sighed Miss Jonquil, who so far had not mentioned the little scene in the breakfast room.

"Such a great thirst," chimed in Miss Jessie, her face darkening a bit. "Just think, the last of Brother's Scotch whiskey."

"It went to Brother," said Miss Jonquil, thoughtfully. "In a way."

Miss Jessie folded her hands. "I suppose so.

"Bunk," I said.

Miss Jonquil turned to glare at me. "How dare you!" she said. "Lord Duppa isn't even out of sight yet!"

The surprising strength of that rheumy gaze didn't faze me a bit. I said, "For your information, Jonas came and spoke with me last night. He's been in the white room all this time, and he doesn't know a blessed thing about Lord Darryl Duppa's silly Ouija board."

Miss Jessie's face bloomed. She clasped her hands together. "Brother!" she whispered.

But Miss Jonquil glowered at me. "Teller of false tales!" she spat.

I supposed I'd gone too far, calling the Ouija board silly—and, by implication, Lord Duppa—but I was still plenty miffed about the other night. "Miss Jonquil, your brother is back inside my head, as of last night. I never 'lost' him," I said with emphasis, "but in any case, he's found now."

Miss Jessie's eyes flicked nervously between the two of us, and her hands were clutched to her heart. Miss Jonquil paid her no mind. She drew herself up and tilted her narrow head back so she could stare at me down her skinny nose.

"All right," she said, smiling as smug as a backstreet bully. "Produce him."

I was still annoyed five days later, when Sam and I set out for the east. I was livid with Jonas, for not showing up—for *still* not having shown up—despite all my cajoling and pleading. He was there, all right. He just wouldn't do me the favor of putting forth the effort to talk to his sisters. You'd have thought he would've wanted to!

And I was irked at Miss Jonquil, too, who all the rest of that day—and the days that followed as well—smirked every time she saw me. It wasn't much of a gesture, that little dry smirk, but it was just enough to make me so gol-dang peeved I could hardly think straight.

I'll give Miss Jessie the benefit by saying she had chosen to take the neutral ground. The truth was, she just agreed with everybody. When she was talking to Miss Jonquil, Miss Jonquil was one hundred percent right, and when she talked to me, I was. Miss Jessie must have got pretty sick of patting hands and saying, "There, there. You're absolutely right," all those times.

When Sam and Nezzy and I left to meet the stage, armed with a recent telegram from one of Mr. Barnum's lieutenants giving us the name of our hotel in Baltimore and letting us know the train tickets were waiting, Miss Jessie came out on the porch to wave good-bye. She give us each a peck on the cheek and Nezzy a chuck under his chin.

Miss Jonquil didn't. I saw her as Mr. Alvarez drove us off in Jonas's fancy buggy, all tight-lipped and staring after us from a window high in the south turret.

I didn't hear a peep out of Jonas on the stage ride or on the train, either west or east of the Mississippi. By the time we finally pulled into the depot in Baltimore, I was awful nervous. Here I'd bet all my marbles on Aisha's prophesy coming true, but now I was beginning to have serious doubts. If Jonas wouldn't come forward and say howdy to his own sisters, what on earth had made me think he'd stick his head out for a bunch of total strangers who bought tickets?

A man named Mr. Leonard Strider met us at the station. He said he worked for P.T. Barnum and was our front man, whatever that was. Slender and maybe thirty-five, he was clean-shaven and had shortish, sandy hair, which he wore slicked back above little gold-rimmed glasses and a wide brow. I remember thinking that he wasn't so tall as Johnny

Devlin or so long-legged, and not nearly so good-looking, although he had a pleasant enough voice.

Of course, back then I was comparing every man I met to Johnny Devlin. Waiters and porters on the train, diners in the restaurants where the trains stopped, passengers who were total strangers to me, and now Mr. Strider. It wasn't their fault that none of them measured up.

Anyway, Mr. Strider treated us like visiting royalty, which made me feel all the worse that I couldn't raise Jonas. He attended our luggage, even seeing that Nezzy got out of the baggage car first thing, and that he was walked around to loosen his joints.

He tipped everybody right and left, ferried us through the throng and into a closed coach, and off we went. Personally, I would've enjoyed seeing some of the city. It was dark and rainy that day, but still, I'd never been in a big town before. However, Mr. Strider seemed to have the idea that things like that were old hat to me, and I was too depressed about Jonas to correct him.

It was fair close in that coach, what with Mr. Strider insisting the curtains be drawn and the windows closed (and what with Nezzy smelling ripe from being crated), but we finally stopped in front of the biggest danged hotel I had ever seen. Mr. Strider whisked us through the lobby and we didn't get stopped once, which is saying something when you're pulling a smelly cheetah on a leash. We didn't even pause at the desk. He just snapped his fingers at this person or that, and took us straight up the stairs to our suite.

He opened the door with a flourish, then stepped back, gesturing for me and Sam and Nezzy to go in ahead of him. "Only the best for Mr. Barnum's stars," I heard him say as I walked past him.

I remember thinking that Mr. Barnum was surely going to be bankrupt before the month was out, if he put all his carnival acts up in similar places.

First off, the whole thing was carpeted within an inch of the walls, and those rugs weren't cheap, either. Nebuchadnezzar took advantage of it right away and threw himself down, rolling around and scratching his back and purring, and spotting the carpet with all sorts of unmentionable stains.

The sitting room was awful big, I'd say about twenty feet by thirty, and there were big windows all along one wall that let in a ton of light and led out to a terrace. Sam had headed straight there.

Doors led off the sitting room on either side to the bedrooms, I supposed. The furnishings were awful fancy but comfortable-looking—mostly in greens and golds and a little bit of dark blue here and there—and smack in the center of it stood a lean, middle-aged waiter with black shoes so shiny that Sam could have shaved in them.

"I am Carl," he said, in a clipped German accent, once he'd gotten an eyeful (and noseful) of Nezzy, "und I will be your waiter. Feel free to order room service at any time, day or night." He handed me the menu, saying, "As you can see, our bill of fare contains a wide variety, all prepared mit de utmost care by our Paris-trained chef, Walter Vanderstoob. You may summon me at any time."

And then he gave a crisp bow and left.

"My goodness," I said.

"Vanderstoob? A Dutch chef?" said Sam, who was done inspecting the terrace, and just coming in the doors. He was in a real good mood, mostly on account of we were finally off the train. He got sick. "What's the world coming to? They'll have red-Indian chefs before you know it!"

Mr. Strider was overseeing the bellboys with the baggage, but he said, "Oh, certainly not! That sort of thing would never happen, I assure you."

And then his head came up real sudden, like he'd been lulled by Sam's white-man clothes and cultured demeanor, but had just remembered he was part Indian. The flush came brightly up his neck and stopped just short of his cheekbones.

"Oh dear," he said, and patted his wide brow with a big white handkerchief. "I'm so sorry! I didn't mean, that is . . ."

Sam waved his hand. "Think nothing of it, Strider," he said in a nonchalant fashion. "You know, no one ever thinks a Navajo can whip up anything decent. They always expect grubs in the chocolate mousse and beetles in the soufflé."

Strider laughed, but it kind of broke in the middle and fell off to nothing. He fingered his collar, then said, "Your, ah, first performance is this evening, Mrs. Newcastle. Mr. Barnum has had costumes prepared, but we won't have time for final fittings today. So, if the both of you could wear something of your own? I'll be here at seven to pick you up."

I nodded, picturing myself sitting red-faced, in my plain yellow dress, in front of a roomful of people and yelling into thin air, "Dad blast it, Jonas! Come out from betwixt Plato's feet!

"By the way," Strider added, "it's a sold-out crowd tonight. Fifteen hundred people." I felt my heart rise up into my throat, but he just kept talking. "The papers have been full of you. I expect there'll be the usual rabble-rousers in the crowd, but I'm sure you know how to deal with that. Well, I'll see you this evening, then!"

I lifted a limp hand, waving him good-bye, and as he left, Sam came up behind me. "The usual rabble-rousers?" he said. Nezzy followed him and flopped down on the carpet next to me.

"You got me," I said, staring at the door that had closed behind Mr. Strider. "I only hope there'll be some rabble to rouse. Or some rouse to rabble. I mean, I hope to Clancy that Jonas sees fit to make an appearance."

Sam put his hand on my shoulder. "Don't worry about that now," he said from behind me. "If Jonas doesn't want to come out and play, well, that's the way it is. We'll just go home with our tails between our legs. I'll get a job cleaning shitters on the reservation, and you can go to work for Darryl Duppa, pouring his drinks and telling him life's grand and he's wonderful."

I sighed. "Sometimes, Sam, you can be real irritating."

"I know." He rubbed my back for a second, then gave me a little slug on the arm. "Right now, worry about giving Nezzy a bath. The sooner the better."

*   *   *

True to his word, Mr. Strider showed up at seven o'clock on the dot. We were ready for him. Well, mostly: We looked the part, anyway.

Sam wore his Navajo duds and deerskin boots—his best ones with the beading—and lots of silver squash blossoms and bracelets. I'd never seen him rigged out fancy before, and I've got to say that he looked good enough to be a king, or at least a prince.

He had Nezzy on his best leash, with his best turquoise-studded collar, one that Mr. Alvarez had tooled for him, with the stones and silver set in by hand. I had on my good blue dress—with turquoise trim to match Nezzy's collar—and my hair was piled on top of my head. The three of us fairly reeked of lavender hotel soap.

"Ready?" chirped Mr. Strider, and I wanted to say, "No, not by a long shot, and why don't we sit down and think this over?"

But Sam said, "As ready as we'll ever be," and gave me a little push, and so the four of us—counting Nezzy—set out for the theater.

It had been drizzly off and on all day, and our coach's wheels crunched over wet pavement and brickwork. And all the way there I kept calling, *Jonas! Jonas, come out!* in my head. I even tried calling Aisha, but it was no use. Nobody was paying the slightest bit of attention to me, and I was thinking that it was just like Jonas to show up within yelling distance and then refuse to show himself. If he'd gone clear away I think it would have almost been better, for to have him right there with me and hiding at the same time was a torture on my nerves.

We came to a stop outside the back door of the place I was to speak. It was the Jewel Box Theater, and there were giant pictures of me—well, I guess it was supposed to be me—out front and "Prophet Annie Tonight!" was in two-foot letters across the marquee.

I felt like the top of my head would fly right off at any minute and I was almost in tears, just from the idea of telling Mr. Strider he'd have to give all those people their money back. I swear, I would rather have been bit by a desert rattler ten times over again than to break that news. Why, when Mr. Barnum found out, he'd likely have a heart attack and die, and it would be all my fault!

I thought about how smug I'd been the morning after Jonas showed up again. I'd thought all my problems were solved, or at least coming to a fast resolution. Well, I'd been an arrogant little fool, and look where it had got me.

Mr. Strider stepped down from the coach and held his gloved hand up to me, but I couldn't take it.

Best to get it over with now, I thought. Best to just say it out and go back to the hotel and pack our bags, and leave on the night train and lick our wounds in private.

So instead of taking his hand, I sat back in my seat and said, "Mr. Strider, I can't."

His smile wavered a tiny bit. "Pardon, Mrs. Newcastle?"

Sam made a face at me, a horrified what-in-the-name-of-God-are-you-doing? face, but I closed my eyes. "I said, I can't do it. I can't control Jonas."

Strider said, "Beg pardon?"

"I mean that I can't call him up," I repeated, my eyes still clamped shut. "I can't just put a saddle on him and ride him around. I can't put him on a leash. Mr. Strider, I can't take him out of my pocket and tell him to hop!"

"That's all well and good, Mrs. Newcastle," he said, like he didn't understand a blessed thing I'd said. "Come along, now. If you'll just accompany me toward the stage door . . ."

I got down somehow, and I think I was walking toward the steps up to the door, but I couldn't feel my feet moving. "Please!" I gasped, "I can't do it!"

I was having trouble getting enough air, and I was sure the top of my skull was going to fly away any second. I hoped it would take me with it.

"Nonsense," said Mr. Strider, and gave out with a feeble laugh, like he was trying to make light of the situation but was secretly just as scared as I was, albeit for different reasons. Although the night was cool, out came that big white handkerchief again. He wiped at his neck and said hopefully, "These preshow jitters are commonplace. I'm certain you'll be right as rain just as soon as you get out on stage."

That was the exact wrong thing to say to me. "Sam!" I cried at the same time my knees gave out. I slithered downward, and it was only Mr. Strider's hand on my arm that kept me from sitting all the way down in that puddly alley.

Sam grabbed my other arm and hoisted me up. For a second there it was a tug-of-war, what with Mr. Strider intent on pulling me up the stage-door steps, and Sam tugging me back toward the coach.

In the end, Sam won and pushed me up inside the coach, where I sat on the seat with a thump. Nezzy followed and sat at my feet, although he looked a mite confused. From inside came the sounds of an orchestra starting to play, and I raised my head.

"They hired a band?" I said weakly.

"Mr. P. T. Barnum has indeed hired an orchestra, Mrs. Newcastle," said Mr. Strider, suddenly looking the next thing to fierce, which was probably about as close as he ever got. "He has hired publicists and musicians and taken advertisements in the newspapers. He has invested good money— and quite a bit of it, I might add—in renting the hall and hiring seamstresses and scenic painters and paying your fares all the way from New Mexico—"

"Arizona," I said.

"Wherever!" Mr. Strider snapped. "Mr. Barnum has parted with a great deal of time and effort and cash to bring you here to meet this audience tonight, and he has paid me a considerably more modest amount to put it all together. I will not allow a little stage fright on your part to put my family out on the streets!"

I had begun to cry, and I couldn't say a thing lest I explode. But Sam spoke up right about then. He said, "My dear Mr. Strider, this isn't a case of stage fright. Annie can't call up Jonas—the late Mr. Newcastle, that is. He's being obstinate."

Strider looked thunderstruck. "What?"

Patiently, Sam said, "The spirit is not with her, if you get my meaning."

Mr. Strider sputtered while, inside, the orchestra started a second tune, and outside, it started to mist. He finally reclaimed the ability to form words, and shouted, "My God, man, are you telling me she thinks this is *real?* Oh, I should have listened to Boyd. He wired me, you know. Warned me! But I didn't listen. I thought it was all sour grapes!"

He sat right down in the middle of the alley, and pounded his fist on the pavement. Water splashed up, but he didn't seem to notice. "Mr. Barnum is going to be furious! A lunatic! He's gone—we've gone—to all this trouble for a delusional little lunatic! Oh Lord, Lord, Mrs. Strider and all the little Striders, cast onto the street! What will I do about poor Joey, tell me that?"

I had some control over my tears by then, and said, "Mr. Strider, I'm not crazy, and I'm sorry about your family. Surely Mr. Barnum will—"

"You don't know!" he cut in, "You just don't know!" It had started raining for real by that time, and the water poured off his narrow hat brim, soaked his suit, ran over his face. "He can be an ogre, I tell you, a veritable ogre if you cross him hard enough! Oh, my poor little Mary and Daisy and Theodore! Oh, my poor Mrs. Strider!"

"What about Joey?" Sam asked. I noticed that at some point, he'd climbed inside the coach, too. He was a dry as a lizard.

"We'll just have to give him away!" cried Mr. Strider, and buried his face in his hands. "It's either that or the knackers," he mumbled hopelessly through his fingers.

"Mr. Strider!" I said, shocked out of my tears. "Just because you've had a little bad luck, you can't mean you'd give away your own little boy!" I was certain I'd heard him wrong about the butcher.

"Well, of course not!" he said angrily, looking up. "Joey is our old buggy horse."

I reached across and laid a hand on Sam's knee. "I suspect we'd better go in. Maybe I can think of something else. Maybe I could dance for them. Can you sing?"

"Christ," Sam grumbled, and stepped down into the rain.

A moment later we were inside, and I was toweling off Nezzy's back and feet. Mr. Strider looked like something the cat had dragged in after fierce battle in the water trough.

The orchestra was a good deal louder now, and they were going into their fourth or fifth number by the time Sam and Nezzy and Mr. Strider and I reached the wings.

Strider rubbed the towel over his hair one last time and handed it to a stage hand. He ran his fingers through it to smooth it, saying, "Thank you, thank you! You can fake it, you'll see. Everybody does!" and then he stepped away from us and out onto the stage.

"Oh cripes!" I whispered. "I can't fake it, Sam! Mr. Boyd asked me to do the same thing. I couldn't do it then, and I can't do it now. I'll just have to be honest with them, that's all. They'll surely understand."

Sam blew out air through his lips and shook his head. "I don't know, Annie. Couldn't you just try to fake it a little bit? Take a peek." He lifted back the curtain a smidge so that I could see the audience.

Well, I darn near collapsed again. One thousand and five hundred people is a lot of folks, and it sounds like a lot when somebody says it like Mr. Strider had to me. But seeing those fifteen hundred people all sitting there, waiting, was something else entirely. It looked like all the people in the world were out in that theater, and they had all put on their fancy clothes and jewels just to see me.

I swallowed hard.

Ha! barked a voice from inside me. *Look at that turnout!*

"You evil old goat!" I cried, then slapped a hand over my own mouth. On stage, Mr. Strider turned with a little squish of water and looked at me like I'd just set off a firecracker. Several people in the audience tittered, and Sam was grinning.

"Are you satisfied, nearly giving me an apoplexy?" I whispered, still talking to Jonas. "Will you be nice and talk to these people about flying machines or the stars or the Hun or something? Or do you want to see me tarred and feathered and run out of town on a jeweled rail, and your name turned into a laughingstock?"

It wouldn't be me *they'd laugh at,* he said, all huffy.

"Who else?" I said. I could tell Mr. Strider was coming to the end of his speech. The best and fastest way to get something out of Jonas, to my way of thinking was to appeal to his vanity. Or in this case, disappeal to it, if that's a word. I didn't have time to mess around. "They might laugh at me for a spell, but I can deal with it. After all, I'll be all the way out in Arizona. What would I care?"

Sam was waving his arms and shaking his head and mouthing, "Don't make him mad!" but I just kept on talking.

"For years," I said, "folks'll be saying that rigged games, or forged signatures, or any sort of a pig in a poke is as phony as Jonas Newcastle. That's right, *Jonas* Newcastle, no Annie about it. And it'll serve you right!"

There was a long silence, and for a second I was afraid I'd gone too far and lost him, but then his voice same, soft, *I was only fooling with you, Annie, honestly.*

I crossed my arms. "Well, you had best not be fooling with me anymore. Aisha said they could take you anytime. For all I know, this could be your last chance to talk to the living."

From the stage, Mr. Strider said, "And now, ladies and gentleman, I present to you the prophet, Annie Newcastle!"

Applause rose like a thunder coming over the cornfields, and Sam and Nezzy and I walked out on stage while Mr. Strider squished his way to the wings. Two chairs were set out, one at center stage—with a little table beside it with a glass and water pitcher—and one over to the side a bit. I stood in front of the one in the center and Sam, taking Nezzy's leash, went to the other. Sam was looking at me hopefully, and I gave a little shrug of my shoulders, as if to say I didn't have a single clue as to what was going to happen.

A hush had fallen over the audience. I had never in my life seen so many people, and every single one of them was staring at me, real expectant. It was surely the world's most well-dressed lynching party.

"My name," I began, "is Annie Newcastle, who some have called prophet. Thank you for coming to see me. Soon you will be listening to the spirit of Mr. Jonas Newcastle, my late husband who died on our wedding night."

"Speak up!" cried a man in the back, and I repeated the first part of my speech, only louder.

"Mr. Newcastle was a colonel in the army," I went on, "where he fought the Sioux. He ranched cattle in the Arizona and New Mexico territories, and he owned the Little Devil, the Aztec, the Iowa Princess, and the Buckshot mines in Arizona."

So far, it was the speech I always used to give when I was with Boyd's. Back then, I'd just sit down and Mr. Newcastle would take over, but he wasn't coming forward tonight. So right after the part about the Buckshot mine, I started improvising, so as to stall for time.

"I have come here tonight with my friend Sam Two Trees, who is one half Navajo and the best chef west of the mighty Mississippi, and who was adopted by the late Mr. Newcastle when he was just a little boy. Sam, say hello."

Sam threw me a nasty look, but he stood, held up one hand, palm to the audience, said, "How," and sat down.

I would've swatted him with one of his precious iron skillets right about then, had there been one handy. But there wasn't, so I just resolved to get even with him later.

Gesturing, I said, "And this is Nebuchadnezzar, who is my pet African cheetah. Nebuchadnezzar was willed to me by a dear friend, Aisha, who was herself from Morocco by way of New York City, and he is my tame pet. He also keeps the birds from smacking me on the head."

I had stalled about as long as I knew how. I sat down in my chair and took a deep breath, and thought, *Jonas, if you're going to do any talking, now's the time.*

There was no answer, but I crossed my fingers, mouthed a quick prayer, and announced, "I will now welcome the spirit into my body. Ladies and gents, I give you Jonas Newcastle."

16

A minute went by, then two, and each seemed like an hour. I could feel perspiration beading on my forehead. The crowd was starting to get restless, and somebody in the back got up and started sidling toward the aisle.

"Jonas!" I hissed under my breath. "Jonas Newcastle!"

I'd do it if you'd quit fighting me, you little harridan! came the answer, plain as day.

"I'm not fighting you!" I growled between my teeth. "Hurry up!"

You are, so! he insisted, and then I felt my foot twitch—spasm, more like—and then it went numb. Just like old times.

I breathed a sigh of relief as he cried, *Bully! Almost in! For the love of God, just relax or we'll be here all night!*

I asked no questions. I just let go.

Up came the numbness, up my legs and my arms and my torso and finally my neck and face, until I couldn't feel anything anymore, not even the chair I was sitting in. Usually, it was right about here—sooner, actually—that I'd just leave my body and float off to the holding porch for a little thera-peutic nothingness. But this time, I stayed.

Jonas was talking. I figured it was through my mouth, though I couldn't feel my lips move or my jaws opening

and closing. He stood up, and I went right with him. It was
sort of like being a little fly inside of my skull, watching and
hearing everything, but unable to do anything but observe
the proceedings.

Jonas spoke about the benefits of eating oranges. "Toward
the end of the next century," he pontificated, "a man named
Paula or Pauling or some such will discover that oranges
contain an important vitamin that naturally enables the
human body to fight off and prevent influenza and colds.
Zinc, too. Yes, indeed, take lots of zinc. Of course, a goodly
number will perish from influenza before that, yes indeed,
particularly about thirty-five or forty years hence, while
we're at war with the Hun.

"It reminds me of the time I was panning for bright metal
down along the Gila River, which is in the Arizona Territory.
Must have been 1875 or thereabouts. Solly Culhaine, my old
master-at-arms from the Sioux campaign, came running into
camp one day with a big bagful of lemons. Now, where
he'd got those lemons in the middle of the Arizona desert
was a mystery . . ."

Since I didn't much care about Solly Culhaine and the
lemons, I stopped listening—it was just that easy. I don't
mean that I just ignored him: I mean that I didn't want to
hear anymore, and I was suddenly deaf.

That sort of brought me up short, and I decided maybe
I *did* want to hear again, and *boom!* There was the old
blabbermouth talking, plain as day.

It was quite a revelation, finding out I could turn him
off and on like that. Well, change the level of what I was
experiencing, I should say. Jonas didn't skip a beat. He was
walking us all over the stage and making grand gestures
with my arms and orating to beat the band.

I made the sound go away again so that I could think
over this development. Maybe I was doing what Jonas had
been able to do all along. Maybe I could slide in and out,
too, sometimes feeling everything he felt—physically, I
mean—and sometimes part of it, or not at all. I experi-
mented a bit—not so much as to disturb Jonas's lecture, for
I was grateful beyond words that he'd shown up to give

it—but enough that I was pretty gol-danged impressed with myself.

I was having so much fun slithering around, in fact, that I lost track of time. Before I knew it, Jonas was looking at my watch pin—we'd been there two whole hours, already—and taking questions from the audience.

I settled in to have a listen.

Most of the questions were the same as folks had asked back at the ranch, at the beginning. People wanted to find something they'd lost or catch a husband or set up in business or make a "killing" in stocks. But Jonas didn't answer questions like that at the start, and he didn't answer them now.

He finally got tired of being asked where so-and-so lost her cameo locket, and said, "My dear ladies and gentlemen! This evening, I have spoken about the next great war: a worldwide war which will last for years. I have spoken about the taming of the savage Indian and his transmutation into an upstanding citizen. I've told you of the rise of the colored man to prominence, of women in the White House, of unimagined wonders in medicine and mechanicals and thinking machines, of wondrous inventions, and fractal geometry. Yet the only questions you have for me concern mundane trivia. Is there no one here with a question worth answering?"

I was real impressed. Of course, I'd missed most of his talk, and it sounded as if he'd given them a good one, but it also sounded like they were more concerned with getting their sister married off or making a fast buck than they were about important things.

Then a man, over on the left side and toward the back, stood up and waved an arm at us.

Jonas pointed my finger at him and said, "Yes, my good man. Have you a worthy question for me?"

"I do," the man said, right out. He was youngish and not too well dressed, and his handlebar mustache did nothing to muffle the smug, superior edge to his voice. "Are you familiar with spiritualism?" he asked. "Theosophy? With the works of Madame Helena Petrovna Blavatsky?"

Well, that was a new one. I'd never so much as heard the name, and thought that from the sound of it, she might be a Russian princess or something.

But Jonas said, "Yes, I am."

"Are you a believer, Mr. Newcastle?" asked the man. "It would seem to me that you'd have to believe now." Several people in the crowd laughed, but most of them just looked puzzled.

"I do not hold with table tapping or floating trumpets or rampaging ectoplasm," Jonas said, and I was surprised that he sounded angry. "Some of the spiritualist beliefs, as well as the theosophist doctrine espoused by Madame Blavatsky, seem sound. But the rest?" He shrugged his—my—shoulders. "Although I cannot truly say beyond my own experience of dying, I believe the rest of it to be so much charlatanism and claptrap."

"How can you not believe?" cried the man, hopping up to stand on his chair. He raised an angry fist. "I say it's you who's the charlatan!"

The crowd buzzed for a second, but Jonas held up a hand. "Silence!" he barked, and the audience quieted. "And who are you," he asked the man, "to accuse me of humbuggery? You, Charlie Webster, who never in your life held a job for longer than seven months running and who sends home not a penny to his ailing mother, but who can find a dollar whenever necessary to buy a young lady's attentions down at the wharf? You, Charlie Webster, of 72 Raymond Street, second floor in the back, who rode here tonight on the back stoop of a trolley without paying the fare, and who sneaked into this assemblage through an open window in the prop room? Why should anyone listen to you, who's only come here to incite trouble?"

The man had colored up early in Jonas's tirade, and by the time Jonas finished, Charlie Webster was heading for the nearest exit. A light dusting of applause broke out, then swelled into a storm. Some folks even got to their feet and whistled. When at last it died out, a rotund, middle-aged woman got to her feet.

"Mrs.— I mean, Mr. Newcastle?"

Jonas nodded my head. "Yes, my good woman?"

"Mr. Newcastle, my name is Mary Dodge—that's Mrs. Ralph Dodge," she said in a soft southern drawl, "and I would like to say that I found your talk tonight both edifying and elucidating." There was some more applause, but Jonas quieted it with a gesture. He did have command, I'll say that for him.

"Thank you, dear madam," he said, and gave a half-bow.

"I'd also like to say that I am a member of the Theosophist Society," she said. "I joined up in '75, right at the start. And Mr. Newcastle, I have never witnessed a more convincing exhibition of necromancy in my life."

Jonas cocked our head. "Hardly that, madam. Hardly raising the dead. My body is moldering in the Arizona dust as we speak. One might be more correct to call it a temporary possession of my wife's person. A visitation of flesh, if you would. She is an excellent medium."

While I was busy being taken aback by the compliment, several people said "ah!" at the same time, and Mrs. Dodge said, "Thank you. And for anyone in this room who's got their doubts, I happen to know Charlie Webster personally. He comes to our local meetings, sometimes, and everything Mr. Newcastle said about him is true. Well, I don't know about the trolley or him sneaking in through a window, but the rest of it's on the mark. Nasty little troublemaker, that's Charlie."

There was a bigger "ah!" from the crowd.

A fellow toward the front stood up and said, "Mr. Newcastle, could you speak a bit about what it's like to be . . . what it's like on the other side?"

Jonas paused a moment, like he was thinking. I was interested in this answer, too, since I didn't much see how he could answer it, being caught up in a clerical error and all, and never having got clear over there to see it.

At last, he said, "It's very bright. Next question?"

Well, it went on like that for a good hour more, and then another half hour after Jonas retired and it was just me. I felt like I didn't really give people their money's worth, since I'll be dogged if I knew what they were talking about half the time, but I guess Jonas had done such a good job that they were happy.

Mr. Strider, his poor suit still damp in places, was fair jubilant as we rode back to the hotel. Mrs. Strider and the children were saved, not to mention old Joey, and he said he'd never seen such a marvelous act in all his life, with the possible exception of the Marling triplets, who played three-cornered catch using the suction of their noses while they each juggled six razor-sharp hatchet blades and sang "God, the Father of Us All" in three part harmony.

"It wasn't an act, Mr. Strider," I said as he helped me down from the coach out front of the hotel.

"Call me Lenny," he said happily. "You need some assistance, Mr. Two Trees?"

Sam was already halfway down the deserted block with Nezzy, headed for the nearest alley so that Nezzy could relieve himself there instead of the rug, which he had earlier. At home, we just left the door open for him.

"No," he called back, and then he and Nezzy must have found the alley, because they ducked out of sight.

"Lenny, then," I said. We entered the lobby, and while he waited for our key, I tried again to explain. "It wasn't an act, Lenny. There really is a ghost."

"Yes, I know, Annie," he said after mumbling something to the desk clerk. I had given him leave to call me by my first name directly after the performance, when I was in high spirits.

He took the key in one hand and patted my fingers with the other. "You told me."

I clenched my teeth a couple times. "Lenny, you're not listening."

We started up the stairs, and he said, "Yes, I am. The ghost is real. He speaks through you. Jonas Newcastle knows the future because he goes to the white room and reads it or eavesdrops or something, and then he tells it through your mouth." We came to the door, and he opened it and ushered me inside ahead of him. "When he's not mad at you, that is. Correct?"

"Correct." I sat down in one of the sitting room chairs

with a thump. It was no use. Lenny Strider had decided I was a card-carrying loon, adrift on the lake of raging—if harmless—insanity. But so long as I brought in the audiences and gave them what they wanted, he was willing to row my boat.

He sat down across from me, and pulled off his gloves, then reached into his pocket and brought out a little leather-bound notebook. "Tomorrow, you have fittings at eleven o'clock. I can tell you right now that the seamstresses will be busy. The dresses they made are much too large." He looked up. "Mr. Barnum was under the impression that you were a taller woman."

He turned back to his notebook. "We have one more show here in Baltimore tomorrow night, and then we leave for Philadelphia. You have three days off, then two performances, then it's on to New York."

He looked up again, an almost religious look coming over his features. "Mr. Barnum will meet us in New York. You'll like Mr. Barnum."

I perked up a tad. I said, "Earlier tonight, you said he was an ogre."

"I did not!" he replied, suddenly sanctimonious. "I would never say such a horrible thing about a gentleman like Mr. P. T. Barnum!"

"Fine," I said. It was clear to me that Lenny Strider had a curious grasp of things. I let him be.

He then read me a long list of show dates that I forgot just as quick as he said them out, because I had something else on my mind. "Lenny?" I said, when he paused in between cities. "Where's everybody else?"

He put down the notebook. "Beg pardon?"

"Everybody else," I said. "I thought I was joining up with a circus. Mr. Barnum's circus."

"Heavens, no!" he said, and then he began to laugh.

I didn't see what was so gol-darned funny about the question, and I said so.

"Oh dear, Annie," he said, wiping his eyes. "No, no! You are under contract to do exhibitions, which is a far better thing than playing the circus. Oh my goodness, *far* better!"

I had read that "exhibitions" thing on the contract, but I'd thought it meant giving lectures in the sideshow and such. Maybe a special booth. I said, "Well, what are exhibitions?"

"Just what you did tonight," he replied. "I suppose you're too young to remember Jenny Lind, the Swedish Nightingale?"

"I've heard of her," I said. She was pretty famous.

"Well, Mr. Barnum did for her just exactly what he's doing for you. Exhibitions. And if you're going to put on a show anything like the one I saw tonight, you're going to be very, very rich."

There was a knock at the door, which I thought was strange. Why would Sam knock? But Lenny got up and answered it, and ushered in Carl, our German waiter. He was pushing a tray on wheels, and when he got to the middle of the room, whisked off the white cloth that covered it.

"A late supper, madam," Carl said, all clipped and dignified. "As you ordered."

I shook my head. "I didn't order—"

"I did," broke in Lenny, digging in his pocket for a tip. He handed some coins to Carl, said, "That will be all," and then to me, said, "Well? What do you think?"

I stared at the tray, crowded with plates of chopped eggs and chopped onions and little fancy-cut pieces of toast and so on, and at the big bottle of champagne in its cooler. I bent over to get a closer view, then sniffed at one of the plates.

"What's that?" I asked, pointing to some stuff that looked like piles of black and amber jelly, but smelled more salty.

"Caviar!" said Sam, who must have just come in the door. He was smiling ear to ear. He bent to take off Nezzy's leash, saying, "Annie, if this is the way Mr. Barnum treats his employees, I don't believe you should ever leave him."

Well, the caviar was a letdown. Even with Sam bragging it up while he piled it on the bread pieces—toast points, he called them—with chopped eggs or chopped onion or sour cream or all three, and swallowed it down with big, happy smacking sounds, I couldn't bring myself to try it.

He shouldn't have told me it was pickled fish eggs, I guess.

Sam shoveled it in that night, and the next night, and the next, because we were such a hit that we got held over for a third performance. Jonas was real cooperative. I suppose he had finally found the ideal lectern for his speechifying.

The ideal audience, too. Folks that paid two dollars and fifty cents a seat were a lot different than most folks who paid a dime at Boyd's.

Oh, they heckled him some, but he told me he didn't mind. It was to be expected, he said. Of course, it helped that he had access to such an arsenal of handy put-downs. The smart boys who got up to say something disparaging had their whole shoddy history related just like that other sorry case, Charlie Webster.

And Jonas? Jonas minded his p's and q's and showed up every night. Otherwise, he mostly kept to himself. This was because he'd been hiding and listening for a good part of that time since we left Arizona, the time when he was in me but wouldn't talk. He'd listened to my thoughts and words, off and on, all along the train ride to Baltimore, and he'd come to a decision.

You can have him, Annie, he'd said out of nowhere, the second afternoon in Baltimore. *You can have your Johnny Devlin, and see if I care.*

I had just started knitting a sweater for Johnny, as I recall, and Jonas startled me so that I missed a stitch.

"You don't mind?" I said. "After all that mess in Arizona, that getting mad and running off and hiding in the library and leaving me high and dry, now you're saying you don't care?"

I can change my mind can't I? he said, all in a huff. *At the time of my death, this was still a free country. Besides,* he added, a bit softer, *I've been thinking. Had a lot of time to think.*

I didn't say anything.

It wasn't you I was in love with, Annie, he said. *Not that you aren't just lovely. A beautiful ripe peach, just waiting for me to—*

"Get to the point," I said, cutting him off. He was getting that Saturday-and-Wednesday-night tone in his voice again.

So hard, he muttered. *You're so hard. Not like my darling Frieda at all.*

I threw my knitting on the floor so sudden it scared Nezzy. "So you finally admit it!" I cried, jumping up as the cat ran into the bedroom. "It *was* her you wanted the whole time! Why, you nasty old geezer!"

I don't think we have to resort to name-calling, Annie, he said, sounding like a schoolmaster. *And I already admitted it. Months ago!*

"Don't take that tone with me," I shouted, "and don't patronize me!" And then I got myself a bit more under control, and added, "I knew I was right. Grandma Frieda, all along. But why in creation did you do it?"

Fall in love?

I shook my head. "No. Why'd you play up to Mama the way you did, and for all those years? Why'd you write her all those letters and have her send pictures of me. Why couldn't you just leave it alone?"

There was a pause, during which I sat down again, and finally, in a small, small voice, he said, *I was lonely, all right? I missed my Frieda. It wasn't my fault she was already married to your grandfather when I first laid eyes on her, you know. And I don't for a second believe any of that nonsense you made up about her having a temper, Annie. My little Frieda wouldn't have raised her voice for anything. I tell you, from the first moment I saw her . . .* His voice, or at least the one I was hearing in my head, trailed off.

"But why'd you write Mama?" I insisted. "She never loved Papa as much as you, she never loved *anybody* as much! She saved every single one of your letters, did you know that? And she never saved any of Papa's, not even a scrap! Didn't you know you were breaking her heart? Didn't you realize what it'd do to the rest of us, to have her pining her whole life for a hero in Arizona that she couldn't have?"

Oh! he said. *Oh, Annie, I didn't realize! It's just that Velda was so . . . loud. So angry all the time. And I never could*

*have lived so near your Grandmother, bless her. Oh, I loved
her so! I still love her.*

"I figured that part out already," I said impatiently. "But
what about the letters and the pictures? Why couldn't you
just leave me alone?"

You were so like her, Annie, he said, his voice growing
thoughtful, even tender. *Even when you were a child, I
could see her in you. Your eyes, your hair, the tilt of your
nose, that crooked little smile . . .*

"My smile is not crooked!" I grumbled.

Yes, it is, just a little, he insisted gently. *I had your mother
send pictures because . . . well, because I could. Because I
knew she'd do whatever I asked. The same way she promised
me she'd keep you pure and send you to me when you were
old enough. Of course, she didn't do so well with that one.*
Umbrage had crept into his tone, and I could just see him
squaring his shoulders. *Tommy Boone, indeed!* he huffed.

"What's done is done, Jonas," I said, going back to my
needlework again. I almost told him that Aisha said
Grandma Frieda was there, on the other side, which I took
to be heaven. But since I didn't know which way Jonas
would go, once he got disentangled from all that bookkeeping nonsense, I kept my mouth shut about it. No use getting
his hopes up.

"I forgive you, I suppose," I said. "But it was a mean and
selfish thing, what you did to Mama. What you did to all of
us." My needles went *click-click-click,* taking the brunt of
my anger. "If Grandma Frieda had known what you were
up to all those years, she would've set after you with a
rolling pin."

Oh, no, he said. *Not my Frieda. Not my little plum tart.
But can we get back to the matter at hand?*

I looped another stitch. "Since I'm about to lose my lunch,
what with you talking about my sainted grandmother like
that, I'd say the sooner the quicker."

Good, he replied. *As I was saying, you can have your
Johnny Devlin. If you ever cross paths with him again, that
is. Although God only understands the attraction. Just a
gold-dipped ruffian, that's what he is.*

"You have your opinion," I said, "and I have mine." And then I looked up, all of a sudden, the needles quiet in my lap. "Jonas, you can see things about folks. I know you can. I was there last night, remember? I want you to tell me for true if I'm going to wed him."

How should I know? he said, a little testy. *I don't even know how I knew those things about that man, that Charlie Whatshisname.*

"Charlie Webster," I said.

Whatever. And before you have one of those fits, Annie, I'm being totally honest with you. I have not the slightest idea where that information came from. I just opened up my mouth—your mouth, I mean—and there it was.

I sighed. "Honest Injun?"

Cross my heart, he said.

"You don't have a heart, Jonas. Not anymore."

Don't be smart, Annie, he grumbled. *It's not attractive.*

Right about then, Sam came in with Lenny Strider who was still being overly nice to him on account of that "red Indian chef" thing, and Jonas retired to a corner of my mind. But that business about his knowing the details of those hecklers' lives—without knowing he knew—chafed on me.

A couple of nights later, while we were on the train to Philadelphia, when it was late and the car was nearly deserted, I asked Jonas why, if he could somehow tap into the dirt on a fellow without hardly trying, he couldn't answer people's questions about missing ear-bobs and such.

It's a waste of time, Annie, he said. *A pure and simple waste. Folks should be concentrating on the big issues. The science of chaos, for instance, or cold fusion. Not on paltry things.*

"Well, it wouldn't hurt you to answer just the important ones," I said, staring out the window. Whenever Jonas started talking about all that scientific nonsense, I just got lost. I added, "I mean, just the questions folks seem to think are important. You might not care whether somebody's sister is going to move to Texas or Maine, but it's a problem of fair staggering proportions to the fellow who asks it."

Pish! he said. *Start answering questions like that, and that's all they'll ask. I know people. Is that a town yonder?*

Lights were glowing softly on the other side of a hill we were passing, outlining its black shape with a faint halo. "Either that," I said, "or a forest fire."

Very funny, he said, dryly.

I said, "Then quit trying to change the subject. How do you know things if you don't know you know them? What I mean to say is, how do you know you can't tell somebody where she lost Aunt Martha's filigree bracelet if you don't try?"

You're hopeless, he groaned. *I just can't, that's all. I've told you already, I don't know why. All right?*

I knew not to push the point. I said, "All right, Jonas. Good night."

He said, *And you can stop trying to screen those thoughts you keep having about Devlin. It doesn't do any good, you know. Besides, I already said I'd be big about it.*

I chuckled under my breath. I hadn't been trying to hide my thoughts about Johnny from Jonas. If anything, I'd been trying not to think about him too much. If I let myself, it'd be Johnny Devlin day and night, and I'd have no room for anything else.

But I said, "Thank you, Jonas. I appreciate it."

All right then, he said. *Good night, Annie.*

"Good night, you old devil," I said, not unkindly, as I felt him recede into some musty, disused corner of my brain. I went back to my knitting.

"Talking to yourself?"

I looked up to see Lenny Strider smiling down at me. He'd be accompanying us for the whole tour, since Mr. Barnum had wired to change his title from front man to talent liaison. He slid into the seat opposite me.

"No, just talking to Jonas," I replied, concentrating on my knitting. It was a dark green wool, which I planned to mix in with a softer color on the front of the torso. I thought it would be past glamorous with Johnny's sea-colored eyes, and I almost had one sleeve done.

"Oh, yes," he said, winking. "Jonas. Of course."

I sighed and put down my needles. "How's Sam?" I asked, mostly to change the subject. I already knew how he was: hanging his head over observation deck's railing, throwing up that last batch of fish eggs and chopped onion. He'd been sick for almost the whole trip out from Arizona.

"Fine, I guess," said Lenny. "He emptied his stomach out, I guess, because he went up to the kitchen car."

That sounded a bit odd to me, but I decided to let it rest. I said, "Lenny, on that list you have, the one with all our engagements? What's the farthest west we get?"

"Denver," he said, without troubling to look at his notebook. "I tried to convince Mr. Barnum to include San Francisco, but . . . well, I might yet convince him."

"When do we go to Denver?"

"Next month," he replied. "The middle part of April, I believe." A hand went to his breast pocket. "I can give you the exact dates if you wish."

I stopped him with a shake of my head. "Don't trouble yourself. I was just curious. But could I have a copy of that schedule for my own?"

"Certainly, Annie, certainly," he said. One eyebrow went up. "I hope you don't mind my saying it, but I'm surprised. You didn't seem very interested in your itinerary the other evening."

I said, "Things change," and got busy with my needles again.

The whole time we were in Philadelphia, I kept picturing that line that said, *Denver—12–14 April* on the schedule Lenny had copied for me. Colorado was fairly close to Arizona Territory, I told myself when Lenny took us to see the Liberty Bell and the place where the Declaration of Independence was signed. If Johnny had come to see me in Utah, mightn't he stretch it to Denver? After all, he probably wasn't wanted up in Colorado. It'd be like a vacation for him!

By the time we'd had the tour of Philadelphia and seen all the historic landmarks, I had myself convinced that Johnny really would come for me in Denver. He'd walk right into the auditorium, big as life, and despite all the people in the audience, he'd doff his hat and bow from the waist, and say, "Begone from this place, Jonas Newcastle, for I have ridden through hard country to make Annie my wife."

Well, all right. I suppose I had it a touch theatrical—when it came down to it, I couldn't imagine a man like Johnny Devlin saying a word like *begone*—but that was the way I'd made it up in my mind.

By Denver, we'd have plenty of money to keep the sisters fixed up for the rest of their lives, and to send Sam to Paris or Timbuktu or Rome, wherever they had the best cooking schools in the world. And enough that there might be some left over for me.

Kind of a dowry, you might say.

So that is why, by the time I gave my first show in Philadelphia, I did so with a new respect for Jonas Newcastle. For the first time, I felt easy about thinking my own thoughts, and this relieved me more than I had conceived that it would.

When we finished up in Philadelphia—which is some Greek words smashed together, Sam told me, to mean the "City of Brotherly Love"—after playing to standing-room-only crowds (and another held-over show) and headed for New York City, I was excited and expectant.

Jonas was getting housebroke, so to speak, I was going to meet Mr. Barnum, and Denver—and Johnny Devlin—was in my future.

17

Our first day in New York we had no commitments other than a chat with the gentlemen of the press, which was scheduled for the middle of the afternoon. So we set out to see the sights. Of course, Sam had his heart set on seeing the Stock Exchange first thing, but I let him go by himself. I went to the theater.

We were booked into the Burbridge Exhibition Hall, and Lenny said that we were sold out—three thousand seats worth—for the whole of the three days we were to play there. For my part, I didn't see as how I—or Jonas, I mean—could make myself heard with a crowd that big.

"No fear," said Lenny as our hack stopped in front of it. "Acoustics, you know. You project just fine."

My brows went up. "I what?"

Lenny laughed and helped me down to the sidewalk. He said, "You're loud enough, I mean."

New York was sure a busy and supernatural place. The streets had been congested on the way from our hotel, and the sidewalks were crammed with all sorts of strange and curious people. I had never before seen a man in a green leprechaun outfit and a sign on his back saying, "O'Brien's Balm is Best," or an elegant couple bickering in what I took to be Russian, or a grown woman with a feathered hat three feet high and the teensiest, fluffiest dog I'd ever seen under her arm, and all of them walking down the street in the broad daylight.

Of course, I probably looked pretty strange myself, seeing as how I'd brought Nezzy.

To the accompaniment of blaring street noise and a couple of horses that reared in their harness and whinnied at the sight of Nebuchadnezzar, Lenny steered me around a couple of Irishmen sparring for a fight—and the Irish policeman leaned up against the building and watching nonchalantly—and led me inside the hall.

The theater was dark and cool, and smelled like must and mildew and something sugary. A man in a uniform draped in braid walked over. For a minute I thought he was going to throw us out, the way he eyed Nezzy. But he said, "May I help you?" real polite. Keeping an eye on the cat, of course.

"Yes," said Lenny. "I am Leonard Strider, in the employ of Mr. P. T. Barnum. May I introduce the prophet, Annie Newcastle?"

Well, right off, the man in the braid knew who I was. He bowed, which sort of embarrassed me, and said, "A pleasure, ma'am. I'm George, the Burbridge's head doorman. And this," he said, pointing to Nezzy, "is the famous Nebuchadnezzar, I take it?"

I hadn't realized that Nezzy was famous, too, but I said, "Yes, it is. Call him Nezzy, for short."

"Nezzy, then," said George. "Would you like to see your dressing room?" And then he looked over at Lenny and whispered to him, "Mr. Barnum's here, Mr. Strider." He pointed over his shoulder. "In the manager's office."

"In person?" said Lenny. He looked even more impressed than I felt. "Really? I wasn't expecting him until tomorrow!" He looked at me and grinned. "Say, this is splendid! Wait'll I tell Mrs. Strider! Why, he must have heard how well we're—I mean, how well *you're* doing!"

He rubbed his hands together in anticipation. "George, could you tell him we're here? And while we're waiting, I'll show Mrs. Newcastle around the theater."

George said he'd be happy to and went on his way, and

Lenny took me and Nezzy into the theater, the way you'd go in if you were going to see the show.

There were a sea of seats lit by gas jets along the walls, and overhead, a balcony. Lenny said there was a second balcony above it. We walked down toward the stage, peered into the empty orchestra pit, then over to the side and up the stage steps.

At Lenny's urging, I went out on the stage, out in the center of it, in front of all those red velvet drapes. There must have been a million yards of velvet in those things. Gas jets at the ready, all the footlights stood like little brass sentries, studding the rim of the polished maple floorboards. Overhead, frescoed cherubs ringed with gilt danced and flitted.

And when at last I looked out over the area where the audience would be sitting, at that first ocean of seats and the two tiers above it, my legs gave out. I mean, I just went *plop*—sat down right in the middle of the stage on my fanny, all unceremonious, and for a moment, I didn't care.

"Criminy," I whispered.

Lenny Strider, who'd been preoccupied with something in the corner, turned toward me. "Did you say something, Annie?" he began, then stopped himself and stared at me. He probably decided that sitting right down on the floor was something I did all the time—something connected to my delusions of Jonas—because he said, "I'm going to go see what's keeping Mr. Barnum. This is quite an honor, you know, Annie, quite an honor!" and didn't even comment on my position.

While he practically skipped his way up the center aisle, I tucked my legs and sat there, Indian style. I couldn't get up quite yet. The reality of it had set in too hard and too fast.

Three thousand people. Twice as many as I'd played to in Baltimore.

"Criminy," I repeated. "Criminy sakes."

"Yes, it is quite a number," said a voice. Not Jonas's. Nezzy's head came up and his ears perked.

"Aisha!" I looked all around, but I didn't see anything, not even the tiniest glimmer of gold dust.

"You will not see me, dear Annie," she said. "I am too far."

"What do you mean, 'too far'?" I asked. "I can hear you fine."

"I am too far down the path, little one," she replied. "But what of you, and what of Jonas? He is cooperating, is he not?"

I nodded, though there was no one there to see it. "Just fine. Jonas is being real accommodating. I mean, he talks when he ought, and gives the folks a good show for their money. And he's leaving me alone, if you know what I mean."

"Excellent." It sounded like she breathed the word more than said it. Nezzy cocked his head, twisting it back and forth. His keen eyes searched the area, but he couldn't seem to find anything.

"Take advantage while you can, little one," she said, her voice growing fainter with every word. "Soon everything will be put right." She said something else, I think it was "take care of Nebuchadnezzar" or maybe "don't swear at Nebuchadnezzar," although the first was a lot more likely. And then she was gone.

Nezzy stretched out on the stage, rolled over on his back and began to purr, but to be frank, I was a little mad. I didn't know why she had bothered to show up at all if that was all she had to say.

But then I looked at Nezzy's contented, slit-eyed expression and listened to those big, rumbling purrs, and I knew why she'd come one last time. Not to see me, so much, but to say good-bye to Nezzy.

I tell you, I got kind of choked up.

I hadn't too long to ponder it, though, because right about then a set of doors opened up in the back, and two figures came in, silhouetted by the bright light at their backs. The more slender one, I recognized as Lenny. The blockier figure had to be himself, Mr. P.T. Barnum.

I got to my feet and dusted my skirts as the doors closed behind them and they began to make their way toward me. Mr. Barnum looked a pleasant enough man when he got close enough that I could see him clear—at least, he was grinning awfully wide. He had gray hair, and sparkly eyes behind little gold-rimmed glasses, and a bit of a tummy. I don't know what I had expected, but he seemed older than I'd pictured him. In fact, I didn't put him too much younger than Jonas.

He sure had more get up and go, though.

"Mrs. Newcastle," he said, pumping my hand after Lenny had made the introductions, "I can't tell you what a pleasure it is to finally meet you! Just a delight!"

"Likewise," I said.

"Lenny tells me you packed them in like sardines in Baltimore and Philadelphia," he said, finally letting go of my hand, but still wearing that big smile.

"Every seat in the place was full, if that's what you mean," I replied. "This sure is a giant theater. You really expect to fill it up for three nights running?"

Barnum laughed. It was a big, loud boom of a laugh that must have reached all the way to the lobby, and I saw Nezzy's whiskers twitching from the corner of my eye. Mr. Barnum paid no mind, though. "Ah, my dear Mrs. Newcastle!" he said. "I expect to fill it for five nights running!"

"Call me Annie," I said. "But we're only booked for three nights."

He waved his hand. "Details, details. Five nights, you mark my word. Say, Strider, there's nothing booked right after us, is there?"

"Sir?" Lenny replied, so tense he was practically standing on his tiptoes. "No, sir, no conflict."

"You see, Annie?" Barnum said with a grin. His hands held his generous stomach. "Five nights. Now, where's that Indian you travel with?"

"His name is Sam Two Trees," I replied, a little annoyed at the "that Indian" comment. "And he's down at the Stock Exchange."

If I'd let any of my mad creep into my voice, Barnum didn't seem to notice. Either that, or he was too polite to let on. He said, "Good, good! The Stock Exchange, then. A man after my own heart! And I trust this is Nebuchadnezzar?"

I calmed right down. I guess so many people had made wisecracks about Sam since we got back east that I was overly defensive.

He was pointing at Nezzy, and I said, "Yes sir. You can pet him if you want. He's real tame."

Barnum looked at the white tip of Nezzy's tail, going *thump-thump-thump* on the polished boards, and said, "Uh, perhaps later, Annie, perhaps later. Right now," he said, turning back toward Lenny and me, the smile fair blooming on his face, "we have things to talk about. Lenny, how much of Gotham has she seen?"

"I haven't seen any of Gotham," I said, before Lenny could speak. "Is that another part of New York, like Brooklyn?"

Barnum broke out in that big laugh again. "Come children! I'll show you the city, and then it's back to the hotel to meet with the gentlemen of the press!"

Well, we did the town from the inside of a coach, with Nezzy hanging out the window. Mr. Barnum said I had a tight schedule and couldn't take the time to stop, but perhaps I could the next day. We clopped past the *New York Tribune* "Founded by that great American visionary, Horace Greeley," said Mr. Barnum, and confided, "A personal friend"), and the Young Men's Christian Association ("A wonderful organization," proclaimed Mr. Barnum. "Builds character!"), and the place they'd started building the Brooklyn Bridge.

While we rode, I guess Mr. Barnum got to sort of liking Nezzy, who picked his lap to lean across. It wasn't too awful long before Barnum was scratching that cat behind the ears, calling him "kitty-cat," and remarking on how he smelled like lavender.

I guess the scent of that hotel soap clings to fur like nobody's business.

Anyway, we also went past the house a fellow named Vanderbilt was putting up on Fifth Avenue, although the word *house* seemed too paltry for its description—it looked more like an elegant hotel. Mr. Barnum said Mr. Vanderbilt had sunk three million whole dollars into it, and he was still richer than Croesus.

We went through the theater district—which was easy,

seeing as how we started out on the edge of it—and dallied round one side of the famous New York Central Park. I was impressed with how big it was. I'd always thought it would be more like a big town square—you know, something you could throw a ball across, with folks cantering their park horses and trotting their fancy buggies around the outside.

But this was hundreds of acres and all planted wild-looking, but with benches. There were paths for people to ride and walk, Mr. Barnum said, but you couldn't see them from where we were on account of all the trees and bushes.

Lastly, he took us for a late lunch at a little restaurant he knew, called Antoine's. He said we had just time for a bite before we had to go back to the hotel.

The maître d' made a big fuss over Mr. Barnum and gave us a special table, and the chef himself came out and shook hands with him.

"Does this happen all the time?" I whispered to Lenny.

"Without fail," he whispered back. "He's a great man." Pride and awe were in his voice, like he was soaking up as much as possible of Mr. Barnum's light while he could.

Mr. Barnum introduced me to every person that so much as said hello, and gave them complimentary passes to my show. When I whispered in his ear that there couldn't be any seats left, on account of it was sold-out, he said to me, "Annie, there's no such thing as sold-out. Why, it's not even starting to get full until the floor's packed solid and they're hanging from the rafters!"

We ate our lunch, although for French cooking I decided I liked Sam's better, and then we went back to the hotel.

Now, I've spoken about our hotel in Baltimore, and how it was fancier than fancy, but I have to tell, this one was even more grand. Our rooms were enormous and really fine, and the lobby was all filled up with ferns and flowers and plants and sofas and chairs, and everything but the plants and the leather, it seemed, was mahogany or gilt or glass or polished brass. Big marble pillars rose up here and there—I expect they needed them to hold the ceiling up, since the lobby was fair big enough to turn a locomotive around in. I was as impressed as all get-out.

I was still impressed when we walked in with Mr. Barnum.

Right there in the lobby was a knot of men who looked like they didn't quite belong there: men with pencils stuck behind their ears, men carrying notebooks and cameras. After the first one saw us, it seemed like the whole crowd of them got up and swarmed around those pink marble pillars—and over us—like bees.

I was scared at first. I mean, for all I knew they were from the Theosophist Society and had come to bludgeon me on account of Mr. Newcastle's remarks, which he had made several of at every performance.

But Mr. Barnum tucked me under his arm and held up a hand, and smiling, said, "Gentlemen! Gentlemen! A little room, if you please!"

They did back off some, and set up their cameras on tripods and just about blinded us with the flashes. Afterward, the questions flew fast and furious. How old was I? When did Mr. Newcastle come to me? What times were the shows? Did I favor Madame Janette's Face Cleanser? Could I "do" Jonas now?

Mr. Barnum put the kibosh on that right away, saying they had to come to the performance. But then they started asking him questions about the circus, and the new partnership with James Bailey. They asked about Iranistan ("His house in Bridgeport, Connecticut," confided Lenny) and books and politics, and somebody asked if I was as great a star as Jenny Lind.

"Apples and oranges, gentlemen!" he said. "Why, how could one compare the wonders of an evening sky with a soft, sunny day in June?"

That seemed to appease them, although I didn't know whether I was supposed to be the June day or the Big Dipper. And then the questions came back at me.

Had I ever fallen on my head? What kind of cat was Nezzy, and how did you spell *Nebuchadnezzar?* Was anyone else in my family a medium or did they lift tables or float trumpets? What size shoe did I wear?

I did my best to answer politely, although a lot of the questions were silly and didn't have squat to do with Jonas.

But then a fellow in the back with a big, black mustache called, "Hey Annie, where's your tame Indian?"

Just like that, I was flooded with mad. Lenny figured it out quick—maybe he saw my hands balling into fists, maybe he saw my nostrils flare. Whatever he'd seen, he grabbed me from behind, by both shoulders, and said, "Mrs. Newcastle is accompanied by her friend and her late husband's protégée, Mr. Samuel Two Trees. Mr. Two Trees, who is one half Navajo Indian and one half British stock, is a scholar and a gentleman. Mrs. Newcastle would appreciate it if you would refrain from calling him a 'tame Indian.' "

Well, I couldn't believe that speech had come out of little old Lenny! I mumbled, "Thank you," at the same time the man who'd asked the question turned red and apologized.

A bit of a pall had fallen over the crowd, but Mr. Barnum stopped it from getting ugly. "Well, boys," he said, sweeping out an arm, "there you have her, the astounding Prophet Annie. Come to the show tonight and take her in, and if you don't believe she's the eighth wonder of the world, I'll eat Nebuchadnezzar!"

Everybody laughed except Nezzy, and Barnum continued, "Mrs. Newcastle will be embarking on a tour of the east and the middle west," he announced, handing out passes. "And when she returns to New York, there'll be a parade, mark my words!"

Somebody asked what his next big act was going to be, and he put a finger against his nose. "That would be telling!" he said with a grin. But when they pressed him, he replied, "All I have to say to you, gentlemen, is one word: *Jumbo!* Now boys, Mrs. Newcastle is tired. Let's let her retire, shall we, and we'll see you at tonight's show!"

Well, Mr. Barnum had predicted we'd be held over for two extra nights and he was right, though he wasn't there to see it. The day after my first performance, he said he had to see a man about an elephant, and got on a boat headed for England.

The newspapers were kind to us, even if they were a little strange. One of them ran my story under the headline,

"SPOOK OR SHAM," and another had the title "GHOST GIRL GETS GOTHAM'S GOAT." I thought those were a little silly—I hadn't even seen a goat in months—but there you are.

I had expected trouble from the religious crowd. I got it, to some extent—picketers outside and inside, and folks holding up signs with Bible verses written on them, or "Repent!" But Jonas handled it just fine, slicker than butter down a hot ear of corn, you might say.

He had something on everybody. He told me that every person has something secret—maybe it doesn't seem bad or perverse to other folks, but it's something he's real embarrassed about, and has never told. So when Jonas started talking about people, saying things he couldn't know, they got plumb nervous—even the Bible thumpers—because they thought any second he was going to hit on their big secret. They just turned tail and ran.

I wouldn't really tell anyone's secrets, Annie, he said one night when I asked him about it. I think we were in Dayton, Ohio, by then. *In the first place, that's none of anyone's business. In the second place, they might retaliate against you. And in the third place, well, I don't know what they are. The secrets, that is. Wherever that information comes from, what I say is all there is.*

"You big fake," I said, shaking my head.

He chuckled. *It works, doesn't it?*

I had to admit that it did. Still, I suppose those folks were the most convinced of Jonas's veracity—and the least likely to admit it.

The cities pretty much blurred together. Terre Haute, Champaign, Lexington, or St. Louis, they all looked like the inside of the same smoky theater, the same gilt-edged hotel.

There were exceptions, of course. Chicago stood out. First, because somebody walked a pinto pony right into the lobby of our hotel, and second, because a bunch of spiritualists tried to hold a séance and call up the departed in the middle of Jonas's speech. I guess they didn't feel Jonas was departed enough for them, and were going to see that their spooks put him in his place.

Sam got up and walked right out into the audience. He put his fist smack through their Ouija board, and those trumpet floaters scattered like flies off a screen porch. I guess Sam must have been thinking about Lord Darryl Duppa at the time, because he had a big grin on his face when he came back and sat down.

Washington stood out, too—Washington, DC, I mean—because I got to meet the newly inaugurated President of the whole U-S-of-A, James A. Garfield himself. It was a private audience at the White House arranged by Mr. Barnum, I guess, because there were lots of photographers. He didn't say much to me—just asked how was I and did I like their fair city—but I was sure impressed.

And at least he didn't ask me if Jonas could locate his dead Aunt Betty's silver nutmeg scraper.

As the days went by, we zigzagged our way north, then south, always a little farther west than the previous zig or zag. When we played Des Moines, I half-expected some Sycamore folks would come up. After all, it was only about seventy-five miles, and they could have taken the train, easy. But not a soul in that audience did I recognize, though I looked and looked for Uncle Tad's kids, Emmy and Mike. I cried and cried. Funny that it bothered me as much as it did, but there you are.

I knew then that Iowa wasn't the place for me, no matter how nice it was to see her just coming into spring. My place was somewhere else. Maybe Arizona, maybe someplace I hadn't been yet.

In Springfield, Missouri, we finally crossed paths with the Barnum (now Barnum & Bailey) circus, and out of the blue, one Mr. Montana DeFrois showed up at our hotel to take us to see it. Mr. Barnum had sent him special, on account of he'd remembered all the questions I'd asked about it while we were riding around New York that day. Mostly about the trains and such. I do love a train.

Mr. Montana DeFrois took me and Sam and Lenny and Nebuchadnezzar out to the place where they were set up, and I tell you, it was a sight!

Elephants, lions, tigers, and monkeys chattered and roared

and trumpeted from everywhere, and folks dressed all in spangles moved about on horseback or afoot with a sense of purpose. Folks in costume tumbled or somersaulted past us, crying, "Hup hup hup!" and not one soul even blinked at Nezzy on his leash!

The smells reminded me of Boyd's, only better. I know it's strange to say that you like the smell of manure mixed with peanuts roasting mixed with popping corn and the smell of sugary things and sawdust, but I sure did. I hadn't realized how much I missed being with Boyd's.

They were getting ready for the performance and, as a man with three blue merle cowdogs—one carrying a basket in his mouth, and all three up on their hind legs—went past us, Mr. Montana DeFrois asked would we like to sit in and see it. Right at the same time Sam and Lenny said, "Yes!" I said, "No."

Everybody looked at me, and I said, "Well, I'd rather see the train. I can always go to another circus, but when else will I get to go back where the public isn't welcome?"

Montana DeFrois, who was all decked out in a ten-gallon hat and white leather chaps and a fringed white jacket that I just knew Johnny Devlin wouldn't be caught dead in, said, "Your wish is Mr. Barnum's command, little lady!"

He sent Sam and Lenny off toward the big top with another fellow, and then the two of us and Nezzy set off walking. Pretty soon we were at the side yard and I was staring up at the circus train.

Oh, it was painted wonderful from end to end! There were paintings of fantastic tigers jumping through flaming hoops, and tightrope walkers, and ladies dancing the ballet on the backs of galloping horses, big as life. Lions roared through palm jungles on one car. Zebras and giraffes thundered across the African veldt on the next.

Montana DeFrois boosted me up into one of the horse cars, and showed me how the stall doors swung to the side, to allow them to be loaded and unloaded. Each stall had a name painted or chalked on it: Arrow and Sunny, Taffy and Rosemary, Silky, Dash, Augie, and Jumper. On and on they went, so many names that you were surprised anybody could keep them straight.

But Montana said, "There's four teams a'horses to the car, and several more cars just like this one. The circus is just one big family, Annie, and our horses is part of it. Why, I wouldn't go nowhere without my Rainmaker!" He pointed out the sliding doors into the fading light, and down the hill to the circus's remuda, which was abuzz with activity. "There, the big paint horse. Black an' white. See him?"

I picked him out right away, although the corral was jammed with horses and people riding them off or saddling them or putting them in harness. "He's handsome," I said.

"You bet your backside," said Montana, offhanded but proud, and helped me down from the car.

He showed me up and down the line: the office, the private cars where the show's stars bunked, the regular berth cars where everybody else stayed, the cat cars, and the elephant cars. The giraffe cars had special hatches in the roofs so the giraffes could stick their long necks out and catch the breeze.

"What do you do if you come to a tunnel?" I asked.

"Shut the hatches," he said, like I was feeble.

There were cars that carried snakes and lizards and other small animals, all in baskets or boxes or cages that could be toted by hand. There were cars that carried zebras and camels and ostriches and llamas, and rhino and hippo cars. The monkey cars stank even though they were spotless, and I remarked on it.

"It's hard to keep the stench off a monkey," said Montana thoughtfully, and moved on down the line.

We saw so many animal cars that I lost count. And that wasn't all. There was a car that carried nothing but food for the animals, another that carried food for the people. There was a poster car (for the transport of circus posters and the cooking up of the paste the men stuck them up with), and cars that carried canvas or poles or rope, or harnesses, both fancy and workaday, for the horses and elephants and oxen and water buffalo.

There was even a car that carried nothing but costumes. A

steady stream of folks ran to and from it, bringing bright little scraps of costume to be fixed or altered or shored up, or holding their shoulder straps in one hand or something. When we peeked in, three harried seamstresses were busy at work.

"Virginia!" said one plump woman, who was digging frantically through a pile of little pouches and sacks while the sweat dripped off her nose. "Where in the hell have you put my dark green sequins with those little gold jiggers round the edges?"

"Bugger off, Pet!" replied Virginia, who looked to be the next thing to be buried in somebody's tutu. And then Virginia said that Pet could take her sequins and stuff them where the sun didn't shine, and Montana hurried me along before the situation escalated.

And then there were the flat cars. They toted all the fancy, curlicued, and gilded wagons they used in parades and for putting on the show itself. Of course, all the wagons were in use down by the big top right then. I could imagine what it would look like when they were all loaded up, though, and I could imagine what it would be like to be a little kid, standing in a field, and seeing that big circus train coming down the tracks on a spring afternoon, all golden and shining and painted up, and bringing magic with it. And all of a sudden I wanted that kid to be mine, mine and Johnny Devlin's.

Oh, please! said Jonas, real disgusted. I guess he must have been lurking around on the tour. *Any more of this nonsense and I'll be sick.*

Stop sneaking up on people, I thought right back at him. I didn't speak because I thought it might disturb Montana, who was waxing on about the pony carts. *A girl can have thoughts, you know. Besides, we made an agreement.*

Yes, he said, *bring that up. I know we made a pact, but do you have to think about him* all *the time? A man has limits, you know.*

"You wouldn't know I'm thinking about him at all if you'd retire to your corner like a good ghost," I said right out loud, and Montana stopped talking and looked at me.

"Ma'am?" he said, with his eyebrows knotting up.

"Sorry," I replied. "Nothing." And then, to Jonas, I added,

Tonight's your night off. Don't you want to go read some-
thing in the white library?

Hmmph! he snorted, and was gone, just like that.

By the time Montana and I finished the tour, the sun had
set and the circus proper was in full swing. We walked back
to the big top in the dusk to the sounds of animals roaring,
the calliope whistling gaily, the barkers chanting a mile a
minute, and the audience gasping or applauding or laughing, or all three at once.

Since we didn't have a show to put on that night—Mr.
Barnum not wishing to go into competition with himself, as
it were—Montana took me inside the big tent, to where Sam
and Lenny were sitting in the front row.

If they didn't look a sight! There they sat, Sam staring at the
trapeze artist in the center ring and Lenny laughing at the
clowns over to the side, and both of them had a big pink
spun sugar in one hand and a bag of peanuts in the other.
For a minute, they looked just like a couple of kids. Then, I
guess the circus brings out the kid in everybody, doesn't it?

Of course, I'd missed the big parade of acts that opened
the show, as well as about the first quarter it, but I sat down
with them. Montana got me some spun sugar, too, and I
had a high old time.

Afterward, we tramped through the sideshow. It was mostly
like the one at Boyd's, except the acts were more classy and
there was deeper sawdust in the aisles. We were just about to
take our leave when a voice called out in a southern drawl,
"Annie? As I live and breathe, it's Annie Newcastle!"

Well, if it wasn't Mona the Fat Lady! She got down off her
platform and waddled toward us, all smiles and chins, and
I ran up to her and gave her a big hug. And after she'd said
hello to Sam, she said hello to Nezzy, too.

"This big ol' pussy cat saved my mama's genuine sapphire
hat pin," she said, hugging him. "You done chased that
mean old robber up a tree, didn't you, puss-puss?"

Nezzy chirped, and rubbed his face against her wide
bosom.

"What're you doing with Barnum, Mona?" I asked. "Did Mr. Boyd go under?"

She shook her head. She was still rubbing Nezzy's ears. "Boyd's still goin' strong, blast his ornery hide," she said. "I finally had enough and I up and quit, and what do you know? The next week, I gets me a telegram from Mr. James A. Bailey and Mr. P. T. Barnum their very own selves, askin' do I want a job. Well, I should say so!"

She suddenly stopped and rubbed at her eyes. "Aisha told me it was a'comin', yes she did, she tol' me afore the accident. And I didn't believe her."

She started to blubber right there in the sawdust aisle, and Sam and Lenny heaved her up. She sat down on an iron-banded keg, and said, "In a minute, Harry," to the barker who wandered over, probably to ask why his star wasn't on stage. And then she told us as how Boyd still held a grudge against me for leaving.

"He bad-mouths you every chance he gets," she said, "and calls you . . . what is it? A rhinestone-studded fake, that's it. And sometimes a half-set plaster saint what needs to be dropped down the well. That old monkey's butt'd take ads out in the papers if'n he thought he could get away with it. Course," she added with a disdainful sniff, "he's a'feared of Mr. Barnum takin' him to court and such. Why, you're famous, Annie, you and Mr. Newcastle! I read about you in all the papers!"

Then she looked up, her face all shiny and glowing, probably as much from the exertion as the excitement, and said, "That Mr. Barnum's a real pip, ain't he? Why, I'm makin' double the best I ever did with that skinflint Boyd, I'm gettin' to see the country by rail, and—" She blushed, and looked around like somebody'd hear her. "And I'm even keeping company with Wallace Smike," she whispered. "He's the elephant trainer, and he likes big ol' gals."

She sat up straight with some effort, and grinned. "Yessir," she said, "ol' P.T.'s a pip!"

18

"There's your new schedule," said Lenny. He set it on the table in front of me, smiling.

"What?" I said, picking it up. It shivered in my hand. "What new schedule?"

He sat down across from me. "Mr. Barnum's very pleased. Very pleased, indeed! He's added twelve cities to the tour, including," he added proudly, "San Francisco. My hometown, and the place of residence of Mrs. Strider and all the little Striders."

"But Denver's moved!" I cried, staring at the paper in horror. "It's moved all the way to May, and the end of May at that!"

Lenny took off his glasses and held them up to the lamp, making a pointed study of the lenses. We'd had our own private railway car since Topeka, through the courtesy of Mr. Barnum. I was beginning to see why he was so thoughtful.

"Lenny?" I insisted.

He put his spectacles back on and peered over them at me. "Actually, it's been changed for some time. Since a week before Mr. Barnum sent the Pullman." He ran his fingers lovingly over the tabletop. "Solid mahogany," he said.

"You told me," I said. Actually, he'd told me at least six times about that table, and about the upholstery, and about the piping to the washroom, and about every single, solitary thing on that gol-danged car.

I love trains and everything about them, I really do; but if he told me one more time about the fold-down writing desk or the etched glass doors, I figured nobody'd blame me for tossing him off the observation deck.

Sam just shut himself off in his room whenever it looked like Lenny was about to give his Pullman lecture.

Anyway, I said, "Why'd you change it? You know I've been marking the days till Denver!"

"Well," he said, leaning over to stop the window shade from jittering, "this way Denver will be all the sweeter, won't it? Not that I have the slightest idea why you're in such a toot to get to Colorado. Nothing but mountains. Besides, you wanted to get west of the Mississippi."

"No," I said, a little testily, I guess, "I wanted to get west of Kansas. West of Colorado, too. And south of it."

Lenny looked up and to the side for a second, then said, "New Mexico?"

I sighed. "Arizona Territory."

Jonas popped out—which he often did on the train rides between speaking engagements—and started sing-songing, *Annie and Johnny-Devlin-the-murdering-thieving-kidnapping-bride-stealing killer, sitting in a tree, k-i-s-s-i-n-g. First comes—*

I snapped, "Oh, shut up, Jonas!" and Lenny leaned back and gave me one of his usual "looks." By that, I mean that he'd lift his eyebrows up real high and kind of stretch his upper lip down, and turn his head away, so that he was facing me three-quarters. He did it every darn time I mentioned Jonas in any sort of a real sense, and he looked as though . . . Well, I thought he looked as if he'd just realized there was a big old bug in his last bite of apple pie. Jonas said he looked more like a constipated bullfrog.

I thought it was cute at first. I don't think he knew he was doing it. But by this time it was beginning to wear on me.

Before he could open his mouth—either to spit out the bug or tell me how happy he was for me that I had Jonas,

I said, "Crimeny, Lenny! You're set on making me mad today, aren't you? First you tell me the schedule's changed—and without even asking me if you could do it, for heaven's sake—and second, I'm sick and tired of you not believing in Jonas!"

"Why, Annie!" he said, shocked. "Mr. Barnum changed the itinerary, not me, and of course I believe in Jonas!"

The front door to the car opened, and Sam, wiping the soot from his vest, came in from the observation deck just in time to hear me holler, "You do not! You always say you do, but you don't mean it!"

You tell him, Annie girl, Jonas cheered.

"You shut up!" I said.

"I'm sorry!" cried Lenny.

I raised my fists and hollered, "Not you, Lenny! I was talking to Jonas!"

Lenny stood up and backed away, clear over to the wall. Well, it wasn't far. Those cars aren't very wide.

Sam leaned against the wainscoting and lifted a brow. "Family spat?"

"Sam," I said, "will you tell this pinstriped weasel that Jonas is real?"

Sam looked at Lenny, deadly serious, and said, "Jonas heap big real. Me no lie." And then he brightened and asked, "Anyone for lunch? I've been in the kitchen car, up to my elbows in an utterly uncollapsible eggplant soufflé. And if they don't do the impossible and flatten it, it'll be ready in about a half hour."

I threw up my hands. "You can go to the devil, both of you!" I shouted. I pointed a finger at Sam. "You with your 'heap big' and 'how,' and playing dumb when it suits you and then making like . . . like . . . like the King of France's cook. And you Lenny, blaming everything on Mr. Barnum when you know darn well that you've been wanting to extend this tour, and you just pestered him till he did it. And I'm sick of you thinking I'm just a harmless little crazy person. Jonas is as real as either one of you, as real as anybody. I can't help it if I'm the only one who can hear him. I can't—"

And then I stopped talking, because, across the room from Lenny, the vase on the sideboard, a vase filled with pink roses, was slowly lifting into the air all by itself.

Sam and Lenny followed my gaze, and we all watched with our mouths open as it slowly glided through the air and across the Pullman. It hovered in front of Lenny for a second, went up about an inch, made a wide, slow circle round his head, then crashed to the floor.

"Mother!" said Lenny, real high and strange, and then his eyes rolled back in his head and he just crumpled up.

Sam went to him right away, but I stood there like I'd taken root. I whispered, "J-jonas? Did you do that?"

I heard him utter a weak word or two, something I couldn't quite catch, and then he tucked himself away.

"Annie? Annie!" Sam growled from the floor. "Are you going to stand there all day, or are you going help me get him up?"

Once I got cooled off, I realized that Lenny had done me a big favor by booking all those extra cities, including more western towns that would take me even closer to Johnny Devlin's home territory than Denver.

Also, after Jonas's floating vase trick, Lenny was a die-hard believer. He pussyfooted around me the rest of the day, asking, "Is he here? Is he here?"

As for Jonas, he'd just about exhausted himself with that demonstration. He didn't show up until the next evening, when we were in Omaha and I was just about ready to go onstage and tell everybody they could have their money back.

Never let it be said that Jonas Newcastle passed up a crowd of people waiting to be talked at, though. He came roaring out and orated for a good hour and a half before he folded.

He told me later that his little exhibition of levitation had near to done him in for good. *Never make me do that again, Annie,* he said with a shudder that I felt.

"I didn't make you do it the first time, you old rapscallion."

You most certainly did, he huffed. *Tried to kill me!*

"Too late for that," I said, and put away my knitting. Jonas went off to sulk.

We kept on traveling, and getting interviewed by the press, and doing shows to sold-out crowds. As we got farther and farther west, I kept thinking that maybe Johnny'd be in this city, come to this show or the next one. But he didn't, not in Abilene or Amarillo, not in Las Cruces, or even in Tucson.

When he didn't turn up at the Tucson show, right smack in Arizona, it near to broke my heart. It was Iowa all over again, only so much worse I didn't think I could bear it. Oh, Jonas gave a good lecture like always. What I felt didn't affect him, curse his hide. But I was on the inside, searching every face in the crowd to no avail.

That night, and for a good week after, I cried myself to sleep. It was pretty sniffly during the days as well, and Sam tried to comfort me, but it didn't help.

Finally, he said, "Annie, you're not feeling so bad about Johnny as you are for yourself. What did you think? That once you tied up Johnny Devlin your future would be made?"

When I thought about it later, that Sam was sure one smart Indian. But right then, I snapped, "I don't know what you're talking about!"

Sam just shrugged.

I knew Johnny wasn't in jail. At least, I didn't think he was. I'd been following the papers real regular for any news of him and he hadn't been mentioned. I was sure there'd be some sort of notice if he'd been put in prison—or worse, hanged.

I kept on looking in the papers, though. Sam picked them up regular, and since in those days he was only interested in the boring financial pages, I had the rest of it to peruse at my leisure.

Still, I came up empty. Oh, I saw where the Arkansas Claw—otherwise know as the fiend, Badger Jukes—had escaped a posse along the California border by jumping down into Mexico. They printed about another Tackett—not Ike or Gobel, but Jubal, who was a full brother to Gobel, if I remembered right—who'd been lynched for cattle rustling somewhere near the town of Gila Bend. But they never mentioned Johnny, not once.

Jonas was no help at all. *Don't ask me,* he'd reply, making out like he was real bored with the entire situation. *How the devil should I know anything about a thieving saddle tramp?*

By the time it was almost halfway through May and we'd worked our way to the west coast, then north to San Francisco, I had just about decided it was useless. It'd been a girlish fancy, that was all, I told myself. Johnny Devlin never loved me, I'd just imagined it. After all, he'd never once so much as kissed me. He'd never said a word to lead me to believe that I was anything but just another girl to him, albeit a charlatan and a faker.

Just another carnie.

Just another liar.

Just another girl to unload before his life had a chance to get complicated.

No. I couldn't lay the blame on him, not any of it, not unless a man could be blamed for being handsome or growing up kind. I'd taken a half of a toothpick and built a two-room cabin, like my papa used to say. The whole thing had been in my mind, not his or anybody else's. Likely I had made no impression at all. He probably didn't even remember me.

And Aisha had been mistaken, or I'd mistaken her meaning. All the good things are set in stone, she'd said. Well, maybe my running into Johnny Devlin again wasn't a good thing. Not a bad thing, either, just a thing that wasn't going to happen until I was maybe fifty years old and we passed on the street, and I puzzled over that vaguely familiar face. Fate, I decided, had something else planned for me.

Still, I was awful blue when we got to San Francisco. I was even dressing somber and sad, though I didn't realize it at the time.

Lenny Strider invited me and Sam for dinner that first night in San Francisco. He said we'd have plenty of time to make the theater—Jonas had to give a lecture that evening—and that Mrs. Strider and all the little Striders were counting on it.

We met the whole crew, a more polite and neat and clean bunch of kids you'd *never* want to meet—and I mean never, and saw their house. It was a fine three story in a good neighborhood, painted bright green on the outside with about four different colors of trim, and decorated real precise on the inside, everything in its place, just so.

After we had all remarked on how lovely it was, and how pretty the mimosa trees in the backyard were, the two littlest Striders—Daisy was seven and Theodore was six—went upstairs with their nanny, and the rest of us trooped into the dining room and sat down to dinner.

"Mr. Strider says your stage act is quite electrifying, Mrs. Newcastle," said Mrs. Strider, in the way of conversation. She was big on the formalities, and had already reprimanded the maid sharply for serving somebody from the wrong side.

I looked up from my stringy pot roast just as Lenny said, "Oh my, yes! She killed them in Santa Barbara."

Mrs. Strider frowned. Flicking her eyes toward their daughter, Mary, she cautioned, "Language, Mr. Strider!"

Lenny colored a bit. "Yes, dear," he said. "Sorry. What I meant to say was that Mrs. Newcastle—and Mr. Newcastle—are very entertaining and educational, as we shall all see at tonight's performance."

"Really, Papa?" said little Mary, dimples sinking into her cheeks. At nine, she was the eldest of the new generation of Striders, and had been allowed to dine with the grownups. She was chubby and had beautiful skin, and her pretty long blond hair was tied up in blue ribbons. "Really? Can we?"

"Speak when you're spoken to, Mary," said her mother sternly. "After all, it's not often you're allowed to dine downstairs. This is a very special occasion." Then she turned to her husband and said, "I don't remember discussing this, Mr. Strider."

Poor little Mary muttered, "Sorry, Mother," and turned her attention back to her peas and carrots. Right then I felt awful sorry for her, about as sorry as I'd felt for anyone besides myself in the last couple of weeks, which was saying quite a bit. Plus, her dimples reminded me of Johnny Devlin all over again.

"I don't believe the show is fit for Mary to see," Mrs. Strider was saying. Then she turned to me and said, "Nothing against you, Mrs. Newcastle. I'm sure that deep down inside, you're a decent enough woman, possibly even Christian. Mr. Strider speaks highly of you. However, I don't believe I want Mary witnessing your performance. She might believe it's real."

Lenny almost choked on his carrots. "My dear," he began, but I cut him off. I decided to change the subject.

"Mary?" I said, and she looked up. "Mary, have you ever seen a real live elephant?"

She glanced at her mother, who nodded, as if giving the poor child permission to speak, and then she said, "No, ma'am. Father works for Mr. P. T. Barnum, but not in the filthy circus."

Right then and there, I knew that it was the mother speaking through the child's mouth, but Sam said, "What?"

I kicked him under the table—not hard, but enough to get his attention—and said, "She probably means that her mother's told her the circus isn't sanitary. Isn't that right, Mary?"

The little girl nodded, and at least Mrs. Strider had the decency to look a little embarrassed.

"Well," I said, "that's all well and good, but sometimes unsanitary things can be a lot of fun, if you wash your hands and wear gloves. Why, Mr. Barnum has llamas all the way from Peru, and a hippopotamus from the jungles of Africa! Zebras and giraffes, too, and ostriches, which are the biggest birds there are!"

Mary's fork was frozen in midair, and her face glowed with excitement. "Really, Mrs. Newcastle?" she breathed. "How big?"

"Taller than your father," I said, and when she gasped, I added, "Even taller than your father with you on his shoulders! They lay eggs this big!" I spread my hands wide. I admit I exaggerated the size by a bit, just to see her amazed expression. "They have long, long necks and they can't fly, and when they're frightened, they stick their heads down in the sand so they can't see what's spooking them."

"Mrs. Newcastle," Mrs. Strider broke in, all disciplinarian. "I don't believe ostrich eggs are a fit subject for the dinner table."

Well, I shut up and we finished eating, although why anybody would serve a dry old pot roast with carrots and peas and potatoes when they lived in a place like San Francisco was beyond me. All the time we'd been working our way up the coast, Sam had concocted wonderful meals of fish and crabs and lobster and shrimps, anything he could buy fresh. Having finally talked Lenny into letting him rig a little kitchen in the Pullman, he had ever since been cooking up a storm.

He'd miraculously lost his stomach troubles the minute we'd moved into our private car, too. He said it must be the public transportation that made him sick, not the trains themselves.

At any rate, we suffered through the meal, although Lenny ate like he was starving. It's pretty amazing what things a person can get used to and miss. Afterward, we repaired to the carriage house to meet Joey, mostly to get away from Mrs. Strider obsessively pushing the bric-a-brac back into place.

Joey turned out to be a handsome fellow. The years had left him sunken over the eyes and grizzled on his once-chestnut face, but he whickered to Lenny, and ate carrots and apples from our hands.

At last, the children were put to bed ("Probably in cast-iron nightshirts and back braces," a disgusted Sam whispered to me) and we and the Striders repaired to the Chelsea House Theater, which was the place Jonas was supposed to speak that night.

We got there early, of course, being as Jonas and I had to see the stage and Lenny had to check in at the box office. After I met the stage hands and Jonas had seen the place, I said, "Mrs. Strider? Would you care to accompany me to my dressing room?" Sam started to tag along, but I said, "Just us girls, if you don't mind, Sam."

He wiggled his eyebrows at me, but he leaned back against the wall and rolled a cigarette.

Annie, don't be a troublemaker, Jonas said, although his warning had an undertone of glee, like he was rubbing his spirit hands together in anticipation.

He had good cause. If he'd been listening in on my thoughts during dinner, and then those I had on the ride to the theater, he knew I'd had a real revelation, one which I was about to share with a woman who more than likely didn't want to hear it.

"Sit down, won't you Mrs. Strider?" I said as she stepped inside. I followed her and shut the door behind me.

She settled herself primly on the chaise, both feet on the floor and her back straight as a rod, and said, "Yes, Mrs. Newcastle?"

I plopped in a chair across from her. "First off," I said, "My name's Annie. I'd appreciate it if you'd call me that."

"All right," she said. "Annie."

"That's right," I said. "And what's your first name?"

"It's Lorna," she replied, "although I'd rather you didn't—"

"Fine," I said, cutting her off. "Lorna it is. Lorna, I'm going to tell you a little story. It's sort of like a parable, only it's true. Are you with me so far?"

She looked irritated, but she nodded.

Now, I'd been doing a lot of thinking—I guess I'd been mulling it over for months, and had just realized it that night. It snuck up on me after the fact, if you will, but when it caught up to me it was sort of like waking after a blow from a sledgehammer: Everything's just the same, only you've got a real different perspective on it.

"Lorna," I said, "would you agree that a sin is a sin?"

She looked kind of surprised, but she said, "Yes. I suppose so."

"Good," I said. "And would you agree that all sins are equal?"

Her brow furrowed. "Well, there are little sins, and then

there are big sins. Murder, I should think, is a very large sin. A little white lie is a very small one."

I figured she'd make it hard on me. "Well," I said, "we're talking about a big sin, here. A sin that changed a lot of people's lives for the worse. See, long ago, there lived a little girl by the name of Velda. She was pretty and blonde, but she had a terrible, terrible temper. She hollered and yelled and pitched fits at folks, even the folks who loved her, for nothing. Some people'd say that the mad gave her a good feeling, but I don't know.

"Anyway, it cost her the man she loved, this temper of hers. He said she yelled too much, that she was too loud, and he went all the way across the country to get away from her.

"It eventually cost her the life of the man she married, who threw himself in front of a train because he couldn't bear her tirades anymore. It even cost her the love of her daughter, who grew up thinking that she couldn't do anything right, because this sin of Velda's, this terrible temper, poisoned her daughter's mind.

"Even after Velda died, this daughter let all sorts of folks just push her around. She was molded so weak that she went off to marry a man she'd never met, just because she'd promised her mother. And when he died on their wedding night, being quite a good bit older than she, she was such a fearful little weakling that his spirit hopped right into her head and haunted her, and she couldn't get rid of him, no matter what."

Mrs. Strider tipped her head and said, "And what, may I ask, has this to do with me? I don't believe the last part for a moment, either."

I leaned forward on my elbows. "You should believe it, Lorna. You should believe it with all your heart, because Velda was my mother, and I was and am that little pantywaist daughter. My mother's temper crippled me and killed my father and alienated practically the whole town of Sycamore, Iowa. She didn't mean to do it. I mean, she didn't set out with those things in mind, but she did it all the same. Why, I only just realized that I used to think about Mama all the time, think about what she'd say or do, and secretly blame my temper on her. I didn't even have a life of my own, Lorna, not to speak of. I was just my mama's audience.

"And you, being so strict with those kids? It's every bit as much a sin as my mama's temper ever was. Don't take me wrong. I don't mean any disrespect to you or to Lenny. But you can see in those kids' eyes that they're scared to death of displeasing you. They're scared now, but later, when they're older, it'll turn into something else."

I sat up straight. "I don't believe you'd admire what it's going to turn into."

Lorna stood right up and looked down her nose at me, and for a minute I was reminded of Miss Jonquil. "Well, I never!" she said.

Oh, let me have at her, Annie! piped up Jonas.

I pushed him back. I said, "Lorna—Mrs. Strider—it's probably none of my business, but I don't want your kids to grow up scared of their own shadows. They're too nice for that."

She set her lips tight for a moment, and then she said, "Did you ever stop to think, Mrs. Newcastle, that it is *because* of the way I'm raising them that they're so nice?"

"No," I said. "I think they're just mortified they're going to put a foot wrong. And that's not the reason to do things."

"Well!" she said. Then, "Well!" again. And she turned on her heel and stomped straight out of my dressing room and slammed the door behind her.

I just stood there and shook my head, once my ears stopped ringing from that bang the door made. I admit I was probably too quick to be meddlesome, and had stuck my nose in where it wasn't wanted. I figured I only had so much time before we moved on, though, and that I might not see Lorna Strider again.

By the looks of things, I was right about that part, anyway.

The trunks had been delivered and I changed into my costume—I chose a pretty rose-colored dress for that night, all glittery with sequins around the neck, but tasteful—and started powdering my face. I'm not one for makeup of any sort on the street, but when you're on the stage you have to put some on, or else people in the back can't tell that you have eyes.

I finished my face, and seeing as I had about twenty minutes before the curtain went up, I decided to step out in the alley and have a breath of fresh air. To sort of clear out my head, you know?

It was foggy outside and there were no birds about. I stood beside the door, at the top of the steps, so that I wouldn't lose the theater entirely. I could hear people moving on the street out front, on their way to see Jonas and me.

"They say she talks about flying machines and pictures that come through the air on invisible waves!" said one lady beyond the fog.

"What cheek!" said a man. "I wonder if there's somebody on the balcony, throwing down Currier and Ives prints."

"Bah," said another. "Vivid imagination, if you ask me. Nothing else. It's a crime to charge for such a thing."

And then the woman said, "But you've paid to see her all the same, haven't you, Horace?" and then she and the first man laughed.

I was glad I couldn't see them. Not because I would have done anything—folks were entitled to their own opinions, I supposed, and the only ones whose opinions I really cared about were folks I liked—but because talk like that always made Jonas fighting mad. Even then he was pushing at my arms and legs, trying to get in and go give them what for.

"Stop it, Jonas," I muttered.

Blast them anyway! he cried. *The overeducated, overstimulated rich brats!*

"That Horace sounded like he was about your age," I said with a grin. "Well, your age when you kicked the bucket."

He did not! If this was the army, I'd have them horsewhipped!

Well, we could have passed the night away arguing in the alley, but it was about time for me to go in. I felt bad about Mrs. Strider, but not nearly bad enough to take back what I'd said. I'd meant it, every word, and from my heart.

And I was feeling terrible sorry for Mama. Sorry that she'd hated her life so much, sorry that she couldn't have seen the good in it and Papa and me and herself. And mostly, I was sorry that Aisha hadn't mentioned Mama's name when she talked about the folks watching over me up in heaven.

Whether that meant that Mama was busy doing the Lord's work elsewhere, or that she was maybe taking heavenly classes on how not to get mad all the time, or worse, that maybe Mama wasn't in heaven at all . . . well, there was nothing to be done about it. Even praying wouldn't help at this late date.

I had come to the place I stood at that minute, understanding-wise, with no big jolting revelation. I had just slid into it, and it was a good fit.

You know, I felt taller, too, like I'd just put down a big load of bricks.

I was just turning to go back inside when I heard voices behind me, quite a bit closer than the last batch.

"This be it, I tell you!" said the first voice. It was a woman's voice, I thought, and it sounded sort of familiar, but the fog sometimes plays tricks with sounds, echoing them around and such.

"Ouch!" came a second voice. "You dasn't have to go pushin' me into the wall!"

I clapped a hand over my mouth to keep from laughing out loud.

"Oh, get up, willya?" said the woman's voice. "They's steps someplace over yonder . . ."

And then I saw a figure through the fog. No details, just an outline of a slight man with one arm in a sling, it looked like. The woman's voice, coming from somewhere behind him, I guessed, said, "Excuse me, ma'am, but is this here the Chelsea House Theater, where that Prophet Annie gal's goin' on the stage?"

I said, "Yes, it is. This is the stage door, though. You'll have to go out front if—"

And then I remembered that the show was sold out. Like usual. Well, Mr. Barnum handed out passes to every Tom, Dick, and Harry who crossed his path. Why shouldn't I extend the same courtesy to this couple? I was feeling magnanimous.

I said, "The tickets are all sold out, but if you fellows would like to see the show, you're welcome to come in and stand in the wings. Backstage, I mean, next to the curtains."

"Thankee kindly, ma'am," said the woman's voice—I still couldn't see her for the fog—and the slight man started up the stairs.

I had a sudden bad feeling—like a punch in the gut—when he mounted the second step, and Jonas cried, *Run!* when he reached the third.

It was too late, though. Badger Jukes—still with a voice like a girl's and minus the skunk smell—lunged forward, with Gobel Tackett right behind him. The last thing I saw was something flashing in Badger's upraised claw, and then there was nothing.

19

When I came to, the first thing I sensed was a closeness. Not only of the stuffy air, which fairly reeked of pine and urine, but of my surroundings. It was darker than the inside of a black hog at midnight, so dark that I couldn't have seen my hand in front of my face, if I could have got it there.

First off, I was lying down. I was also thirsty. And not just the I-think-I'll-get-a-glass-of-water kind of thirst. I was so dry that when I licked my lips, it sounded—and felt—like the rasp of sandpaper. My arms were stiff, and the walls so close on either side of me that they pressed my arms to my sides and scratched them. Raw, unpainted, splintery wood, I knew. Not even sanded.

I twitched and squirmed and finally got one arm worked free from my side. I raised it overhead, out in front of me, but it didn't get far. Bare wood met my fingers before they'd gone a foot from my body.

Terror gripped me, and Jonas, in a frightened little voice, not like himself at all, said, *Are we finally dead, Annie? Have the fools buried us?*

We were in a coffin, all right. But, I realized, a coffin that was moving. Moving on wheels, probably in the back of a wagon, moving over ruts. I was being transported, sure as shooting, and I whispered, "We're not buried yet, Jonas. Hang on."

I pushed at the lid, then pushed again, harder, and a thin slice of daylight knifed over my hand, half-blinding me. "Criminy," I whispered, blinking. "Well, it's not nailed shut, that's for sure. I bet they've got a padlock on it."

In darkness again, I mulled this over, a situation compounded by my throbbing head. It took me a minute to remember that I'd been walloped, and then a minute more to remember who'd done the walloping. And with the remembering came a surge of pure, undiluted anger that I felt as a physical thing, like a fire churning through my veins, like lightning shooting through my fingertips.

"That *scum!*" I shouted, though my parched throat only sounded it as a hoarse rasp. "That no-account, lobsterhanded, feebleminded, white trash scum!" And then the back of my head commenced to pound like nobody's business, precluding any more tirades.

Calm down, said Jonas. *Anger isn't going to get us anywhere.* I suppose he was feeling relieved just to find out we weren't planted underground.

I wasn't so easily satisfied, though. While I couldn't get a hand around to the back of my poor head, when I tried to raise it up a bit, pain cut through the my skull like a blade. I eased off. It felt like it was stuck to the boards. I knew then that I'd bled quite a bit, and the blood had dried and glued my hair—and likely my torn scalp, too—to the coffin floor.

This may sound pretty disgusting, but let me tell you, it's not half so disgusting as when it's your scalp and your hair.

Where do you suppose we are? asked Jonas, oblivious to my hurt. *Those filthy skunks! Why didn't you run when I told you to?*

"Run to where?" I muttered crankily. My mad had eased off some, but I was still pretty dang-blasted annoyed. "The only place I could run was into the theater, and I would've had to move away from it first to get the gol-dang door open!"

You could have jumped over the rail, he grumbled.

"Yes," I said, "you're right. I could've jumped right over the rail and broke my leg when I landed and therefore have gotten into an even bigger mess than I am right now in this blasted coffin going who-knows-where. But at least I would have tried, wouldn't I?"

There's no need for sarcasm, Annie, Jonas said, real clipped.

Despite my aching head and the pine scent, which was just about overpowering, I smiled a little. "Then there's no need to second-guess what I can't patch up, is there?"

I was satisfied when he didn't answer. For somebody who had started out all lecherous and pigheaded and single-minded—not to mention nasty—Jonas had mellowed a good bit since he came to me at the first. Well, he was still some of those things and a few others, but all in all, I held the reins now.

I said, "I'm going to try to get my knees up and push at this lid. Jonas? Are you still there?" My throat not only felt sandpapery, now it felt raw.

Yes, he mumbled, like he was real annoyed with me. *Go ahead. Kick the damned thing. You're part mule, anyway.*

I didn't respond. Instead, I tried bringing my knees back and up, but the lid was too low. "Dad blast it!" I growled through my teeth, and then I kicked, as hard as I could.

Well, I'll be danged if one of the lid boards didn't loosen a bit! I could see a sliver of sky, right where my foot had kicked the top.

I got pretty excited, I guess. "Look at that!" I whispered. "We'll be out of here in no time!"

Maybe, said Jonas. *Maybe not.*

"Why do you have to be so blasted cantankerous all the time?" I said. My voice was tamped down to a scratchy whisper, now. "At least I'm *doing* something!"

I braced myself for another kick at the lid, but Jonas said, *Wait!*

I was about to ask him what for, but then I knew. The wagon or coach or whatever we were on was slowing down. "What is it?" I whispered. "Where are we?"

Just a minute, said Jonas, real caustic-like. *I'll go look.*

"Oh, you're a card," I muttered as we came to a full stop. Somebody hopped down to the road, jiggling the wagon a little, and I heard the sound of their boots on gravelly dirt. They came closer, then stopped. I held my breath.

Somebody banged on the side of the coffin, which just about scared me silly, but I shoved my fist in my mouth and didn't call out.

"Aw, you're crazy," said Badger Jukes's voice. "It looks dandy." The bootsteps started again, this time going away, and then the coffin tilted slightly as he climbed back on the wagon.

"Could'a swore," said the second man. Gobel.

"You could'a swore Johnny was dead back at Three Forks, too," said Badger, disgust in his voice. "You could'a swore you plugged him twice and he fell off'n that cliff. But no, he turns up a fortnight later, bigger'n life and lustin' for blood. So don't tell me as how you could'a swore nothin'."

Gobel grunted by way of a reply, and we started moving again.

I tell you, my heart was beating faster than a snare drum in the Veterans of the Civil War parade. Johnny Devlin almost murdered by Gobel? And now Johnny was out for their blood?

I knew I shouldn't pay attention. I mean, I had enough to worry about already, what with being snatched away five minutes before I was to go on stage and not even knowing where I was or where I was headed, and boxed up tight with my own waste in a stinky pine coffin to boot.

I started wondering if Sam was following me already, and then I wondered if Lenny had to go out on the stage and announce to everybody that I'd been kidnapped and so would therefore be unable to entertain them that night, and if they'd thrown tomatoes at him.

Oh, who cares! snarled Jonas. *We've got to get out of this box and get away, or at least get to a pistol!*

"How can we?" I growled back. "Even if I could kick this lid off, the open place'd be down by my feet. It'd take me a good half hour to worm my way out. Even Gobel and Badger would figure out something was afoot by then. And even if I *did* get out and get to a pistol, I can't shoot worth beans!" I tried to cross my arms, and got a splinter in my elbow for my trouble.

You don't seem very worried, he said. *You don't seem to even care! For all you know they plan to take us out in the middle of nowhere and bury us alive.*

"No," I rasped. "They won't do that. Least, I don't think so. If they wanted us—I mean me—dead, why didn't they just cut my throat in San Francisco? Why go to all the bother of loading me on this hearse—"

Hearse? Jonas breathed. *Do you really think it's a hearse?*

I snorted. "Jonas," I said, "for somebody who's been deceased since last August, you sure are afraid of funerary trappings. Why, you're already in the ground!"

I just don't want to go down a second time, he said. *What if you die? Die of thirst? Suffocate in an unmarked grave? What'll happen to me then?*

I sighed. "Jonas, I don't think they're going to murder me at all. I think they're going to hold me for ransom. After all, haven't I been in all the papers? Sam's keeping track of the money, but I expect we're pretty rich by now."

My head was hurting worse than before, and what little of the lid I could see now was beginning to look real wobbly.

"Jonas?" I said, and my voice sounded strange to my ears. "Jonas? I think I'm going to . . . going to . . ."

I passed out.

When I woke, what little light had been let in by the loose board was gone. My head didn't hurt so bad and for some reason, my mouth wasn't so dry as before. But I felt heavy and achy from not moving for so long, and I realized I'd do about anything to get out of that box.

"Jonas?" I whispered. "Jonas, where are you?"

He didn't answer. He was off somewhere, and I couldn't really blame him. I would have gladly gone with him, if I could.

I listened for some sound that might tell me what was going on. There weren't any voices, just some cicadas singing. I figured they'd made camp and gone to sleep.

I gave the loose board a tap with my foot. It didn't budge. I gave it a little bit of a kick, and I heard a soft creak, like a nail coming loose. I began to push up, real steady, with my foot, which wasn't easy because my leg was aching something fierce, and my hip joint didn't want to work very good. But slowly, slowly, I felt it give, and before long, a star peeked through my coffin lid.

I let my leg drop then, resting it. The next part was going to be harder, because to get the board to budge any further I'd have to push at it from the level of about mid-thigh. The only things I had to push with were my hands, and they weren't working worth a darn. Also, my arms weren't long enough.

I pondered this, all the while thankful that I could see that star, and that a little more air was coming in to take the piss and pine smell with it. And then it came to me in what you could only call a blinding flash. If my arms had been working better, I would have slapped myself alongside the head.

I didn't have to take off the whole lid to get out: I only had to loosen up the one board that the hasp was attached to!

I felt along the lid with a half-numb hand, and sure enough, found the place where the extra nails came through that held the top half of the hasp. Further exploration found it to be a short board, cut on angles and put in where the coffin kind of belled out at the sides.

If I could free up that one board, I could just lift the lid and climb out. Well, crawl out. My climbing muscles were about shot.

I began to push. I pushed so long and hard that several times I almost gave up, but then I'd think, what else did I have to do, and I'd push some more. And finally, the board began to give. It creaked against the nails that held it to the cross-beam, but it slowly raised up, a fraction of an inch at a time.

At last I had it pushed far enough that I could get my hand out. I gripped it by the edge and pushed toward the outside, and the nails on the perimeter let out a screech. I stopped and held my breath, listening for sounds that might betray one of those two polecats waking up, but there was nothing.

I eased the board free and carefully dropped it over the side. It hung there, probably dangling by the padlock.

"Dear God," I whispered, "please let this work," and I pushed upward on the lid.

It lifted back on its hinges slick as a cellar door, only not so creaky.

Slowly, every stiff muscle in my body complaining—not to mention my scalp, which felt like it was ripping off—I sat up. I had tears in my eyes from my head hurting so much, but I scrubbed them away.

The coffin I was sitting in was in the back of a old buckboard. The horses that had been pulling it were tied out and dozing in the moonlight. A few yards from the wagon there was a pile of ash and half-burnt limbs and saguaro ribs that had once been a fire, and Gobel Tackett and Badger Jukes slept beside it. Other than that, there was a whole lot of nothing in all directions.

Gobel must have been on guard duty, for he was sitting up with his rifle across his knees, but he wasn't such a good guard. His head had sunk down on his chest, and he was breathing real slow.

Shoot the fools! said Jonas all of a sudden, and I grabbed the side of the casket.

"Do you have to keep scaring me half to death?" I hissed under my breath.

Hush! he said, real commanding. *Just get a gun and shoot them both.*

"I'm not some corporal or sergeant you can push around, Jonas," I whispered as I made my achy muscles carry me over the side of the coffin. The bed of that wagon was ankle-deep in little bird bodies, which made me real sad. It was bad enough they had to suicide themselves, but you'd think either Badger or Gobel would think to sweep them out every once in a while.

I closed the lid, replaced the board I'd pried free, then eased myself down off the buckboard. "Besides," I said, creeping stealthily—if creakily—toward the horses, "I don't have a gun. And I couldn't shoot anybody, even if I had one. Not even this trash."

Just then, Gobel roused.

I froze. He wiggled his backside down in the dirt, leaned his head back into the rock he was sitting against, and began to snore softly, his mouth open.

I waited a couple of minutes, till I was sure he was settled back into a deep sleep, and then I swiped a couple of full canteens off the buckboard and crept over toward the horses. I coaxed one into his bridle before he was full awake, and started to lead him away, but Jonas said, *What are you doing? Take them both!*

He was right. With a horse, they'd be able to track me down before I got two miles. I didn't even know which direction to go.

So I clipped a lead rope to the second horse's halter, and after some struggle, got mounted on the first one. This is no easy feat when your whole body feels like you've been dragged through three miles of cactus and you've got no saddle to hang on to. I had to tiptoe with those horses quite a good ways away from camp to where I could stand on a rock.

Finally mounted and leading the extra horse, I set off into the wilderness at a walk. My joints were so sore that I couldn't go any faster for a while, and the horses were not what you'd call real cooperative. Two different times the riderless horse just stopped—and I didn't—and I was jerked from my mount, adding to my long list of hurt body parts. At least they were too lazy to take off running, for if they had, my goose would have been cooked for sure. But both times I had to lead them until I found something to stand on.

I was following the trail of Gobel and Badger's wagon, following it backward. It had seemed to me that they had to have set out from someplace civilized, and I was going to find it. It also seemed they had come a long ways, because I didn't believe northern California was supposed to be this dry or cactusy. I began to wonder just how long they'd had me locked up in that box.

According to my stomach, it must have been three years because it was hurting terrible from being empty for so long. I'd already poured a whole canteen down my gullet. This probably wasn't a very good idea, but I'd been so starved for fluids that I feared I'd pass out again.

Jonas wasn't much help. He said I'd roused one time that he remembered. Of course, he didn't recall being in the coffin—or being anywhere, really—he only remembered Gobel forcing water down my throat. If they had done that once, they might have done it more. For all I knew, I might have been gone from the Chelsea House Theater for a day or a week.

By the time the sun started to creep up over the horizon, all orange and yellow and red and purple, Jonas estimated we had been on the move for about two and a half hours. I stopped only to tear a big hunk from my skirt, fold it several times, and then wrap it round my head like one of Aisha's turbans, to keep the birds off. They were already starting to dive at me. I kept moving—sometimes at a walk, other times at a slow jog—until it was about midmorning, by the angle of the sun, and then I reined in.

What are you stopped for? said Jonas. He'd been quiet for a while. *We've got to keep moving, trooper! Put a good distance between ourselves and those slimy cutthroats!*

"Jonas," I panted, half-swoony. I half-slid, half-fell off the horse, the empty canteen and the other—now only half-full—banging my side. Two dead sparrows slithered off with me.

"I'm sick," I said. "There isn't a single part of me that doesn't hurt. Half my hair's matted to my head with dried blood, and I think I left the other half in that casket. I've got splinters in my arms and hands, and blisters on the blisters on my backside from this bony nag. I'm thirsty, I'm stiff, I'm sore—also bruised from falling off this gol-dang horse two times. I'm half-starved to death, I've got beak punctures in my nose and my neck, and on top of it all, I smell to high heaven."

I slid the horse's bridle off, then looped it 'round his neck and tied him to his harness mate. "I am going to rest. I'm going to get some sleep, if I can. And then, and only then, am I gonna move on."

Jonas didn't answer, probably because he knew I had my mind set. And if he'd opened the switch—or however that worked—and stuck a metaphysical hand down into the waters of my body, then he knew I wasn't lying. If anything, I had understated things. I felt like I'd have to get better to die.

And so I led the horses into the shade of some scrub oak and tied them as good as I could. I gave them a little water and apologized to them because it wasn't more. Then I drank a mouthful myself and dragged my carcass over to the next patch of shade.

I was asleep before my head hit the ground.

Somebody was kicking me.

"How should I know?" came a voice through a fog of hurt.

The kick came again, this time to my rib cage. I groaned.

"Made a sound," the voice, familiar and female—no, male—said again. "She's alive, all right. Good thing for her."

Why was it good for me? I wondered. If I'd been dead, had they planned to kick me some more? Maybe slap me around a little?

Somehow, this struck me real funny. I giggled, but it came out more like a whimper. I still had my eyes closed. My eyelids, like every other part of me, seemed bruised and sore. I felt like I must be red and blue and purple all over.

Jonas? I said, in my mind. *Where are we? What's going on?*

I haven't the slightest idea where we are, he answered, all cross. *And as for what is happening, I believe Badger and Gobel have caught up with you. I told you to ride on! You stopped too soon and slept too long, and now you're going to get us killed.*

I am? I replied. My brain was foggy and sore, too, and so I couldn't come up with any snappy answers, let alone make sense of the questions.

Also, somewhere out there in the fog, the voices were talking again. I don't mean ghostly voices, but the voices of those two pea brains, of Gobel and Badger. I couldn't make out what they were saying—it was more like they were talking in off-kilter tones instead of words—and then somebody picked me up like a sack of potatoes and threw me across the bony old withers of a horse.

I just pulled back into myself, and I would have lost consciousness again altogether if not for Jonas stepping to the forefront.

"What do you—?" he began to speak through me. But then the full effect of my bruises and such must have slammed into him all at once, because he hissed, "Good Christ in heaven!"

I wondered if Jonas had my eyes open, and no sooner had I thought it than I could see what he saw: nighttime on the desert. I had slept away the whole day and part of the night, and by the light of a full moon I saw Gobel Tackett snugging my arms to my feet with a rope they'd passed under the horse's belly, and then snugging the whole business to the horse's mane.

I was going to die—I knew it right then. I was going to end my life kicked to pieces beneath the belly of a roan-colored no-name nag in the middle of the desert, with nobody around who cared enough to bury my carcass.

Jonas sensed my fear, and said, "Say, there! Don't you realize I'll slip under the horse's belly? I can ride sitting up, if you don't mind!"

"Let 'er up, Gobel," said Badger. He was standing behind me so I couldn't see him, but he sounded as mean as always.

Gobel let out a deep sigh, and began to loosen the knots he'd tied.

"Thank you," said Jonas. "Thank you very much."

"You sure is a lot more polite than the last time," Badger said. He stepped around the horse to where Jonas (and I) could see him. He was scratching his side with that horrible claw. "What come over you, Missy?" He curled his lip into a sneer that I guessed was supposed to be a come-hither gaze. "Maybe you got you a hanker for me or Gobel."

"I should say not," snapped Jonas. "And I'd appreciate it if you didn't call me 'Missy.' Colonel Newcastle will do."

Gobel, who had finished untying us, froze. Badger stopped talking—and sneering. He did this nervous little dance from foot to foot. After three little hops, he said in a broken voice, "What'd you say?"

We got down off the horse. Well, I say "we." Jonas had control at that moment, just like he did in the lectures. I was only along for the ride.

Anyway, we got down, and Jonas barked, "Stand up straight, soldier!" And I'll be diddly danged if they both didn't snap to! Of course, they didn't salute or anything, but they stood up taller. Poor Gobel's mouth was hanging open.

Jonas addressed himself to Badger Jukes. "I suggest you stop your pussyfooting, man, and get to the point. Why have you brought me to this desolate landscape?"

Badger didn't seem to be listening. He said, "Is you Jonas Newcastle? The haunt? I means, the ghost? For real?"

Something about Badger's tone had me antsy as all get-out, but Jonas answered right back, "I most certainly am 'for real,' as you so eloquently put it. What is it that you gentlemen wish from me? I have a show to run and a schedule to keep," he added, a little too uppity for the circumstance, if anybody had asked me, "and this nonsense has already inconvenienced me to a staggering degree."

I was right about it being too uppity. A look came over Badger's face, a look that was as crazy as it was mean. He stepped 'round the horse (for Jonas had been talking to Badger and Gobel from the opposite side of the beast's back) and right up to us, and before I knew it, his gun was cocked and its barrel was pressed hard against the center of our forehead.

"Aw, golly whillikers," Badger mimicked in that high, girlish voice. "Gobel, we has disturbed her schedule. His schedule, I mean. Hey, what d'you call a Yank colonel in a red dress with glittery stuff sewed on it, anyways?"

Gobel, at least had the sense to be unnerved. He gulped, but he didn't say anything. I was getting pretty nervous, myself. Jonas had underestimated Badger and was playing him for a fool, and I racked my brain for anything that might be of use.

"I think you calls him a nancy-boy," said Badger, answering his own question. That one eye just kept staring in at his nose. It was hard not to be fascinated. "How does I know you're really him," he went on, "and this ain't just the gal usin' her feminine wiles? Answer me that, nancy-boy."

Jonas, the pigheaded fool, crossed our arms over our chest and said, real snide, "You'll just have to take my word for it, you moronic troglodyte."

A look of undiluted fury flashed into Badger's eyes and stayed burning there. He pushed the pistol deeper into our forehead, half-screaming, "What's that mean? You call me a name?"

I was kind of curious myself, but this wasn't the time to be asking questions, because Jonas answered right back, "Fine. Why don't you go ahead and kill me. I'm already dead. Of course, you'll kill Annie, too. Pity. But, to tell the truth, I don't really care much for this vessel. Female, you know. Have to piss sitting down, of all things. I'd much rather move into one of you."

Gobel, goggle-eyed, whispered, "B-badger?"

Badger had eased off on the pressure from the pistol, but he still held it to our forehead. He looked square at us— well, at Jonas—and said, "What'd you mean, move into one'a us?"

Calm as anything, Jonas said, "What do you think it means?"

Badger shifted on his feet again a couple of times before he said, "Aw, you can't do that."

"Can't I?" said Jonas, smugly.

Now, if I'd had a gun and a less beat-up body to assume control of, I would have winged the both of them on general principles. But I didn't, so I whispered a little something at Jonas.

He perked right up. He said, "You boys ever pick up those mojos from Evil Eye Harrison?"

Gobel's eyes got bigger, if that was possible.

"W-what you talkin' 'bout?" said Badger, his claw twitching.

"Well," said Jonas, "even if you had gotten them, they

wouldn't have done you any good. Mojos mean nothing to me. I eat them for breakfast, grind them up under my feet, powder them for fertilizer! So go ahead, pull the trigger! Send me rocketing from this inferior female body, set me free to invade—"

"Oh no you dasn't!" announced Badger all of a sudden, and holstered his pistol. "We ain't so dumb as you think. You ain't gonna trick us into settin' you loose so's you can worm your way into one'a us. I ain't'a sharin' my earthly body with no dead Yankee colonel!" It was his turn to cross his arms.

Jonas shook our head. "You're too smart for me, boys," he muttered, staring at our feet. Then he looked up. "Well, I should have known you would be. That was genius, the way you made off with the girl."

Badger smiled. Well, I think it was a smile. "Well," he drawled, "we— Hey! Didn't you call me a name about a minute ago? A trog . . . a trogditty or somethin'?"

I was crossing my mental fingers that Jonas wouldn't get his back up again, because for once he was playing them right on the money. But there was no need. Jonas, bless him, had found out that the honey of flattery soothed a wild pig a lot better than whacking him with a two-by-four.

Of course, the two-by-four is a whole lot quicker if you've got the element of surprise, but we weren't afforded that luxury.

"Please," soothed Jonas, "forgive me. Let us sit for a moment. I don't suppose you have any food? I didn't notice it before, but this body is famished."

Badger seemed to relax a little. "I reckon it—I mean you—should be. You ain't et for two, two and a half days. Gobel's gived you water, though. Hey, Gobel!" he called over his shoulder. "You bring anythin' to chew on?"

Gobel produced some goat jerky and hard tack, and Jonas and Badger sat themselves down.

"Two and a half days?" said Jonas, chewing after a long drink from the canteen. "What verve you gentlemen have!" Badger's face started to knot up and Jonas quickly added, "Such flash! Such dash! Such flair!" For a second, he sounded like his old buddy Lord Duppa. I guess they'd had more in common than I thought. "I imagine," Jonas continued, "that we've managed to travel a bit in that time?"

"Bet your ass," said Badger proudly, and dug another chunk of jerky out of Gobel's tote with that claw of his. He handed it over to Jonas, who managed to take it without flinching, and confided, "We's down to Arizona Territory."

I thought, *What?*

Jonas thought, *Hush!* straight back at me, then said, "My goodness! Arizona! However did you manage that in such a short time?"

Gobel, who had so far been silent for the most part, ventured, "We said you was my dead sister. We come down from San Francisco on the freight train. Badger put his . . . um . . ." He nodded toward the claw hand. "He wore himself a sling," he finished up.

That's why I was in that horrible coffin, Jonas, I thought. Desperately, I added, *Oh, Jonas, we're so far from San Francisco that nobody'll find us!*

There, there, child, he thought back at me, and strangely enough, I took some comfort from it.

"Gracious sakes," said Jonas. He took a long drink of water. "And now that we're in Arizona, what sort of plans do you have for me?"

Badger curled his lip again. "Well, see, we was plannin' on havin' you tell us when ol' Fortesque Potter was gonna ship his gold. 'Ceptin' Fortesque had hisself a little accident and won't be makin' no more shipments."

So Johnny had killed Potter after all. I felt my heart sink. Why'd he have to do it? Maybe Potter'd stolen the mine from his papa or something, but still, that didn't give him leave to murder a fellow. All my common sense and self-recrimination to the contrary, I still had it bad for Johnny, and the news that he'd killed somebody near to broke my heart. Not so much for the man who got killed—Potter was a low skunk, after all—but because Johnny would surely perish on the gallows for his crime.

Listen up and quit feeling sorry for yourself! Jonas thought at me in a bark.

"—and now that Johnny's after Gobel an' me," Badger was saying, "I reckon we'd better lay low for a while. Go where nobody's lookin', if'n you gets my meaning. So what I wants from you, Mr. Big Deal Dead Yankee Colonel, is— Say, you might'a said some spooky words before, about the mojos and all, but I been thinkin'. You could'a heard about them from somebody else. How does I know you ain't just that gal, pretendin'?"

Jonas sighed, and I felt suddenly odd, like something had just brushed past me. "Your name is Badger Arnold Jukes," he said. "You were born in Arkansas thirty-two years ago to Hummingbird and Branch Jukes, who were double first cousins and had problems of their own. During the War Between the States—"

"The War of Northern Aggression, you means!" cut in Badger, all cranky and cross.

"Whatever," said Jonas. "You had three brothers and two sisters, all deceased, and most of whom died before the age of ten days. During the war, you came across one of your Missouri cousins, Bumble Jukes by name, and murdered him even though he was fighting on your side. Last year, you killed another Missouri cousin, Weevil Jukes, as he rode home from testifying at a trial."

Badger drew himself up and laid his claw, the thumb twitching, over his heart. "The worstest Jukeses got exiled to the wilderness of the north country a long time ago. We of the Arkansas Jukeses has sworn an oath to cut 'em down if'n we sees em'."

Jonas was silent for a moment. Finally, he said, "My dear boy, is any of this impressing you at all?"

Gobel had his mouth hanging open again, but Badger slowly shook his head. "Nope," he said. "You could'a asked my mama, or anybody from down our way in Arkansas."

I wondered how in the world Badger thought I'd have the time—or the desire—to go all the way to Arkansas and ferret out his mother. But Jonas just said, "All right," with a sigh. "I didn't want to have to do this. You might want to move in closer."

Badger scowled. "Why?"

"Because you might not wish Gobel to hear what I have to tell you."

Badger furrowed his brow, but after a minute he said, "All right, I reckon. Gobel, you draw a bead on 'er, and commence to blastin' should I tell you."

Well, Gobel pulled his gun and Badger leaned in, and Jonas pushed my skirts out of the way and leaned to Badger's ear and whispered in it. I will not recount what he said, since, being a lady, I don't speak of such things. I will say, though, that after Jonas had spoken, Badger leapt back like somebody'd just set a firecracker off in his pants. He grabbed his crotch with both his hand and his claw and cried, "Nobody knows that! That's private! You been snooping on me!"

"Hardly," said Jonas, real bored-like, and took another bite of jerky. For my part, had I been in the body at that moment, I would have turned bright red and stayed that way for a week.

"Badger? You want I should plug him?" Gobel asked, confused by the proceedings.

"No, goddamn it," snapped Badger. "He's real enough. Damn and blast your hide, you old spook!"

Jonas shrugged. "You wanted proof. At least I asked you to lean in before I told you a certain appendage was shaped like a—"

"Shut up!" Badger cried.

"Like a what?" asked Gobel.

Badger yelled, "You shut up, too!" And then he sat right down. "All right, Mister. Or lady, or whatever you are. Like I said, we ain't gonna be goin' for no paltry ol' gold shipments no more. No payrolls or no banks, neither. No sir, we has decided to go to the source."

"The source," Gobel echoed, nodding his head.

"We wants you," Badger said, his voice as whispery as the night, all of a sudden, "to talk to them other spooks—kinda gather 'em all together-like for a little confab—and find out where the lost El Galgo mines is. We wants you should take us there."

*   *   *

Now, I'd heard the mines called El Galgo mentioned once or twice by Lord Duppa, but I figured they were a legend. They were some legendary digs supposedly started by the Spanish back in the 1500s. This was when they came up from Mexico to seek the Seven Cities of Gold.

Of course, they didn't find squat in the way of golden towers and streets, but according to legend, they did run across a rich vein of ore. Some people said that El Galgo had fed the coffers of Spain single-handed for five or six years, until Apaches wiped out all the miners and successfully blocked any access to it. Well, tortured and killed everybody who tried to get near the place, to be precise about it. Eventually the Spanish gave up and, so the story went, even forgot where it had been.

And so when Jonas agreed to take those two no account peckerwoods to it, I just about had an apoplexy! Oh, I kept my mouth shut until everybody settled down for the night, but then I let Jonas have it with both barrels.

"You don't know where that gol-dang mine is, Jonas Newcastle!" I whispered. He had vacated the body and left it to me to be burdened by the ropes binding my hands and feet. "And furthermore," I added quietly, "you're a coward, leaving me to suffer through the night tied up like this. You might at least have picked some of the splinters out of my arms and hands."

Such a complainer! said Jonas from the relative safety— and comfort—of the back of my mind. *Honestly, Annie, if I'd realized you were so particular about things, well . . . Sometimes I ever wonder what I saw in you. Even Wednesdays and Saturdays weren't all that—*

"Stop trying to change the subject," I hissed. To my left, Gobel turned over in his sleep. I watched him twitch for a second before I said, "Jonas, how in the heck are you going to take them to that stupid mine when you don't even know where it is? Nobody knows where it is because it isn't anywhere! And what are they going to do when they find out there isn't an El Galgo? Did you stop to think of that?"

And who said I didn't know where it was? he replied sleepily.

"It doesn't exist!" I whispered.

Doesn't it? He made a yawning sound, although I didn't know how. *Well, Annie, in the morning, just start them northwest, toward Tupper's Pass. You do know how to find northwest, don't you?*

"Of course I do," I said through clenched teeth. "But why do I have to do it? Where are you going to be?"

Oh, he said offhandedly, *I thought I'd sleep in a bit. Good night, dear.*

"Jonas!" I whispered. "Jonas, you coward! Come back out here!"

But he was tucked away, folded into some dark and silent corner of my mind. I knew he wouldn't come forward until he was good and ready—which left me alone with my bruised body, those two idiots, and a mind full of unanswered questions.

I lay there for a long time, sagging against my ropes and trying to ignore all those itches I couldn't reach, and thinking—against my will, I swear it—about Johnny Devlin.

I'd about got myself talked into believing that I didn't mean anything special to him. Well, I thought I had. But a person could wonder about another person, couldn't she?

I wished I hadn't missed that snatch of Badger's speech about Old Man Potter getting killed, because I was scared to death Johnny'd done the killing, and Jonas had left before I got around to asking him.

Of course, for all I knew, Johnny had murdered fifty people before I met him. I just didn't like to think of him killing anybody after.

That sounded so stupid that I would have kicked myself if my legs hadn't been bound up. I stared up at the stars and whispered, "Annie, you are sure a fool."

And then, right out of nowhere, Jonas said, *He didn't kill anyone, all right? And now, for the love of all that's holy, will you please go to sleep?*

"Honest?" I asked, my eyes filling with happy tears.

Honest. Now, tuck up. Big day tomorrow.

The next day found me tied up in the back of that buckboard—which we'd gone back for—and getting sunburnt fast. Also chock full of dead birds, since with my arms bound I couldn't disentangle those that got their little beaks or talons stuck in my turban. I comforted myself that at least I wasn't in the coffin, although they had brought it along. I didn't want to ask why.

It was real slow going, seeing as there was no road and Gobel had to get down about every five minutes and move a rock or chop some brush or something. However, despite the delays, they insisted on taking the wagon.

"For haulin' our gold, stupid," Badger snapped at me when I asked.

I just kept my mouth shut after that.

About midday, they found a road, and we started to make better time. And sometime in the late afternoon, they stopped to rest the horses again and give them water. Gobel pushed me down off the buckboard, and took off my ropes so that I could relieve myself behind some bushes. I was grateful for that. My stomach was all topsy-turvy from not having eaten for so long, and then Jonas wolfing that goat jerky and hardtack all at once. I was in the bushes for a considerable time.

I snagged my dress on some thorns coming out, but it was already too late to save it. After two and a half days in a casket and then a half on horseback and the rest in the wagon, and it was ripped and torn and stained and generally ready for the rag bag. I was smelling riper all the time, too.

Course, it didn't much matter, seeing as how Gobel Tackett and Badger Jukes were the only ones around to smell me. I doubt they could smell much of anything over their own considerable stench.

Badger was waiting when I came out of the brush. I was pulling sparrows and warblers out of my makeshift turban. Staring at me with his one good eye, he had a Winchester rifle swinging loose in his good hand. "Hurry up," he said, all high and kind of surly, and waved the rifle over toward Gobel and the horses. I walked on over there ahead of him, and stood in the shade of a mesquite tree, beside the wagon.

The landscape had changed since we started out that morning. We'd been in flat old scrub desert—greened up with spring and, I guess, for desert, it was coming lush. But gradually we'd got higher and the land had started to roll some. Now there were trees here and there—sometimes whole groves of paloverde and the like—and a patchy ground cover of scrubby shrubs three and four feet high.

I could see mountains in the distance to the north, east, and just hints of them to the west. The ones to the north were the nearest, all purple and blue and losing their haze. We were close enough that I could see just the last patches of snow on their peaks.

I was getting a tad colder, too. My dress had short little cap sleeves, and now my arms were not only sunburnt: They were goose-pimply in between the splinters. I tried rubbing them to warm myself up, but it only drove the splinters in deeper.

Anyway, I went over and stood under the tree, where Gobel was crouched on his heels. He held out a grubby hand. "Jerky?" he said.

I took the piece from him, wiped it on a relatively clean spot on my dress, and took a bite.

"Reckon we'll eat hot food tonight," he mumbled, not looking at me. "Badger'll shoot somethin'."

I recalled that butchered tortoise when they'd made off with me before, and a shudder ran through me. I sure hoped there weren't any tortoises around here.

From behind, Badger's claw gripped my shoulder, and I jumped. He turned me toward him, and demanded, "Is you him yet?"

"Pardon?" I said, although I knew what he meant.

"I said, is you him? Who's in there? Who'm I talkin' to?"

I sighed. This had been going on all morning. I ducked a bit, to keep a finch from diving into my forehead, and said, "I told you. I can't just call him up like you'd draw water up a well. Jonas comes in his own time."

Badger stood there a moment, rocking back and forth on his heels, tensing and relaxing his little lips. Then he drew his pistol and aimed it right at my stomach. I believe I sucked in some air, but I didn't flinch. You didn't dare, with Badger.

"You know what I'm thinkin', lady?" he said. "I'm thinkin' I'm tired of you just sayin' 'northwest, northwest, Tupper's Pass.' And I'm thinkin' that mayhaps that spook can jump outta your carcass and into one'a us if'n you dies, but mayhap he can't. But I'm also thinkin' that I could sure inconvenience him some if I was to gut-shoot you."

I swallowed hard and started calling Jonas's name in my head with a certain degree of desperation.

"See," Badger continued, "I figures you wouldn't die. Not right off. Oh, you'd be beggin' somethin' fierce for me to finish it, but I couldn't kill a sweet little thing like you outright. No, ma'am, it'd prob'ly take a good week, week and a half afore the septics'd carry you to Jesus. By then, Mr. Dead Jonas Newcastle will've taken pity on you an' come on forward."

"N-no he won't," I said. "He'll just go off to that white room and leave me to suffer, and you won't get anything for your trouble."

"Ain't gettin' nothin' for it now, so far's I can see," he said, all sassy. "Just northwest and more northwest, when all the time I keep thinkin' we should'a been headin' south. Meskin's don't wander too far from home, even when they's lookin' for gold. El Galgo's closer to the border, and I means the Meskin one, not the Canadian."

"But . . . but . . ." I stuttered. I had to think of some way to convince him we were on the right track. And then all of a sudden, I got an idea. If Mrs. Krupp, the schoolteacher we'd had when I was in the sixth grade, had been there, I would have kissed her hairy old face for drilling us on all those maps.

I said, "This used to be part of Mexico. It's only—" I batted at a lark. "It's only been in the U-S-of-A since the fifties when we fought the Mexican War. Why, all those years ago when the Spanish came looking for the Seven Cities of Gold, practically the whole west was theirs! Or it was the Indians'," I added, "depending on how you want to look at it."

Badger just stared at me, like he hadn't understood a word I'd said.

Gobel, scratching his ear, piped up, "I think she's onto somethin' there, Badger. I seems to recamember—"

"Shut your hole!" hollered Badger, and he turned back to me with a reddening face. I could almost see the mad boiling up just under his surface.

"I knows all about the Meskin War, Missy," he said, "so don't go givin' me no history lessons. Wherever they drawed the border back in them days, I still thinks you's playin' us for fools."

He paused, as if thinking, and after a minute said, "No, I thinks either the haunt comes out right now, or I'll just plug you. We'll leave you for these goddamn birds and the coyotes, and me an' Gobel'll be down across the Meskin border 'fore they finishes you off. Don't reckon he could jump in us then, could he, Gobel?"

Gobel shook his head, although he didn't seem real sure about it.

I'd used up all my jaw ammunition, and I was so scared that I had to go to the outhouse again, even though I'd just been. Voice cracking, I said, "D-don't you want to find El

Galgo? Jonas wouldn't steer you wrong. I'm leading you there!"

Badger scowled and cocked the gun. It was pressed so tight against me that I felt it through my rib cage as well as heard it.

"I dasn't think you's leadin' us there nowhere," he said, frowning. "I believes you an' that spook is leadin' us in a wrongly direction, and has made you a plan to get us lost out here in the wasteland, and then . . . Well, I don't rightly know what happens next. Mayhaps you thinks you can sneak out while we lie dying of thirst. Mayhaps you think you're gonna get the gun and plug me. Or mayhaps that old haunt wants I should just shoot you through the head so's he can have a finer vessel."

He stood up a little straighter. "Well, he ain't gettin' me. My vessel's my own. And if he don't show up by the time I counts to five, he ain't gettin' you no more, neither. One. Two."

I was frantic. Jonas was nowhere to be found, and I started praying.

"Three," Badger continued. "Four." He smiled.

Duck! cried Jonas.

He didn't have to say it twice. I leapt to the side and hit the dirt so fast I landed rolling and tumbled clear under the wagon.

I heard a gunshot, maybe a rifle, and a ricochet as it hit the metal wheel rim next to me. I scrambled to the far side of the wagon and hunkered down just as three more shots were fired from the distance, and Badger and Gobel began to fire back.

Will you open your eyes? Jonas shouted over the blasts. *I can't see a damned thing!*

"You don't need to holler!" I shouted back. "You can't get any closer to my ears than you already are!"

Open-open-open! he cried again, his voice filled with blood lust and excitement.

I peeked out one eye. Badger and Gobel were on the other side of the wagon, maybe twenty or twenty-five feet out. At least, they were firing from there. A broad copse of bushes

was in the way, and all I could see of them were little wisps
of spent gunpowder smoking, riding up on the breeze.

Nobody's firing back at them, Jonas said. At least he didn't
shout it.

I thought he'd gone crazy. I said, "What do you mean,
nobody's shooting back? Why, I heard the gun blast myself!
Why'd you think I jumped all the way over here? What'd
you warn me about if there wasn't any—?"

Stop being so cranky! Jonas said impatiently. *Good God,
Annie. You're as bad as Velda ever was! What I meant to
say was that he—Say! Everybody's stopped now.*

I registered the sudden silence, all right, but I whispered,
"You take that back! I'm nothing like my mother!"

"Hey!" called Badger's voice, from the brush. "Hey! Who's
doin' the shootin'? Show yourself!"

I held my tongue—and Jonas held his—while we waited
for whoever was out there to answer. They didn't.

I heard Badger and Gobel arguing about something, I
couldn't tell what, and then Badger yelled again, "Hello out
there! *¡Hola, amigos! Habla,* um, the *Españolish?* You speak-
a the Mex?"

No answer.

"Why'd you say that?" I hissed at Jonas. "Why'd you say
that about me and Mama? Not only was it not nice, but it
wasn't true. You just beat everything!"

Will you hush up and listen? said Jonas. *He's out there!*

"He who?"

"Apache?" called Badger, and now he sounded as scared
as I'd been when he had that gun to my stomach. "Me friend
to Apache! Famous claw hand! Bring white woman, give
present to your chief! Mescalero? Jicarilla? Chiricahua?"

I hissed, "Now he's going to give me to the Indians!"

That saddle tramp, Jonas said, trying to sound peevish.
He didn't quite pull it off though.

"What?" I said, still focused on the possibility of spending
the rest of my short life in a tepee with somebody named
Buffalo Hump.

I said, it's that saddle tramp.

"*My* saddle tramp?" I breathed.

"Answer me, damn it!" yelled Badger.

Yes, Jonas allowed, *your saddle tramp. All right? Aisha said—*

"You talked to Aisha?" I butted in. First Johnny, and now Aisha! It seemed like everything amazing was happening all at once.

All superior, he said, *For your information, Annie Newcastle, I get around a good bit. Aisha's too far away to talk to you anymore. But she can talk to me, though now I can barely hear her. At any rate, she told me to send you this way. She said that your Johnny was coming south, hunting for those two morons.*

This didn't quite sit right with me. I hated to be arbitrary, but I said, "Jonas, how'd you know he'd be exactly here? No offense meant, but Arizona's a pretty big place."

"Navajo?" hollered Badger, in desperation. "Paiute? Yuma? Is you red or is you white?"

Jonas chuckled, like he'd just pulled off a good trick, and said, *I knew where we were, dear. I knew that a northwesterly direction would take us within shouting distance of Tupper's Pass within a day. And I knew—through Aisha you understand, because personally, I don't care one whit—that Johnny would be riding down through Tupper's Pass and coming out this end.*

I was grinning like it was Christmas. "Jonas, you really do beat everything!"

Well, he sniffed, *I do know the Territory like the back of my hand.*

"Funny," I said. "You didn't know it so well when they had me down south, up in those foothills."

Hush, he said. *If something had gone wrong and we'd had to find a mine, I would have directed them to my old Iowa Princess. Silver, she was, till she played out. Still, a dangerous place, the Iowa Princess. Been boarded up for years. If you don't know precisely where to step—*

"Afternoon, boys," said a voice that sent shivers all through me. It was real close, so that his words just came out conversational. "Well, I reckon it's getting on more toward evening."

I couldn't see where it was coming from, and neither could Badger or Gobel, I guess, because their heads popped up from the scrub, then went back down—then up, then down again—just like a couple of gobblers at a turkey shoot.

"That wasn't very nice, what you did," Johnny went on, like he was kind of bored. He clucked his tongue. "Kidnapping that little gal again. Shame on you. Well, you'd best throw out your guns, boys. You don't want to end up like old Ike, do you?"

I'd been so engulfed in my own problems I hadn't so much as thought about Ike Tackett. Where was he, anyway? I'd thought he and his brother Gobel were just about joined at the hip.

Gobel said, "What about Ike? What you meanin' Johnny?"

"Gobel, Gobel, Gobel," Johnny chided. His voice seemed to be coming, so far as I could tell, from off to the side, out in front of where those two yahoos were crouched down. "You don't know? Why, I thought for certain you were in on it!"

"In on what?" yelled Gobel.

Badger piped up, "You ain't gonna trick us with your . . . tricks, Johnny Devlin! We has got the gal and we's got her pet spook, too, and you ain't a'gonna split us down the middle by castin' aspersions. So just go on your way and we won't plug you."

"In on what?" insisted Gobel. "What about Ike?"

Johnny said, "That's a real kind offer, Badger, but I don't believe I can take you up on it. See, when you killed Ike and dropped me over that cliff and left me for dead, you sorta pissed me off. You can understand that, can't you, boys?"

"Now, Johnny," said Badger, a touch of agitation in his voice, "I weren't the one what dropped you over that there cliff."

Johnny replied, "Ah. It was Gobel, then. Well, I'm sorry about accusing you, Badger. You must've been busy at the time, shooting Ike in the back and all. Funny thing. That was the first time I'd ever seen him take off his bullet charm since he got it from that *curandera*. Guess he forgot to put it back 'round his neck when the lead started flying."

Oh, that was good! said Jonas. *Bully for him! I might just be able to stand him after all.*

I ignored him. I was too busy holding my breath, for there was a silence in the scrub. Then Gobel's voice came, sounding all pinched and quiet. "That true? You done that, Badger?"

The bushes started shaking, then thrashing, and then there came the report of another gunshot. I jumped at the sound and, for my trouble, got banged on the head by the underside of the wagon.

The bushes went still, and there was another long silence. Finally Johnny, his voice speaking from an entirely new direction this time, clucked his tongue and said, "Now what have you two simpletons gone and done? Somebody dead over there?"

"You's a real card to draw to, Johnny," came Badger's voice, except it didn't sound like he was making a joke, and it wasn't coming from over by the scrub anymore.

It sounded more like it was coming from behind me this time, and when I heard a stick break, I shouted, "He's moved!" before I thought.

Something jerked me out of my crouch beneath the wagon's edge, jerked me away in a tumble and back into the brush.

Unhand us, ruffian! cried Jonas, but it was on the inside of me, where it did no good whatsoever.

I looked down. The goat jerky Gobel had given me was rising up in my throat, I saw Badger's claw arm fast around my waist. I didn't think. I just commenced to beat on it with both hands.

"Let me go!" I hollered, and pounded on that claw some more, but he was powerful strong for such a little, skinny man, and his grip only got tighter. "Let go! You're going to squeeze me in two!"

And then he not only snugged his grip, he moved it upward, so that I couldn't get any air back into my lungs. I panicked. I started to sputter and cough and gasp, except nothing came out, no air, no sound.

I heard him yell something at Johnny, but I couldn't make out the words because Jonas was shouting at the same time, *Use your elbow! No, the other one! Christ, girl, you're hopeless! Kick backward! Kick him in the knees!*

I tried, I swear. But every time I shot my elbow back, it met with nothing but air, and the same thing happened when I tried kicking.

Judas Priest! Jonas growled. *Let me take over! We've only got a few seconds before you pass out!*

I let him. In fact, I don't remember ever leaping out of that body so fast as I did on that occasion.

From my small corner, I watched dizzily as Jonas hauled back with one elbow—I'd been using the wrong one, I saw that right away—and shoved it into Badger's rib cage so hard and fast that I heard bones cracking. I didn't know if they were mine or Badger's, since I was only watching from inside, and I didn't much care to find out just then.

Badger let us go, just like that, and doubled up and screamed like a cat with its tail in the thresher. Jonas took us in a big gulp of air, and then, before I could even think about it, he bent low and threw his shoulder, full bore, into Badger's unprotected side.

There was a lot of rolling and tumbling, so much that I was fair dizzy, but Jonas seemed to know what he was doing. He'd knocked the wind right out of that fool, and we ended up on top, straddling him, and then it was Katie bar the door!

Jonas pummeled his face with my fists, shouting, "You imbecile! Moron!" as dead birds fell from the turban to Badger's face. Jonas squeezed Badger's sorry sides with my knees, slapped his cheeks and broke his nose. "The El Galgo mines indeed!" he hollered. "I'll lead you there over my dead body, you cretinous ass!"

I would have corrected him, except just then I became aware of a pair of boots—big, dusty, fancy-tooled boots—standing about four feet over to the side. *Jonas?* I thought at him. *Jonas, stop walloping Badger and look up.*

Jonas gave him one last lambast to the chin—Badger was
unconscious by this time, of course, so it didn't really matter—and looked right up those boots, up those long-legged
pants, up that silver belt buckle and pale blue shirt, and
leather vest, and right up into Johnny Devlin's sea-green
eyes.

"Am I interrupting?" he said, those dimples sinking partway into his cheeks.

Christ, thought Jonas, and just like that I was spewed out
again and into my body. *I was having such a good time,
too!* he said, all disgusted. *I suppose you'll get all lovey-
dovey now.*

"Shut up, you old degenerate," I muttered under my
breath, and then I realized I couldn't think of a gol-danged
thing to say to Johnny. Sweeping a mockingbird from my
shoulder—it was a small one—I just looked up at all that
gorgeousness and gulped.

"Well," said Johnny, his dimples sinking deeper, "nobody's ever called me an old degenerate before. I suppose
it depends on your perspective."

"I—I—I—," I stuttered. Boy, did he ever have good ears.

He stepped up and put his hand down to me, mindless
that he could be stabbed by diving birds. "Why don't you
hop up, and we'll see if you've killed him all the way dead."

My knees were so wobbly that he had to lean me against
the wagon two times before I stuck.

Honestly, said Jonas while Johnny knelt to Badger. *Get
some control of yourself.*

I whispered, "I can't help it."

Johnny looked up from Badger and said, "He's still alive.
Sorta." He stood up again, and dusted his knees and his
hands. "You beat the wadding out of him, all right. You
must be a whole lot stronger than you look."

He just kept staring at me, till Jonas said, *Well, nod your
head or* something, *girl!*

I said, "Th-thank you," and then I felt about as dumb as
a duck for having picked that to say when my heart was so
full. And then my cheeks flushed extra hot at just the
thought of telling him those things out loud.

He studied on me for a moment, never losing that little grin or those dimples, and then he said, "You're sure a lot more quiet than the last time." He pointed down at Badger. "He had a gun, didn't he?"

I nodded. "And a rifle."

"Rifle's in the wagon," Johnny said. "Gun must've got knocked out into the brush during the fight. Well, I guess I'd better check on old Gobel. Kinda hate to lose him."

"Why?" I said, all of a sudden finding my tongue. "He shot you twice and knocked you off a cliff! I heard him and Badger talking about it."

Johnny pursed his lips for a second before he said, "True, but he only winged me. And it was a short cliff. This piece of trash, on the other hand?" He gave Badger a little kick, and Badger moaned. "He'd kill his own mama for a three-cent nickel."

I didn't say anything, but inside my head, Jonas piped up, *Peckerwoods, the both of them. Reb trash. If I'd had just one more minute I could have—*

"What's the coffin for?" Johnny said. I guess he'd just noticed it.

"They put me in it," I said. "I was in it for two and a half days." And then the fullness of that statement—and everything that went with it—hit me full force, and I started to cry. I didn't want to, mind, but I couldn't stop myself.

The next thing I knew, Johnny's arms were around me, and he was comforting me. He told me it was all right and that I was safe, and he'd get me back to civilization. I only cried harder. Of course, after a while I was crying because he was holding me and I'd never been so happy in all my life, but I was bawling like a baby all the same.

Finally, after a couple of soggy minutes in his arms, I got another good whiff of myself. "I smell terrible!" I wailed, and that set me off on a new tangent of tears.

Johnny actually laughed, though I don't know how he could, considering the stench rolling off me. "C'mon," he said, and lifted me up. He walked around the back of the wagon and set me inside, saying, "We can get you cleaned up, princess, don't you worry." And then he gave me a little tweak on the nose and walked off, over toward where Gobel lay.

Gad, said Jonas, all disgruntled and grouchy. *Why don't you just strip to your petticoats and throw yourself at him?*

"Oh, hush," I said, sniffling. "And now that I remember it, you were sure shy about coming out when Badger was going to gut-shoot me and leave me for the coyotes."

I was only being judicious, my dear, he said, up on his high horse again. *Judicious. He who is wary is wise.*

"He also gets gut-shot," I muttered. There was no arguing with Jonas. If I hadn't learned anything else these past few months, I'd at least learned that.

I looked over in the direction Johnny had gone. I'd thought he'd be right back, but I didn't see him. I was searching the scrub when I noticed it.

Uh-oh, said Jonas.

"Badger's loose!" I cried, rising to my knees and gripping the side of the buckboard. "Johnny!"

There was no answer of any kind. Nobody shushed me or shot at me, and I craned my head all around, looking for movement in the scrub, looking for a sign of anyone.

And then the bushes came alive, out about ten yards from the place Gobel's body lay. They trembled and roiled, the motion going north, then south, then toward me, then away. I saw Johnny come up, then Badger, then Johnny again.

Somebody must have kicked hard and missed, because a whole creosote bush, roots and all, sailed up in the air.

And then I saw the knife. That's what they were fighting for, a knife that glinted in the sun. It rose in Badger's shaking hand, shaking because Johnny held his wrist. It wrenched this way and that, then disappeared, then rose and fell again, this time with deadly determination. And then the bushes stopped moving.

Breathing shallow, I half-fell off the wagon. Badger's rifle was in my hand.

"J-johnny?" I said. It had happened so quick that I hadn't seen whose hand held the blade on its last thrust. I took two steps, then three, to the place where I'd tussled with Badger. I called to Johnny again.

The scrub moved and I held my breath. And then he stood up, and I slapped a hand over my mouth.

"Jesus," said Badger, wobbling from side to side. "Ol' Johnny was tough enough, but damn, Missy, if'n you don't fight like a man!"

And then I noticed the knife grip, sticking from his side, the blade buried in him and probably corroding to beat the band, if life is fair.

He took a step toward me, just one, and I raised the rifle in my shaking hands. And then he stopped stock-still. "Why'd the birds stop singin'?" he said, plain as day, and then he fell straight forward, like a fence post would if you dropped it.

This, said Jonas happily, *is marvelous.*

I was already moving toward the place the fight had been. Bushes grabbed at my skirts, cactus tore them, but I kept going, giving wide berth to Badger. I passed within a foot of him, though. His watery little eyes were dead and staring.

And then I came upon Johnny. He was lying there so still and quiet, I knew he must be dead. I knelt beside him, birds slipping from my turban to his chest, and kissed his handsome face and beautiful hands and cried, "Oh, don't be dead, Johnny, please don't be dead! Jonas, is he gone?"

I felt the back of his head and found the place he'd hit it on a rock, and then I closed my eyes and pleaded, "Has he crossed to your side? Please send him back if you can! Oh, Jesus, don't take my Johnny from me! Jonas, please help!"

And then I felt Johnny's hand tighten on mine, and I opened my eyes and looked into his face. He was grinning at me like the cat who swallowed the canary bird. Which he might well have done if there'd been wild canaries in Arizona and if he'd kept his mouth open long enough.

"Say," he said. "You really do believe in that ghost of yours, don't you?"

I blushed, and Johnny added, " 'My Johnny'?"

I was horrified. I know a person shouldn't be when they've slipped and let another person know how they truly feel, but this was so gol-danged important! I opened my mouth to say something, then changed my mind and closed it. I just knew he was thinking I was a crazy little fool, and I didn't want to compound it.

But he was grinning at me so smug, so teasing, that I figured I couldn't do myself any worse than I already had. I swallowed hard, opened my mouth again, and this time I said, "Johnny Devlin, I love you. You may think I'm crazy, falling in love with somebody that I've only ever met but once, but I can't help it. Aisha told me that only the good things are carved in stone, and Sam showed me those hawks, the ones that hunt in packs in the desert, and I think that you and me are carved in stone, and that maybe we're like those hawks."

He tried to say something, but I laid a hand over his mouth. "Maybe you and me would've always been alone, even in a roomful of people. Maybe that's how it would have been if we'd never met. But I came to the desert, just like those birds. Well, maybe not just like those birds. They come because they're hungry and there's good hunting, and I came because I was weak. But I met you, that's the important thing. And I guess I knew from the very first, from the time I saw you in the crowd in New Mexico, that I was meant for you, and you for me. Aisha was right. We need each other, Johnny Devlin. At least," I ended, falteringly, "at least, I need you."

He gazed up at me, his face gone from amused to serious. He reached up and gently pulled a dangling sparrow from my turban. "Annie?" he murmured. "Who's Aisha?"

I threw my head back and just shrieked. My mouth was still open with the cry when I felt Johnny pulling me down, and then he was kissing me so good and so thorough that I realized I'd never been kissed before, I'd only been pecked at.

"Criminy," I breathed, once he was finished.

Well, it came around that he told me he couldn't stop thinking about me, either. He told me that it had happened for him back in New Mexico, too, and that he'd gone up to Utah just to see me, thinking it would get me out of his mind.

Except, he only had it worse. When Ike and Badger and

Gobel kidnapped me at Christmas, he said he near about died, just thinking about what they could have done to me.

"Been trailing them," he said, stroking my hair, "on account of what they did to Ike. I got a late start because I got stove up a bit. But I thought it'd be at least another week, ten days, before I ran across them."

So when he pulled out his spyglass and came across Badger and Gobel driving that old buckboard straight toward him, he thought it was his lucky day. Until he saw me, that was. He said that right then, he wanted to murder them both instead of just killing Badger and knocking Gobel around.

That made me feel real warm.

We talked late into the night by the little fire he built, with the late Badger Jukes and Gobel Tackett stacked like kindling in that coffin they'd brought for me. He pulled out my splinters and gave me enough water for a spit-bath, and we talked and we laughed and we talked some more. And I found out that I genuinely liked Johnny, not because he was good-looking or tall or had a kind way about him. The first is pretty parents, and the last can be acted. But he was, deep down, a nice man. That's something rare.

I wanted to be with him, like lovers, in the worst way. I know he wanted the same. But I said, "Johnny, when you make love to me the first time, I don't want to sell tickets."

He looked at me a little strange, and then a look of understanding passed over his face. "Ah," he said, smiling gently. "Your Jonas."

And he didn't press the issue, bless his eyes.

At sunup, he dug a hole and buried Gobel and Badger right there in the high desert. Gobel got the coffin, and Badger had to make do with an old blanket.

After they were covered up, Johnny leaned both hands on the shovel and said, "Lord, they're yours now. Do what you want with 'em." And then he added, "I got him for you, Ike."

He turned to me and said, half-sheepish, "Well, Ike wasn't much for brains, but he was a good man on the trail. Decent shot, a fair cook, and nobody ever got bored when old Ike was around. He always had a story to tell about that family."

We left the buckboard where she stood and rode back the way Johnny'd come, leading the extra horse behind us. He gave me the use of his saddle horse, the one I'd admired back at Christmas, because its saddle wouldn't fit on either one of the team. He said he wouldn't have me riding bareback in my condition.

I wasn't inclined to argue.

And Jonas?

He just disappeared. Oh, I knew he was still lurking around. I was still full up with the spirit, so to speak. But not a word did he say to me.

I got to thinking that he was just trying to lull me into a false sense of security, so that he could skim the milk, so to speak, if and when me and Johnny made love. I wasn't falling for it, though, no sir.

By the time we made camp the second night, I'd found out a lot more about Johnny. He talked about his home and his upbringing, as I talked about mine, and I saw that his had been more cultured. He came west with his mother when he was twelve, his father having sent for them, and the whole family lived high off their digs. Johnny's father even had seventeen men working for him at one time!

When he was eighteen, he got sent back east to college—he was like Sam in that way, except he didn't cook and he stayed for the whole shooting match, right up to and including graduation. He was all set to get a job with some big company back in Philadelphia when he got word that there'd been trouble at the mine. Both his folks were dead.

Of course, he came back lickety-split.

"That fat old weasel, Fortesque Potter, had taken over Dad's operation by then," he said, poking at the fire with a touch more savagery than was necessary. "I tried everything legal, but he had the deed and it was his word against mine. So I . . . I found another way."

"Robbing his shipments," I said. I was cuddled into his shoulder. Having stopped at a stream midday to bathe all over and wash out my tattered dress, I was feeling a good deal more chipper and smelling like a whole new woman, even if my dress was still damp in places.

Johnny nodded. At least, I felt his jaw nodding into my hair. He said, "Except I was a fool. The only thing that happened was that I became an outlaw, just as bad as Potter."

I looked up, into his face. "It wasn't the same! You were only trying to get back what was yours!"

"In theory, yes," he said, ruffling my hair. "In practice, I'm afraid not."

He'd run into Ike by way of saving him from a lynch mob down in Sonora—well, it wasn't a big lynch mob: just three drunks with a grudge and a rope. But after, Ike had just started tagging along. I guess he believed that if somebody saved your hide, you were beholden to them forever. Anyway, Ike's brother Gobel showed up with Badger in tow, and they started tagging along, too. The papers started calling them the Devlin Gang, and then the papers associated them with Billy the Kid over in New Mexico (on account of Badger) and the Clantons in Tombstone (on account of Arvil Tackett, Ike and Gobel's half-brother, who Johnny never rode with, let alone met), making their reputation all the worse.

"Hell," he said, disgusted, "I never met any Clantons. If the papers are even half truthful, I would have been on Wyatt and Doc's side."

Maybe Sam had been right after all about famous people knowing one another.

"The problem is," he went on, "that now I'm wanted for killing Ike."

I started to open my mouth, but he beat me to it. "No, sugar," he said, "even if I'd taken Badger in alive he'd never have confessed. He'd have hung us both out to dry just for spite. Wasn't smart enough to see it any other way, the dumb bastard. But there's paper out on me. Guess I'll have to go down into Mexico for a few years."

He suddenly smiled. "Darlin'," he said, "do you speak any Spanish?"

"You proposing?" I asked, blinking back tears. "Jonas and birds and the sisters and all?"

He kissed me.

Like Aisha said, the good things are set in stone.

POSTSCRIPT

APRIL 1943

Naturally, me and Johnny got married. And I suppose, if you're romantically inclined, you're real happy now and don't care about the rest, and I should just be a nice old lady and say "the end." But if you're still worrying about Sam and Nezzy and Lenny and the sisters—which you should be, because there was a lot to worry about—let me put your mind at rest.

First off, while we were out there in the high desert all that time ago, Johnny decided I should finish my contract with Mr. Barnum. I was half-expecting it, but I was still sort of surprised. I'd thought maybe we'd just run off down south of the border, and that would be that.

But Johnny had the clear head that I, in my romantic stupor, didn't. He said he had plenty to keep him busy, and that I should go back to San Francisco and finish the tour, and that he'd meet me in Nogales, Mexico, come July. That was when I was scheduled to make my last appearance before we renegotiated the contract with Mr. Barnum.

And then he took me up north, to where the railroad went through, and bought me a clean dress and put me on a train, a ticket to San Francisco in my hand.

"Good journey, darlin'," he said on the platform, and kissed me, then whispered in my ear, "Don't forget—Nogales."

I cried near all the way to San Francisco, I missed him so much. But still, I had faith that Fate had good things planned for us. Jonas finally popped out about halfway up the coast, but he was awful grumbly and only said about four words to me.

When I got to San Francisco, having wired ahead to Sam that I was unharmed, he and Lenny met me at the train and hurried me into a cab.

"Where have you been?" insisted Lenny, his high forehead sunk into furrows. "Are you crazy? We've had the police looking for you! The whole countryside's been having fits, and then you just wire 'I'm fine' and 'I'm coming up there'? Mrs. Strider told me about that little discussion you had, you know. Being kidnapped's one thing, but kiting off five minutes before showtime because someone's put you in your place is just—"

"What?" I said. "Did she say that?"

Sam had the sense not to be exasperated with me. Maybe he thought it strange that I'd disappear for seven days and then just turn up on the train, all full of smiles, but he kept his opinions to himself.

When we were alone, I told him what had happened, the whole of it, from waking up in that awful coffin to being kissed good-bye on the platform.

"Well," said Sam, "what are you going to say happened? I don't suppose you can tell the truth."

I nodded. "Not all of it. Not without getting Johnny in a heap of trouble."

Sam mulled this over for a minute, and then he said, "Just say part. Leave the coffin part in, though. Lenny'll like that."

So I told the police I had been kidnapped by one Badger Jukes and one Gobel Tackett, and been transported south via frieght train in a cheap pine casket. I told them about waking up in the desert, and about escaping, and then I told them that I didn't recall how I'd got back to civilization.

The detective sort of scowled, like he didn't believe me,

and then asked where I'd got the money to take the train, and where I'd got clean clothes.

"She wired me," Sam piped up.

"We sent the money," Lenny announced, "through the courtesy of Mr. P. T. Barnum, her employer and mine, who was much distressed by her absense, and is jubilant over her safe return."

"Uh-huh," said the detective with a raised brow, but he left it at that.

The papers were full of the story. They posed questions as to what had really happened in those seven days, and made a big to-do over the coffin part, which pleased Lenny no end. Sam was right about that part. But I stuck to my story when questioned. I plain didn't remember, I insisted, and we went on with the tour.

Jonas behaved himself, pretty much. In fact, he was almost jovial right up until the middle of June, when we'd worked our way back to Minneapolis. We'd given three shows and were about to move across the river to do one in St. Paul when, in the coach, he started talking. It was odd right from the start, since Jonas usually went away for the rest of the night or at least a few hours after he'd given a lecture.

"You sound funny," I said to him. "Maybe you better go rest some more."

I'm about to, Annie, he replied, weakly but happily. *I'm about to go for good and all.*

All of a sudden, my back got real stiff. I said, "Jonas?"

Sam and Lenny, who'd become accustomed to me talking to myself—well, talking to Jonas—had been absorbed in their own conversation, but Sam stopped in mid-sentence and stared at me.

I'm going to fly away, dear Annie, said Jonas, *just like the old song says. They're waiting.*

"Oh, no," I breathed. "Jonas?"

It's so bright! he said, his voice growing more distant with every word, but more jublilant, too. *So bright! Ma? Is that you, Ma? Forgive me, Annie. Forgive us all!*

"Annie?" said Sam, his hand on my arm.

"What's going on?" Lenny asked, over his glasses.

I searched for him for another moment, but it was done. I felt light as a feather again, so light I thought I'd float through the roof of the carriage and out over the city.

I said, "He's gone."

Softly, Sam said, "Oh, Annie." He put his arm around me and gave me a little hug.

"What?" said Lenny. "Who's gone? You don't mean, that is, it isn't . . . ?"

"Sorry, Lenny," I said, and I wasn't surprised when my tears came. Jonas Newcastle had been an almighty thorn in my side, that was for certain, but I'd miss the old coot. I'd half got to liking him.

Once we'd got Lenny through about three rounds of the vapors and put a half bottle of bourbon in him, he contacted Mr. Barnum and called off the rest of the tour. Even though it only amounted to three more cities, poor Lenny got fired and went home to his stiff-backed children and starched wife and regimented household. I guess Mr. Barnum wasn't all sweetness and light after all. Sam and I headed home to the sisters, home to Arizona.

The sisters came out on the front porch to greet us as we drove up to that god-awful black castle, and when I got down from the buggy, Miss Jessie gave me a big old hug.

"Welcome home, dear," she said, and daubed her eyes. and then she whispered, "Sister's glad to see you, too, really, but she's . . . she's proud."

So I walked up the steps to where Miss Jonquil was standing, arms stiff at her sides, and I smiled wide and said, "Oh, Miss Jonquil! It's so good to see you again!" I gave her a smile, and she commenced to weep right then and there.

"I'm sorry I was cruel," she said as I hugged her tight. "I'm just a mean old lady, that's all."

I was inclined to agree, but I said, "No, Miss Jonquil. Just a little pigheaded, like your brother. We all are, sometimes."

Later, they asked me about Jonas, how it had been when he left. I guess maybe they were secretly worried he'd go down instead of up, but I said, "He sounded, well, peaceful, you know?"

They held each other's hands and cried, but I noticed they weren't sad tears. Quietly joyous, more like.

July rolled around and I made ready to go down to Nogales and finally meet up with Johnny, and spend the rest of my life happy as a mule knee-deep in clover. Sam and I told the sisters I was going off to marry a man I'd met while I was touring, and who Jonas had approved of. Actually, that was the pure truth. I guess we just left out the part where his name was Johnny Devlin.

Well, all right, I lied. I told them his name was Johnny Dearborn, and he ranched in Mexico.

But anyway, they approved and I guess I got the family blessing. I sort of wanted it, too.

After a teary scene with the sisters on the front porch, Sam drove me down to catch the stage at Phoenix. I can't say I was looking forward to his good-bye. After all, if he went away to Paris, I'd probably never see him again. But while the Wells Fargo men were loading my bags, he pressed a thick envelope into my hand, then held it, both his hands wrapped around mine.

"Little Annie Newcastle," he said. "Be happy. And don't fail to follow the directions."

And then he hugged me so tight I'd thought I'd bust. The second he released me, he turned and walked straight away. I just stood there, my eyes brimming as I watched him amble down toward the buggy. After, when I was on the stage and it was pulling out of town, I looked back and saw his face. He was crying, too.

It was about a quarter hour before I remembered the packet I held. The envelope was plain, with no writing, but when I opened it and pulled out the contents, I just sat there with my mouth gaping.

Sam had been busy. Behind my back, he'd been taking notes on everything that Jonas said, and had put near all the money I'd earned—at Boyd's and on tour with Mr. Barnum—into the stock market. There was a long list of which stocks he'd bought for me and how many shares, and the dates before which I should sell them. The name of the stockbroker I should contact in New York was written out, and there were also passbooks from banks in Phoenix and New York. They were savings accounts made out in my name, and showed a combined balance of more than thirty-two thousand dollars.

And there was a note. It said, "Don't worry about me or the sisters, Annie. I took a share for them, and a touch for myself, too. At current market prices, and by my figuring, you should be worth about $176,000. But if you follow the directions on the enclosed list, you'll be worth considerably more in time, and I do mean considerably. Be outrageously, intensely, wonderously happy, Annie. Every time I make Apple Charlotte, I'll think of you."

It was signed, "Your forever friend, Sam."

I was teared up practically all the way to Tucson.

By the time we pulled into Nogales, I was dusty and sore from three days on the stage, but full of anticipation. Waiting on the street was Johnny, the handsomest man in the whole world and all shined up for the occasion. We got married that afternoon, and honeymooned all night and half the next day until neither one of us could so much as lift a finger.

"Jonas must have left," Johnny said, rubbing my belly lazily.

I laughed.

"Miss him?"

Now, I thought that Johnny was just doing a real good job of pretending to believe in Jonas, and I was inclined to forgive him. After all, Jonas had moved on and I had no way to prove that he'd ever been there. So I played along with it, pretending to believe that he believed, and said, "Yes and no."

He lifted an eyebrow, and I said, "Yes, because I really sort of got to like the old curmudgeon, once he was halfway housebroke. He was pretty much all-the-time company. Well, except for when he was tired, or when he was ornery or peevish. Or when he was just mad at me for doing or thinking something he didn't approve of."

Waiting, Johnny smiled, those dimples cutting deep creases into his handsome face.

"And no," I continued, "because I fell in crazy in love with you. Our future's a duet, not a trio."

"Sing with me, Annie," he whispered, and well, I suppose you can guess what happened next.

In the morning, we set out north on horseback with a pack mule, just the two of us, just Mr. and Mrs. Johnny Devlin.

"Aren't you afraid to cross back up into the territory?" I asked.

"No," he said, grinning. "I'm not afraid of anything today. Besides, I've got something to show you. It's a wedding present."

I tipped my head. "A wedding present?"

"For both of us. From Jonas."

"What?"

He just kept grinning. "You'll see."

Three days later, we had ridden ourselves not only up over the border, but to an enormous maze of a canyon. We spent a whole day just riding through the twisty channels: some vast and wide, and some so narrow you had to pull your legs up out of the stirrups to keep from getting them scraped. I was so thoroughly turned around I couldn't have gotten out of there if you paid me, but Johnny seemed to know just where he was going.

At last, in the late afternoon, he stopped and dismounted. I followed suit, and we ground-tied the horses.

"Come on, darlin'," he said, taking my hand, and led me up a gravelly slope where, a long time ago, somebody had cut steps into the rock.

"Where the Sam Hill are we?" I asked. We'd come so far and I'd got so mixed up about directions that I was kind of scared.

"Just a few more feet," he said with a grin. Well, who could resist those crinkly green eyes? I followed him.

At the top of the worn steps, there was an opening in the rock, a natural cleft. Johnny picked up a lantern that was sitting just inside, and lit it.

"You've been here before?" I asked.

"Shhh," said Johnny, and led me inside. "Watch your step,

Annie," he warned, and while I was busy watching my feet, he turned the lantern up.

I blinked, and thought that it seem like an awful lot of light from just one lantern, and then I looked up and gasped.

"El Galgo," said Johnny.

Gold was everywhere. Big fat streaks of it ran along the crooked, sloping walls, the convoluted floors, the ceiling high above me, and reflected the lantern's light like a hall of mirrors. You could see where somebody had mined it out. Mined it a lot, for rotted scraps of canvas sacks were here and there, and rusty pick heads and such. But they hadn't even touched it. There was enough gold to last for twenty lifetimes, or forty; enough gold to keep whole countries afloat for years.

"How . . . how," I stuttered.

"Jonas," he replied, then he added with a grin, "Sit down, Annie, before you fall down."

I sat.

He hunched down next to me, and said, "I know you don't really believe that I believe you about Jonas. And, all right, to be honest, I didn't at first. But that last night, when we were camped, you woke me up."

"I did?"

He nodded. "Right in the dark, hard middle of the night. And you said, 'Listen up, boyo, because I've got something to say to you.' I knew right away that it wasn't my Annie talking."

"What'd he say?" I asked, amazed that Jonas could have just up and walked in while I was asleep, and not even wakened me. It sort of gave me the shivers.

"Well, first he gave me a lecture on wedded bliss."

I flushed hot, and chuckling, Johnny said, "We'll discuss that some other time. But finally, he made me write down a bunch of directions to this place. Latitude and longitude, which didn't do me a whole hell of a lot of good. And directions by landmark, which did."

"You never said a word!" I cried, and it echoed several times off all that gold. I slapped a hand over my mouth and whispered, "Sorry."

Johnny ran his big thumb gently over my jaw. "Well, I still didn't really believe. That was, until I rode in here and took a gander." He looked up at the glinting ceiling, then down the long natural cave. I couldn't see any end to it, just gold reflections going on forever.

He turned to me. "I believed then."

Later, he showed me the running dog in the rock, outside, above the entrance. Well, it was a place where lighter stone made a pattern in the darker that sort of looked like a skinny running dog. "El Galgo means the greyhound," he said, looking up.

He told me that Jonas had said he wasn't to claim it, just take out what he needed and let the rest lay, and that was what we did. Well, I suppose "needed" is a relative term.

We traveled all over the world in the years that followed. We went to Paris three times to see Sam, and then to New York to see him after he started working in the hotels there, in all kinds of famous and celebrated places you've heard of. He was so rich that he didn't have to cook, of course. He just loved it.

Sam never married. He had a good friend though, who he met in Paris. Jacques LaCroix was his name, and he and Sam lived together till the day Sam died. He couldn't cook a lick but he sure could eat, and we got to liking him about as good as Sam, himself.

Johnny built us a big fancy house, too—bigger than Jonas's castle—up in Denver, and we were pals with all the right people. I can't say as that was my favorite part, although I really did like Gini Peters and her husband, Dix. They had retail stores, and Gini set fire to about everything she touched, but they were good people, about the best in Denver.

As bad as we wanted them, we were not blessed with children. I got real down in the dumps about it and sulked for years, but one morning I woke up and everything was all right. I mean, I felt like it was okay that we couldn't have kids, and that maybe we could do for somebody else's. It was just that sudden. We opened a home for orphaned boys there in Colorado, and another for girls, and financed them for years. We even adopted three kids ourselves, two girls and a boy.

John, Jr., is a lawyer over in California, now, and his son, Jackie, just came into the business with him. They come to visit every few months. They do what you call show business law, or maybe it's theatre law. I don't know. Anyway, they get to meet all kinds of movie stars and they bring me autographed pictures, and keep talking as how I should move out to Hollywood and live with John, Jr., and his wife, Althea. Or, they say, if I want to be more my own person, I could live in their pool house, which has got two bedrooms and a fireplace. Live a little more high on the hog, you know?

I just laugh and say fiddlesticks. I've chugged enough champagne to last four lifetimes, glittered enough for six. My high-on-the-hog days are finished and done. Simple's how I like it now.

Our girls, Meg and Milly (Milly's the oldest), both got married and have a passel of kids between them. They married for love, I'm proud to say, and not for money. Of course, they don't get out to see me much, Meg being in Scarsdale and Milly being all the way over in Europe, but we write all the time. I've got so many pictures of kids and grandkids and great-grandkids around this place that it's practically a fire hazard.

You know, I always wondered if maybe Aisha hadn't come to me that night—the night when I got better, all of a sudden—and whispered a ghostly pep talk at me, kind of like she had done for Nezzy. Maybe she scratched me behind the ears. I like to think so.

Anyway, after the stock market went belly-up in '29, we moved back to Arizona. We were going by the last name of Dearborn by then and had been for ages and ages, so as to circumvent any trouble that might arise from anybody snooping after Johnny Devlin or Prophet Annie Newcastle. Of course, I'd followed Sam's instructions to the *T* and was clear out of stocks by then. I'd moved most all my money to land investments outside Chicago and Los Angeles, per

Sam's instructions, and was watching my bank account get fatter and fatter.

In fact, Johnny only had to go down to El Galgo with a pick and a sack about three times. My "Sam money" kept us in steamship tickets and champagne.

I gave a lot of thought to telling John, Jr., and the girls about that glittering hole in the ground, but in the end I kept my mouth shut. They've had plenty all their lives, and they'll have plenty more when I go, enough that they can pass it to their kids if they don't go hog-wild and try to buy England or something.

No, I think I'll just let El Galgo be. It's too late, anyhow. I buried Jonas's directions to the place in Johnny's breast pocket.

Anyway, after Johnny passed on and left me alone, I got myself a small house. It's a nice one, one I can take care of myself. And nobody on the block knows I've got money tucked away. They just think I'm that crazy old lady with a stuffed cheetah by the Philco.

Oh! I forgot about Nezzy! He lived six more years, bless his chirpy old heart. He was wild for Johnny and we took him everywhere. He even went all the way to Paris with us and traveled 'round the world on a steamship. But one day, back in Denver, he crawled up the stairs and came into my room, then licked my hand and died, just like that. I guess his sweet old heart just gave out.

Johnny had him stuffed. I was dead-set against it at the time, since all I could think of was that rapscallion, Mr. Boyd. But now I'm glad. It's real comforting, having Nezzy right there where I can go in and have a word with him. Well, just his shell, really. But he's not using it anymore. He doesn't mind.

Well, I guess that's about it. If you have some old magazines lying around, you might see an occasional picture of me and Johnny, all covered in confetti and waving from a ship, or us going into a theater or posing with some prince or polo player. They used to take our pictures a lot. And you know, nobody ever recognized either one of us. A suit and tie and bank account for Johnny—and glittery dresses and smart haircuts for me—sure hid a multitude of sins.

And once I scaled down, got the little house and started dressing plain like I used to when I was young, and tying my hair back in a knot, why, I was invisible again.

Funny, the way that all worked out.

Like it was preordained, or something. Set in stone.

We later heard that Lenny Strider had got back on his feet right away, when he landed a job managing a fancy gaming house right there in San Francisco. He ended up owning several different nightclubs, all of them real high-tone, and got to be quite a wealthy man. I always wondered how Mrs. Strider took to it.

And the castle? Miss Jonquil and Miss Jessie lived on there for another twelve years, bless their hearts. We went to visit them several times, and on each occasion, Johnny hired carpenters and stone masons to shore up that monster of a house. It was crumbling fast, sort of like the sisters. After they passed on (Miss Jessie two months before Miss Jonquil), it was about a year before we could get down there, and looters had stripped the place clean.

I just looked up at it, all black and empty and hulking there in the middle of nowhere, the wind whistling through its broken windows, and said, "Let the desert have it back, Johnny."

Well, I suppose I should end this, now. Odd to end your story when you haven't ended your life yet, but that's the way it'll have to be. I suppose the kids are going to be sort of upset when they read this—finding out that their mama was in a carnival telling the future, and that their daddy was on the outs with the law and all—but I don't think they'll take it too hard. They're good kids. As good as if we'd made them ourselves, like Johnny used to say.

As for me, I reckon that Jonas was what you'd call a major force in my life, all of it, which is a pretty gol-danged astounding accomplishment for somebody who I only knew alive for a few measly hours.

Sometimes I think back on the bad things he brought me,

from childhood on up, and I get so mad I could chase that ornery son of a mule down the block, whomping him with a twig broom every other step. But then, I think on the good things that happened because of Jonas—all those carnival folks I got to spend time with and meeting up with Johnny and knowing Sam and Nezzy and such—and I get to thinking more kindly of him. Sort of scamp-like, I guess.

And the predictions? Jonas was right about a lot of things, I've got to give him credit. Flying machines and motorcars and the radio? They've all come to pass (except for the lady president and flying to the moon and such) despite how improbable I thought they were.

I guess a lot of other people thought they were improbable, too. Folks just came and paid their money for the oddity of it, I suppose, because hardly anyone remembers Jonas's prophesies, let alone his name. Let alone mine.

Well, hardly anyone, aside from that Ezra Bind Todd person I talked about in the beginning, the one who said such wrong-headed things about me in his book, *Curiosities and Freaks of the American West, Volume III: The Amazing Powers of "Prophet Annie" Newcastle*. To hear him tell it, I was hand in glove with those spiritualist people, and had assistants behind every curtain, vomiting up ectoplasm and wafting gauze through the air and sifting through the crowd, picking their pockets so's I could tell them all about themselves.

Bunk and horseradish.

Well. Like I was going to say before I got off on that Mr. Todd, it seems to me that all those years ago when we toured the East Coast for Mr. Barnum, I remember a few fellows who came several times, in different cities, like they were following us around. Scribbling on pieces of paper, they were. As I remember, Jonas was talking mostly about coal and oil and gasoline and hydroelectricity and nuclear power around then. And cold fusion. I never did figure out what that was. I suppose I didn't need to.

Anyway, years later, when Johnny and I were sailing to Europe for the umpty-umpth time, I recognized one of those men, one of those scribblers.

He was a lot older, of course, and I'd only seen him three times and long ago, but I knew him right off. He was coming down into the main dining room as I remember, and on his arm was a woman all decked out in jewels. I heard somebody whisper that he was John D. Rockefeller, and that he owned Standard Oil and was the richest man in all the world.

I had to laugh. Somebody besides Sam did take Jonas serious, after all, and made a good go with what he said. I wonder what the old spook would've said to that.

Probably, "Good show, Annie! Bully for him!"

Bully for us all, I say.

OCAIN & SONS
PUBLISHERS
NEW YORK CITY, NEW YORK

August 19, 1943

Mrs. John Dearborn
312 Desert Quail Drive
Tucson, Arizona

Dear Mrs. Dearborn,
Thank you for letting us consider your most un-usual and fanciful Western novel, PROPHET ANNIE. I sincerely commend you for writing it. A manuscript of this length would be a daunting task, even to a writer much younger than yourself.

However, while I am impressed with the time and effort that obviously went into PROPHET ANNIE, I'm afraid I cannot recommend it for pub-lication by this firm.

As you know, the war has created a paper short-age. We have cut our lines back by 25% for the duration, although even in peace time we, at Ocain & Sons, do not publish speculative fiction, fantasy, or "spook stories."

While these elements could be edited out, I'm sure you'll understand that there would not be much story left. I'm afraid I would have a very hard time, indeed, selling this book "as is" as a nonfiction title.

Best of luck taking it elsewhere. Should you ever write a realistic novel—say, one with more gunplay and Indian attacks, and none of this mysticism or circus stuff—I hope you will send it to us. Westerns are very popular now.

Best wishes,

Frank Cohen

*Franklin L. Cohen
Senior Editor*